MW00966530

REFLECTION
PUBLISHING

Divine Invasion

Michael L. Monhollon

ISBN 0-9657561-0-6 LC 97-91836

Divine Invasion
was produced and prepared by
Reflection Publishing
1 Hendrick Drive
Abilene, Texas 79602

Printed in the United States of America
1 2 3 4 5 6 7 8 9 10

Cover Illustration by Keith R. Davis
Cover Design by Imagination ii

This book is printed on acid-free paper.

For Seth and Joshua

CHAPTER 1

Six corpses, entirely nude, hung rotting in the morning sun. They had been there three days, but the last of them, the strongest, had expired just hours ago, at daybreak. The grass about the low crosses had been trampled flat by Roman boots.

"Why do they have to put them so close to the road?" Herodias asked querulously. The height of the crosses was little greater than the height of the men hanging from them. The feet of one were perhaps a cubit above the ground, eighteen inches. The feet of the others would have dragged the ground but for the iron spikes driven through the lapped feet and into the post. Despite her words and her tone of disgust, she leaned closer as the royal chariot passed by the crosses, the stench of decay, of voided bladders and emptied bowels, filling her nostrils. "All Jews," she said. "Of course they would be."

Crucifixion was a cruel death, never inflicted on citizens of Rome.

"It's needed as an object lesson to would-be revolutionaries," Herod Antipas said. He, unlike his wife, had no interest in the circumcisions of the dead. Using his teeth, he pulled the stopper from an amphora of wine. He drained half of it, gulping repeatedly without drawing breath. The flies were thick, and buzzards perched on the crossbeams of the crosses within easy reach of the vulnerable eyes. God, these Romans were brutes, Herod thought.

Neither Herod nor Herodias said anything for perhaps a mile. The silence was broken only by the jingling harness of the horses, the creak of the chariot, and the tramping feet of King Herod's military escort.

"Did you know about it beforehand?" Herodias asked him.

"Know about what?" He had finished the jar, and droplets of wine hung in his reddish, square-cut beard and stained his tunic. "Oh, the crucifixions. No." Though nominally a king, he was more accurately a tetrarch, a satellite prince without the same royal dignity. Perea was his province, as was Galilee, but the two provinces constituted only a fragment of his father's kingdom. Just as his father had held his kingdom at the pleasure of the emperor, so Herod Antipas held his tetrarchy. The emperor's legionnaires would rarely consult him before inflicting the penalty for insurrection.

"They should always consult you," Herodias said. "You should insist on it." Her hair was dark and straight, jewels glinting from the hanging tresses.

"Maybe I will."

"And maybe you won't." Her anger showed in her eyes, so dark as to appear utterly black.

"What's that supposed to mean?"

"It means don't merely talk about it this time. Do it."

He regarded her sourly. It was hard for him to believe, sometimes, that he had ever been in love with her, but he had been. There was a time, especially in Rome, where he had come to know her little more than a year ago, when he could hardly get enough of her.

"You shouldn't drink in the mornings," she told him as he tucked the empty ceramic jar beneath the seat on which he sat.

He belched and grinned with satisfaction at her expression of distaste.

"You're not nearly as civilized as your brother," she said.

"So you should have married my brother."

She had, of course. It was his brother Philip she had left for him, and, though Philip (also a tetrarch) had made an early show of mild hostility, Herod had come to believe that Philip was very much content to have inflicted her on him. He reached again under his seat for the last of the jars he had stashed for the journey.

He, for his part, had given up a Nabataean princess, and it was doubtful he had heard the last from her father, Aretas.

"Do you intend to swill wine all the way to Jericho?" Herodias asked him.

"All the way to Jerusalem. I'll have to restock in Jericho."

She made a sound of disgust.

"After the spectacle we just witnessed, I intend to become as drunk as possible." He bent toward her to bestow a sloppy kiss, and she pushed him away.

"I'd suggest you do the same," he said. "Wanton."

Her eyes narrowed, but her lips curved in a smile. "Beast," she said. The sun shone in her black hair, emphasizing its luster.

"Strumpet."

"Lecher."

Peace restored, he held out the wine jar to her, but she shook her head.

He shrugged. "Perhaps it's just as well."

"What's as well? Why?"

"This is my last amphora," Herod said, taking a short pull on it. "I'd hate to have to split it with you." He wiped his mouth with his forearm.

† † †

The preacher — the wild man, some would say, being skeptical even of his sanity — stood in the Jordan River at the Hiljah Ford. Though the day was warm, and the air, beneath the overcast sky, was humid, the water itself was cold. The ford was several miles upstream from the Dead Sea, but the water, nonetheless, was brackish. John's camel-hair robe was bound at his waist with a leather belt, and the swift current rose high enough to keep it wet.

A boy splashed out toward him, struggling against the current, the water rising as high as his chest. Good, the preacher thought. He'd been watching that one.

He gripped the boy's arm. "What is your name, son?"

It was Seth.

"Ah," said the preacher. "The child of promise. 'God has appointed for me another child.' So said Eve." One hand on the boy's chest, the other behind his head, the preacher pushed him down beneath the surface of the water and drew him up again, his hair streaming with water.

"Go," the preacher said. "Go and live a life that is pleasing to God."

"What shall I do?"

"Eh? What's that? What shall you do?" One hand gripping the boy's shoulder with the strength of a pincer, the preacher looked up at the crowd. "Do you need me to tell you how to live a life that is pleasing to God? Are you completely numb in spirit?" Sometimes he thought they were; it was enough to make him despair.

"If you have food," he said, "then share it with someone who has none. If you have two coats, give one of them to someone without any coat at all. Is Judea devoid of those who are poor and afflicted so that there is no good you can do?"

Still their faces were blank, uncomprehending. The preacher looked again at Seth. "Ask God, son. Ask him, and he will tell you what you should do."

The boy nodded.

"Go on now."

There was the rumble of distant thunder, and, casting a nervous glance up at the dark clouds, the boy floundered toward the bank.

A man reached out a hand to help him to shore, lifting him easily onto the bank. "It's all right," he murmured. "The Baptizer was preaching to all of us, not just to you."

The man had a dark beard, a straight nose, and warm brown eyes, almost golden in color. The boy smiled up at him, and the man squeezed the boy's shoulder. Then he entered the river himself, wading out to the Baptizer.

"Would you too be baptized?" John said to him, taking his arm. "You are conscious of the sin in your life?"

"All have sinned, have they not?"

"A strange answer." There was something odd about the man, something familiar and yet unsettling — unsettling even to John, who was rarely unsettled.

"You have not been to hear me before," he said. "How is it that I know you?"

"Do you?"

John drew him close, staring into his face with an almost maniacal intensity. He did everything with an almost maniacal intensity; it was one of the reasons he attracted crowds. "Don't I?" he said.

The man smiled, his teeth straight and white against his dark beard. "We met as children."

"Children!"

"We played together on the streets of Jerusalem when the two of us were only twelve years old."

John searched his eyes.

"Try to imagine me without the beard."

"Jesus. Mary and Joseph's boy."

The man nodded. "Your cousin Jesus."

"Yes."

Jesus' woolen robe and tunic floated on the water, swirling about his hips. The current about them was swift, carrying the gravel from beneath their feet, and several times each had to shift his feet to find purchase.

"Why do you hesitate?" Jesus said. "You are known as the Baptizer, are you not?"

"So I am." John scooped water from the river with his hands, but as he raised them, the sun broke through the lowering clouds, forming a halo about his cousin's head. John blinked, temporarily blinded. From close by came the flapping of wings, but, though John jerked his head, he could see nothing. It seemed to his sun-dazed eyes that the people and the shrubbery along the bank were all in shadow, and he felt disoriented, dizzy.

Jesus' hand, which years of carpentry had hardened into oak, was at his elbow, supporting him. His face seemed unnaturally bright.

"It's you," John said. "You're the one who is to come."

Jesus smiled, a little quizzically. "I hardly see how I can be, as

I'm here already."

John ignored the play on words. He scooped up water and held out his cupped hands to Jesus. "Take it," he said. "I need for you to baptize me. Please."

Jesus pressed John's hands back against his chest. "No, John. You are the Baptizer. It is I who have come to you."

"It would be a sacrilege. You have no need of the baptism I offer."

Jesus extended his hand to the crowd on the bank, still little more than a forest of shadows to John. "Do you see them? They have need of the baptism you offer."

"But —"

"And today I accept baptism on their behalf."

"My . . . my work is over, then."

"Very nearly," Jesus told him. "Very nearly."

† † †

Herod and his party heard voices as they approached the Jordan River, long before the river itself was visible. More accurately, they heard a voice. When the chariot topped the rise that overlooked the Jordan, a crowd of people was visible on the far bank — peasants, most of them, though here and there was the gleam of gold or the flash of a brilliant hue that marked the clothing of a rich man. The speaker was a wild man, hair to his shoulders, beard full and unkempt on the breast of his camel's hair robe.

Herod held up a hand. "Halt," he cried softly, and his captain echoed the command.

The tramp of feet and the jingle of armor and harness ceased, and, in the relative quiet, the words of the preacher could be distinguished: "Today I have seen the one spoken of by the prophet: 'I watched in the night visions, and behold with the clouds of heaven there came one like unto the son of man. He came to the Ancient of Days and was presented before him . . .'"

"What's he saying?" Herodias asked.

"Shh! It's from the Book of Daniel."

Though the day had been dry, the heads of roughly half the crowd were plastered to their scalps with dripping water, and their cloaks were spotted. All eyes were intent on the speaker.

". . . all people, all nations, all languages should serve him . . ."

None of the crowd had yet noticed Herod's party. "It's a Messianic passage," Herod said, softly enough to be audible only to Herodias and to the guards closest to them. "He's preaching the overthrow of earthly kingdoms and the foundation . . ."

"He's a revolutionary then."

"Perhaps, but not necessarily. It's a matter of theological interpretation."

Herodias shot her husband a look of withering contempt.

One of the men nearest to the preacher, one of the better dressed among them, said abruptly, "Who are you to say such things?" His voice was loud enough to carry easily across the river valley. "Who are you that we should listen?"

Herodias said, "You mean a man accused of treason can save himself by means of a fine theological distinction?"

"Shh," Herod whispered, gesturing vigorously.

"You say the day of the Lord is upon us," said the well-dressed man. "Are you then the Messiah?"

The shape of the crowd shifted subtly, though it was not clear to Herod whether in support of the preacher or his questioner. The well-dressed man stood in a crowd of six, all with phylacteries strapped to their left arms, three with another of the black leather boxes strapped to their foreheads as well.

Herod was familiar with the phylacteries: each contained four passages of scripture. Moses had commanded the people of Israel to keep God's law always before them; there were some who took the injunction literally.

"Are you the Messiah?" the well-dressed man said again.

"I am not the Messiah," the preacher said.

"Who are you then? Are you Elijah?" Elijah, generally acknowledged as the greatest of the prophets, had never tasted death — at least, not according to scripture. At the conclusion of his ministry, he had been taken up into heaven in a chariot of fire. Many Jews —

and Herod as well, though he was of Idumaean extraction — half-expected Elijah to descend again from heaven one day to announce the end of time.

"I am not Elijah."

"Are you the prophet the Lord promised Moses?"

"I am not."

Another of the scribes said, "Who then? How dare you presume to baptize God's own chosen people?"

"I preach a baptism of repentance, in preparation for one who is already among you. The hearts of God's people must be cleansed of all unrighteousness."

"Who?" said a member of the crowd. "Who is among us?"

"We are sons of Abraham," said the scribe. It was the Gentiles who needed cleansing, the Gentiles who had to undergo ritual purification in order to become one of God's people. The Jews were His already.

"I will tell you the worth of being a son of Abraham." The preacher hawked and spat the phlegm against a rock outcropping. "Out of that stone God can raise up sons of Abraham."

The graphic insult to their race — to Abraham — left them momentarily speechless. The preacher said, "You have asked me who I am; let me tell you who you are. You pretend to be righteous and holy, wearing your religion on your sleeves as you do, but you are merely politicians. Pharisees and Sadducees and . . . You there — do I recognize in you a member of the ruling Sanhedrin? What a nest of snakes!"

"You can't —"

"But I can. And one is here among you who is more powerful than I, one whose sandals I am not fit to carry. I warn you to flee the coming wrath, for the one who is to come is here. His winnowing fork is in his hand, and he will clear his threshing floor, gathering up the wheat into his barn and burning the chaff in an unquenchable fire."

"Who? Who are you talking about?"

Herod leaned forward to prod his driver. "Advance," he said. "Advance."

Several members of Herod's guard trotted ahead of the chariot and several behind. The bulk of Herod's fifty men flanked him, and Herod's captain rode a charger on the far right. By the time they reached the river, they had the attention of everyone on the far bank. The silence was total, the faces sullen. Herod Antipas was no favorite of the Jews.

His men formed a column to cross the ford. There was no bridge. The road led down into the water at the Hiljah Ford and up again beyond it. The chariot rocked precariously across the paving stones laid across the river bottom in the middle of the ford, the royal couple holding their feet up to keep their slippers dry. The water had a salty smell to it, a stale, unpleasant odor.

With a jolt the wheels of the chariot regained the road on the other side of the Jordan River.

"Herod Antipas." It was the preacher, the wild-looking one in the camel's hair coat. "We've been expecting you."

"Are you John?" Herod said, sounding a little breathless. "The one they call the Baptizer?"

"I am John." His face was gaunt and deeply lined. He was an ascetic who had subsisted for years in the desert on a diet of locusts and wild honey.

"And how is it you have been expecting me? Are you a prophet then?"

John laughed, the sound mocking. His dark eyes seemed to burn in his head like smoldering coals. "Oh, yes. A prophet indeed! Yesterday I saw the king's men laying these paving stones on the river bottom so that your chariot could more easily navigate the ford, and I prophesied to all here, 'The king is coming.'"

"So you are not a prophet?"

"I am the voice of one crying in the wilderness, make straight the paths of the Lord."

"The words of Isaiah," Herod said. "What do you mean by them?"

"I mean that the day of the Lord is at hand. Even now the ax is at the root of the tree. Every tree that does not bear fruit pleasing to God will be cut down and thrown into the fire."

There was something about his eyes; Herod felt the hair rise at the nape of his neck.

"Do not think that you yourself will escape unscathed," John said. "Already a fox has been in your brother's henhouse."

"What do you mean?" Herod said. "Do you speak of treason? Treachery?" Treachery had always been a constant worry, both for him and for his father before him. Of all his father's sons, only he and Philip now ruled any part of their father's kingdom.

"Treachery indeed. Philip's own brother has lain with his wife and rides with her now in the royal chariot."

There was some general laughter in the crowd, though Herod's darting eyes failed to detect a specific culprit. He flushed.

"You will find impudence most imprudent, Baptizer," he said.

John bowed elaborately. "My apologies to your wife, the queen. Or should I say your niece?"

Herod's face had become the color of clay. "You should not," Herod said.

"Have I been misinformed then? She is not the daughter of your deceased brother?"

"Aristobulus was my half-brother."

"I see it now. Your sister-in-law is half a niece and wholly a wife. A talented woman indeed with so many roles to play!"

"This is intolerable," Herodias said sharply. Her narrow face was pinched in anger. "Why do you banter words with this wild man? Guards! Arrest him."

The captain wheeled his horse toward John, a half-dozen of his men falling in behind him. A stone rang off the captain's helmet and he wobbled in his saddle.

Herod stood upright in his chariot, his expression disbelieving, his heart hammering in his chest. The boy responsible stood just a little way from John. It was Seth, his hair still damp from his baptism. Already he had fitted another stone to his sling, and he twirled it casually at shoulder-height, his eyes watchful, his narrow face unsmiling.

John held out a hand palm-downward to the boy. "No," he said. "I will go peacefully."

It was too late. One of Herod's soldiers launched his javelin in an over-the-shoulder throw, and it hit the boy just under the breastbone and hurled him backwards.

Cries of anger and astonishment sounded here and there among the crowd. One Jew drew a sword from a scabbard beneath his cloak, and a stone, thrown from somewhere, caught Herod in the shoulder, sending him sprawling backwards onto Herodias.

"Dolt!" she shouted, pushing at him and kicking at the driver. "Move." The soldier at the reins, ducking his head, spurred the horses.

"Protect the king," the captain shouted, turning his horse after him, and the soldiers retreated in tight formation.

When the soldiers had passed over the rise to the west, the crowd, which had scattered, huddled tightly around the fallen boy. John the Baptizer stood looking at the man who had drawn his sword.

"They won't be arresting you today, Baptizer," the man said grimly. His complexion was dark and smooth, his black beard trimmed close to his face.

"Who are you?"

The man didn't answer immediately, and John turned aside. He had the boy Seth to attend to.

† † †

The boy was lying on his back, the javelin running through his body, pinning him to the ground. He felt no pain, only a mild dismay that he didn't seem to be breathing. He felt as if he were drowning in a warm bath. When the face of the Baptizer appeared above him, the lines of his features wavered disconcertingly.

Seth opened his mouth to speak, but his words, which had a garbled, underwater quality to them, were unintelligible.

The Baptizer's words likewise were unintelligible. Seth found himself looking through John's wavering image at a river valley greener and richer than he remembered it. John faded, and Seth found himself alone in the far country.

† † †

Several miles up in the sere hills northeast of Jericho, Jesus stood with his face turned in the direction of the Jordan River. He had heard no sound — he was too far away for that — but he had sensed something, and it troubled him. "Dear God," he said, softly. "Dear God."

He stood for some time, watching and listening. A crow cawed in the distance, a harbinger of death. Jesus sighed, deeply. "How long, Father, how long?" he murmured.

If an answer came, no one but Jesus heard it. He turned to climb higher into the barren hills.

† † †

John closed the boy's eyes and eased him onto his side. The crowd pressed closely about them. He stood and looked at them, his eyes settling on the dark-skinned man, who by now had sheathed his sword.

"Judas," the man said. "Of Kerioth." He looked down at the boy, and, as if moved by sudden feeling, gripped his cloak by the collar and tore it down the front.

It was a gesture of mourning, and it reflected how all of them felt. Another man tore his cloak, then another.

"He was a brave young man," said someone. All around, men scratched dirt from the earth and ground it into their hair. More cloaks were torn. Some removed their shoes, and some sat upon the ground. A tunic was removed, and a pallet prepared from it for the body.

"How long must we stand for this?" someone said.

John shook his head. "Not long," he said. His eyes focused on Judas. "The day of the Lord is upon us, a day when we will be delivered, not by human hands, but by the hand of God." He looked around at all of them. "On that day," he said in a growing voice, "the Lord with his cruel and strong sword will punish the fleeing serpent. On that day a song will be heard in the land of Judah."

A wailing went up from the crowd, beginning with a single voice and growing.

"On that day Israel's dead shall live; their corpses shall rise. The earth will disclose the blood shed upon it and will no longer cover its slain."

The boy was lifted up on his pallet. John started through the crowd, moving toward the river, and those he passed turned to follow him.

"On that day," John said, holding up his hands. "On that day the trumpet will sound. The earth will give birth to those long dead."

The crowd waded into the river *en masse*. John cupped water in his hands and let it drain through his fingers onto the hair and dripping beards of those around him. He pushed some down totally into the water and with his hand drew them up again.

"The trumpet shall sound. The dead will be raised."

A hysteria had gripped the crowd. Each one plunged down into the river and came up again, his hair and his clothes streaming water.

CHAPTER 2

As the afternoon turned to dusk, Centurion Marcus Antoninus marched from the garrison at Jericho to the Hiljah Ford with half his company. Herod had arrived in Jericho bellowing complaints about the lack of security at the ford, and Antoninus was under orders to take possession of the ford, by force if necessary, and to seek out and capture a long-haired, unshaven barbarian known as John the Baptizer.

"Not publicly, not publicly," Herod had insisted. "The people will riot. He's a great favorite of the people."

"So what? So what if we upset a few Jews?" Antoninus's tribune said.

"It may not be just a few Jews. If we fan this into a full-fledged insurrection, Rome won't look too kindly on either of us."

"Where else but in public can I find him? You think his Jewish friends will point me freely to his door?"

"You secure the ford," Herod said. "If you find John, arrest him. If you don't, let it go. I'll find him eventually. He's well known in my territory beyond the Jordan."

The tribune looked at Antoninus. "Take fifty men," the tribune said. "See to it."

The first travelers Antoninus came upon were Nabataean merchants, two of them, small and dark, each sitting side-saddle on his donkey. Four camels plodded behind them carrying huge sacks of grain, two to a camel, each sack large enough to have held one of the Nabataeans and his donkey as well.

"Stop," Antoninus called out to them in Aramaic, the common language of Palestine.

The merchants stopped their donkeys, and their camels came to a halt behind them.

"You have come from Hiljah Ford," Antoninus said. "What were the conditions there?"

The first man said something in a language incomprehensible to Antoninus.

"What?" he said, this time in Latin. To his troops he called, "Does anybody speak this monkey tongue?"

None of his men volunteered.

Turning back to the merchants, Antoninus said something vulgar about the sexual practices of the Nabataeans' mothers, and the two bobbed their small, dark heads.

He let them go. The Romans were two miles from the Jordan River when they came upon their first group of Jews.

"Stop," he cried again.

The Jews stopped. There were five of them, too few to be any kind of threat, too few to be anything but terrified.

They pressed close to the side of the road, eyes on their own sandaled feet.

"I seek John the Baptizer," Antoninus said in broken Aramaic.

None of the travelers answered him or even raised his eyes.

Antoninus pointed to one of them. "Seize him," he said, and two of his men stepped forward to grab his arms and jerk him forward.

"What is your name, Jew?" Antoninus said.

The man looked up at him. One of Antoninus's men jerked his hood from his head, revealing a dark face and a short black beard. It was Judas.

"What is your name?" Antoninus repeated.

Judas told him.

One of Antoninus's men pulled the scabbard from beneath Judas's cloak, jerking it loose from the fabric that held it. "He's armed, centurion."

"He is. How very interesting. Are you one of the *sicarii*, Judas of Kerioth?"

Judas shook his head, denying comprehension of the Roman's Latin. "I'm not sick," he said.

Antoninus wasn't fooled. "I wasn't inquiring into the state of your health," he said. "I was suggesting you were an outlaw who preyed even on his own people in the name of a misguided patriotism."

Judas lifted his shoulders, turning his hands palm-upward in a helpless gesture.

"Speak up, Jew."

"No, centurion," Judas said plaintively. "These are violent times. I am concerned for my safety, and for that of my friends."

"Were you at the river earlier today? Did you see the man they call John the Baptizer?"

"The wild man? Yes, I saw him."

"Where is he now?"

Judas shook his head. "Beyond the Jordan? I can't say where."

"You can't, or you won't? In what village does this Baptizer reside?"

Again Judas shook his head. "I don't know."

Antoninus stared at him. Judas kept his eyes on the Roman's feet.

"Let him go," Antoninus said abruptly, and his soldiers flung Judas backwards to the ground.

"March."

They passed other travelers on their way to the river and stopped twice more to question them. No one could tell them anything about the Baptizer, and, when they got to the ford, it was deserted.

† † †

"Are you hurt?" Judas's four companions were gathered around him, looking down.

"No. I'm not hurt."

Judas held up his hand, and a man named Simon helped him to his feet. "Roman dogs," Judas said. "They'll pay for that one day."

"Judas Sicarii," Simon said.

Judas looked at him irritably. "What?"

"It's what the Roman called you. *Sicarii*."

"*Sicarii* is plural," said one of the others, who knew a little Latin. "It should be Judas Sicarius, Judas the Daggerman. It has a ring to it."

Judas half-smiled. "For a revolutionary," he said.

Simon said, "We can't stand here jabbering; we have to go back. If they arrest the Baptizer, we will lose the rallying point we've placed so much hope on."

"Maybe the arrest would be the trigger needed to rouse the people," Judas said, disagreeing. "John is a popular figure."

"You heard him, though. He is not the Messiah; he is not Elijah; he is not the Prophet. None of that is going to raise his stature any."

"People are wondering about him, though. People are asking. And you saw the reaction to Herod's attempt to arrest him."

"True, true. And consider the questions: Are you the Messiah? Are you Elijah, returned from heaven?"

"Yes, we can't ignore this John. If the Romans arrest him, we need to act. We'll make camp outside Jericho tonight. Tomorrow, we'll go back to the Jordan to see if we can find out what has happened to him."

† † †

Neither Herod Antipas nor Judea's procurator — a position to which a man named Pontius Pilate had recently been appointed — lived in Jerusalem. The procurator lived in Caesarea-by-the-Sea, a city built by Herod the Great on the site of a settlement known previously as the Tower of Straton. It was a Greek city in every respect, complete with agora, theater, amphitheater, stadium, palace, temple of Caesar, and colossal statues of Augustus Caesar and of Romulus, the mythological founder of Rome. When the procurator visited Jerusalem, which he was compelled to do from time to time, he occupied the Palace of Herod, which had been the primary residence of Herod the Great, the father of Herod Antipas.

Herod Antipas, whose capital city was Tiberius, a city he himself had built on the Sea of Galilee and named for the emperor, visited Jerusalem with roughly the same frequency as Pilate, though it was not located in either of his territories. On the occasions of his visits, he was limited — unhappily — to the smaller, less elaborate Hasmonaean Palace, which had been the home of the dynasty that had ruled Judea during its brief period of independence some generations ago. The palace was located in the upper city, close to the Xystus Gate of the temple.

Herod arrived there two days after the incident at the Hiljah Ford. Once he had time to rest from his journey, to sleep and to bathe and to dress himself in the royal purple, he sent for the high priest of Jerusalem.

Within the half-hour, the high priest was announced, and Josephus Caiaphas entered the throne room.

"What are you doing here?" Herod asked him snappishly. "I sent for Annas."

"My apologies, majesty," Caiaphas said ponderously, giving Herod a slight bow. "I had heard that you sent for the high priest, a title which has been mine now for a dozen years." He was dressed in the Greek style, with a long, seamless tunic and a cloak with tassels on the four corners of the hem. On his head was the embroidered cap of the high priest.

"I was thinking of Annas."

Caiaphas was a big man with a thick black beard and a booming voice. He had physical presence, but to many it was a hollow presence. He was dominated by his father-in-law, who had been high priest before him. His mind lacked Annas's subtlety. His will lacked Annas's resolve.

"Is there a message I could give him for you?" Caiaphas said.

"Yes. I was attacked by the Baptizer and his followers on the road to Jericho only two days ago."

"*John* the Baptizer?"

"Are there others? He incited the crowd against me, and I was lucky to escape with my life."

"Has he been arrested?"

"Not that I know of. We haven't been able to find him."

Caiaphas raised his eyebrows. "He has ceased to preach publicly?"

"I don't know. I don't know, and I don't care. I want him arrested quietly, out of sight of the crowd."

"Ah," said Caiaphas. "Very politic of you."

"Rome replaced my brother Archelaus because he continually riled the people. I won't make his mistake."

Caiaphas bent at the waist slightly in acknowledgment of Herod's wisdom.

"But the point is, I was attacked. Tell Annas that. Tell him I hold him personally responsible."

"Responsible!" Caiaphas echoed. "How —"

"The Baptizer's a priest, isn't he? One of yours."

"He's a Levite. He serves no formal role in the priesthood."

"Perhaps you should give him one. Why has an unsupervised Levite been permitted to develop such a following among the people? It isn't good, I tell you. It isn't safe. I alerted the tribune at the garrison in Jericho as to his revolutionary activities, but I expect you to look into it as well."

"We've been looking into it. A delegation returned from questioning him only yesterday."

"What did they ask him? What did he say?"

"It was inconclusive, your majesty."

"Inconclusive! Tell your people to stay on him until they reach some conclusions. This John is preaching apocalypse: I want to know why, what his motives are. When you find out, I expect you to report to me."

"Certainly, your majesty. Certainly."

"It may be that we'll have to do something to stop him."

† † †

When Herod had left the throne room, he found Herodias standing in the hall. Her arms were folded across her chest, and her slippered foot tapped impatiently.

"Why do you appoint that boob to do your work for you?"

"It would be better if John were dealt with by one of his own."

"The man is a revolutionary. He precipitated an attack on your own person."

"No, you precipitated the attack by thoughtlessly ordering his arrest with all those people around him."

"No one can be permitted to address you as he did. The man must be nailed up and left hanging on a cross in the very place we found him, by the Hiljah Ford."

Herod's lip curled. "You're a blood-thirsty wench," he said.

She stepped against him, looking up. "But an attractive one?"

His smile widened.

CHAPTER 3

The baptism of Jesus occurred in late summer of the fifteenth year of the reign of the Emperor Tiberius. It was in the fall of the same year that he, along with his family and friends, attended a wedding in Cana of Galilee.

There weren't enough chairs at the feast that followed, and Jesus was seated on the limestone floor with his brothers and two of his new Judean friends. The Judeans seemed ill at ease. Neither knew the bride, the bridegroom, or, for that matter, anyone in Cana.

Everyone was dressed in his wedding-day finest. Eating and drinking, people were sitting in the windows as well as on the floor; people were standing; people were sitting on the outside steps leading up to the roof.

It was Judas of Kerioth who first noticed Jesus' mother standing by, waiting for an opportunity to interrupt. She was wearing a blue cloak as if to go outside, though it was only the middle of the afternoon and too early to be leaving. Judas touched Jesus' arm and gestured toward her. "I think your mother wants a word with you," he said. His glance went briefly to Jesus' brothers — James, Joseph, Simon, and Judas — before returning to Jesus.

Jesus looked up, and he smiled when he saw her. "Yes, mother?"

"Come outside with me a moment. There's something I need to talk to you about."

"Just me, or James and the others as well?"

"Just you."

Jesus got to his feet, dusting off his knees and the seat of his cloak. "I'll be back," he said to Judas of Kerioth and his friend Simon.

When he was gone, the Judeans sat looking at Jesus' brothers, no one saying anything. Finally, Jesus' brother James broke the silence. "What did Simon call you?" he said to Judas of Kerioth. "*Sicarius*?"

Judas laughed. "A joke," he said. "A couple of months ago, some Roman soldiers stopped us on the road from Jericho to Jerusalem."

"And they accused you of being one of the *sicarii*?" James glanced at his brothers.

"Why does a Roman dog say anything?" He said it too loudly, and his words attracted the attention of several nearby. They looked at him, and, when he looked up, looked away.

It was Carmeli's wedding day, not a time for inflammatory discussions of the political situation.

† † †

It was late fall, and the air outside, though muggy, was rather cold. A gust of wind swept up a cloud of dust from the dirt street and swept it toward them, Ducking his head, Jesus pulled his cloak more tightly about his throat.

"Yes, mother, what is it?"

The crowd on the steps had thinned, everyone crowding back into the house as the day cooled.

"They've run out of wine," Mary said.

"Here at the feast?"

"I overheard the wedding steward telling Miriam."

Miriam was the mother of the bride. Jesus glanced toward the door, where three men stood watching them, just out of earshot. "Who are they?" he said. "Are they with you?"

"The steward's helpers."

"Ah. And you'd like me to help carry more wine from Naphtali's house." Naphtali was the groom. "I'd be happy to."

"He doesn't have any to carry," said Mary. "All he had was brought last week."

"How about his parents?"

"Miriam would die."

Jesus smiled at her. "What then?" he said. "Should I go out to the vineyard and start picking grapes?"

"I don't know what you should do. Something."

Jesus looked at the sun, already low in the sky. "It's been quite a celebration," he said. "I could tell everyone we've imposed long enough on the hospitality of our host and hostess. I think everyone would leave cheerfully enough."

"Miriam —"

"Would die," Jesus said.

"I'm being serious."

"I know you are." Smiling fondly, he reached out to touch her cheek.

"You'll help her?"

"I —"

One of the men who had been sitting in the window of Miriam's mud-brick house fell backwards into the dirt, and a cloud of dust rose up around him.

Jesus looked from him — lying on his back with his legs sticking straight up, resting against the side of the house — to his mother. He looked back again. The man wasn't moving.

"Just a moment," Jesus said to his mother. He walked over to the man and saw that his eyes were open.

"Are you all right, Eloy?" Jesus asked, looking down.

Eloy blinked up at him. The beard around his mouth was stained dark with wine, and he still held his cup tightly in his hand. He belched. "Hello, Jesus," he said.

"Hello, Eloy."

"Nice party." He seemed peaceful enough, obviously unhurt, and Jesus turned back to his mother.

"It would be hard to argue that people hadn't had more than enough to drink," he said.

Her smile was wry. "I'm going to leave it in your hands," she said.

"I appreciate your confidence in me, but —"

Mary beckoned to the servants, still hovering in the doorway.

"I know you'll think of something," she said to Jesus as they approached. "Make it rain wine, if you have to."

He smiled suddenly. A professed belief in his miraculous powers was something of a joke his family had begun to affect sometime after the death of his father Joseph.

"Would you prefer white or red?" he said.

She touched his arm by way of acknowledging the joke — and dismissing it — then stepped away. The servants had approached and stood looking at him. All three were young, their beards as yet consisting of no more than the wispy beginnings of a moustache and sideburns.

Jesus looked back at them, still smiling as he reflected.

"Well?" one of the boys said. "What shall we do?"

"I'm thinking. My name is Jesus, of Nazareth. Are all of you from around here?"

"Yes," said the boy. "He's Oren. He's Joel. I'm James, the son of Alpheus. Do you know my father? He keeps the synagogue here."

"I do know him. He's a fine man."

"So where are we going to get more wine, sir?" Joel said.

"Would we have any containers for the wine if we had any?"

"Wouldn't any wine we found already be in containers?" Joel asked.

Jesus thought of wine raining from the sky. "I don't know. Do you know where we can find containers full of wine?"

"No, sir."

Jesus looked at the others. "Any of you know where there's wine to be had in Cana?"

Both of them shook their heads.

"Then I guess we ought to start with containers," Jesus said.

James took his arm, drawing him to where he could see through the doorway into the house. "See the stone jars along that wall?" the boy said.

"That's the wine that's left?" Jesus asked him. The jars were of a type generally used for water. Jews who observed the law strictly, as the parents of the bride did, used a lot of water for ceremonial washing, and the jars for the water were huge.

"No. That's the wine that's been drunk."

"Ah."

"All those jars are empty now."

Jesus looked thoughtful. "Why don't the three of you go in and get them?" he said. "Bring them out here, all six of them."

"Okay."

It took them two trips apiece to get them all. The jars were heavy, even when empty, and the three boys were breathing hard after their effort.

"I think we could use some help with this." Jesus went to the door and beckoned for Simon and Judas to join them. Simon got to his feet. He was tall, with hollow cheeks, a dark, jutting beard and a prominent Adam's apple. Judas was shorter and unusually dark, his hair and closely trimmed beard almost blue-black in hue.

"We need to get these six jars down to the well there," Jesus said to them, pointing toward the center of town. Because the water table level was generally low, few individual households could afford to dig a well to the required depth. They relied instead on the town well for their water. "Can each of you carry a jar?"

"Why?" Judas said.

"They're empty and need refilling." Jesus lifted one of the jars himself, hoisting it onto a shoulder. Judas looked at Simon, who shrugged and shouldered one of the others. Judas picked up one, as did each of the boys. The six of them carried the jars down the dirt road to the well in the center of town.

"We're going to fill all these?" Judas asked as they were setting them down. "It's going to take awhile."

"Then it will take awhile. We can take turns with the bucket."

"I don't get it," said James, the son of Alpheus. "Are we going to serve water to the wedding guests when they're expecting wine?"

Simon said, "They are out of wine then. I thought they were running low."

Judas peered into one of the jars. When he tilted it, a little wine puddled at one side. "I can understand the urge to water the wine, but I think you've waited a little late for it."

"They'll know, sir," James said. "They'll know."

Jesus had already pulled the bucket from the well three times, each time dumping its contents into the jar nearest him.

"It doesn't even look like wine," Judas said, rocking the stone jar to swirl its contents.

"It might work," Simon said. "The wedding guests have emptied out all six of these big jars. It has to have dulled their palates."

"Nobody can be so drunk as to mistake water for wine."

"This is taking too long," Jesus said. He was working at the knot that held the rope to the bucket. "We'll lower the jars themselves down. There're six of us. We'll be able to get them back up."

He removed the bar that secured the jar's lid and ran the rope through the holes. "See?" he said, tying a knot. "A great big bucket."

"I'll say," Simon said.

"Help me lower it. We don't want to chip it against the sides of the well."

Simon helped him play out the rope.

"Okay, heave," Jesus said. His clenched teeth showed white through his beard, and the cords stood out in his neck. Simon reached down to grip the rope for the next pull. As he took the weight of the jar, his face turned red and his neck puffed out like a blowfish. Jesus reached down to grip the rope.

When they had the jar up, Jesus and Simon stood panting, their hands braced on their knees.

"You're stronger than you look," Simon said.

"So are you." Jesus looked at James. "Put the lid back on," he said between breaths. "The three of you waddle it back down the street to Miriam's house, if you can."

"Sure. But do what with it, sir?"

"Present it to the steward."

"We can't do that."

Jesus smiled. "Just don't tell him where it came from."

The three boys looked at him.

"Go on, now. If they're already out of wine, they can't stall much longer."

James's face was unhappy. He shook his head, then squatted beside the jar. Joel and Oren helped him lift it. When they got back, Jesus and Judas and Simon had two more jars filled. The boys took one. Judas and Simon took the other. When they got back, Jesus was standing at the edge of the well, holding onto the rope.

"You don't think maybe three jars are enough?"

"Ah, Judas, Judas. When I do a job, I like to do it right."

Simon stepped up next to Jesus and looked down into the well, sighting along the rope.

"I thought maybe I could pull it out by myself," Jesus said. "I was wrong."

Simon and then Judas both grabbed hold.

When they were done, and all six of the jars were again sitting along the wall inside the front room of Miriam's house, Jesus filled his cup with the new wine and drained it. "Ah, that's good. Want some?"

Judas looked at him sourly. "I don't think so," he said.

"Simon?"

Simon started to shake his head, the gesture quick and birdlike, then he shrugged and held out his cup. Jesus filled it with the ladle.

Simon looked down into his cup for a moment, his mouth pursed doubtfully. "This doesn't look like what we put in it."

"Taste it."

Simon took a sip obediently. He looked up at Jesus, his eyebrows climbing his forehead and his black beard bristling. He took another sip, then another, then tilted his head back and drained his cup, his knotty Adam's apple bobbing in his throat.

"It's wonderful," he said, holding out his cup again. "Wonderful. Judas, try it."

But Judas rolled his eyes in evident exasperation and turned away. "If I'd wanted water, I'd have gotten my fill of it while we were out at the well."

Simon's eyes were fixed on Jesus, his expression a mixture of wonder and incredulity. "How did you do it?" he said. His cup was in his hand, half-extended in front of him.

"Still thirsty?" Jesus dipped the ladle in the stone jar and filled Simon's cup for the second time. "Yes, there's nothing like a good wine."

Judas, looking on, could only shake his head.

† † †

Later, at nearly dusk, Jesus and Simon and Judas were several miles outside of Cana, well along on their journey. The road was a good one, paved with cement made from crushed limestone and volcanic ash. It was convex to allow drainage and bounded by a ditch on either side. The Romans had built the road and maintained it to facilitate the movement of troops; the Jews paid for it.

Jesus and his companions heard a shout and turned to see a boy running along the road toward them.

"Who do you think that is?" Judas said, not recognizing him.

Simon said, "I think it's one of those steward's helpers."

"James," Jesus called. "Son of Alpheus."

James stopped when he reached them, panting and out of breath.

"What can we do for you?" Jesus asked, and James shifted his weight from one foot to the other.

"Where are you going, sir?" he said to Jesus.

"Judea for the winter months. We'll come back after the Passover." He raised his eyebrows. "Why do you ask?"

"I was wondering . . . Could I go with you?"

"If you want to."

"Why?" Judas said. "Why would you want to go to Judea?"

James looked at him. "It's the wine, sir."

"The wine? You want to accompany us to Judea because our prank fooled the steward?"

"It was no prank. Old Jotham said it was the best wine of the feast, and he went off with a cup of it to ask Miriam why she had waited until then to serve it."

Judas threw back his head and laughed, his mirth working his throat. James stood looking at him.

"And how much had old Jotham had to drink at that point?" Judas asked him.

James turned to Jesus. "I tasted it myself, sir, and I wasn't drunk. It was my first wine of the day."

"And so now you want to go to Judea?" Jesus said.

"I want to go with you."

Jesus reached out to lay a hand on his curly head. "Welcome, James, son of Alpheus," he said, smiling down at him.

"Has he cleared this with his father?" Judas said to Jesus. "Shouldn't you inquire? Alpheus may not appreciate our running off with his best helper."

"Some things are more important than familial obligation." Jesus winked at Judas, then started off, leaving the others looking after him. Judas looked at Simon and shrugged.

Simon shook his head. "I'm going after him."

First Simon, then James broke into a trot to catch up with Jesus, and Judas followed.

CHAPTER 4

Jesus spent the winter months in Judea, staying in Bethany at the home of Lazarus and his sisters. Each day he walked with his three disciples to the temple in Jerusalem, two miles north and west of Bethany. The temple and its precincts, composed as they were of limestone and marble, were as white as the occasional snow that fell on Jerusalem and the surrounding hills. Each morning, as Jesus and his disciples crested the Mount of Olives across from the city, the temple, with its gold plating and gilded pinnacles, reflected the fiery splendor of the rising sun with such force that it was impossible to look at it for more than a moment at a time.

"It's beautiful," James said, on the first morning.

"Yes."

"The dwelling place of God Almighty," James said, using a name by which God had been known since before the time of Moses, El Shaddai.

Jesus looked at him.

"Look at it," James said. "Who could doubt that God himself makes his dwelling there?"

"Within the walls which Herod built?"

"Within the Holy of Holies," James said, nodding. By now he was used to the searching questions Jesus put to him and to everybody.

"A place utterly dark and empty," Jesus said.

"Yes."

"Visited only by the high priest on a single day a year."

"The Day of Atonement," James said.

They had started down the gray, chalky road that lay along the olive grove which gave the hill its name. The trees, already old, were festooned with burls, gnarled and twisted as if by some ancient agony. The sun was warm on the backs of the men, but a cool morning breeze swept up from the Kidron Valley.

"He must be a lonely God," Jesus said.

"He must?"

"Wouldn't you be lonely if your only visitor was Caiaphas, and he came to see you only once a year?"

Simon, walking on the other side of Jesus, laughed. "I'd be glad the visit came only once a year," he said.

James was thoughtful. As they crossed the narrow stone bridge spanning the brook that ran along the bottom of the valley, he looked back, squinting into the morning sun.

"I guess if I were God, I'd rather live there among the olive trees," he said.

Jesus laughed. James, worried that he — and Jesus — were guilty of some irreverence, smiled uncertainly.

"I think God would rather live there, too," Jesus said.

"He would?"

"And I think the time is coming when he will say as much."

"To whom?" Judas asked, turning back to look at them. "To whom will God address these comments?"

"The voice of his thunder is in the whirlwind," Jesus said, quoting the Psalmist. "His lightning lights up the world. The earth trembles and shakes."

"What's that supposed to mean?"

"When God speaks, you'll find it hard to miss," said Jesus.

† † †

They entered Jerusalem by the Fountain Gate and turned onto a narrow road that ascended toward the temple in a series of steps, broad and shallow, with little open shops on either side. The streets inside the city were paved with cobblestones, cut square on all sides and fitted together with a thin sandwich of sand between. At this hour the streets were crowded with camels and donkeys, with men carrying large baskets of bread or fish or vegetables, with women carrying shopping baskets or water jars balanced high on their heads. Jesus picked his way among them, James beside him, Judas and Simon following behind. Shoppers haggled with shopkeepers over food and earthenware, brass vessels and cloth.

"Is it how you remember it?" Jesus asked James.

"It was even more crowded." He jumped to avoid a side-stepping camel, a little Nabataean merchant balanced high on its back. "If that's possible."

"You were here for the Passover," Jesus said. "It's more than possible."

Great covered walkways, thirty cubits across, formed the perimeter of the temple precincts. They passed between two rows of white marble pillars, each rising six times the height of a man and consisting of a single stone. James, looking up at the ceiling of polished cedar as they walked, was open-mouthed.

Jesus stopped them in Solomon's Portico, that portion of the colonnade that bounded the temple precincts on the east side. He sat down on the stone flagging, and his three disciples sat around him. It was the posture of a rabbi, and several passers-by dawdled near them to hear what this one had to say.

"Moses tells us that we should not hate in our hearts any of our own people: 'You shall not take vengeance or bear a grudge against any of your people, but you shall love your neighbor as yourself. I am the Lord.'" Jesus looked at Judas. "Does that mean we are free to hate our enemies?" he asked.

Judas, sitting, looked around uneasily at those who were standing around them. "Yes," he said. "By implication."

"But God causes the sun to rise on the evil as well as the good. He sends rain on the righteous as well as the unrighteous."

Simon coughed into his hand, and Jesus looked at him.

"Why then does Moses limit the obligation? If he meant for us to love our enemies as well as our friends?"

"Because of the hardness of men's hearts. Moses had to set some minimal standard for his people; but consider — if we love only those who love us, what have we done? Doesn't everybody do that? Even a Gentile, a man with no special relationship to God, will greet his own kinsmen, his brothers and sisters."

A young man, one of the bystanders, said, "And does God expect more from the Jews? What does he want from us?"

The young man wore not one cloak but two, brightly colored. He was obviously affluent.

"Perfection," Jesus said in answer to his question.

"How can a man reach perfection?"

"How does a man love?" Jesus asked him. "How does he reason?"

The man shook his head.

"God loves and reasons, and he shares those capacities with us, guiding us as a parent might guide the hand of a child first forming his letters."

The man withdrew from his purse two gerahs, worth about a half-day's wage. He gave them to Jesus and sat down with them in the small circle. By the end of the day, two others had paid to sit at the feet of the new rabbi. By the end of the week there were twenty. The crowds around the circle grew larger, and Jesus' voice sounded in ringing tones throughout Solomon's Portico.

In the spring, on the fourteenth day of Nisan, Lazarus came with them into Jerusalem. It was the first day of the Passover, Israel's greatest festival, and in his arms Lazarus carried a plump, yearling lamb. It nuzzled his chest, trying to use its lips to draw his tunic into its mouth, and it let out an occasional bleat. Lazarus, though gaunt, was tall and strong; his gait was steady as they descended the Mount of Olives, and his breath came easily. The wind caught at his long, graying beard and tossed it streaming over one shoulder. James, somewhat in awe of the old man, matched his stride, keeping an eye on him and the lamb he carried.

"He's cute," James said.

"Yes. The best of my flock," Lazarus said. "Sleek and fat, without spot or blemish." Such were the requirements of the Passover sacrifice. His lips compressed in a grim expression as he walked along. "The priests get the breast and right shoulder; they'll like that. Shouldn't have to bribe the temple inspectors more than a couple of shekels to let him pass."

"But that's as much as the value of the whole lamb!"

"Aye, outside the temple. But only a tenth as much as they'd charge me for one of their own scrawny beasts."

James looked back at Jesus. Criticism of the temple inspectors amounted to criticism of the priests themselves. Jesus was talking to Simon, no longer paying attention to James and Lazarus.

It was only as they entered Jerusalem itself, coming in by the Fountain Gate in the east wall, that they became aware of the noise. Everywhere there were people in movement. The direction of the crowd was northward, along the valley which separated the two hills on which Jerusalem was built. From the chatter passing back and forth in a half-dozen languages, Jesus and the others learned that Judea's new procurator — its fifth — was on his way to Jerusalem. He was due to arrive that very morning.

Jesus and his friends turned to follow the crowd up the west hill toward the palace and the Genneth Gate beside it. The arrival of a new procurator was not without significance. Though the Sanhedrin — the Jewish Council of Elders — controlled the temple and dealt with many of the city's internal affairs, the Roman procurator was the ultimate authority inside Judea, in full control of the province's military and judicial administration.

"I hope he's better than the last one," Lazarus said. "We could use a procurator who's fair and reasonable."

"Better if he's unfair and unreasonable," Judas said.

"What's the point in that?"

"It's more likely to unite the people."

"Unite the people, or incite them?" Lazarus said. "You're too young to remember any real fighting. The last thing we need is another war."

"I've done my share of fighting," Judas said, and Lazarus eyed him long and hard.

"Aye," he said. "I dare say you have."

High walls encircled the palace and were patrolled by soldiers. The palace itself had been built of many different kinds of rare stone imported from all over the world. The roofs were remarkable both for length of beam and for ornamentation. The gate consisted of two arched doors, tall and massive, and these were closed.

The crowd carried Jesus and the others past the palace and through the Genneth Gate onto the north road. "The procurator himself isn't here yet," someone said. "Only his advance guard."

"Look," Simon said, pointing. Far along the road to the north was a cloud of dust rising brown against the blue sky. The cloud seemed large even at that distance, and it was growing larger as it approached. "More soldiers."

Lazarus had tucked the lamb inside his cloak to shelter it from the press of people. "Aye," he said enigmatically.

Judas put a hand to the short sword he wore beneath his cloak.

An entire legion was approaching to join the one already in Jerusalem. The first cohort, consisting of more than a thousand infantry, had custody of the eagle, the military standard of the Roman empire, a red bird on a field of white. The bust of the Emperor Tiberius topped the pole. The image could likewise be seen atop the legion's standard, the cohorts' standards, the companies'. The second, third, and fourth cohorts, each half the size of the first, came into view, trailing away along the crest of the mountain range until obscured by their own dust.

The feet of the soldiers sounded like thunder on the paved road. The sun flashed from their breast-plates, their oblong bucklers, and their ponderous javelins, tipped with massive, triangular points of steel. The soldiers' faces, visible through open helmets topped with lofty crests, were clean-shaven and proud. As they reached the city gate, they ranged themselves before it, standing in well-ordered ranks as if awaiting inspection.

Coming up behind the first four cohorts of infantry was a troop of cavalry, consisting of one hundred thirty-two horsemen, the first troop of ten. Each horseman had a long broadsword strapped to his back, the great handle visible above one shoulder. The cavalry too fell into rank, the horses snorting and stamping as the horsemen reined them in.

Judas's hand dropped from the hilt of his sword. For the moment he was all but blinded by a black despair. Who could even conceive of building an army of Jews capable of besting a Roman legion? He glanced at Jesus and saw that, instead of watching the troop formations, Jesus was making friends with Lazarus's lamb.

Nearly an hour after the first of the Roman infantry came into view, and the standard of the empire became recognizable, Pilate himself appeared, standing in a war chariot, a hand raised in greeting. Stretching out behind him was a continuous line of cavalry and infantry.

Two men came out from the gate to meet Pilate. One of them wore the mitered cap of the high priest and a long blue robe tied round with an embroidered girdle. Caiaphas. The other wore a linen robe even more luxurious in appearance, though without the same ceremonial significance. This was Annas, Caiaphas's father-in-law and once the high priest himself.

"Greetings," Caiaphas said, holding up a hand. "Greetings, Lord Procurator."

Pilate stepped down from the chariot. He was of medium height, with a spare frame, and he wore light boots and a simple tunic under a coat of mail. His head was bare, his short brown hair combed forward.

"You're the priest?" he said.

Caiaphas bowed. "Josephus Caiaphas, Lord Procurator. High priest of Israel."

An expression of distaste crossed Pilate's face. Though he raised a hand casually in acknowledgment of the introduction, he dropped it again almost immediately.

"May our association be long and peaceful," Caiaphas said.

"Yes," Pilate said. His military attire, combined with his narrow face and the prominence of his cheekbones, gave him a severe look.

"To that end I remind you of the custom of your predecessors."

"What custom is that?"

"Of removing the metal busts from your military standards before entering Jerusalem. It is against our law for any graven image to be brought into the city."

Pilate glanced over his ranked troops, taking in the eagle, flapping audibly in the brisk wind, and the other standards with the bust of Caesar Tiberius ornamenting the top of each.

"Rome dictates your law," Pilate said. "The so-called graven image is the bust of your emperor."

"Be that as it may," Caiaphas said. "His image —"

Pilate's nostrils flared. "You dismiss your Emperor so easily?" he said testily.

"His bust is a graven image forbidden by our God."

"And what does the Emperor care for your God?"

Annas spoke, his voice strong but old, almost dusty with age. "The Emperor cares very much for the peace," he said.

Pilate gestured off-handedly toward the troops still massing behind him. Beyond them rose Golgotha, the place of the skull, a dome-like hill bristling with the empty uprights of a dozen crosses. "Behold the Emperor's peace," he said. "Behold the *Pax Romana*."

"Lord Procurator," Caiaphas said. "You can't . . ."

Again the nostrils flared, and Pilate's head went back. "I can't," he repeated. "Tribune!" he called, raising a hand.

An officer on horseback wheeled toward him. Pilate gave a hand-signal. The tribune wheeled back toward the army, hand raised, and he spurred his horse from cohort to cohort, issuing commands.

"I am not my predecessor," Pilate said.

"We're not suggesting that you should be," Annas responded. "You should, though, think before needlessly inciting the people. We can be valuable to you in your governance of this people, but a large part of our value to you consists of letting you know . . ." He hesitated, searching for a diplomatic turn of phrase.

"Yes?"

"Letting you know what things can be readily imposed on the people and what they won't abide."

A thin smile stretched Pilate's mouth. The first infantry cohort was entering the city behind the standards topped with the bust of the Emperor.

"We're going to have to resist you on this," Annas said. "If we don't, we'll lose the support of the people."

Pilate leaned close to Annas. "Resist me," he said, grimly. "Please. Resist me."

He turned away. Annas looked at Caiaphas. "Lord Procurator," he said, mimicking his son-in-law. "Lord Procurator, you can't!"

"He can't," Caiaphas protested. "The point had to be made."

"'You can't' isn't an expression to use in dealing with these Romans," Annas said.

Caiaphas frowned, but remained silent.

The troops entered the city, marching down the broad street lined with sullen, silent faces.

CHAPTER 5

The preparations for the Passover continued. Men grumbled their hatred of Rome and their bitterness that the holiest of festivals would be so desecrated. Boys issued unrealistic threats against the Romans, and women scolded. Jesus and James went with Lazarus and his lamb into the temple, Judas and Simon having disappeared.

The inspectors charged a fee of two shekels, and they found a discoloration the size of a small coin on the lamb's belly. Lazarus couldn't see it.

"Where?" he said. "That's just the light."

"It's a dark spot, very clearly a blemish," said the inspector.

"There isn't. Move the lamp closer."

"I don't need to move the lamp closer to know a blemish when I see one. Move along."

"How much?" Lazarus said.

"Pardon?"

"How much do you want to pass it? How big a bribe?"

The man drew back his chin in indignation. Jesus nudged Lazarus, nodded with his head. "Look."

James had knelt beside the lamb and was stroking its head. "I think maybe it's just as well," Jesus said.

Lazarus made a face.

"It would be hard on the boy to watch you kill it. I'll pay for the Passover lamb."

"No need," Lazarus said. "I've brought money."

Though the plumpest of lambs would have brought only two

shekels outside the temple, inside a lamb of comparable quality cost twenty. Of course, the lambs on sale at the Bazaars of Annas (owned by the high priest's family) had already passed inspection. "It's an outrage; that's what it is," Lazarus said, as he left with his purchase, the ammonia-like fumes of the animal dung still fresh in his nostrils. "And what am I going to do with that one?"

"Keep it, for now. James will carry it home for you."

There was an edge to Jesus' voice, despite his mild words. Lazarus looked more closely at his face. "You're as angry about all this as I am," he said.

"Yes. The temple is being systematically defiled. The day is coming when it will be destroyed. Not one stone will be left standing upon another."

Lazarus drew back, suddenly uncomfortable. Jesus had a habit of making unexpected pronouncements only loosely related to the subject under discussion. It was as if a door opened at the back of his mind just long enough to give him a glimpse of something that no man could see.

"When?" Lazarus said.

"Pardon?"

"When will the temple be destroyed?"

Jesus smiled sadly at him. "I don't know," he said. "Not my lifetime or yours, I think." He indicated James. "Perhaps in his."

It was as Lazarus suspected: Jesus knew no more than he had said. It was disconcerting, even eerie. Lazarus had never gotten used to it.

They left the court of the Gentiles and all its commerce, passing through the elegant stone partition through which none but a Jew could pass. Pillars at equal distance were inscribed in both Greek and Roman letters: *No foreigner may enter the Sanctuary on pain of death.* Fourteen steps led up to the Beautiful Gate, more than ten times the height of a man and plated with Corinthian brass. This gate opened into the court of the women. The temple proper was still higher up and further in.

The Nicanor Gate, named after a wealthy Jewish donor from Alexandria, was five steps above the court of the women. Jesus and

James and Lazarus passed through it into the court of Israel, forbidden to women. Black smoke poured off the altar just beyond a low wall. To their right, lambs bawled in panic as they were pinned to the floor by means of an iron ring. The stones about them were stained dark with the blood of a thousand sacrifices, of a thousand thousand. Lazarus joined the line, the sacrificial lamb caught up in the crook of his arm. Jesus and James stayed back, James with Lazarus's lamb.

When a horn was blown, Lazarus went with a group of twenty and, kneeling, fastened his lamb in the iron ring so that its body pointed north and south, its head toward the holy house itself, which was beyond the altar. He drew a bronze knife from his belt.

Jesus, seeing James's eyes fixed on Lazarus and his knife, said, "Look up into the temple. Do you know why the first gate has no doors?"

James looked up through the massive gate, plated with gold, into the vestibule of the sanctuary. He was the son of Alpheus, the keeper of a synagogue. "As a symbol of the universal visibility of heaven," he said, "and of the nature of the Lord God, who can be neither shut in nor closed out."

Another gate, smaller, was visible on the far side of the vestibule. It too was plated with gold, with gold vines above it and clusters of gold grapes as tall as a man. Within that gate was visible the seven branched candlestick with its candles continually alight, the table of shewbread with its twelve loaves, and the altar of incense with thirteen kinds of sweet-smelling spices. Beyond all of that, invisible in the gloom, was the gate into the Holy of Holies, its doors closed and covered by a great Babylonian curtain, embroidered with blue and flaxen and scarlet and purple, the design suggestive of the very image of the universe. Beyond that veil, entirely empty and totally dark, was the dwelling place of God.

James turned back just as Lazarus was holding up his lamb so that the blood ran out into the silver vessel held by a priest. When the vessel was full, the priest threw the blood onto the altar, and a cloud of smoke rose up. The hissing of the blood on the altar was barely audible over the chanting of the Levites, "Praise the Lord!

Praise him, O servants of the Lord, praise his holy name," over the groaning of the ropes drawing up buckets of water from the great cistern far below, over the sloshing of the water on the stone floor to wash away the blood. Mingled with all the sounds was the endless bleating of the terrified lambs.

"Do you remember the words of the prophet Hosea?" Jesus said.

James looked up. "What words?"

"I desire goodness and not sacrifice; the knowledge of God more than burnt offerings."

James frowned.

"The old things are passing away. God will establish a new covenant with his people."

The hair lifted at the nape of James's neck. Jesus, discerning the effect of his words, laughed affectionately and slapped James's back.

† † †

Simon and Judas reappeared at the home of Lazarus in time to help prepare the lamb for the feast. They built a fire in a pit lined with stones, impaled the lamb on a spit, and stood turning it over an open fire. Inside, Lazarus's sister Martha was scouring the metal dishes they would use, dipping them first into boiling water and then into cold. When she was done, she sent her sister out to get a stone from the fire; all the wooden dishes had to be rubbed with a red-hot stone. When Mary didn't come back immediately, she sent James after her.

"Doesn't she realize all there is to be done?" she scolded. "I declare, sometimes I can't imagine what's going on inside the head of that sister of mine."

James found her standing by the fire, across from Jesus, watching the light of the fire playing over his features in the deepening twilight as he bantered with Lazarus. Though Lazarus and she were brother and sister, they were separated in age by several decades. Mary had always been the baby of the family. Though now in her twenties, in many ways she still was.

"Martha needs that hot stone from the fire," James said at Mary's elbow, and she started, almost surprised to see that she still held the clay vessel in her hands. Smiling sheepishly, she tugged at her brother's robe.

"A hot stone with which to rub the wooden bowls," she said.

As Lazarus bent over the fire to retrieve it, James said, "It's almost a shame we can't linger over this meal and enjoy it." The smell of the meat was inviting, and the juice of the mutton dripped, sizzling, into the fire.

Lazarus eyed him. "We eat in remembrance of what the Lord has done for his people Israel," he said sternly.

James looked anxiously at Jesus. Jesus winked at him, and James face relaxed into a relieved smile. "We'll get to the history of the occasion at the proper time," Jesus said. "James, as the youngest present, will ask the prescribed questions."

And he did. When time came for the celebration, they stood about the table wearing their cloaks and sandals, Jesus and Lazarus holding their staves in hand. They ate ready for travel, as the Israelites had done at the first Passover when God freed them from the Egyptians. Jesus raised his cup of wine and said a prayer. All dipped their hands into a bowl of water for ritual cleansing, and Jesus presented to each a piece of raw celery, dipped in a bitter mixture of crushed fruits and wine

Jesus nodded to James, who asked the first of the prescribed questions: "Teacher, why does this night differ from all other nights?"

And Jesus told the story of Israel's captivity in Egypt, of the tenth plague inflicted on the Egyptians, the deaths of their firstborn, and the sparing of Israel's when God's angel "passed over" their households.

"On all other nights," James said, "we eat either leavened or unleavened bread; why on this night only unleavened bread?"

When the ritual was concluded, when all was eaten, each carried his own scraps out to the fire and burned them, all in accordance with Moses' command.

"Some day, son," Lazarus told James. "God will deliver us from these accursed Romans just as he delivered us from the Egyptians."

† † †

Far to the east, on the other side of the Jordan River, was another village known as Bethany. The town was largely deserted at this time of year; nearly everyone who could travel had gone to Jerusalem for the festival. The Baptizer, John, had remained, according to Herod's reports, and Herod elected to take advantage of the relative quiet to arrest him. That night Herod's soldiers entered Bethany guided by the light of a single sputtering torch.

There were only five of them, their dark faces bearded and their helmets bearing the insignia of Herod, tetrarch of Galilee and of Perea. It was the beginning of the fourth watch, and no one was awake to mark their progress down the wide, dirt-packed lane.

The soldiers, despite their weapons and armor, made little sound until they reached the small, mud-brick house where John the Baptizer reportedly spent the night.

The officer in command of the group held up a hand, and they all stopped.

"Remember," the officer said in a whisper. "Three people, an old man and his wife in addition to the Baptizer. None must have the opportunity to sound the alarm." He tapped shoulders and pointed, sending one to the back of the house, one to the small window at the side of the house, a third to the outer stairs that led to the roof. He and the remaining soldier approached the front door, the officer counting softly. On ten, he pushed through the door, which creaked softly on leather hinges as it opened and, when they had passed through, swung gently back into place.

† † †

On the last day of the Passover, after sundown when it was again permissible to work and to travel, Jesus and his disciples sat on the roof of Lazarus's house, enjoying the pale light of the half moon and the gradual sharpening of the faded stars.

"Pilate returns to Caesarea today," Judas said. "He has persisted in displaying his graven images within the city walls."

He had hoped to provoke a response from Jesus, but Jesus continued to look out into the darkness, almost as if he were expecting someone, though it was too dark to see his face distinctly. James stood beside him, following his gaze, glancing at him occasionally as if trying to attune himself to Jesus' mood.

"Annas has organized a response," Judas said. "When Pilate goes tomorrow, the high priests' households will follow, and with them hundreds of Jews."

"Many hundreds," said Simon, standing as a taller shadow beside Judas. "Thousands. The people are outraged as they have not been since the time of Antiochus Epiphanes." Antiochus Epiphanes was the Syrian ruler who had tried to stamp out the Jewish faith and to impose Greek ways. The result had been a full-scale revolt and the (brief) liberation of Israel.

"I think we should go with them," Judas said. "Annas and his ilk are interested primarily in appeasement. The people are looking for a leader."

It was as if Jesus hadn't heard.

"A lantern," James said, pointing.

Simon and Judas, instantly alert, stepped to the edge of the roof to peer into the darkness, but only the lantern itself was visible, bobbing and swaying as it came toward them.

"A ghost might carry it, for all I can see," Judas muttered, and his hand strayed to the hilt of the sword beneath his cloak.

Jesus, moving beside him, laid a hand on his arm. "Peace, my friend. There is no need to fear."

Judas turned his head to meet Jesus' gaze. "Your eyes are sharper than mine, Rabbi."

"Indeed," Jesus said peaceably. "Indeed."

When the light of the lantern had come to the very edge of the yard, and the point of a beard was just visible beneath the hood of a cloak, Judas called, "Who is it? Who comes to us under cover of night?"

The head came up, and the lantern, but little more was visible of their visitor than before.

"I seek Jesus of Nazareth," said a voice. "Is he here?"

"He is," called Jesus.

Judas said, "Who seeks him?"

"My name is Nicodemus. I seek an audience with Jesus of Nazareth."

"Audience granted," Jesus called. "Wait there. I'm coming down."

"Rabbi," Judas began, concern in his voice.

"Peace, Judas." Jesus went to the corner of the roof and began descending the stairs.

"I'm not sure I like this," Judas said to Simon. "It's an uneasy time. He should be careful."

"Did you note the richness of our visitor's robe? You don't suppose this might be *the* Nicodemus?"

"The member of the Sanhedrin?" Judas's eyes strained at the darkness, where, below them, Jesus stood close to his visitor. Judas could hear the rumble of their voices, but not the words that were said. "I wonder," he murmured.

The lantern moved to and fro across the field in front of the house as Jesus and Nicodemus walked together.

"What do you suppose it's all about?" Judas said several times.

James, finally, impatient with the fruitless speculation, said to Judas, "Why does Simon call you Iscariot?"

Judas looked at him sharply.

"I never . . .," Simon began, but he trailed off as awareness dawned in his shadowed eyes. "*Sicarius*," he said.

"What does it mean?"

"A Roman soldier called him that once. It means daggerman."

"Because he carries a sword?"

"No, no. Haven't you ever heard of the *sicarii*? Of Jesus Barabbas, who patrols the road between Jerusalem and Jericho? He is the most famous of them. They're outlaws who claim they must steal even from their own countrymen in order to support their attacks on the Romans."

"Zealots," James said.

"Not quite. Not all Zealots are outlaws."

"Are you outlaws?" He looked from one to the other of them.

"No," Judas expostulated. "No! It is a lie with which the Roman dogs attempt to brand all Jewish patriots."

"Look, he's coming." Simon gestured. A dark figure was striding toward them across the yard, the lantern already small in the distance.

Judas, Simon, and James crowded together at the top of the staircase. "Well?" Judas said, as Jesus mounted the stairs. "Well?"

"John's been arrested."

"The Baptizer?"

Jesus nodded. "It's time for us to leave Jerusalem."

"To follow Pilate to Caesarea?"

"No."

"Perhaps it's as well," said Simon. "It's a dangerous time."

Judas exhaled sharply. "Yes." He walked to the edge of the roof, looking out. The lantern of Nicodemus was no longer visible in the darkness. "We knew it was coming, John's arrest."

"His work is finished," Jesus said.

"It's too bad. He could have been useful."

"He was useful." Jesus' tone was sharp.

"I meant —"

"I know what you meant."

"What were the two of you talking about for so long, you and Nicodemus?" James asked, anxious to cut short the argument. "Did you spend the whole time talking about John?"

Jesus turned to him and smiled. "No, not the whole time. We spent most of the time discussing childbirth."

His disciples, puzzled, exchanged glances.

"Some day I'll tell you about it," Jesus said.

"Why did he come to you at night?" Judas said. "Does he too fear arrest?"

"No. Nicodemus is a theologian; such men think more clearly at night."

"The night air?" James asked.

"Or the absence of the crowds, particularly the absence of his peers."

"The crowds are enough to keep any man from thinking,"

Simon said, thinking of the days he had spent sitting among them on the hard stone in Solomon's Portico, the air close because of the press of people and his joints growing stiff.

Jesus laughed. "Yes, it's hard to keep your head in the midst of a crowd."

CHAPTER 6

They left the next day to return to Galilee, saying good-bye to Lazarus and his sisters. Jesus led the way north along the road, and Simon, Judas, and James followed at a little distance.

Simon said to Judas, "Why are we going this way?"

"Ask him," Judas said, gesturing toward Jesus ahead of them.

"Does he know we didn't bring provisions for our trip?"

"I don't know what he knows."

Simon took a breath. "I'll talk to him," he said, and he quickened his pace until he drew abreast of Jesus.

"Master," he said.

Jesus looked at him, nodded. "Simon," he said.

"Do you realize that this road passes through Samaria?"

"Does it?" And he continued walking.

"Master . . ." Though his legs were longer, Simon was having some trouble matching Jesus' stride. "Master, I . . ."

Jesus turned his head toward him again, and Simon fell silent.

"Have you ever looked at a map, Simon?"

"Of course."

"It is true that we can walk a day's journey to the Jordan, go up the river along the other side, and cross back over the Jordan again into Galilee —"

"Yes," Simon said, nodding. "That is the way it is always done. Especially since we must purchase food and water along the way."

"But it's a circuitous route that requires six days of travel. If we walk in a straight line, we can make our trip in three."

"But the Samaritans —"

"Simon. Are you trying to tell me that Samaritans live in Samaria?"

Simon's face cleared. "Yes, that's it. That's it exactly." Israel's northern kingdom — the capital city of which had been Samaria — had been conquered by the Assyrians seven centuries before and its people deported into foreign lands. Unlike the Jews of Judah, themselves conquered and deported some centuries later, the deported Israelites had intermarried and disappeared in the foreign lands, never to return. The Israelites left in Israel, mostly those too old or too young, too weak or too sick to survive a journey, had intermarried with the people the Assyrians brought in from other countries. They had given up their racial and religious purity and their right to be called Jews.

"You're concerned that we've brought no provisions with us from the house of Lazarus," Jesus said.

"Remember the words of the rabbi: 'Let no man eat of the bread of the Samaritans, for to eat of their bread is to eat the flesh of swine.'" Simon, though no scholar, was familiar with those writings and traditions that condemned the Gentiles, and such he considered the Samaritans — Gentiles, and, because of their heritage, particularly odious.

"And the flesh of swine is unclean, forbidden to God's people," Jesus said. All this time he had continued northward, walking at a brisk pace. "I see," he said.

"We can hardly go three days without eating, Master."

"No. We can hardly do that." But he continued walking.

Routed, Simon dropped back to walk with the others. "It does no good," he said. "I can't reason with him."

Shortly before noon, they came to a fork in the road, just short of the town of Sychar. Jesus approached the well and sat on the stones at the edge of it.

"Without a rope or a bucket, we have no means to draw water from it," Judas said. All of them were hot and flushed from the exertions of travel, and Judas was in a foul mood as well.

Jesus put his head over the well, and he felt the cool, damp air against his skin. He sighed. "Ah, what I'd give for a sip of that water."

Judas grimaced in exasperation. "We shouldn't have come this way. We all need something to drink — and eat, too."

Jesus wiped his forehead with his palm, and it came away wet with perspiration. "Fortunately, there's a town nearby."

"I'm not going into Sychar," Simon said.

"Nor am I," Judas said.

Jesus looked at James. James looked startled.

"With you? Wherever you're going, I'm willing to follow."

Jesus shifted his gaze to Judas and Simon.

For a moment, neither said anything. "Oh, of course, if you really want to go into Sychar, we'll go with you," Judas said.

Jesus nodded, smiling briefly. He stood to go, then stopped. "I need to stay here," he said.

"I thought you said . . .," Judas began.

"We need provisions from Sychar," Jesus said, cutting him off, "but you'll have to go without me."

Judas folded his arms across his chest. His feet were planted, his exasperation plain. Simon looked uncertain. James, noting their unwillingness, said, almost before he thought, "I'll go."

Judas said, "Alone? Among Samaritans? You won't be safe." To Jesus he said, "You're not going to let the boy go into Sychar by himself, are you?"

Jesus looked at him and continued looking until Judas's gaze shifted uncomfortably. "If only we had a couple of armed men here to go with him," Jesus said. "The boy wouldn't have to go alone."

"I'll go," Simon said. "Of course I'll go."

Judas's head swung toward him.

In the end, they all three went, leaving Jesus sitting at the edge of the well. He looked after them until the dust of the road obscured them, and he continued watching as another shape came out of the dust — a woman, walking slowly beneath a great clay pitcher.

She stopped at a distance of some dozen paces from the well, her eyes on the ground. After standing a moment, she turned to walk the half-mile back into Sychar.

"Did you come for water?" Jesus said, and she jumped, nearly dropping her pitcher. She stood stock still, without turning toward him.

"Because if you did come for water, it's still here," he said. "I haven't poisoned the well."

Her head turned, and she studied him. After giving her a moment to adjust to his appearance, he smiled at her.

"I myself am very thirsty," he said. "I see you brought your rope with you, and a bucket."

She did a full turn toward him. "What?" she said, not comprehending.

"I'm asking for water."

"From me?"

He smiled encouragingly.

"You're a Jew, aren't you? Am I wrong about that?"

"No. I am a Jew," he said. "Is that a problem?"

She spluttered. "A problem!" she repeated. "You're a Jew, and I'm a Samaritan. Doesn't that sound like a problem?"

He raised his eyebrows. A half-smile touched her features.

"Okay, so maybe it's not a problem," she said. "Sure, I'll give you a drink." Approaching the well, she put down her clay jar and uncoiled her rope and bucket from her shoulder.

"If you knew who I am, you'd ask me for a drink," Jesus said as she lowered the bucket.

"It doesn't matter who you are; you haven't got a bucket." Her own bucket hit the water with a faint sound that echoed far below them. "Or a rope, for that matter. I think the heat must be getting to you."

"Do you think so?" He wiped more sweat from his forehead. He was perspiring freely.

"I don't know what to think. You, a Jew, initiate a conversation with me, a Samaritan woman. You ask me for water; you offer *me* water — what am I supposed to think?" She drew up her bucket, pulling it hand over hand.

"Perhaps you and I aren't talking about the same kind of water."

"There're different kinds of water? No. Water is water, my

friend." She reached down to grasp her bucket and pulled it out. "I just have the one ladle," she said. "From what you've said so far, I don't guess that's a problem, either."

Jesus smiled and took the ladle from her. His head went back, and his throat worked as he drank.

Watching him, the woman said, "So what kind of water are you talking about?"

"Living water."

She stood looking down at him, her fists resting lightly on slender hips. "Do you know who dug this well?"

"Jacob."

"Yes, Jacob. The patriarch. He dug the well, and he drank from it, as did his sons and his livestock. Are you greater than Jacob?"

Jesus handed her back the ladle. "Jacob was a great man — but those who drink this water become thirsty again."

"You want more?" She dipped the ladle again in her bucket and handed it back to him.

"Living water becomes a gushing spring inside you, going on forever."

She looked at him, then turned to look back in the direction she had come. She sat abruptly beside Jesus on the stones at the edge of the well. "Mister," she said. "It is a half-mile from the village to this well. I come here for water every day of my life. I could use some of this living water."

"And how about your husband? Go and get him and bring him here."

She looked sidelong at him. "I don't have a husband."

"But you have had a husband."

"How would you know?"

"Isn't that why you come to this well alone in the heat of the day? To avoid the other women of your village?" The women of Sychar would do as the women of any village did, gathering each morning at the well to pound soiled clothes on rocks, to gossip, to carry pitchers of water home on their heads.

"Okay, I've had a husband."

"More than one perhaps."

Her mouth curled as she turned her face toward him. "You tell me," she said.

Jesus returned her gaze. Nothing happened but that they each sat staring into the eyes of the other. The faintest of smiles had begun to stretch her mouth when he said, "Five."

The smile disappeared.

"And you are now living with a man who is not your husband."

She dropped her eyes. "Just my luck," she said, looking at the ground. "When I've made every mistake a woman can make, who do I meet at Jacob's well but a prophet?"

"A little more than luck, wouldn't you say?"

"What would you call it?"

"Providence."

"You haven't denied being a prophet."

"No."

"A prophet to the Jews or to the Samaritans?"

"God sends his prophets to all his people."

"Huh. So tell me, can God only be worshiped at Jerusalem, as the Jews say, or does he honor worship on that mountain as well?" She gestured toward Mount Gerizim, which rose from the plain immediately to the west of them. Even from there they could see the white of the temple on top of it.

"God is spirit," Jesus said. "Those who honor him in spirit can worship him anywhere."

"So the Jews are wrong."

"No. God is as the Jews believe him to be. Though you Samaritans worship him, too, you don't see as clearly who it is you are worshiping."

"So what's your role?"

"To tell you what God is like. To offer reconciliation."

"I thought it was the Messiah who was going to set things right between God and His people."

"It is." He sat looking at her, and her eyes widened.

"It can't be," she said.

"Can't it?"

A man coughed, interrupting them, and the woman jumped to

her feet. It was Judas, with James and Simon, returned from Sychar.

"Oh," the woman said. "Oh." She bent and began gathering up her rope, not bothering to coil it but merely bundling it to her chest.

"It's all right," Jesus told her.

"Oh. Yes. Yes, of course." And she dropped her rope. "It was a pleasure meeting you," she said, backing. "I mean it was really good to meet you. I mean . . ."

"I know what you mean."

"Good. Very good." She bobbed her head at him a few more times, then turned north toward her village and began walking swiftly away. Jesus' disciples stood looking after her.

"That was odd," Judas said.

"She left her bucket and her water jar," James said.

Jesus nodded. "She was very excited."

"About what?"

Jesus got to his feet without answering, and Simon held out a cloth sack.

"Here. We brought food — some salted fish, some fruitcake."

Jesus held open the mouth of the bag. "Looks good. I don't think I need it now."

"But —"

"You three share it. I've had all the nourishment I need for the moment."

The disciples looked at one another.

"Come on, let's go." He started off on the road into Sychar, leaving them standing.

"Do you think she brought him food?" James whispered.

Ahead of them, Jesus turned back. "Are you coming?"

Judas made a face. "We're coming."

"You're about to see something exciting," Jesus said as they caught up to him.

"What kind of food did the woman bring you?" James asked him.

"No food."

"But . . ."

Jesus grinned at James and rested an arm on James's shoulders.

"My food is to do the will of the One who sent me."

"You mean God?"

"So what exciting is about to happen?" Judas asked.

"Look about you," Jesus said to Judas. "See how the fields are ripe for harvesting?"

Judas did look, and what he saw were fields newly plowed and fields whose grasses were tinged with the first green of spring.

"You're speaking metaphorically again," he said dryly.

Jesus laughed out loud. "Yes, you look at these fields, and you say, 'Four months until the harvest.' But listen, if you had eyes to see it, you would see that the fields are already ripe for harvesting. The seed has been sown, and the reaper is gathering grain. You and I will share in that work."

Simon said, "Master — none of us knows what you're talking about."

"Look."

A crowd had come out from Sychar to meet them, men and women, children in their twelfth year, just short of the responsibilities of adulthood, and babes in arms. One of the men stepped forward ahead of the rest and said, "Rabbi? Shera's been telling us about you."

"That you told her everything she had ever done."

"That you are a prophet," said a woman, stepping forward.

"The Messiah," said another.

The man who had first spoken cleared his throat. "We would like — that is, we would be most appreciative —"

"We want you to come stay with us awhile and teach us," the woman said.

Jesus smiled at her. "I would like that very much," he said.

Anyone looking at his disciples would have seen consternation on the face of James and no expression at all on the faces of Simon and Judas; their faces might have been turned to stone.

CHAPTER 7

After spending three days in Sychar, they continued on to Galilee, going first to Nazareth, Jesus' hometown. Nazareth was a sleepy village nestled in a hollow on the wooded, lower slopes of Galilee. There Jesus' mother and sisters received them graciously and his brothers a little awkwardly, being dismayed to find Jesus still in the company of Zealots.

When the Sabbath came, all the men walked to the synagogue, where everyone sat on benches along two walls. The keeper of the synagogue led them in a brief worship, all reciting the familiar prayers in unison.

"As you know," he said, when it came time for the reading of the scripture, "we have a practice of inviting distinguished visitors, when we have them, to select and read our scripture and to expound upon it. Today we have visiting us one of our own, one who plied his trade in carpentry among us for many years but who has embarked on a new path. I understand he has been teaching in Jerusalem in the temple itself, in Solomon's Portico. Jesus, will you do us the honor?"

Jesus stood, smiling, and stepped up onto the dais at one end of the room. All the members of the synagogue stood with him; no one sat for the reading of Scripture.

Selecting a scroll, Jesus unrolled it and read from the prophet Isaiah: "The Spirit of the Lord is upon me, because he has anointed me to bring good news to the poor. He has sent me to proclaim release to the captives and recovery of sight to the blind, to let the oppressed go free, to proclaim the year of the Lord's favor." He read it in ancient Hebrew, which the keeper of the synagogue repeated in Aramaic, the common tongue. Only the learned could speak and understand Hebrew.

Jesus rolled up the scroll again and returned it to the attendant. Then he sat in the chair on the platform to deliver his exposition of the passage. "Today this scripture has been fulfilled in your presence," he said.

Jesus' brother Simon blinked.

Jesus didn't say anything else.

"What do you mean?" said an old man named Levi, who owned a vineyard just east of town. "You speak very well; tell us what you mean."

Jesus looked around at them. Every eye was fixed on him expectantly. "Today," he said, speaking slowly, "this scripture has been fulfilled in your presence."

"What is he talking about?" Levi said querulously. "Somebody tell me what he's talking about. This is a Messianic passage, isn't it? It refers to the Messiah who is to come?"

Jesus looked at him.

"You can't mean . . .," Levi began.

"'The one who is to come' must of necessity become one day 'the one who has arrived,' don't you agree?" asked Jesus.

Jesus' brother Simon stood, and his brothers James and Judas with him. "But I am your brother," Simon said. "As is James and Judas and Joseph."

Jesus raised an eyebrow. "Where is it written that the Messiah will be an only child?"

"But we know you," said Levi. "I remember you when you were a babe in arms, when you suckled at your mother's breast."

"In the words of Isaiah, 'There shall come forth a shoot out of Jesse, and a branch shall come from his roots.' The Messiah will be born and grow up like other men. He will have a mother to suckle him and neighbors to watch him to grow in favor with God and man."

"This is nonsense," Levi said, crossly. "I'm going home."

"I've just been in Samaria," Jesus said. "In the village of Sychar. So glad were the people there to receive me and my message that I stayed with them for three days."

"So what do we care? What do we care about those heathen devils?"

"Do you remember Elijah, whom God sent to the widow in Zarephath when the famine gripped all of Palestine? Do you think there were no widows in Israel?"

Levi had stopped in the middle of the synagogue. His eyes, though dark, were bright with the intensity with which they were focused on Jesus. Everyone was staring.

"Do you remember Elisha? Do you think there were no lepers in Israel in his time? Yet none was cleansed of his leprosy — only Naaman the Syrian."

Old Levi was trembling, but Jesus continued, relentlessly: "The most honored of prophets receives no honor in his own country, or among his own kin, or in his own house. And those who reject God's prophet cannot receive God's blessing. God will send his prophet elsewhere: to the Samaritans, to the Syrians, to the Gentiles."

Levi rushed him, brandishing his cane like a club. Jesus sidestepped its descent, but the force of Levi's charge sent them both staggering into the wall at the end of the sanctuary, and Levi's gnarled fingers closed on Jesus' throat. Judas Iscariot, stepping up behind Levi, slipped his arms beneath Levi's and brought his hands up behind Levi's head. As he lifted him off Jesus, Levi's skinny legs were kicking like a small child's. "Not as good as the Gentiles, are we?" Levi screamed, his arms waving. "Not as good as the Samaritans!"

Two of Jesus' brothers clutched at Judas. James of Cana, when he tried to help Judas, received an elbow just below his breastbone, and he went sprawling backwards. The crowd of men surrounding Judas seemed to be a single thrashing organism, and there were others who slipped past them to clutch at Jesus, to seize him and lift him bodily and carry him out of the synagogue.

Simon the Zealot, caught in the same pile-up as Judas, saw what had happened, and he shouted, "They've got him. Jesus — they've taken him. He's gone." He dropped to the floor and pushed on all fours through the braced and thrusting legs to the door. James of Cana, still sick from his blow, saw him go. He rolled onto his hands and knees and scrambled awkwardly after him, a forearm pressed hard against his abdomen.

In the street, Simon looked wildly this way and that. He saw no one, but he heard voices, ugly voices, coming from the slope above the town. James appeared in the doorway. "Follow me," Simon shouted to him and sprinted around the corner of the synagogue, his short, black beard jutting forward like the quills of an alarmed porcupine.

From the back of the synagogue, the crowd was visible through the just-budding branches of a grove of fig trees. The crowd was pushing toward a place where the ground dropped away, and Jesus stumbled ahead of them, resisting and giving way and calling members of the crowd by name.

Judas came out of the synagogue, a half-dozen of Jesus' townsmen dragging at him, holding him.

"They're going to throw him off," Simon called out to him, hopping and gesturing with his bony arms. "They're going to throw him off."

And indeed it seemed that they would succeed. They had Jesus on the very edge of the precipice, the ground giving and crumbling beneath his feet, when a burst of light, visible for only an instant, blinded them and sent members of the crowd stumbling into each other. Jesus, himself apparently unblinded, pushed his way through them and came down the hill.

"What happened?" Simon asked him, blinking his own eyes against the dark spots that seemed to swim before him. "What happened up there?"

Jesus took his arm. "Come," he said. "Come," he said to James and to Judas, and they walked down the street and out of Nazareth without saying good-bye to anyone.

† † †

"What happened back there?" Simon asked again when they were perhaps a mile down the road that led in the direction of the Sea of Galilee. "What did you do?"

"Nothing."

"But I saw a light."

"Do you remember the words of the Psalmist concerning those who dwell in the shadow of the Most High and rest in the shadow of the Almighty?"

"No," said Simon testily.

"'For He will command His angels concerning you, to guard you in all your ways,'" Jesus said, quoting. "I've had the passage quoted to me recently, in another context."

"What context?"

"I'll tell you later, when you're ready to hear it."

"You mean an angel saved you?" James asked Jesus.

"Wouldn't that be wonderful?" Judas said. "I too saw a flash of light, reflecting off a glass or a mirror."

"I didn't see any glass," Simon said.

"You need to have seen neither a glass nor an angel to believe one was there," Jesus told him. "The question is, Are you more ready to believe in a chance reflection or in God's providence?"

Simon's mouth worked as he thought about it. "I don't know what to believe," he said.

"Ask Judas. He'll tell you."

Judas looked sharply at Jesus, but said nothing.

CHAPTER 8

They made camp that night by the Sea of Galilee, a lake thirteen miles long by eight miles wide. In large part because it lies 450 feet below sea level, its climate is almost tropical, even in the early spring when in the highlands of Galilee the nights are cold. Jesus rose alone during the fourth watch, well before dawn, and walked along the north shore in silence, feeling a peaceful communion with nature and with the God who had created it.

"'O Lord, my Lord, how majestic is your name in all the earth,'" he murmured, quoting the psalm of David. The surface of the lake was luminescent in the moonlight, and in the distance torches glimmered like fireflies as fishermen plied their trade, the boats themselves visible as little more than insubstantial shadows against the water.

"'When I look at the heavens, at the work of your fingers, the moon and the stars which you have made, what is man that you are mindful of him and the Son of Man that you look after him?'" There was peace to be found in nature, peace in the ancient praises, peace in the presence of the Father. Of his Father. What that meant he was still coming to understand, but he knew that his relationship with the Lord God of Israel was special. It was too wonderful to believe — certainly too wonderful to speak of without being labeled a lunatic — but it was equally undeniable. He had had visions and visitations: For him, the veil between this world and the next was wafer-thin.

He was the Son of Man foretold of old. His relationship with

God had existed long before his birth, and his growing maturity was an adventure of rediscovery. *I will open my mouth in a parable; I will utter dark sayings from of old . . .* He had managed to mask the power that flowed in him, had managed to hide it completely but for Cana and the hillside above Nazareth. And, even then, Simon only half-believed, and Judas not at all.

O Lord, our Lord, how majestic is your name in all the earth! He was filled with the sense of joyous expectancy. Today he was, he thought, to find new companions for his journey. It was a journey the end of which he could not see, but which he knew would be more glorious than he now imagined.

As if to mirror his mood, the sun had tinged the horizon ahead with an orange glow. A crescent of white light appeared suddenly atop the distant hills. It was morning.

Jesus entered the town of Bethsaida in full daylight. Two boats were drawn up against the bank, and five men squatted between the boats, each working with twine to mend the tears in two great nets.

"Any luck?" Jesus asked, stopping near them.

Four of the men looked up; the other, grizzled and heavy, continued working on his net. One of the four sprang to his feet. "No, Rabbi. We worked all night, and we caught nothing."

"Andrew," Jesus said, recognizing him. "We met in Judea, along the Jordan."

Andrew flushed. "Yes. John pointed you out to us."

"The Baptizer?" Another man got to his feet. He was clearly some relation to Andrew, but older — in his forties perhaps — with a neck thick enough and shoulders heavy enough to suggest the power of an ox.

"This is my brother Simon," Andrew said. "Simon, this is Jesus of Nazareth, the one I told you about." Two of the others stood as well. They were little more than boys, awed and awkward in the presence of the prophet.

The man on the ground spoke. "Are we going to mend these nets before going to bed? I thought we were going to mend these nets." He glanced up, then went back to his work.

"You caught nothing," Jesus said. "Perhaps you were fishing off the wrong side of the boat." On the ground, the old man snorted.

"Are you a fisherman?" Andrew said.

"A carpenter. I used to fish, though, when I was a boy, in a stream near my home."

"Huh," the old man said.

"Perhaps we could go out together one last time," Jesus said.

Simon answered him. "There's no point in it. Like Andrew said, we've been out there all night."

Jesus smiled at him. "You won't catch any fish on the shore."

"Or on the lake, not today."

"Maybe today of all days."

Simon's smile was disbelieving. "You want to go out there?"

Jesus nodded.

The old man looked up again. "James," he said. "John. Get back to work."

"But —"

The old man fixed his eye on the youngest boy, and he subsided.

Jesus was looking at Simon, who at last gave a shrug of his heavy shoulders. "Why not?" He lifted the prow of his boat and drove it back into the water, wading in behind it. "You realize," he said, turning back. "You realize that if we catch nothing, there are some who'll doubt you're really a prophet." He cocked an eyebrow.

"Some," Jesus said agreeably.

"You say go, we go," said Simon, and he pulled his boat closer to the shore. "Watch your step now. Can't have a prophet getting his sandals wet."

"No, we can't have that." Jesus rested one hand lightly on Simon's shoulder as he stepped into the boat.

"Whoa," Simon said, steadying. "You need to keep your weight low in the boat. That's it. Andrew? Coming?"

They all got in, and Simon used an oar to push off from the shore.

"Are you going to put up the sail?" Jesus asked.

"No." Simon, slipping the oars into the oar-locks, braced his feet and began to row. Andrew had busied himself readying the nets. "We'll take it out just far enough that there could be a shoal of fish;

we'll give it one cast, and we'll go back in."

"Putting me to the test," Jesus said.

"Isn't that what you wanted?"

"Just don't cast until I tell you."

"Just say the word."

All was silent but for the plopping sound each time the oars hit the water and the subsequent swish of the oar through water and the creak of wood.

"You know why we fish at night, don't you?" Andrew asked.

"Because the water's beautiful in the moonlight?"

Simon laughed out loud. "You've got brass, prophet," he said. "I'll give you that."

"Because the fish are drawn to the light of the torches," Andrew said. "When we see them disturb the surface of the water, we cast."

"Is your net ready now?" Jesus asked.

"It's ready."

"Then drop it right there," he said, pointing.

Andrew saw it, too, and threw out the net, spinning it wide and watching it sink slowly below the surface of the water, dragged by the weights along its edge. He still held the rope in his hand.

"How does it work?" Jesus asked.

"I pull the rope, and it closes the net under the fish," Andrew said. "Then we pull it in." As he said that last, he began drawing swiftly on the rope.

"We've got us a haul," he said to Simon. "I think we've got us a haul." Sitting and bracing his feet, he pulled, and the boat tipped alarmingly, sending Jesus and Simon against the other side of the boat to stabilize it.

"Abraham, Isaac, and Jacob," Simon said. "What did you get there, a whale?" He reached for the rope to help his brother, but each time he shifted his weight the boat began to tip. Andrew himself was reared back across his seat, his head nearly resting on the side of the boat opposite the net.

"I'm not sure I can hold it," he said between clenched teeth.

Simon cupped his hands around his mouth. "Little help," he called in the direction of the shore. "Little help."

They all heard the net rip.

"Ease off there, ease off," Simon said, reaching again for the rope and this time catching hold of it. "Don't lose them."

Help, when it came, was in the persons of James and John in their father's boat. They drew up on the other side of the net, and, reaching out, James looped a rope around the net and tied it off. Then he secured his end of the rope to his own boat.

"What do we do now?" James said.

"Tow it in between us," Simon answered. "Unless you've got a better idea."

He didn't. Andrew managed to tie his rope to a ring set near the stern of the boat. The boat was righted, and Simon sat again at the oars.

They were longer getting back than they had been going out. When they reached the shore, Simon and Andrew and James splashed over the side of the boat and, each grasping a portion of the net, staggered up onto the bank, dragging it with them. The silver fish glinted in the sun, several escaping the net and flopping in the dirt, a couple splashing into the water.

Everyone was grinning hugely: Simon and Andrew, James and John, and Jesus. James dropped to the ground, rolling onto his back and squinting up into the morning sun. Simon, dropping the net, stood with hands on hips watching Andrew help Jesus step from the boat to the shore and then help John pull the boats onto the shore.

"You're all grinning like a pack of jackals," the old man said sourly.

"Look," John said. "Look what we caught."

Simon said, "Yes. I never thought I'd be taught to fish by a carpenter."

The old man stood. "Looks like I'm getting in the way of all this sweet talk. I'm going home."

"Don't mind old Zebedee," Andrew said to Jesus, speaking softly.

"James," Zebedee called, looking back over his shoulder. "John. It's time to go home now."

James and John looked at Jesus, uncertainty plain on their faces.

Zebedee stopped and walked back toward them. “Look,” he said. “When I’m gone, then you can neglect your trade and follow around after every wandering preacher that comes along. Until then —” He jerked his head and turned back up the slope toward the mud-brick houses of Bethsaida.

“No.” The voice was James’s. He stood very straight, and his face was set. “This is something we have to do, Father.”

Zebedee turned back toward them, walking up to James and setting himself in front of him, his feet planted wide. “What do you mean, no?” he said. “Is this man your father? Is he the one who raised you, who taught you the difference between right and wrong, who taught you his trade? Or is he someone you’d never laid eyes on before an hour ago?” He turned to Jesus. “You, sir. You’re a man of God, so-called. Remind my son of the great commandment: Honor your father and your mother that your days may be long upon the earth.”

James and John both looked at Jesus, John anxiously.

“It is not the greatest of the commandments,” Jesus said.

“No?” Zebedee said. “What is the greatest commandment, then?” he said. “God spoke them all.”

“Yes, but not all equally.”

“I’m waiting to hear the greatest.”

When he spoke, Jesus’ voice was soft, its rhythm graceful, almost lilting. “Hear, O Israel,” he said, beginning his recitation of the Shema, the confession of faith with which a Jew rose each morning and went to bed each night. “‘Hear, O Israel. The Lord our God is one. Love the Lord your God with all your heart and with all your soul and with all your strength.’ That is what your sons must consider, Zebedee: Can they love God more by staying with you or by coming with me to witness the dawn of the kingdom?”

The word kingdom was one to raise gooseflesh on everyone there. Zebedee turned again to his sons. “Well, which is it?” he said, his voice gruff.

James and John looked at Jesus.

“Very well.” Zebedee cleared his throat. “Very well,” he said again. He turned to start back up the slope. “A man must do what he must," he said, perhaps to himself. "Be it right or wrong, he must do what he must." He said more, but his voice faded to inaudibility as he drew further away.

"That was hard, Rabbi," John said to Jesus. "That was hard."

Jesus' face was drawn up in compassion. "I know it was."

"Rabbi," Simon said. "You speak of following you, but we can't do that. I, at least, can't do that. You are a man of God, and I'm a fisherman."

"Yes, and today I have shown you how to catch fish. Come with me, and I will show you how to be fishers of men."

Simon shook his head. "What does that mean? Fishers of men."

"It means that the kingdom of God is upon us."

Simon pointed past him. "Are those men looking for you?"

Jesus turned and saw Judas and Simon and James of Cana walking swiftly toward him.

"Yes, I think they are."

"They are your companions?"

"Yes."

"Master," James said as they approached. "We've been looking for you. Judas said that you'd deserted us."

"I won't desert you. Judas and Simon, this is Andrew and Simon. James and John, this is James Bar-Alpheus, of Cana."

"This is going to get confusing," Simon the fisherman said.

"Yes, I see how it could be. How about Big James and Little James?"

James of Cana looked swiftly at his older counterpart. "James the younger?" he said.

Jesus laughed. "So be it. And Simon, I'll call you Simon Peter. Simon —"

"The stone," the fisherman said. It was one of the few Greek words he happened to know. "Because I'm stone-headed?"

"The Rock," Jesus said. "Simon the Rock." He thumped Simon's hard shoulder. "Perhaps I should say Simon the Boulder."

Simon Peter grinned down at him. "Okay," he said. "Simon the Rock. Who here's had breakfast? Let's carry these fish up the hill into town, and we'll have some."

† † †

Simon Peter lived with his mother-in-law in a two-room house with mud-brick walls and a thatched roof. He was evidently a good fisherman. Though dirt floors were common in Palestine, the floor in their house consisted of thin slabs of basalt, albeit cracked here and there and a trifle uneven. Simon's straw pallet was in the front room, in a corner.

The tiny window in the back room was covered, and the room was dark, even at mid-day. A woman lay on the pallet against the far wall, her hair matted and disheveled, her cheekbones prominent in her thin face.

As Jesus entered the room with Simon, a long, hacking cough racked her frame. When it was over, she said in a weak voice, "Is that you, Simon? Who is it you have with you?"

Jesus dropped to a knee beside her bed. "My name is Jesus," he said.

She held out a bony hand to him, and he took it in his. "Leah," she said, giving him her own name. "I'm afraid I don't look like much. You'd hardly believe I'm only two years older than Simon."

"I would believe it," Jesus said. "But you've been sick, and it's taken its toll on you." He laid a calloused hand on her forehead.

"How long have you been like this?" he said.

Another fit of coughing left her too weak to answer. Simon answered for her: "Since the autumn. We're afraid —" He broke off.

Leah's breath was rasping. "Go ahead and say it," she gasped, panting. "— afraid she doesn't have much longer."

Jesus jerked his head at Simon, motioning him out. "I'll sit with her awhile," he said.

Simon nodded and retreated into the other room. Jesus looked down into Leah's face. Her eyes were dark shadows in the darkness.

"How long has Simon been a widower?" he asked.

"Two years. In the last two years, I've buried a husband and a daughter."

He nodded. "It's been hard for you — though I think you've reached a turning point."

"Have I?"

"From now on, things will be better for you."

For a time she didn't answer. Her breathing had quieted so much that she might have fallen asleep. "If you say so, sir," she said.

"I say so." He sat holding her hand and looking down into her face.

"Just now I do feel better," she said. "It seems the pain in my chest isn't so bad as it usually is."

"No?"

"No. If you'll believe it, these are the easiest breaths I've taken in months."

He squeezed her hand.

"As a matter of fact . . ." She struggled to sit up, and he helped her, slipping his arm around her and drawing her up in the bed until she could lean her back against the wall. "Ah," she said. "That's better." She emitted a little chuckle, and, out in the front room, Simon's head swung toward the back of the house. "Oh. I should have been sitting up all along, I guess." She met Jesus' eyes.

"There's something special about you, isn't there?" she said.

He smiled. "There's something special about you, too," he said.

"I almost feel like getting up and making everyone some breakfast. It sounds like Simon has quite a crowd out there."

"I can pour a little water in your basin there, and you can wash up. If you'd like."

"I would." She nodded, coming to a decision. "Yes, I think I'd like that."

† † †

Jesus came out into the front room supporting her with a hand at her elbow, another about her waist.

"Leah," said Simon Peter, clearly stunned.

She smiled at him. Her hair was combed, and her face washed, and, with Jesus' support, she swayed only slightly on her bony legs. "You've got some fish to clean, if you want them for breakfast," she said.

Simon stared.

"I don't know what we'll do with the rest of them. Salt them, I guess, if we want them to keep."

"We . . .," John began and stopped. "We were going to take perhaps half of them to our house, so our mother could take them to market."

"We do so appreciate Salome," Leah said. "She's been a blessing throughout all of my long illness.

"If one of you can make me a fire, and you, Simon, clean those fish, I'll get to work on something to go with them."

"Do you think —"

"Oh, I think," she said. "I think. You can't know what a blessing it is to be up and doing something."

John stepped toward her suddenly and embraced her thin frame. "Leah," he said. "Leah, you're better. I'm so happy." Jesus, who let go of her as John took her, stepped away from them.

"I am better," Leah told John, as she smiled at Simon Peter over his shoulder. "I really am better."

CHAPTER 9

Pilate stood in the palace gatehouse, looking out over the mob. "How many of them are there?" he asked his tribune.

"Forty-five hundred as of this morning," the tribune said. "I think more have gathered since."

"Five thousand?"

"Maybe."

More than a thousand Jews had followed him from Jerusalem to Caesarea, and more had gathered daily, choking the streets between the palace and the artificial harbor, which had been constructed by Herod the Great of large stone blocks. For five days they had obstructed commerce and shouted their demands.

Pilate shook his head. "They won't give up. Tell me, what's so offensive about a bust of Caesar?"

The tribune shook his head.

"It amounts to treason," Pilate said. "An unwillingness to tolerate the emperor's likeness."

The tribune said nothing. Pilate continued to look out over the crowd of Jews, his mouth curled in distaste. By Jove, how he hated these superstitious barbarians, their long hair and their unshaven faces! "Intolerable," he said once, indistinctly.

"Pardon, sir?"

Pilate came to a decision. "Send a man down to them. Better — go down yourself. Tell them I'll meet with them to discuss their grievances. Tell them to gather in the great amphitheater. I'll meet with them at noon."

The tribune saluted, striking his breast plate with his fist, then extending his arm. He turned on his heel and left. Pilate listened as the sound of his boots on the stairs faded to scuffing, then was gone.

† † †

Caesarea's amphitheater was a round, free-standing building with an arena and seats placed around it in concentric circles. Pilate's tribune delivered the message to Annas and the others of the Jewish leaders, and Annas spent the rest of the morning spreading the word that Pilate had at last agreed to meet with them. As noon approached, they crowded in through the gates and down the radial walks into the arena.

The circular shape of the amphitheater was dictated by the specific forms of entertainment that Greeks and Romans cherished; that is, gladiatorial games and *venationes*, contests of beasts with one another, or of men with beasts. At noon, five thousand Jews were milling about the arena, talking and shouting to one another, all anticipating their victory. By one o'clock they had begun to get restless. They looked up at the ranks of empty seats that surrounded them, and some crowded near the gates.

At two, Pilate appeared in the podium, the seat of honor in the first gallery. Only a few saw him at first, but those few pointed out the procurator to others and gradually the whole assemblage lapsed into silence. They stood in ranks before the podium, craning their necks and looking up.

"Subjects of Rome," Pilate said in a high, crisp voice that carried over the arena. Beside him stood his tribune and a handful of soldiers. Pilate's salutation and the show of military force produced sporadic mutterings among the Jews. Pilate waited for silence.

"Subjects of Rome," Pilate said again. All around the arena the great doors were swinging shut, closing off the exits. "This foolishness will cease, and it will cease now," Pilate said.

No one among the Jews said anything. Soldiers had begun to file into the first and second galleries, a full two companies of them.

"I am giving you one chance to disperse. You will return to your homes, to the cities and villages from whence you came."

A voice sounded from among the Jews, old and reedy, but weighty with authority. "What of the graven images?"

Pilate's eyes scanned the crowd, seeking the speaker. He spotted him a little to his right. On the old man's robes was the insignia of the Sanhedrin, the ruling body of the Jews in Jerusalem. Pilate had been hoping it would be Annas.

"There," he said, pointing. "Kill him."

The tribune nodded to one of his men, and the soldier launched his javelin. In the arena the old man fell back with the shaft of the javelin protruding from his chest.

"Who else has a question?" Pilate asked the Jews. In the utter silence, the old man coughed and a stream of blood ran out over his lips as he died. "If you do not pledge — here and now — to desist from this rioting and this endless petitioning, then not one of you will leave this arena alive."

Among the Jews, there was some rustling of clothing, some shifting of feet. A sound rose up like a collective sigh.

"Am I understood?" Pilate said.

There was no answer. A smile tugged at a corner of Pilate's thin mouth.

"We are prepared to die for our God," said a voice, crackling with authority. The voice belonged to Annas, standing far back in the crowd. As Pilate focused on him, Annas stepped up onto a block left in the arena from a previous entertainment. "If you would kill some of us, you must kill us all," Annas said. He gripped the collar of his tunic in both hands, and he tore it open, revealing a desiccated chest bristling with white, curling hair.

Pilate extended a finger toward him, and the tribune beside him looked at him questioningly. Pilate opened his mouth to give the order that would end Annas's life, then he hesitated. The arena was filled with the sounds of ripping cloth as tunic after tunic was torn down the front. Everyone was tearing open his clothing and exposing his chest.

"Kill him?" the tribune asked.

Pilate was staring out over a sea of naked chests, over five thousand bearded faces, upturned and defiant. He was looking at the leadership of the Jews, those who, out of self-interest, were most willing to collaborate with Rome. If he killed them all, he would indeed be relying on his legions to keep the peace.

Pilate moved his head fractionally, staying his tribune. "What's this about really?" he called to Annas. "It can't be about a few metal busts."

"That's exactly what it is about," Annas said. "Graven images of a man whose claims to deity are codified in your own law."

Pilate listened with his lower lip caught in his teeth.

"Our people will not tolerate the graven images of a foreign god," Annas said.

"And if I promise henceforth to remove them before entering Jerusalem?"

"If you make such a promise, we will disperse," said Annas.

There was a silence. The eyes of the Jews and of the Roman soldiers surrounding them were all on Pilate.

He nodded once, decisively. "Very well," he said, and, turning on his heel, he strode away.

† † †

It was Thursday by the Roman calendar when Simon's mother-in-law began her recovery from her wasting illness. At midday on Friday of the following week, they were on the roof of the house, enjoying the heat of the pale sun as they ate their lunch of fish, nuts, and dried fruit. John sat on the edge of the flat roof with James of Cana; the two were kicking their legs as they ate. They were almost done when a man called to John from the street. "John! Is Andrew here? Or Simon?"

It was Philip, a sometime resident of Bethsaida whose casual attitude toward work left him free to travel all over Palestine. He had been with Andrew at the Jordan when the Baptizer pointed out Jesus.

"They're both here," John said. "Who's that you have with you?"

The man with him was a big, barrel-chested man with a full beard and a thick mane of reddish hair. James recognized him at once. "Nathaniel," he said.

"Little James."

Jesus, who had been squatting beside Simon Peter as he ate his lunch, walked to the edge of the roof. "Philip," he said. "I thought I recognized your voice."

"I told you I'd see you again in Galilee," Philip said.

"You did, and I didn't doubt you." He raised a hand to his mouth and bit into his last dried fig. "I take it that's Nathaniel with you."

"It is, sir," Nathaniel said, his face upturned and eyes squinting against the sunlight.

"You look familiar."

"I was at Carmeli's wedding in Cana."

"So you were," Jesus said, nodding. "Greetings."

"I don't think we had the opportunity to speak on that occasion."

"No. What would you have of me?"

"Knowledge, if you're the prophet Philip says you are."

"Which prophet does he say I am?"

"He wasn't specific."

Jesus laughed.

"Pardon my doubts," Nathaniel said, "but, as far as I can tell from Scripture, no prophet is to come from Galilee."

"Or especially from Nazareth?"

"I find no mention at all of Nazareth."

"You are a straight-talking Israelite, Nathaniel. Was it the improbability of a prophet coming from Galilee that you and Philip were discussing as you sat under the fig tree?"

Nathaniel looked at Philip, then back up at Jesus. "Master," he said, and his voice cracked.

"Come on up," Jesus said, nodding toward the stairs. He met them at the top and picked the twig of a fig tree from Nathaniel's hair, the twig studded with green buds. He held it out to Nathaniel, smiling. "Someone as easily impressed as you are will be a pleasure to have around," he said.

† † †

Philip and Nathaniel brought news of the events in Caesarea: Pilate had backed down; the stature of Annas and Caiaphas and the other priestly families of Jerusalem had been immeasurably enhanced. Judas, especially, was distraught.

"They're nothing but Roman toadies," he said. "These insignificant concessions, though, will increase their influence. It will be all the harder to arouse the people."

"Who says we want to arouse the people?" Nathaniel asked. "We don't want a war, not with Rome."

"We are God's chosen people," Judas said. "It's not right that we pay tribute to heathen oppressors."

"It's not a question of right and wrong. It's a question of practicalities. We won't throw off the yoke of Rome until the Messiah comes."

"And what then?" Judas asked, not daring even to glance at Jesus. The hopes he and Simon harbored were something he was not yet ready to discuss. "What can even the Messiah do if Annas and his cronies have the confidence of the people?"

Nathaniel studied him just as he might an unusual species of insect. "What can he do?" he repeated at last. "What can he not do? Do not the scriptures say, 'Behold, he comes with ten thousand of his holy ones to execute judgment upon all and to destroy the ungodly'? That 'they shall seek to hide themselves from the presence of the Great Glory, and the children of the earth shall tremble and quake'?"

"The Book of Enoch," Jesus said, and everyone looked at him. "Hardly ancient wisdom."

"Enoch? Perhaps not. But the same theme runs throughout the prophets. Take Isaiah, speaking of the day of the Lord: 'All hands will be feeble, and every man's heart will melt —'"

"Literally, do you think?" Jesus said, interrupting. "What does he mean by a melting heart?" He knew, of course, of the tradition to which Nathaniel referred. For centuries Palestine had been buffeted by the world powers, overwhelmed repeatedly by military forces so great that some Jews had despaired of rescue by merely human means. They had come to believe that time itself was divided into two parts: the present age, which was wholly evil, and the age which was to come. Separating those two ages would be the day of the Lord, a day on which a Messiah, pre-existent from all eternity, would sweep down from the heavens and drive his enemies before him.

"The author of Enoch was quite right in thinking that the Jews were beyond the help of any human agency," Jesus said. "He was wrong, though, in his ideas as to what form the divine invasion would take."

Nathaniel was looking at him expectantly, waiting for some citation of authority. When he realized that none would be forthcoming, he blinked and looked at those around him. Jesus had assumed an authority greater than that of *Enoch*; only Nathaniel seemed aware of the enormity of what he had just done.

"A divine invasion?" James of Cana said tentatively. "What sort of invasion?"

They stayed up talking well into the night, and no one went home to sleep, not even those with houses in Bethsaida. Ten men stretched out shoulder-to-shoulder and head-to-foot across the front room of Simon Peter's house, taking up every bit of floor space.

Simon Peter awoke stiff and cramped in the early hours of the morning, before the first watch, and he pulled himself up into sitting position against the outer wall. As he combed his fingers through his hair, he looked around at the crowd of sleeping strangers, each a shapeless mass hunched under a single blanket, and he wondered if his life would ever be the same again. He yawned and smacked his lips. As dawn approached, a little light filtered around the canvas that covered the room's only window. How many houseguests did he have now? He counted and came up one short of the expected total. It was several minutes before he realized who was missing:

Jesus himself, the cause of all that had happened to him these past several days.

Simon let himself quietly out of the house. It was the Sabbath, a day when no Jew could lawfully work, and no one was about. Simon reentered the house.

"Andrew," he said, shaking a sleeping form. James the son of Zebedee turned his head and blinked up at him, eyelids heavy with sleep. "Oh. James. Sorry."

"What is it?"

"Jesus is gone. Which one of these lumps is Andrew?"

Andrew sat up. "Simon?" he said, blinking at his brother. Beside him, Judas came awake, pushing up on one elbow.

"He's gone again, has he?" Judas said. "Where this time?"

Simon didn't much like either of the Judeans, having seen little to overcome his natural prejudice against them. "I don't know where," he said irritably. "If I knew where, I wouldn't be in here asking, now would I?"

Andrew struggled to his feet. The others were stirring, rolling onto their backs, sitting up, throwing aside their blankets. "Thank God it's morning," one of them, Philip, said.

"Don't be profane," said Nathaniel.

"You mistake a heartfelt call to prayer for casual profanity."

"I call it like it sounds."

Soon they were all crowding through the door.

"This way," Andrew said. "When I got up yesterday, he was coming from the lake." Andrew led the procession down the wide dirt road toward the water's edge.

"Where?" said Judas when they got there. "I don't see him."

"Up there." It was Philip. He pointed to a pile of jumbled rock that rose to an elevation of thirty feet or so above the surface of the lake. Weeds of all kinds and a number of stunted, twisted trees were growing up through the rock, the trees leaning out toward the lake, into the gusting, onshore breeze. Jesus was crouched at the top of the rock pile where the wind had swept it clean. The morning sun, just breaking above the horizon on the other side of the lake, shone in his face, and the wind blew his hair.

"Jesus." Philip waved his arms.

Jesus looked down and saw them. "Good morning." He stood and bounded toward them, his feet finding the stones in his descent as surely as a mountain goat's. "You're up," he said. He looked around at them and grinned. "All of you."

Simon Peter shifted his feet, glancing down and then up again to meet Jesus' eyes. "What were you doing, Rabbi?" he said. "Why do you go off by yourself each morning?"

"Ah, but I wasn't by myself."

Heads turned as some looked for a heretofore unnoticed companion. Others exchanged glances.

"How about all of you?" Jesus said. "What have you been doing? Have you washed? Have you eaten?"

"No, Master. We woke up, and we came out here to find you."

"Very devoted of you. Why don't we all walk down to the river where it feeds the Sea of Galilee and bathe there? We can be on our way."

"On our way where?" asked Andrew.

"And what about breakfast?"

Jesus reached out and tousled James's hair. "We'll breakfast in Capernaum," he said.

"Capernaum? But that's six miles," Nathaniel said. It was, he thought, a significant objection, because travel was one of the thirty-nine types of work prohibited on the Sabbath.

"I have an open invitation to speak at the synagogue."

"But the law . . ." Nathaniel trailed off, silenced by Jesus' eyes — mild, and yet, it seemed to Nathaniel, dangerous.

"The law tells us we must rest on the Sabbath," Jesus said.

"Yes." Nathaniel nodded vigorously. "As God Himself rested on the seventh day."

"Come with me then, and I will give you rest."

"But —"

"Is there any among you who would find an hour-and-a-half's walk along the lakeside unduly onerous?" Jesus asked them. "No?" He turned back to Nathaniel. "How then is it work in any meaningful sense of the word?"

Nathaniel opened his mouth to state the obvious — that the oral traditions defined travel as covering any distance over something less than a mile, however onerous or easy — then he closed it again. His eyes shifted away from Jesus, and he shrugged.

Simon Peter, who had been looking from Nathaniel to Jesus, began to smile, and the smile broadened until they could see every tooth in his head. "A little hike on the Sabbath?" he cried. "Wonderful! Marvelous! I get so stir-crazy on the Sabbath, sometimes, I think I'm going mad."

"Let's go then," Jesus said, "before madness strikes us all." He started off around the lake, and after a moment's hesitation, his disciples followed, the youngest, John and little James, running to catch up with him and walking abreast of him along the shore.

† † †

They reached the synagogue in Capernaum at the end of the first watch. When the others began to arrive, Jesus and his disciples were already seated on the benches that circled the four walls.

Jairus, the master of the synagogue, paused in the doorway, his eyes scanning the row of strangers. His gazed fixed on Jesus, and a smile flitted briefly across his features. "Jesus," he said. "It's been a long time."

"You seem almost surprised to see me."

"To tell the truth, I thought perhaps you'd been arrested, as John was. The word is that Herod's holding him in the dungeons below his palace at Machaerus, on the shore of the Dead Sea." Jairus shook his head. "The threat of unrest has the authorities on edge, from Herod and Pilate to the chief priests in Jerusalem. Any popular figure must be on his guard."

The possibility of danger had not occurred to Jesus' newest disciples. Simon Peter and James and John, the sons of Zebedee, glanced at Jesus uneasily.

"At least you can refrain from personal attacks on the king," Jairus said.

Another man came into the synagogue. In contrast to Jairus's oiled locks, this man had dirty, matted hair that stuck out from his head in spikes. His eyes lighted on Jesus, and his head seemed to retract into his neck like a turtle's.

Jesus' eyes focused on him. "Hello, Jonah," he said, and Simon Peter, who had listened to Jesus' exchange with Jairus in growing apprehension, looked from Jesus to Jonah and back again.

Jonah didn't answer Jesus' greeting. His eyes never leaving Jesus, he moved crablike along the wall to the row of benches opposite him.

"Who is that?" muttered Simon Peter without moving his mouth.

Jesus glanced at Peter. "Jonah," he told him. "You must not spend a lot of time in Capernaum."

"I can't say I'm sorry," Peter answered. Jairus graciously pretended not to hear.

† † †

When it was time for the services to begin, Jairus introduced Jesus and offered him the scroll of Malachi. Jesus, unrolling it, read: "Surely the day is coming that will burn like a furnace. It will set the arrogant on fire, and every evildoer, and they will be as stubble. Not a root or a branch will be left to them, says the Lord God Almighty. But for those of you who revere my name, the sun of righteousness will rise with healing in its wings. You will go out and leap, like calves released from the stall."

He looked up and saw the eyes of Judas and Simon, the Judeans, upon him. With a sigh he closed the scroll and sat down to expound upon the text. "You have all heard of the preaching of John the Baptizer," he said. "Now that he has been arrested, the day of which Malachi prophesied is upon us, the day on which the Lord will separate the wheat from the chaff, the wicked from the good. Each must repent of the evil that is in his heart. Each must turn from his evil ways . . ."

He was interrupted by Jonah, who throughout the service had become increasingly agitated.

"Of what do you repent, Rabbi?" he said. "Of what do you have to repent? We know who you are, Jesus of Nazareth. We know."

"We?" Jesus said.

One of the men of Capernaum said, "He's never been quite right, not since childhood. He's my brother."

"He's possessed," muttered another man. "That's what Jonah is."

Jonah, on his feet, put his hand to the back of his head. "Did you call me Jonah?" he said in a high falsetto. "I'm Jonina, his sister." He bobbed his hip. "I'm a girl." His voice changed. "Did I say a girl? I meant to say hyena." He cackled madly, bobbing his head. He stiffened suddenly and, craning his neck, began goose-stepping about the synagogue, his sandals slapping on the stone floor. "Did I say hyena? I meant to say ibis, the sacred ibis of Egypt. Did I say ibis?"

"Enough!" Jesus said, his voice sharp and authoritative, and Jonah fell silent, his body stopped in mid-gesture.

"We know who you are," Jonah said again, in a voice nearest to his own. "I know."

One of the men of the synagogue said, "It is the demons." His tone was hushed. "The demons have taken him."

"You're the Messiah," Jonah said. "The anointed one. The holy one of God."

"Enough," Jesus said again, more softly.

Jonah teetered, as if unbalanced by the merest breath of air. One leg came off the ground, and he collapsed abruptly. The man who had identified himself as Jonah's brother came off the bench in a futile effort to break his fall.

"Please," he said, looking up. "He's been so ill."

Jesus knelt beside them, and with one hand he reached out to Jonah. "Be gone," he said, placing the palm of his hand against Jonah's cheek. "Be gone, woman and hyena and jackal and ibis. Be gone all of you, and leave this man in peace."

Jonah, staring up at him, began to shake. "They're going," he croaked. "Oh. Oh. They're going." His hand gripped Jesus' forearm squeezing until his knuckles were white. He relaxed slowly. "They're gone," he said. "They're gone." He shook himself and tried to sit up. He succeeded, Jesus supporting him on one side and his brother on the other.

"They're gone," he said again, looking around at the others with wide-eyed amazement, and they returned his gaze with an amazement equal to his own. Then all eyes turned to Jesus.

CHAPTER 10

Jesus stood slowly, the crack of his knee sounding loud in the silence. Jairus was the first to speak. He cleared his throat and said, "What was it that Jonah called you?"

Jesus smiled at him. "He obviously was out of his head."

Another man said, his voice hoarse, "It was not Jonah who spoke, but the demon."

Still another: "Not one demon, but many. And you spoke to them and banished them."

Jesus' eyes became sad. "You may find the banishment short-lived." Reaching out a hand to Jonah, he pulled him to his feet.

"Master," Jonah said, standing shakily, his eyes on Jesus.

"Jonah. Go and sin no more."

"What do you mean, the banishment may be short-lived?" asked the man who had last spoken.

"Master," Jonah said, his eyes remaining on Jesus.

"Jonah. If you do not enter into God's kingdom, whatever evil spirits possessed you will return and each will bring with it seven spirits more wicked than itself. Do you understand? A man's soul cannot remain empty and swept clean. Something must fill it. Seek God and His kingdom, or you will find yourself worse off than before."

Jonah nodded, slowly and soberly. "I will," he said. "Thank you."

Jesus smiled gently, giving him a brief nod.

Jonah walked unsteadily to the door of the synagogue, pausing for a moment in the doorway to look back.

"You are not far from the kingdom," Jesus said.

A slow smile spread across Jonah's features in answer to Jesus' own. Then he walked through the doorway and was gone.

"Well," Jairus said. "Well, well."

Another man said, "When you say that the day of the Lord is upon us . . ."

It was nearly an hour before Jesus got away, and even as he left the synagogue, many of the men of Capernaum crowded close to him. Everyone was talking excitedly.

"Perhaps the kingdom is upon us, and perhaps it isn't," one man in the crowd said to another. "It can't do any harm to watch and wait, I always say. Watch and wait and we will see what comes."

Jesus' disciples — those who had come with him to Capernaum — grouped together, staying as close as possible to each other and to Jesus.

"Look there," Simon the Zealot said softly into the ear of Judas. "The doors and windows."

The women of Capernaum stood in their doorways, children about their feet and hanging from the windows of the mud-brick houses. A few men were visible, too, coming toward them.

"What does it mean?" asked James of Cana, who had overheard. "Where did they come from?"

Judas shook his head. "He draws them. Somehow."

They turned a corner, then, and saw Jonah ahead of them, standing in the open space around the city's well. "I'm all right," he was saying. "I'm in my right mind, and I owe it all to a man called Jesus, who is preaching here in the synagogue." He spotted Jesus at the head of the crowd coming toward him. "There he is! There is the man who healed me. The man who spoke to the demons which possessed me and commanded them to leave."

Necks craned from the doorways. Heads turned this way and that. A small crowd of boys ran toward them, calling out to each other and to their fathers, who stood around Jesus. The women came out of their houses.

"They're going to mob us," said Philip, just loudly enough to be heard over the noise of the crowd. "We need to get out of town and into the open."

They were headed that way, walking faster as they went, but as they neared the outskirts of Capernaum they saw Jonah again, now standing with the tax collector at the toll booth on the road to the east. Jonah was pointing, and the black beard of the tax collector bristled as he craned his fat neck, searching the crowd for the man of whom Jonah spoke.

"Levi," Jesus called.

The tax collector started. Though Jews did not travel on the Sabbath, others did, which was why he was at his booth. His habitual breaching of the Jewish law made him as unpopular as did collecting taxes for Rome in the first place.

"Levi! Your house is one of the largest in Capernaum. I have need of it."

"My house, Master?"

"Your house." The crowd pressing around him was no longer silent. Voices called questions, and hands reached out to tug at his robe.

"But what . . . what should I . . ." Levi's pudgy hands indicated the toll booth.

"Now, Levi."

He came out of the booth, a fat man with his distended abdomen straining at his tunic. "This way, Master."

Jesus caught Simon Peter's eye and gestured with his head. Simon Peter linked arms with him and applied his shoulder to the seemingly amorphous crowd. It shifted subtly — far enough for them to make the turn off the main road in pursuit of Levi.

This street was narrower, and the pressure of the crowd against them increased. The younger James whimpered. The noise of the crowd had grown to a dull roar, any words indistinguishable.

"Must have . . . every person . . . in this blessed town here with us," said Simon Peter, driving and pulling them through the bottleneck of the narrow lane.

"Here. In here." Levi was ahead of them, on the stoop of a large house.

"Follow him," Jesus said.

Jesus mounted the stoop and entered the house with Simon Peter, John, and the younger James crowding in close behind him.

"Quick, bar the door," said Simon Peter.

"No." Jesus' eyes swept the room. "May we place the couch up on that heavy oaken table?"

Levi nodded, his hands clasped in front of his expansive stomach. "Anything, Master."

Jesus bent to one end of the couch, nodding for Simon Peter to take the other. They lifted it onto the table. There were people all around them, now, filling the courtyard without, filtering through the door as a couple of boys, unable to compete with the press of people, climbed through a window.

"Let's swing this whole thing back against the wall," Jesus said. He and Simon Peter lifted, the veins in Jesus' neck standing out and even Simon Peter's face reddening with the strain. When the table was against the wall, Jesus stepped up onto it and sat down on the couch.

"Good people of Capernaum," he said in ringing tones that silenced the general hubbub. "Why do you follow me so closely? Is it because you find your friend Jonah restored to his right mind?" To call Jonah a friend was to speak euphemistically; Jonah was unbalanced, and as such was an outcast, a pariah. "No, you have glimpsed a treasure half-buried in a field. Do you feel it, the sense of tremulous expectation? In your joy you would sell everything you have to buy that field. The kingdom of heaven is a pearl of great price. A gem merchant, when he glimpses it, will sell everything he has to possess it." A shaft of sunlight broke through the roof to shine on Jesus' face and to outline his hair. Several in the crowd, their excitement at a fever pitch, mistook the light for glory, blazing down from heaven. When Jesus raised his eyes, everyone else looked up as well.

The sun was coming through a hole in the mud-caked reeds that made up the roof. Beyond the hole were people, several of them, standing on the roof. Another mat of reeds came away, expanding the hole, and chunks of mud fell down into the house.

"Hey, you there," Levi called angrily. "That's my roof. Hey!"

The men on the roof moved something over the hole, blocking the sunlight. The something was a man tied to a stiff pallet, his legs angling in through the roof. The sunlight appeared about him again as he was lowered into the house, suspended by ropes. He came to rest on the floor of the house directly in front of Jesus. He was pale and thin. His legs were sticks, emaciated and useless.

"Good sir," he said, his voice cracking. "Good sir."

"Yes, my son?"

"Pray for me, Rabbi. Will you pray for me?"

"What would you have me pray?"

"It is said that the prayer of a righteous man can accomplish much, and I have been like this all of my life."

Jesus looked down at him, his brows knit together, his expression compassionate.

"I have sinned. I have sinned as have my fathers before me. It is my sin which has done this to me."

"Has it?"

"Rabbi, I feel the weight of it. It is a restless burden that never goes away."

"Be at peace, then. Your sins are forgiven you."

Exclamations of surprise echoed back and forth among the crowd, accompanied by the hiss of much whispering.

"Jesus," Jairus said in a scolding voice, "only God may forgive sins."

The paralytic twisted his neck toward the sound of the voice.

"You think I speak idly?" Jesus said. "No. Rejoice with me, for this day God has given to one man the power to forgive sins."

"You refer to yourself, sir? That would be blasphemy."

"Which is it easier to say to this man, 'Your sins are forgiven' or 'Arise, pick up your mat, and walk'?"

Jairus smiled condescendingly. "A man may say either of those things easily enough," he said. "With little effect in either case."

"I suppose he may." Jesus looked down at the paralytic before them. "What is your name, son?"

"Jether, Rabbi."

"Arise, Jether. Pick up your mat and walk."

All eyes were on Jesus; then gradually, one set at a time, they turned to the young man, the paralytic. Jether's larynx bobbed in his thin neck, and tears welled in his eyes. "Rabbi, I cannot," he said.

"By faith a man may do all things," Jesus said. "If a man has faith the size of a mustard seed, he may say to a mountain, 'Move from here to there,' and the mountain will move. I say now to you, 'Get up.'"

Jether's face had become the color of raw liver. His mouth opened, and, as tears started down his cheeks, his face crumpled into a mask of abject misery. "Rabbi, I cannot," he repeated.

"If you say you cannot, you cannot indeed. Would you be a cripple all your life?"

A sob broke from him, sounding no more human than a donkey's bray. He rolled to his side and with his hand drew a knee up under him. For some time he lay like that, his face pressed hard against the limestone floor, tears working their way out of eyes squeezed tightly shut and dripping from his face to the floor. Except for the sound of his labored breathing, the room was silent.

Jesus got down from the elevated couch and knelt beside him. His hand gripping Jether's thin upper arm, he said, "Come on now. Let's get up together."

Jether lifted his head.

Jesus smiled encouragingly. "Come on," he said.

Jether drew his other leg under him. There was a gasp from someone nearby: Jether had moved the leg without help from his hands. Jesus pulled him up, and Jether staggered as his foot turned so that the sole of it touched the ground. Jesus held onto him until he was on both feet, standing hunched and swaying.

"You did it," Jesus said to him. "You're standing."

Jether looked at him, his mouth half-open in stunned disbelief.

"Go on."

Eyes wide with fright, Jether straightened.

"Reach down for your mat."

Slowly, he stooped for it, groping, Jesus still holding to his arm. He stood again with his mat. He looked out over the watching crowd. He took a step toward them, and the crowd scrambled back as if he were a corpse risen from the grave, clearing a path for him all the way to the door.

Jether looked back at Jesus, and Jesus nodded. “Go on,” he said.

Jether turned and, tottering, went out.

The path through the crowd closed up again. All eyes were on Jesus. Old Jairus was staring, too, his arm out and his finger extended, trembling, toward Jesus. “You,” he said. “You healed that man.”

“What happened?” said another voice. “What did you do?”

“It’s some sort of trick.”

“A trick?” Jesus said. “How long has Jether lived among you?”

“Heal me, Master,” came a quavering voice. “Heal my crippled hands.”

“Come with me to my house and bless my child.”

The crowd closed on him, hands reaching out from it to grasp and clutch at him.

One of the hands was Levi’s. “This way, Master,” he said. “This way.”

Jesus followed him into the next room, and from that room to the next. His disciples struggled after him, pushing at the crowd that followed.

“Through the window,” Levi said, and Jesus stepped up onto a carved chest of reddish mahogany and from there to the sill of the window.

CHAPTER 11

They did a forced march north along the road that skirted the Sea of Galilee — Jesus' disciples stealing uneasy glances at him, the boys, John and the younger James, breaking into a trot from time to time to keep up with the pace of the men, the crowd thinning and falling further and further behind.

"That was incredible," Simon Peter said at last, breaking the silence.

Jesus glanced at him. "Do you mean that you don't believe what you saw, or that you wouldn't have believed it had you not seen it?"

"Oh, I believe it," Simon Peter said. "I believe it."

"But you wouldn't have."

"No." He shook his head.

"And yet some will. Some will hear of it and believe, not having seen."

"How could they?" asked the younger James.

"It takes an extra measure of grace."

"How did you do it in the first place? Did that take an extra measure of grace as well?"

"Yes. Yes. What you have witnessed is the very grace of God pouring itself out upon men."

James shook his head, and his curly hair bounced around his head. The other disciples pulled their cloaks more tightly about themselves and quickened their pace.

"So where are we going?" a man asked, and everyone turned to look.

"Who are you?" said Judas.

The man cleared his throat and waved his hands in embarrassment. "My name is Thaddeus. I guess I, uh, followed you folks through the window at Capernaum."

"What do you want?"

"To go with you. Where are you going anyway?"

Jesus waved a hand. "Gennesaret," he said. "Magdala. Cana. Jotapata." He started walking again, and the others followed.

Thaddeus laughed, still sounding self-conscious. "Sounds like you're making the grand tour."

"I am. Do you still want to come?"

He shrugged. "Sure."

"What do you mean, sure?" Judas asked. "You don't have anything more important to do than to go traipsing all over the countryside?"

"Evidently not." He smiled weakly, bobbing his head vaguely in all directions as if thereby to render himself less objectionable.

"We're delighted to have you, Thaddeus," Jesus said, and he bumped Judas's hip with his own to silence him.

"What about me?" Levi said in his high-pitched voice. "May I come, too?"

Everyone looked at him. Judas said, "Don't you have any taxes to extort?"

"I never . . ."

"Don't tell me you never. Just look at you! Who in Palestine has the opportunity to get fat? We're an occupied country. Only those who curry favor with the Romans are able to prosper."

Levi looked down at his vast expanse of stomach, bouncing a little with every step. "Perhaps a little traipsing would do me good," he said.

Jesus' hand closed on his shoulder, and Levi looked at him anxiously. "I think a long hike will do you all kinds of good," Jesus said.

By degrees Levi's face relaxed into a smile of relief.

† † †

Simon Peter had never imagined that, when he left his home in Bethsaida that Sabbath morning, months would pass before he saw it again. Walking south along the west coast of the Sea of Galilee, they went first to Gennesaret, where they stayed several nights with a woman Jesus seemed to know from somewhere, a wealthy widow named Susanna. Jesus taught at the synagogue and was well-received.

"You ought not confine your preaching to the synagogue, Rabbi," Susanna told him in her customarily sharp, clipped tones. "Not many women attend. Oh, I know they *can* attend; I know even that women are encouraged, sometimes, to attend; but the fact remains that not many of them do. You want to know where you ought to be preaching? The village well, early in the morning. You want your message to reach women and children — and you should — then that's what you need to do."

Hers were the sharp opinions of an older woman, and Jesus smiled at her affectionately. "You know, Susanna, I don't know what I'd do, sometimes, without you to tell me."

"Humph," she said, not quite certain whether or not she was being made the butt of a joke. Jesus laughed. Her mouth twitched, and she smiled at him.

He did preach one morning at the well at Gennesaret, attracting a crowd of several dozen. His words aroused interest, but no more: He refrained from healing any paralytics and from speaking to demoniacs.

Gradually his disciples began to relax into their role as the pupils of a celebrated teacher.

† † †

When they left Gennesaret, they continued south along the shore of the Sea of Galilee. They approached Magdala early one morning, walking along the shore where fishermen were returning from their night on the lake. Their womenfolk were there, too, cleaning fish and salting them, and their sons were mending nets. Jesus called out to people and greeted them. Some looked at him askance, without speaking; others responded with a wave of the hand and a friendly word or two. As the morning grew late, Jesus led his disciples up the hill toward the village of Magdala.

"Do you know somebody here as well?" Simon Peter asked Jesus, who shook his head.

"Not a soul."

"Susanna gave us provisions enough for the noon meal. After that we're on our own."

"Not completely," Jesus said. He nodded to the women gathered at the market stalls along the street.

"What do you mean, not completely?" Simon Peter said.

Jesus was looking about him, evidently enjoying the soft breeze and the sunshine. "Peter, Peter," he said, pausing with his hands clasped behind him to take in the scent of baking bread coming from a nearby shop. "Have you learned nothing from me yet?"

John and his brother James were walking together at the rear of the disciples. John elbowed James and nodded. "Have you been watching her? She was following us from boat to boat down by the lake. Don't look!"

James jerked his eyes forward. Trying not to move his mouth, he said, "How can I tell you if I noticed her if you won't let me look?"

"I mean look without appearing to," John said. "Out of the corner of your eye."

James tried it. "Where?"

"By the corner stall. She stopped when you looked at her. There! She's moving again."

"I see her."

She was walking with her face turned toward them, one hand extended fearfully in front of her to ward off obstacles she might otherwise run into. "What's that on her face?" James asked.

"Dirt, I think." Her face was streaked with it. Her eyes, impossibly wide, seemed rimmed in red. "Notice who she's focused on."

"Do you think she's a danger to him? Should we warn him?" Jesus had stopped at the well. He sat, hands braced on his thighs, and smiled cheerfully around at those crossing the square. Judas and

Simon Peter drew the water, each drinking some and offering it to the others, then setting the bucket down at Jesus' feet. Judas plopped the ladle into it so that Jesus could help himself.

The woman scurried forward, her head ducked as if to avoid being struck by the rays of the sun, the hood of her cloak pulled halfway over her face.

"Stop her," James cried, and ran forward, followed by John in close pursuit.

The woman was too quick for them. She dropped to her knees in the dirt by Jesus. Her hand closed on the ladle he was reaching for. She scooped it full of water and, looking up at him, handed him the ladle as James skidded to a halt behind her, throwing up a cloud of dust, and John ran into him.

Jesus, in the process of taking the ladle, looked past the woman at them. "Thirsty?" he said. He extended the ladle.

James, his face reddening, shook his head.

"No," John said. "We just . . . we . . ."

Jesus smiled down at the woman. "Thank you for the drink," he said.

She ducked her head, nearly drawing it down into her shoulders, but she gave him a tentative smile.

"What is your name?" he asked her.

James had edged around so that he could get a better look at her. When he saw her face, he was startled to see that she was young beneath the dirt, perhaps no older than he himself.

"Mary," the woman said.

"My mother's name is Mary."

Her smile was shy.

"Is there anything I can do for you, Mary?" Jesus asked her.

She shook her head with quick, birdlike movements; then, abruptly, a sob broke from her, and she fell forward over Jesus' feet, her hair falling about them, her shoulders shaking in her grief.

James started forward, but Jesus checked him with a look and a shake of his head. He laid a hand on her back and let her cry a little. When she looked up at him, her tears had cut pale tracks through the grime on her face.

A number of women had drifted over from the stalls in the marketplace. "She ain't right, mister," said one. "Never has been."

A merchant, who had come over himself to see what was attracting all his customers, said, "She has a devil, sir. More than one of them, if you ask me."

"I didn't ask you," Jesus said.

"Your feet," Mary said. "So very dusty."

"I've come a long way."

"Allow me. Please." And she ladled some of the water over his feet, washing away the worst of the dust.

"Thank you very much," Jesus said, gravely.

"Wait. They're wet." Casting about her for a cloth and not finding one, she bent forward again and began wiping his feet on her long, dark hair. A woman in the crowd clucked disapprovingly.

"She's just smearing dirt back on his feet again," James said under his breath to John, and John poked him.

"But who is she?" James said.

"You heard her. Her name is Mary."

"But that doesn't . . ." John poked him again, and James fell silent. Jesus was helping Mary to her feet.

"We're about to have lunch," he said. "I'd like for you to join us."

She nodded, almost imperceptibly, her eyes locked on Jesus' face.

† † †

In Tiberius, the capital city Herod Antipas had built for himself, they spent two days and two nights at the home of Joanna and Chuza, the steward of Herod himself. Herod was absent, and Chuza was with them almost constantly, providing for meals and mended clothes, listening to Jesus and providing for his every need.

"How do you know these people?" Simon Peter asked Jesus.

"What people? Joanna and Chuza? I just met them at the same time you did."

"Then why —"

"Why did they take us in? Remember what I said about the pearl of great price: A man will sell all that he has to possess it."

"But —" Simon Peter tapered off. Jesus was a man of uncommon charisma, he thought, and that was that.

† † †

The fortress at Machaerus, on the Dead Sea, had been destroyed by Rome in subjugating the Jews and was later rebuilt by Herod the Great. Herod Antipas, his son, had a large villa there that sat atop a barren mountain on the eastern edge of the Dead Sea. Though Herod had always liked the desert oasis, Herodias hated it. Machaerus was far too isolated. On their first return to it in many months, Herod went nightly to his dungeons to visit John. More and more it seemed to Herod that John's voice was the voice of a prophet.

"They say you are Elijah," Herod said to John on one such visit.

He didn't look like the greatest of the prophets. His hair and beard were matted from his captivity, and his clothing reeked of human waste. Always thin, he had become emaciated, gaunt. He was kept in a cell the size of a tomb, only just large enough to lie down in, and was permitted to leave it only when Herod wanted to talk. On such occasions, the stone was rolled back from John's cell, and John was led by torchlight down a subterranean passage far from the reach of either breeze or sun.

"I am the son of Zachariah and Elizabeth," he said. "There are those living who watched me grow up."

"'Lo, I will send you the prophet Elijah before the great and terrible day of the Lord,'" Herod said, quoting Malachi. "And you tell us you herald the coming of the Messiah. Wouldn't that make you Elijah?"

Herod sat flanked by his guards, and John stood before him, his feet planted wide. "Not in the sense you mean."

"Either you are Elijah, or you are not," Herod said.

"Or I am Elijah, and I am not. Reincarnation is a concept of Eastern mysticism, not of Malachi."

"Ah," Herod said. He leaned forward, and his eyes seemed to flicker in the torch-light. "I thought as much."

John moved his head, surprised as always at Herod's apparent fascination. He had little faith that it would do him any good.

"Elijah was the greatest of the prophets, was he not?" Herod asked. "Or perhaps that's a matter for debate. At least we can say that he was the first of the great prophets."

John said nothing.

"When Malachi says, 'Elijah will return,' perhaps he means that prophecy will return to God's people. There has been no prophet in Palestine for four hundred years. Until you."

John's face remained impassive.

"Well? What do you say to that?"

"So I am a prophet. Do you mean to release me then?"

Herod shrugged, his face contorting in irritation. "I mean, what do you think of my theory?"

"Because if you're not going to release me, then this prophet is prepared to return to his cell."

A scowl tightened Herod's mouth.

"And when you return to your villa —" John paused.

"Yes?" Herod said. "Yes?"

"You might consider the consequences of holding a prophet of the Lord God prisoner in your dungeons." His voice crackled for a moment with its old authority.

Herod's eyes widened.

"Especially a prophet foretold of old."

"Are you threatening me?" But his voice quavered.

John only smiled, thinly, the fire fading from his gaze. He turned and stood facing the door until a guard moved to open it.

† † †

After Tiberius, Jesus and his disciples left the shore of the Sea of Galilee and struck off into the interior, stopping for a time at Cana, where James's parents, Alpheus and Mary, put them up, and for a time in Jotapata. They returned to Bethsaida by a circuitous route, skirting the northwest border of Galilee and stopping in Baca, in Meron, in Gischala and Thella. They were on the road some miles north of Bethsaida when Andrew dropped back and gripped Jesus' arm. "Listen," he said. "Do you hear it?"

It was a bell, ringing monotonously somewhere up ahead.

"It's getting closer."

"A leper," Philip said. "Unclean."

Jesus turned toward him with a pained expression. "Which of the men made in God's image would you call unclean?" he said.

Philip retreated to walk again beside Nathaniel. As the leper came into view, ringing his bell and wearing the required placard, Philip muttered, "Well, that man," in a voice too low for anyone but Nathaniel to hear. The leper's threadbare robe was torn in places, showing the tunic beneath, and he was dragging one sandal, its strap broken and hanging, the foot bleeding, leaving dark smears on the surface of the dirt road.

When the leper saw Jesus and his disciples coming toward him, he left the road and stopped in the brush to one side of it, waiting for them to pass. The hand that held the bell was missing two fingers; the places where they had been were unhealed sores. The pigment had come out of his skin in splotches, making his face, with its single, yellowed tooth, a mask of horror.

Simon Peter, Philip, and the others crowded forward, quickening their pace even as Jesus hung back.

The leper lifted his bell again and let it fall so that the clapper hit the side with a muffled ding. "Unclean," the leper said in a hoarse voice.

Jesus approached him, stopping when he was only a pace away. The man regarded him with his one good eye, the other being stained a milky white. "Do not endanger yourself. There is no point."

Jesus inclined his head. "No point in compassion?" he said. "No point in simple human contact?"

The leper shook his head. "Not for me. Never again for me."

Jesus held out a hand to him, palm up, and the leper drew back reflexively.

"It's all right," Jesus said, leaving his hand extended. "It's all right."

The leper met his eyes and, after a moment, reached out slowly to clasp Jesus' hand in his own three-fingered claw. Jesus smiled encouragement, and the leper returned his smile uncertainly, exposing the yellowed tooth.

"What is your name, sir?" Jesus asked him.

"Simeon."

"The Lord bless you, Simeon. May the Lord bless you and keep you; may the Lord make his face to shine upon you and be gracious unto you; may the Lord lift up the light of his countenance upon you and grant you peace."

"Thank you, sir." There were tears on his face.

"You're welcome, Simeon." Jesus smiled, then turned back toward the road.

"Oh, Simeon," he said, turning back. "Don't mention this to anyone."

Simeon shook his head. "I wouldn't do that, sir. They would shun you, too."

"God's speed to you, Simeon." And he left him there beside the road.

CHAPTER 12

When Jesus caught up with his disciples, their faces were unsmiling. He fell into step again beside Simon Peter, who drew back to keep from touching him.

Jesus shook his head. "Peter, Peter," he said, and Simon Peter glanced at him and away, his expression grim. Jesus looked around at the others, none of whom would meet his eyes.

"Does none of you know the benefits of compassion?" he asked.

"Master," said Simon Peter. "Compassion is all very well, but you have endangered us all."

"What about compassion for us?" Judas said. "Do you have no compassion for your friends?"

"And what calamity has befallen you that you should be the object of compassion?"

Judas's lips compressed in annoyance, and they walked for a little way in silence. John, tugging at Jesus' sleeve, said, "Is there no danger of contagion, then?"

Jesus looked at him and sighed. "Very little, I think," he said.

"You don't know?" The voice was Judas's. "You think?" To the others, he said, "He doesn't know whether he's exposed himself and all of us to a slow, wasting death."

"There is a power loosed in the world," Jesus said. "Wait awhile and see what —"

"Ho!" a voice called in the distance, interrupting him. "Ho there!"

Jesus stopped, and Judas and Simon Peter ran into him. "Hold up," Jesus said. "Who was that?"

"There," said John, pointing.

A man's head appeared coming over a rise behind them, then his shoulders, then his torso. "Ho there," he called again.

Jesus turned back to meet him, his disciples straggling after him. The man broke into a run, staggering his last few steps and falling to his knees in front of Jesus.

"Master," he said.

Simon Peter's eyes had focused on his left foot, where his sandal hung by a single strap. "He's taken the leper's clothes," he said.

The man raised his eyes to Jesus, and a shock passed through Simon Peter's body and lifted the hairs at the nape of his neck. It *was* the leper, his blind eye healed, the pigment in his face miraculously restored. Though two of the fingers still were missing from the right hand, the sores were gone.

Jesus reached down to grip his shoulder and raise him to his feet. "Greetings, Simeon," he said.

"Master."

"You will need to find a priest to examine you and to offer the sacrifices required by Moses."

"Yes, yes. Of course. Please, sir. Is it permitted to know your name?"

"Jesus of Nazareth. But I'd like for you not to tell anyone what happened here."

"Jesus. Of Nazareth," the man repeated.

"Remember," Jesus said. "Seek out a priest. Tell no one."

Simeon nodded. "Of course, of course," he said. "Thank you. You have saved my life."

Jesus smiled at him. "Very likely," he said. "Go on now."

Simeon leaped to his feet and, after clasping Jesus to him with reckless enthusiasm, took off running along the road ahead of them toward Bethsaida.

"Well," Jesus said, looking after him. "We had best get on to Bethsaida ourselves." And he started off.

His disciples followed, but at a distance, and they whispered among themselves.

† † †

They were still a mile outside the village when Andrew saw the crowd of people coming toward them. "Look," he said.

"I don't guess Simeon kept his good news to himself; what do you think?" Jesus said.

"Does that mean the leprosy will return to him?" John asked him.

Jesus shook his head. "No. Secrecy was a request, not a condition."

"What are we going to do? If we continue on into Bethsaida, we'll be mobbed just as we were in Capernaum."

"Jesus! Jesus of Nazareth," came a chorus of voices.

"Let's get off the road. This way," Jesus said. But as they left the road, the people coming from Bethsaida toward them broke into a dog-trot. There seemed to be about fifty of them.

Jesus and his disciples angled across the broken ground toward the Sea of Galilee, already visible below them. Simon Peter said, "If we can stay ahead of the crowd for perhaps ten minutes, we can be at my boat, if by some miracle it's still where I left it."

"Then I guess we'd better stay ahead of the crowd," Jesus said. He broke into a run, gathering up his robe and his tunic to keep from tripping over them.

"Master," Peter called, pounding after him. "This doesn't seem very dignified for a prophet."

Nathaniel, breaking into a run himself, laughed out loud.

"There'll be nothing dignified about what will happen if they catch us," Jesus said.

Simon the Zealot passed Jesus and Simon Peter, his robe flying and his long legs pumping. The cries of the crowd grew louder, not quite masking the more immediate sounds of the disciples' labored breathing and the slap of their sandals on the hard, sandy ground. They reached the shore of the lake and turned along it toward Simon Peter's boat, now visible in the distance.

"We're going to make it," Simon Peter huffed between gasps as John and James and James the younger passed him. "We're going to make it." And they did, piling into the boat headfirst and feetfirst, James and John splashing into the water with Simon Peter to push off.

About twenty yards off shore, Jesus said, "Drop the anchor."

The crowd was gathering along the shoreline, a few splashing in, but none making a serious pursuit. "The crowd's grown. There have to be a hundred of them," said John.

"Men of Israel," Jesus called, standing up in the boat and nearly upsetting it before recovering his balance. "Men of Israel, whom do you seek?"

One of the men on shore, a young man, called, "The one who healed Simeon the leper."

Another said, "Jesus of Nazareth."

"You have found him," Jesus said. "I am Jesus. What do you want of me?"

The question produced a general hubbub, each man turning to his neighbor to confer. Finally, a voice rose above the rest. "Bless us, Master," it said.

"In what way are you in need of a blessing?"

"I am poor," cried a voice.

"I'm hungry," cried another, a woman. "I slave and struggle to keep food on the table for my son and myself, and still there is not enough."

"My wife is dead."

"Who among you is poor?" Jesus cried, holding up his arm.

A dozen hands were raised.

"Blessed are you who are poor," Jesus said.

"Will you fill our purses?" There was general laughter, and Jesus smiled.

"No, I have not the means to do that."

"Then what is the good of your blessing?"

"Though I can't fill your purses with coin, I can give you something infinitely better." He raised a hand, palm outward. "Blessed are you who are poor, for yours is the kingdom of heaven. Blessed are you who hunger, for you shall be satisfied, if not physically, then spiritually, which is more important."

"Such cant," Judas said in an undertone. "I'll be surprised if they don't stone the boat."

Jesus' head turned a fraction of the way toward him, but his words, when he spoke, were addressed to the crowd. "Is there no blessing to be found in poverty and hunger? There is so much suffering: Is it all meaningless? No. Just as your arm may be strengthened by the strain of toil, just as gold is refined by fire, so your character is formed in the crucible of suffering. Without it we are all fat toads, self-satisfied, cruel, and self-indulgent."

"What about my wife?" called the widower. "Did sickness consume her so as to improve my character?"

There was a scattering of laughter, but Jesus ignored it.

"And hers, perhaps. The path to God is not an easy one. Your wife toiled, and she suffered —" He paused, almost as if listening. "And she sits today in God's own presence, and angels minister to her needs."

Silence. "I miss her," the man said at last, his voice so choked with emotion that it almost failed to carry to the boat.

"Yes. I know. You mourn, and you will be blessed by it. Though it seems impossible, the time will come when you will again laugh."

"Bless me," called another. Jesus recognized him.

"A blessing on you, Dothan." Jesus said. "Blessed are you when people hate you, when they exclude you and insult you. Rejoice, for great is your reward in heaven."

In the following silence, Dothan looked with some embarrassment at those around him, but everyone was focused on Jesus. Someone called, "Instruct us, Rabbi," and a chorus of voices took up the cry.

"You want me to tell you how to live?" Jesus held up a hand. "Moses has given you the law, has he not? Why don't you obey it?"

He looked from face to face, but no one answered him. "Is it because the law seems cold and lifeless to you?" He pointed to a man dressed in purple linen. "Nathan," he said.

"Me?"

"You. Would you have the Lord as a living, breathing presence in your life?"

"Of course, Rabbi."

"Sell what you have, and give the proceeds to the poor. You heard me bless the poor. There is a dark side to the blessing: You are rich; if you cling to your riches, then you have already received all the comfort you will ever have. You are well-fed, but the day is coming when you will be hungry indeed. You laugh now, but one day you will mourn and weep."

Nathan's face flushed. "I come seeking a blessing, and instead you give me a curse?"

"The curse was yours already. I give you the opportunity to exchange it for a blessing."

"It's not an opportunity, but an ultimatum."

"What greater prize could there be than the kingdom of heaven?"

Nathan turned away. "Go to hell," he muttered audibly.

There was a silence, Jesus looking from face to face among the crowd. "I offer the blessing to each of you," he said. "Would you be perfect, even as your father in heaven is perfect? Love your enemies. Do good to them that hate you; bless them that curse you; pray for them that mistreat you. If someone slaps you, turn to him the other cheek. If someone takes your cloak, give him your tunic as well. Give to everyone who asks you, and if anyone takes what belongs to you, do not demand it back. Treat everyone just as you would want to be treated yourself."

"Not our enemies, surely!"

Jesus smiled at the one who had spoken.

"It makes no sense, you say. Let me ask you: if you love just the people who love you, what special service have you done to God? Everyone loves those who love them, every Gentile, every tax collector, every villain. If you are good only to those who have been good to you, how are you different from anybody else? If you lend only to those who can repay you, what have you done? Even the most corrupt among us lend out money expecting to be repaid. But love your enemies; do good to them; lend without expecting to receive anything in return . . ."

"And then what?"

"Yes, what then?"

"If you do these things, your reward will be great. You will be sons of the Most High God, who is Himself kind to the ungrateful and to the wicked. God has given you much; it is only thus — by doing something you don't have to do, by doing a kindness you don't even want to do — that you can return to him something of what he has given you."

He talked to them for a total of less than an hour, but they were big themes for him, themes he would return to again and again. When he was done, he gestured for Simon Peter to raise anchor and head out onto the Sea of Galilee. He himself sat heavily on the bench in the bow of the boat.

"You look tired," John said to him.

Jesus smiled at him. "Do I?"

"The preaching takes energy from you just as the healing does."

"I think you're right," Jesus said. "I think I'll take a nap."

"Where are we going?" Simon Peter asked. "Hadn't you better tell us that first?"

"Back to Capernaum? If we get there after dark, we can make our way to Levi's house easily enough. How would you feel about a slew of houseguests, Levi?"

"I'd be honored." Levi cleared his throat, conscious of the unsmiling faces around him. "I wonder if I could go by the name Matthew from now on. You all know what my past is. I know there are some of you that can never forgive me for it." He deliberately avoided looking at either of the Judeans, Judas or Simon. "I'd like to make a break with my past."

"Why the name Matthew?"

Levi looked at James, the son of Zebedee, who had asked the question. "It was my father's name."

"Matthew, then," Jesus said. "Very good." He slipped out of his cloak and began to fold it. "Will someone wake me when we reach our destination?" He lay down along the bench, his arm and the folded cloak pillowing his head. The arm of the cloak he draped across his face, shielding it from the light.

† † †

James and John, Simon Peter's old fishing partners, helped with the sail. "Those clouds are coming from the west," James said to Simon Peter. "We're going to be sailing right into them."

"We'll make it." The wind caught the sail, and Simon Peter leaned back on the rope to hold the slender mast upright.

"If you say so." Simon Peter, a good fisherman, was the best boatman on the Sea of Galilee. James had seen him cutting through waves choppy enough to have swamped him and John and Zebedee. Peter would be leaning far over the side of his boat to balance his mast, his silhouette visible against the occasional flash of lightning as he ran ahead of the storm.

The wind changed abruptly on them, whipping the boom across the boat so fast that it caught John in the back of the head and sent him sprawling.

"It's taking us out to sea," James said as Simon Peter dropped the rope that held up the sail. The wind, though, had filled the sail and kept it from dropping. Simon Peter gripped the canvas, pulling at it, lifting himself off his feet in his effort to lower the sail.

"Little help," he called, and James and Andrew gripped the sail beside him. They got it down, and the waves turned the boat broadside, rolling it with each swell.

"Look," James said, pointing.

Rain was sweeping toward them like a dark curtain, dimpling the surface of the waves, the shore invisible beyond it.

"Uh oh," someone said.

"'Uh oh' is right." Simon Peter gripped the rudder and, grimacing with the strength of the effort, turned the boat into the waves. A few large, cold droplets fell about them, and then the rain was coming down in sheets, plastering their robes and tunics to their bodies and their hair to their heads. Simon Peter found it impossible to guide the boat; the best he could do was to keep it from foundering. "We'll have to ride it out."

"Can we ride it out?"

A flash of lightning illuminated the clouds above them. One second passed, then two. Thunder crashed down, loudly enough that even Simon Peter flinched.

"We're pretty exposed out here," he said.

Another flash of lightning and another blast of thunder — this time only a second apart. A wave broke over the side of the boat, which kept turning against the waves despite Simon Peter's best efforts with the rudder.

James gestured toward Jesus, only just visible through the dark rain. "How can he sleep through this?"

The Judeans were no sailors. "We're going to die out here," called Simon the Zealot, half-standing, staggering this way and that like a drunkard as he made his way toward the bow of the boat. "Master, we're all going to die."

Lightning blinded them, and the thunder was simultaneous. Simon clutched at Jesus' tunic. "Master, wake up. Wake up. Don't you even care that we're all about to die?"

Jesus swung his legs off the bench, freeing his head from his cloak and making an effort to sweep the sudden deluge of water from his face as he sat up. The rain was a gray mist, obscuring the vision and numbing the ears as it drubbed against the planks of the boat. The crack of wood sounded from the back of the boat as the rudder broke off in Simon Peter's hands.

Jesus stood up, swaying precariously with the wild rocking of the boat, and stepped up onto the bench on which he'd been resting. A jag of lightning touched the water roiling and foaming about them, and it suffused the lowering clouds with light. Jesus, stretching out his arms, was silhouetted against the luminescent sky as the thunder blasted overhead and the rain beat down on their upturned faces.

"Abba!" he shouted. "Father." He sounded happy, even delighted. "Thanks be to you who gives to the son of man all dominion over the animals that slither and burrow and run —" He staggered, nearly pitching overboard. "— over the fish of the sea, over the very elements themselves."

A wave broke over the side of the boat, half-filling it, and Jesus fell backward into the boat. "Peace," he called out, raising an arm, laughing. "Be still."

"He's gone mad." The voice belonged to Judas, who was floundering with the others through the water in the bottom of the boat, his grasping hands seeking purchase as the waves broke over the side.

Jesus, regaining his feet, turned toward them. "Peace," he said to them. "Peace, be still."

The wild light faded from the sunken eyes of Simon the Zealot. Jesus waded through the knee-deep water and helped Judas to his feet. The boat seemed to be rocking less violently now, perhaps because of the stabilizing effect of all the water in the bottom. A golden light lit up the sky behind Jesus' head, a calmer, steadier glow than the lightning. John and his brother James turned to see the sun shining through a rift in the clouds. Within minutes the sea was calm, even glassy, its surface undisturbed by the merest ripple.

"Good God," Simon Peter said, looking out on it.

"Don't be profane," said Nathaniel automatically, helping Andrew and James with the daunting task of bailing out the boat.

"I wasn't being profane. I said God was good, and I meant it."

Jesus, smiling, reached out to lay a wet hand on Peter's head in benediction. "He is good."

"I have to say I agreed with Judas for a minute," Simon the Zealot said, looking at Jesus. "I thought you'd taken leave of your senses."

"When instead I was enjoying them to the fullest."

"How could —"

"Because I love weather."

"Good weather," James said. "At least that's what I like."

"Ah, but God made the rain and the lightning just as he made the wind and the sun."

"And too much of any will kill you as sure as drowning," said Simon Peter.

Jesus laughed.

"What just happened?" began James the younger, looking around at the others. He felt the conversation had strayed far wide of the point. "Did he or didn't he —" He broke off. Jesus was looking at him and grinning broadly.

"Well?" James asked him.

CHAPTER 13

They entered Capernaum at night, bone-weary and their wet clothes chafing them. They went directly to the house of Levi — now Matthew — and he brought out such food as hadn't spoiled during his long absence: nuts, dried fruit, a little salted fish. They fell asleep in chairs, on pallets and couches and, primarily, on the limestone floor.

"We need some time to ourselves, to rest," Jesus said the next morning.

"I can go out for provisions," Matthew said. "No one need know you're here."

"Let me go," Thaddeus said to Matthew. "Your appearance in the village might attract attention. Everyone knows Jesus left from your house, and that you left with him."

Matthew nodded.

Thaddeus went out and returned with a boy leading a donkey burdened with large quantities of grain and fruit and fish stuffed into rough burlap sacking. Peter, Andrew, James, and John carried it all inside, and the boy departed. Some time later, the noonday meal was laid out on the great oaken table, Jesus and his disciples sitting and reclining about the table to eat.

"I thought you were discreet," Matthew said to Thaddeus, and all eyes followed the direction of his nod to the window, where two or three boys peered in from the outer courtyard.

"I thought I was."

The boys watched awhile and left and later returned with two or three of their fellows. Matthew went out to shoo them off, but Jesus, realizing his intention, went out after him.

"It's all right," he said.

"But they'll —"

"It's all right. The last thing we want to do is make children feel unwelcome in our company." He smiled at the youngest, a plump little boy with brown eyes and dark, curly hair. "What's your name?"

"Samuel."

"Samuel! That's a mighty important name for such a little fellow."

The boy ducked his chin and smiled at the ground.

"Did you know there was a prophet named Samuel?" Jesus squatted in front of him, and the other boys clustered around him just beyond arm's reach. "What's that you've got behind your ear?" Jesus asked Samuel. "Do you have something behind your ear?"

The boy shook his head.

"I think you do. I think you have a —" He reached out and tugged at a lock of Samuel's hair just behind the ear. "— a lepton!" He pulled back his hand and turned it palm up to reveal the small bronze coin. "What do you think about that?"

The boy reached out for it solemnly, taking it tightly in his small, pudgy fist.

"Do you see any coins in our ears, mister?" one of the others asked.

"Well, I don't know. Let me look. No, nothing behind that ear. Nothing behind the — no, I was wrong. What's this?" He withdrew his hand and turned it over to reveal another bronze coin.

"Do me, do me," the others shouted, one or two of them jumping up and down in their excitement.

"Okay, okay. Line up here. I'll check behind all your ears." When each had been enriched a lepton's worth, Jesus said, "Okay, now, off with you."

"Can we come again tomorrow?"

He smiled. "You may come again tomorrow."

When he turned to go back inside, he saw Matthew and Judas

standing together at the door, each wearing an identical expression of disapproval.

"From the look of you, I'd think you were twins," Jesus said.

Judas, his scowl deepening, glanced at Matthew.

"Don't you think they'll go home and tell their families?" Matthew said. "To hear there's a man at my house performing magic is going to sound familiar to some of them."

"I suppose it will, but it can't be helped."

Judas said, "It could have been helped. I could have come out and sent them away."

"Ah, but I couldn't let you do that."

"Wouldn't the end justify the means?" Matthew asked.

"No end can justify uncharitable means."

Matthew looked at Judas, who shook his head.

† † †

When they sat down to supper that evening, there were more than a dozen people in the courtyard, several of the boys who had been there that afternoon, three or four women, a half-dozen grown men. Jesus acknowledged them with a wave of his hand and, after he had eaten, went out and spoke to them for a couple of hours.

The next day some of those returned and with them perhaps a dozen others, curious to see the man who had cast the demons out of Jonah and who had healed the paralytic. Jesus again went out and spoke to them. He held their babies, smiling and speaking into their solemn faces. He took the gnarled, arthritic fingers of the old between his hands and prayed for an easing of the pain. He touched the twisted back of an old woman. The crowd of visitors grew from day to day, people coming from as far away as Chorazin and Gennesaret, Bethsaida and Magdala, until the courtyard was overflowing from the first watch until late into the evening.

† † †

Herod was still in Machaerus, staying in his villa by the Dead Sea with Herodias and all his household.

"Why waste your time with that wild man?" Herodias said to him one evening after his return from the dungeons. "You always come back with the stench of him in your hair and clothing. I think he's affecting your mind as well."

Perhaps he was. Herod went because he was compelled to go, because John had fanned his lifelong interest in Messianic prophecy into a consuming passion.

"What of the Gentiles?" Herod had said to John, when the prophet stood before him that evening. "When the Day of the Lord ushers in the age which is to come, what will happen to the Gentiles?"

John stood slightly stooped, already aged a decade from the hardships of prison. His weathered skin had paled beneath the grime on his bony hands and narrow face, and he held his arms close against his sides as if he were in pain. He looked up at Herod, but said nothing.

"'Let all the inhabitants of the land tremble, for the day of the Lord is coming. It is near, a day of darkness and gloom, a day of clouds and thick darkness,'" Herod said. "Joel. The book of the twelve. The suggestion is that many will suffer."

"Yes."

"But surely not God's own people."

John's eyes were red-rimmed and bloodshot. "God's people have turned from him. They are apostate."

"And the Gentiles, will they be destroyed completely?"

"Unless Israel can be saved."

"But Israel's salvation is to be the destruction of the Gentiles," Herod said.

"No. The Lord intends Israel to be his instrument to redeem the Gentiles. Isaiah says, 'I will give you as a light unto the nations that my salvation may reach the ends of the earth.'"

"Does he not also say, 'I will trample the nations in my anger'? 'I will crush them in my wrath, and I will pour out their lifeblood on the earth'?"

"'Turn to me and be saved, all the ends of the earth,'" John said.

"'For I am God, and there is no other. To me every knee shall bow, every tongue shall swear allegiance.'"

"'They shall come to Israel in chains and bow down,'" Herod said. "Isaiah again."

"'The nations shall come from the ends of the earth to Jerusalem to see the glory of God': The Psalms of Solomon. 'The Son of Man will be a light unto the Gentiles.' Enoch."

"There would seem to be two strands of prophecy concerning the Gentiles," Herod said.

"Why do you care? What are the Gentiles to you?"

A smile twisted Herod's face. "I serve Roman masters," he said.

"Rome! If it's Rome you're interested in, fear not; Rome will be destroyed. Look to Daniel. 'After this I saw in the night visions a fourth beast, terrifying and dreadful and exceedingly strong. It had great iron teeth and was devouring, breaking in pieces, and stamping what was left with its feet.'"

"The fourth beast is Rome?"

John nodded. "'And as I watched in the night visions, the beast was put to death, and its body destroyed and given over to be burned with fire.'"

"'And as I watched,'" Herod said. "'I saw one like a son of man coming with the clouds of heaven.' Who is this son of man?"

John said nothing.

"You know and I know that Israel cannot defeat Rome by merely human means. It will require the might of this apocalyptic figure of Daniel's, the one seated at God's right hand."

"'To him was given dominion and glory and kingship,'" said John. "'That all peoples, nations, and languages should serve him. His dominion is an everlasting dominion that shall not pass away. His kingship is one . . ." John broke off.

Herod was crying.

† † †

Jesus and his disciples had been in Capernaum for a week when Jairus appeared, flanked by two men foreign to Capernaum, from the look of them foreign to Galilee as well. Their dress identified them as scribes, masters of the law.

They pushed through the crowd and stepped through the doorway into the house, Jairus following in their wake and members of the crowd peering past them into the house.

The faces of the scribes were cold and stern. "We're here to speak with Jesus of Nazareth," one of them said. Behind him, Jairus's face showed his discomfort.

"I am he."

Matthew stood just inside the door, bobbing his head at his distinguished visitors and wringing his hands.

Jesus said, "And who are you? Envoys of those hypocrites in Jerusalem?" He swung his feet to the floor, but remained seated.

Jairus looked appalled.

One of the scribes cleared his throat with a sound like the meshing of iron gears. "We come from the High Priest himself."

Jesus nodded. "Correction noted." But his tone was dry.

The scribe's eyes scanned the front room, taking in Matthew and Simon Peter and the other disciples, taking in as well the big oaken table, which still held the plates and scraps of the noon repast. "This is a fast day," the scribe said. "Yet we see you've been eating."

"I have," Jesus said. "Moreover, I've encouraged others to do so."

"Why?"

"Do the wedding guests fast while the bridegroom is with them?"

The scribe raised an eyebrow disdainfully.

"No, there will be time enough for fasting when the bridegroom has left them."

The scribe looked from one end of the room to the other. "Has someone been married here, or are you mad?" He turned to Jairus: "Is he mad? He babbles like a madman."

Jairus looked at Jesus and shrugged helplessly.

"Whose house is this?" the scribe demanded.

Jairus, locating Matthew, pointed. "That man, Levi. A collector of taxes."

The scribe's eyes widened. "A tax collector," he said with heavy emphasis. Again he scanned the room, eyeing Jesus' disciples. "And no doubt the rest of these men are sinners of a similar type. What pretender to holiness would eat with such men?"

"Perhaps it takes genuine holiness," Jesus said, rising at last from his couch. "Of course, I can understand your being more familiar with pretenders."

The scribe seemed uncertain whether or not he had just been insulted.

"Everything you do is for show," Jesus said. "You make your phylacteries wide —" He gestured to the leather boxes strapped to their arms and foreheads. "— and the tassels on your garments long. You love to be greeted in the marketplaces and to have men call you 'Rabbi,' 'Master.' Don't you know that you have only one Master and that all men are your brothers?"

The scribe's face had gone pale. Drawing himself to his full height, he said, "You show by your words that you are unfamiliar even with the definition of holiness —"

"Or choose for your own reasons to ignore it," said the other.

"As the prophet Ezra told the people Israel," the first scribe continued. "'Make confession to the Lord, to the God of your ancestors, and do his will. Separate yourselves from the people of the land . . .'"

"Woe to you, you teachers of the law. You're shutting the door to the kingdom of heaven in the faces of your fellow men. You don't want to go in yourselves, and you want to be very sure that everyone else is going to be damned with you."

"How dare you —" The scribe was too overcome with anger to complete the thought.

"God is like a shepherd," Jesus said. He looked around to include his disciples and those who were looking in at the door and window. "If even one of his lambs is lost from the others, he will leave his flock and go in search of it."

The second scribe, sneering, said, "You blaspheme, sir. What do you mean by comparing the Most High God to a miserable shepherd?"

"Better a shepherd than a teacher of the law. You travel over land and sea to win a single convert — and when you do, you turn him into twice the son of hell that you yourselves are." Again reaching out to the others in his audience, he said, "God is the great physician. Will he go out to the sick or to the well?"

"A good answer," said Nathaniel. "Let them answer that, if they can."

The two scribes were too enraged, apparently, to say anything at all. Jairus, shocked to the core by Jesus' attack on the scribes, was filled with dismay.

"Two men went into the temple to pray," Jesus said, "a man of the law, and a tax collector. The tax collector, who knew he was a sinner, beat his breast and tore at his hair as he pleaded to God to have mercy on him. The other, the man of the law, looked with scorn at the tax collector and said, 'I thank you, O Lord, that I am not a miserable wretch such as that one. I thank you that I am such a worthy fellow.' Which prayer will God hear?"

"Amen," someone called.

The first scribe turned to Jairus. "It is clear at any rate how he is able to cast out demons."

"If indeed the reports be true," said the other.

"For is not Beelzebub the prince of demons?"

The second scribe nodded.

"It is by the power of Beelzebub that he casts out demons."

Jairus looked fearfully at Jesus.

"How can Satan cast out Satan?" Jesus said. "If a house is divided against itself, how shall it stand? If Satan has taken up arms against himself, then his end has come."

"How then —," Jairus began.

"How can a man enter a strong man's house and plunder his property?" Jesus said, completing the question. "He must first tie up the strong man; then he can do as he likes with his property."

"Listen to him! He himself is possessed," exclaimed the first scribe.

"Careful, Scribe," Jesus said. "Careful. The gates of hell loom close."

"We don't have to stand here —"

"Those who cannot distinguish between the spirit of God and the spirit of Beelzebub are damned already," Jesus said.

The first scribe turned abruptly on his heel and strode from the house. As he swept through the door, the other scribe followed in his wake.

Jesus looked at Jairus, who remained standing just inside the doorway of Matthew's house.

"You will hear from them again," said Jairus.

"Yes."

"You could have been more conciliatory," Jairus said.

"I'm not sure I could have. It's unwise to be conciliatory in the presence of evil."

"Evil? They are men of the law."

"Yes."

Jairus looked at him searchingly, then he too turned and left the house. Jesus' disciples stood looking at each other, at the floor, at the people crowding the doorway and the window — at anyone and anything but Jesus himself.

CHAPTER 14

Herod Antipas was entertaining that night in honor of his birthday. He had invited the leading citizens throughout his tetrarchy to a great feast, hoping the celebration would make the remote villa at Machaerus more tolerable to Herodias. His hope was in vain.

"What joy can I find in men at table?" she said.

"But —"

"I'm not coming. I'll be a wife to you again in Tiberius, not here."

He would have liked to return to his capital city on the west shore of the Sea of Galilee. The problem was John, and the difficulties involved in transporting him to Galilee. The people were convinced he was a prophet of God. Since his arrest, sympathizers had kept up a continual vigil outside the walls of the fortress. They were present day and night. Though tonight, on his birthday, Herod was making an effort to forget them.

Pillars lined all four sides of the great hall of Herod's palatial villa. The pillars created a passageway around its perimeter and provided numerous places of ingress and egress for the scores of servants coming and going with huge casks of wine and carts burdened with rich food. There were exotic meats and fruits — and pastries built into great towers of ostentatious confection. Before the night was many hours old, wine and chocolates and the juices of exotic meats had stained the lips and tunics of the host and his guests. They rested between courses as the dancers swept through the hall in a long, undulating line. Trailing long strips of gauzy fabric, the dancers entered from one side of the room and exited between two of the pillars on the other, then entered again from a third side. The faint percussion of cymbals, almost imperceptible at first, grew louder until it marked time for the weaving arms and the dancing feet.

A gauzy streamer encircled Antipas, brushing his clothes and hair, and he guffawed with boozy pleasure. A harp rippled, and the veils of the dancers dropped to the floor in rapid succession. The harp sounded again, and, beginning at the other end of the line, the robes dropped in sequence.

The dancers were all women, flowers woven into their long hair. Anklets and bracelets jingled on their bare legs and their upstretched arms as they advanced on the dais where Antipas reclined on his couch. Herod cackled with delighted anticipation, but the line broke just before it reached him, and the dancers fanned out through guests.

It was midway through the dance when Herod noticed Salome, the fourteen-year-old daughter of Herodias, standing at the edge of the banquet hall. She was dressed in white. One of her slim-fingered hands rested against a pillar, and her eyes were on the dancers.

Herod held up his goblet to his steward, Chuza, who had come from Tiberius to organize the feast. Chuza bent immediately to fill the goblet. Herod tossed back the wine and again extended his goblet. As Chuza refilled it, the lead dancer advanced on Herod, a taunting smile on her sculpted face. Her head shifted from one shoulder to the other in time to the beat of an unseen drum. Her long, bare arms moved in front of her body, weaving, reaching, as she mounted the dais. The percussion changed, becoming faster, lighter, and the dancer clasped her hands above her head, exposing her abdomen. Her hips gyrated wildly.

"Ooh," called several of the guests, and the sound was followed by general laughter.

Herod groped with his goblet for the table and, not finding it, let the goblet fall to the floor. The dancer leaned backward to touch her hands to the floor and, pushing off with her foot, swung down off the dais.

Salome's eyes went to Herod, whose face was flushed and perspiring. He beckoned to her, and she came to him.

She stood before him, slim and straight, like her mother in face, but only just developing in figure. Her eyes were large in her narrow face, innocent and fawnlike. For Herod, the music and the dancers and the laughter of his hundred guests faded into the background.

"You're a dancer," he said hoarsely.

She shook her head.

"Your mother tells me you're quite good."

A shy smile touched her lips.

"Dance for us on my birthday."

Her head turned toward the hall, the men reclining on couches, the dancers just exiting through the pillars on the far side.

"Do this for me, and ask what you will of me in return," Herod said.

Her eyes cut toward him. "Mother wouldn't like it."

"The devil with your mother. Herodias is a jealous old crow."

Again the half-smile, not shy this time, but full of mystery. Herod rose from his couch. "Gentlemen," he said, clapping his hands for their attention. "Salome, the daughter of my wife, Herodias, is to dance for us this evening."

There was applause, a few catcalls. Salome curtseyed, that enigmatic smile still playing about her lips.

"Salome?" Herod said. "Can you begin, or do you need some time for preparation?"

"A quarter-hour to get into my dancing costume."

"Granted then. Granted!"

She departed, and he dropped back onto his couch and reached for his goblet. "Steward!" he said. "More wine."

Actually, he didn't feel quite well. Currents of indigestion roiled his bowels, and, when a burst of flatulence escaped him, it did so with a sound like a clap of thunder. Most ignored it, but there was scattered applause.

"There are few sights and sounds more revolting than those of men eating and drinking," Herodias said, dropping down on the foot of Herod's couch.

"Herodias!" Herod said, blinking at her in some alarm. "You came to my party."

"I understand my daughter is to be on display this evening."

"You said she was good. You should be proud of her."

"Instead of being a jealous old crow?"

"I didn't mean . . ."

"I know what you meant."

"Then she won't be dancing? She has to dance. I've announced it. If she doesn't dance, it will make me a fool."

"I think your foolishness is something beyond Salome's ability to augment or diminish," Herodias said.

Herod's face flushed dark. "If Salome won't dance, then why are you here? You've said men disgust you."

"I want to see how she does with an audience."

"You mean . . ."

A drum beat started up, three long beats and two short, three long beats and two short. The crowd fell silent. A flute sounded, its song at first sedate, then increasingly frenzied. Herod, suddenly uneasy, felt his pulse quicken. A figure more geometric than human cartwheeled across the room and disappeared again on the other side. The percussion became metallic, the clash of weapon on shield. The flute was joined by another, then another. Salome came from the back of the room, flipping from hands to feet, hands to feet, her body a blur in the torchlight. She ended her run directly in front of the dais in a full split, her hands upraised. Her hair was pulled back from her face into a hard knot, and streaks of dark makeup marked her face. Though her garment was flesh-toned and form-fitting, the effect was more animalistic than feminine.

Salome rolled to her side and pushed up into a handstand, scissoring her legs forward and backward. When she dropped into a walk, she pawed twice at the ground before each step, lifting and dropping her shoulders in time to the music, her arms unnaturally stiff at her sides. At the end of the room, she turned and pointed at Herod, who still reclined on his dais. She swept her open palm back and forth as if striking him.

Her next run toward Herod culminated in a double flip, in

which she drew her knees to her chest in the air and straightened in time to land on her feet on the dais itself. She repeated the slapping gesture, the breeze she generated stirring the very hair of Herod's beard. She strutted first one way, then the other before his couch, her hands on her boyish hips. Herod's tongue appeared briefly between dry lips.

Salome placed the instep of one tiny foot on Herod's shoulder, and his chest constricted so that he found it impossible to breathe. Slowly, slowly, she lifted the slim leg so that the toes pointed toward the vaulted ceiling. She gripped her ankle and pirouetted slowly, her torso arched, her delicate ribs showing through her thin clothing.

For Herod the world ceased to exist but for the girl. The music of the dance was all of a piece with the movements of Salome. Time slowed as she jumped and turned and moved her arms. The torches themselves had ceased to flicker.

Herod started, aware, suddenly, that the music had stopped and the dance was over. Salome stood motionless before her audience, one foot in front of the other, her arms upraised. His face was wet with tears as he rose to his feet. He looked around as if lost, his eyes passing over his guests and servants, over Herodias, over Salome herself. Finally, he swept the wine and grapes from a silver tray and picked it up. He dropped heavily to one knee before Salome and presented her the tray. "Instruct me with what gems and precious metals I may adorn this tray. Ask what you will of me, and I will give it."

The half-smile again touched her face, enigmatic and mocking. "Anything?" she asked as she took the tray.

"Anything you ask," he said, "up to half my kingdom."

As he got to his feet, his guests began to shout, stamping their feet and pounding their tables in acclamation. Herodias gestured, and Salome went to her, bending her head to receive instruction. She went again to Herod, and he put an arm about her, raising his hand for silence.

"Well?" he said to her. "Tell me — tell all this audience — what it is you wish."

She held out the tray to him. Only gradually did the crowd fall silent.

"I ask that you present the tray to me again," she said.

"Yes?" he said. "Adorned with what?"

"Adorned with the head of one they call John the Baptizer."

Herod felt he had been struck in the chest. The audience was silent. "Adorned with what?" he said again.

"Adorned with the head of John the Baptizer."

All eyes were on him. He wet his lips and laughed, though the sound was tremulous, devoid of its usual heartiness. "Ask for something else," he said. "A ransom in diamonds. Rubies, perhaps. Pearls."

"I want the head of John the Baptizer."

Herod shook his head, bewildered. Herodias stood, drawing his eyes. "Is the king not a man of his word?" she asked.

The eyes of his guests were on him. He started to say something, but lost the sense of it as soon as he had begun to speak.

Herodias arched an eyebrow.

Herod cleared his throat.

"I repeat," she said, stepping to Salome and resting a hand glittering with jewels on her thin shoulder. "Is the king not a man of his word?"

He grinned foolishly, shrugging his beefy shoulders. "Herodias," he said pleadingly.

She shook her head and stepped off the dais, guiding Salome with her through the courtiers of Herod and the important men of Perea and Galilee.

Just as she had reached the far end of the room, Herod called to her. "Wait," he said.

Herodias turned with Salome.

"All right," he said.

"Yes?"

"As you ask, so let it be done," he said.

CHAPTER 15

The crowds that surrounded Matthew's house became larger, denser — and more frantic to catch sight of Jesus, to touch him, to hear him speak. The only times he could leave the house occurred early in the mornings, well before first light, when he would go out alone to walk along the shore of the Sea of Galilee, to gaze out at the torches of the fishermen far out on the water.

The crowds troubled him. They were responsive — he was, after all, performing signs that had not been seen in Israel since the days of the prophets — but the response was different in kind from what he had hoped, from what he had expected. His call to the Kingdom, so reminiscent of John's, was not being answered. There was, here and there, a desire to answer it — a desire for genuine repentance — but the ability to achieve it seemed entirely absent.

He often walked for miles in the early hours before dawn. He prayed, he thought — and he felt increasingly a sense of waiting. The current pattern of his ministry would not last, though what would replace it he did not yet know. Of one thing he was increasingly certain: Human beings were lost. Man could not find his way back to God, even with God standing and beckoning to him.

It was on one of his early morning walks that Jesus came across Simon Peter. Peter stood by the water's edge looking out at the glittering torches.

"Are you looking for me?" Jesus asked him.

Peter shook his head, his eyes still on the water, then he

shrugged. "I knew you were out here. I'm not sure what I was looking for."

"You miss it, sometimes, don't you?" Jesus nodded toward the water, and Peter sighed in response. He looked down at his hands, rough and calloused, the knuckles of the fingers large with hard use, and he held them up.

"I'm a fisherman," he said. "It's what I've always done; it's what I'm good at. I feel out of place indoors so much of the time, listening to religious talk and helping with the crowds."

Jesus nodded. "I understand."

"Do you?"

"Look at my hands. All my life I've been a carpenter."

"And you miss it?"

"Sometimes. The smell and feel of the wood, the muscular fatigue of a good day's work . . ."

"Do you ever think about going back to it?"

Jesus shook his head — a little sadly, it seemed to Peter. "I'm doing my Father's will."

"God's will?"

"Yes. And there's satisfaction in that, too."

"What about me? Am I doing God's will?"

"Yes."

"Are you sure of that?"

Jesus looked at him. "I am sure of that," he said.

Peter nodded reluctantly.

Jesus put a hand on his shoulder. "You won't be forever without the joys of fishing. Remember? I promised you that."

"Ah, yes." Peter chuckled, almost to himself. "I'm to be a fisher of men. Do you think it will have the same satisfactions for me?"

"I do. A man who has hunted for sailfish in the Great Sea, would he return to fishing for minnows in a shallow stream?"

Peter had never fished in the Great Sea, much less for sailfish. "Fishing for men is like hunting for sailfish in the Great Sea?"

"And more," Jesus said. "And more."

† † †

The crowds no longer remained in the outer courtyard. They pressed into the house. They reached out their hands to Jesus — and even to his disciples — and they picked up such small items as could be concealed easily beneath their robes, thinking to keep them as souvenirs or talismans. During the day it was impossible for Jesus to confer with his disciples alone, impossible to rest, impossible even to eat. He had added a twelfth disciple, choosing a man named Thomas out of the crowd according to some criteria known only to himself.

One day a woman standing in the midst of the press of people in the doorway called out to Andrew, the disciple standing nearest her, "There are people here to see Jesus. They say they are his brothers."

Someone behind her shouted something.

"And his mother," she added.

Andrew pressed toward Jesus and bent close to him to pass on the news.

Jesus straightened, and the crowd became immediately quiet. "Tell them to come in," Jesus called to the woman in the doorway.

She passed the word back, and, beyond her, Jesus' message echoed across the courtyard.

"They want you to come out to them," she said at last.

Jesus shook his head. His smile was a sad one. "I can't go to them; they must come to me."

The answer echoed back toward Jesus' waiting family.

"Are they coming?" Jesus asked.

There was more calling, more craning of necks. "I don't think so," someone said.

Andrew leaned close to him again. "Maybe you ought to," he said. "Your mother, your brothers."

"Who is my mother?" Jesus said. "And my brothers? You are all here. Those who do the will of God are my mother and my brothers."

"That seems rather cold," said Judas, severely.

"Does it? My family has heard of the work I am doing, and they come to restrain me, thinking I'm not in my right mind."

"Are you?" someone asked.

Jesus' eyes sought out the speaker. "I am here to start a new family, a spiritual family. It will of necessity disrupt some of the old ones."

"That can't be good," Judas said. He spoke in a role to which the crowd had become accustomed — that of devil's advocate.

"I have come to set brother against brother, to set father against son."

Nathaniel, who of all the disciples was closest to being a scholar of the Scripture, felt a chill working along his spine. Jesus' words echoed those of Zechariah and Enoch, of the greatest of the rabbis: He was describing the Day of the Lord. He was laying out, however obliquely, his Messianic claim.

"You are to call no man father," Jesus was saying. "For each of you has but one father, the one in heaven, who waits for your return. Listen, God is like a man who had two sons. The younger of them said to his father, 'Give me my share of the inheritance now . . ."

† † †

Early the next morning, before the crowd had yet become large, a young man came into the house, going from one room to the next until he came upon Jesus.

"Joseph," Jesus said, recognizing his brother.

"Hello, Jesus. You've hurt Mother, you know."

"I know. I'm sorry."

"It's not like we brought ropes along to tie you up. All we wanted was for you to come home with us."

"My work is here."

"Are you sure?" Joseph looked at Judas and Simon the Zealot, whom he had seen in Cana and again in Nazareth, at Simon Peter and Andrew, at the corpulent Matthew. "Why not leave it for a short time? A rest might bring you new energy."

"Or a new perspective?"

"Look," Joseph said. "It's the time of the Feast of Dedication, and the entire family's going to Jerusalem for it. Why don't you come with us? From all reports, you've been doing all kinds of wonderful things. Why waste it all on a Galilean backwater like Capernaum?"

"I agree with him there," Judas said. "You've been doing great things. You should be in Jerusalem."

Jesus glanced at him.

"Why the self-effacement?" Judas said.

Joseph, not liking the turn the conversation was taking, said, "I was thinking of a quiet celebration of the festival, all of us together as a family."

"You go to the feast," Jesus said. "You and mother and the rest. It is your time for feast-going. I can't go without entering the public eye, and it's not yet time."

"When will it be time?" Judas said.

Joseph, looking back and forth between them, said, "Time for what? What are you planning?"

Jesus smiled, the crinkles deepening around his eyes. "Wait and see," he said mildly. "Wait and see."

† † †

Simon Peter woke while it was still dark. A hand was on his back, pushing at him, and he peered upward at the shadowy figure beside him. "Jesus?" he said.

"Yes. We're leaving for Jerusalem this morning. Help me wake the others."

"But I thought you said —"

"We're going secretly, leaving under cover of darkness."

"But why —"

"God wants me in Jerusalem. I don't yet know why."

Peter sat up, rolling his head about on his shoulders to relieve his cramped muscles. Jesus moved on.

"Andrew!" Peter said, poking at his brother with his foot. "Andrew, wake up."

Andrew rolled onto this back and raised his head to look at him.

"We're setting off for Jerusalem this morning. Jesus wants to get away before daylight."

Andrew groaned.

Soon everyone was astir. Because Jesus had warned him not to wake the servants, Matthew commandeered John and James to help him gather together such provisions as he had for the trip, and he walked this way and that, giving instructions.

They left Capernaum an hour before dawn. The stars overhead blazed in the black velvet of the sky, and the cold wind cut through their layered cloaks and tunics.

"This is important; this is good," Judas said several times. "We should be in Jerusalem."

"What Jesus' brother said to him made sense," said Simon the Zealot. "There is only so much that can be done staying house-bound in Capernaum."

"This may be where it all comes together," Judas said. "This could be a real beginning."

James the younger, disturbed by their talk, quickened his pace in order to catch up with John and Peter, who were walking with Jesus.

"Your teeth are chattering," Jesus observed when James joined them. "Keep up a good pace and move your arms back and forth." He demonstrated as he walked.

"I would," James said through his clicking teeth. "But my arms seem to be frozen in place against my sides."

"It will warm up at daybreak," Peter said. "Just keep moving."

James nodded bravely, but the ground was hard and unyielding and almost unbearably cold through the soles of his leather sandals.

† † †

They passed through Magdala at mid-morning, and the woman Mary glided out from one of the shops to fall into step beside Jesus. More than one of the disciples failed to recognize her; James, who did, was a little staggered by the change in her appearance. Her dark hair was clean, and it shone in the cold morning sun. Her dress was neat. Her eyes were no longer shadowed, but bright and clear.

"What happened?" James said to John, pulling him aside.

"I imagine it comes of talking to Jesus. That often seems to cause a change in people."

"Is she coming with us?"

John glanced at Mary, who, beyond her first, shy greeting, had said nothing to Jesus, but who kept glancing up at him in apparent awe as they walked.

"I wouldn't mind," he said. "She's pretty to look at."

James looked at her, too, surprised, almost, by the delicacy of her profile, by her soft, clear skin, by the flush of cold in her cheek. "She is, isn't she?" he said.

† † †

Mary didn't accompany them far beyond the borders of Magdala. They stopped for the night in Tiberius, the city of Herod Antipas, at the home of Herod's steward, Chuza, and his wife Joanna, where lights shone in the windows.

After long knocking, footsteps sounded in the interior of the house, and Chuza pulled open the door himself, holding up a lantern to see their faces.

His own face was a shock, smeared with black ashes. "It's John," he said, recognizing Jesus. "The Baptizer. Herod has beheaded him."

† † †

They talked long into the night. At some time during the third watch, when all the travelers had gone to bed but Jesus and Simon Peter, Chuza said to Jesus, "Master, I have no wish to offend you."

"Speak freely," Jesus said.

"I was with John before he died. His last words were of you."

"And his words troubled you." A statement, not a question.

"He said to ask you, 'Are you the one who was to come, or are we to wait for another?'"

A look of pain entered Jesus' eyes. He sighed. "It is not the first time I've had word of John's question. Didn't he get my answer?"

"It has not been easy for John's disciples to reach him. Nor can I now take him back an answer."

"Now he has his answer. I am sorry he could not have had it when he faced his death."

"He had heard you no longer baptized," Chuza said, making John's question his own.

"That I drank wine and ate rich food?"

"Yes. And that neither you nor your disciples kept the fast days, nor did you wash your hands as the law prescribed."

Jesus exhaled noisily. He suddenly looked very tired.

"Master?" Chuza said.

"Have you not witnessed the fulfillment of Isaiah's prophecy?"

Chuza's expression was blank.

Jesus began in a low voice that seemed to gain strength as he spoke. "And on that day," he said, "the eyes of the blind shall be opened, and the ears of the deaf unstopped. On that day the lame shall leap like the deer, and the tongues of the speechless shall sing for joy."

It was a familiar prophecy, one charged with emotion, and Chuza's eyes brimmed with tears.

"Haven't these signs been done in your presence?" Jesus said. "Don't the blind see and the lame walk?"

"Master?" said Peter, and Jesus turned to him. "It is said that John taught his disciples to pray."

"Yes?"

"Being with you has made me more and more aware of God's presence. I can feel him poking at me and prodding me. I'd like to know what to say to him."

Jesus smiled. "Say to him what's on your mind. If something's troubling you, deal with it openly in God's presence."

"Yes, but —"

"You need a model."

"Yes."

"Pray with me then." The focus of Jesus' gaze shifted, and he seemed to see beyond the walls of the room. "Father," he said. "Our Father who art in heaven . . ."

CHAPTER 16

It was hard for Simon Peter to get used to applying the term "Father" to the most high God, the Lord of Hosts, the great "I AM." He tried it several times on the journey to Jerusalem, and each time he felt presumptuous, almost blasphemous. At times he found himself watching Jesus as Jesus prayed, squatting alone by the fire or breaking bread and passing it among his disciples. He wondered about the presumption of Jesus. He called God "Father"; he violated the Jewish law seemingly at will. He presumed greatly. Did he feel presumptuous, as Peter did? Peter shook his head. He thought not — and who was the more presumptuous, the man who felt presumptuous, or the man who did not?

Then there was the title Jesus kept applying to himself, the one taken from the book of Daniel. Though Peter did not read himself, he had heard the passage quoted many times, especially over the past few months, had heard Judas and his friend Simon discussing it while standing apart a little way. *As Daniel watched in the night visions, he saw one like a son of man coming with the clouds of heaven.*

"And he came to the Ancient of Days, and was presented before him," Peter repeated to himself.

As he studied Jesus, he took in the flashing smile with the strong white teeth. The hands with their short, blunt fingers, calloused and hard from years of working with wood. The rough, Galilean homespun.

This was the man who called God "Father," and who called himself the Son of Man.

† † †

The waters of the pool by the Sheep's Gate were supposed to have healing properties. Laman, though he was old, couldn't name anybody who had actually been healed in the pool, but the rumors were sufficient to keep the five columned porches around the pool crowded with invalids. Some, like himself, were crippled with arthritis. Some had been lame from birth. Some were blind, some deaf . . .

On a bad day, Laman's swollen knees were the size of melons. On a good day they weren't much better: not so painful to the touch, perhaps. His hips and his ankles, his elbows and wrists — each bothered him to some extent. At a given point in time any could qualify as the joint that throbbed most with distracting pain.

Each day Laman sat with his eyes on the surface of the water. Most of those on the porches were similarly occupied; even the blind had someone to watch for them. Again, rumor had it, or tradition had it, that when the pool bubbled, its healing properties were the greatest. Rumor had it that the first person in the pool after it began to bubble would be healed completely of all his infirmities.

Laman didn't know. He'd never been first in the pool. Usually the mad dash and hop and shuffle had begun before he even realized the water had begun to boil. The person first into the pool likely had some minor complaint, a recurrent headache or a persistent pimple — nothing that required the supernatural properties of the pool.

Supernatural? Maybe. There were those that said the Lord sent his angel to stir up the water at certain seasons, that it was the angel that accounted for the healing properties of the pool. Others drew attention to the persistent smell of sulfur: a little gas bubbling to the surface, that was all. Nothing supernatural. No one was healed, only deluded for a while, perhaps.

Still, one had to live one's life with hope or without it — and with hope was easier. Laman badgered his family to carry him to the pool earlier and earlier, until some days he was the first one there.

His rheumy old eyes remained focused on the pool for many hours, until the sun was high in the sky and the still air beneath the roofs of the porticos was hot, until all the people walking and standing made it impossible to see the water.

It was early on such a morning that a stranger came and sat on the steps beside him. Laman's initial feeling was one of irritation. Here was another competitor, from the look of him one well able to beat Laman into the pool.

"Does the angel stir it often?" the stranger said, after a time.

Laman glanced at him. "Not often," he said. "Not so often that I myself have ever made it first into the pool."

"You have been here often then," the stranger said.

"Often enough. Every day for the past several years."

"How many years since the rheumatism first infected your joints?"

"Thirty-eight."

"A long time."

"You're a boy; you can't imagine how long."

The stranger's smile was only just perceptible beneath the thick, black beard. "Because I am not thirty-eight myself, you mean."

"At least you don't look it."

"No. You can't have been much older than I am now when the rheumatism struck you."

"I wasn't," the old man said, eyeing him appraisingly. "About your age, I would think."

"You want to be made well?"

"It's why I'm here." Beyond the stranger, a few bubbles broke the surface of the pool, but Laman failed to notice.

"Thirty-eight years is a long time to adjust to being a cripple," the stranger said. "Thirty-eight years of others taking care of you, of others showing special concern."

"I would give all that I have to be made well again." The stranger's clear, brown eyes were unsettlingly direct, and Laman doubted for the first time the truth of what he was saying. It was true, he thought, that any healing would be a mixed blessing. With a start his head jerked toward the pool, where the waters were roiling as if a great fish thrashed just beneath the surface. How had he not heard it?

Panic filled him. “Sir,” he said. “Sir, if you would help me.” He struggled onto his hands and knees and lurched against a pillar in his efforts to rise.

“You don’t need my help.”

“Sir, for the love of God —” Already it seemed to him that the pool’s disturbance had lessened.

“For the love of God,” the stranger said, but he continued to sit impassively.

Laman stood hunched against the pillar. The waters were still, the opportunity past.

“You are on your feet,” said the stranger. “Are you in pain?”

Laman looked down at the twisted claws that were his hands. “Not as much as usual,” he admitted. He relaxed his hands and saw with some surprise that they looked like just that, hands. The skin was liver-spotted and papery to be sure, as befitted the hands of a man nearing seventy, but beneath the skin the hands were healthy and unremarkable. He turned them over feeling something akin to awe as he examined them. He looked up at the stranger.

“You did that. You healed me.”

“Did I?”

“What . . .” Laman felt confused, dizzied by the years that opened suddenly before him. “What do I do now?” he asked.

The stranger laughed. “What indeed?”

Laman stared at him, his bewilderment still showing on his face.

“Pick up your mat and take it with you. Return to a productive life.”

“Yes. Yes, of course.”

Moving slowly by force of long habit, his eyes never leaving the stranger’s face, Laman stooped for his mat.

If there was pain in his knees or his hip, he was unaware of it.

† † †

Laman went in search of his family. Though his joints were free of pain, still he was an old man, his muscles weak from lack of exercise. The festival crowd frightened him. It seemed to be an angrier, noisier, more violent crowd than he remembered — though perhaps it was merely because for the first time in years he found himself moving among them. His gait was steady, and he met the gaze of people eye-to-eye as an equal, not having to look up, not having to beg.

Crossing into the temple precincts, he saw Roman soldiers patrolling the perimeter in what seemed to him unusually large numbers, even for a feast day. To his right, broad steps led up to the Beautiful Gate and the court of the women, which only Jews were allowed to enter.

"Hey, you there," a voice cried out as he walked, but people were talking and calling out all around him and he paid little attention. A thin man with a long beard lying gray and full on the breast of his rich robes was coming down the steps toward him. "You there." Laman turned only when a bony, long-fingered hand gripped his shoulder.

"What do you mean by carrying your mat on the Sabbath?"

Laman looked down at his side, following the direction of the man's gaze. Yes, he was carrying his mat as he walked, though it was a thin mat, not heavy at all — such a little thing that he scarcely noticed.

"Do you hear me, old man? What do you mean by it? Can you not speak?"

"I can speak." Laman looked up into man's eyes, which were dark and angry. "What's more, I can walk as well, after thirty-eight years."

"Yes, but why are you carrying your mat?"

"The man who healed me told me to carry my mat."

"The man who healed you!"

"I told you, I've been a cripple for thirty-eight years. Until this morning I was unable to walk."

"Someone healed you and told you to carry your mat? Who?"

"I don't know who. A stranger."

"Is he here in the temple? Can you point him out to me?"

Laman looked about them obligingly, but he didn't see the stranger. "No," he said. "I'm sorry."

"I, Nathan, a priest of the temple, tell you it is unlawful to carry your mat."

Laman dropped it at his feet.

"You can't leave it there."

"What else am I to do with it? You say I can't carry it away, and yet I can't leave it either."

"Don't bandy words with me."

"I'm sorry, is that unlawful as well?"

But the priest turned on his heel and strode away.

† † †

Annas and Caiaphas had another problem, a big one. That morning they were escorted into the great hall of the palace, where Pilate was holding court. They waited until he had finished hearing the case before theirs and had rendered his decision. Pilate's chief administrative assistant beckoned to them, and they approached.

"Yes?" Pilate said, lounging on his throne of brass and ivory. "What is it this time?"

"We've come to protest the raiding of the temple treasury."

"Ah, yes. I thought you might have."

"I thought we were agreed," said Annas. "The city's public works are the responsibility of the civil government. Of Rome."

"The temple will be a primary beneficiary of the new aqueduct," Pilate said. "You know that."

"What we know —," Caiaphas began.

"Indeed," Pilate said, overriding him. "Were it not for all the cleansing necessitated by your continual sacrifices . . . You spill gallons and gallons of blood every day of the year, and it requires many more gallons of water to wash it all away. The current aqueduct is simply not sufficient."

What he said was true: it was not sufficient. The current

aqueduct, running from the spring of Gihom to the Siloam reservoir just inside the city walls, had been built by King Hezekiah of Judah some seven hundred years before. Seven hundred years. The needs of the city had grown, and the new aqueduct, when completed, would bring water to Jerusalem all the way from Solomon's Pools, outside Bethlehem five miles to the south.

"The public works should be paid for with public funds," Annas said.

"The new aqueduct is going to stretch for miles — not a third of a mile like the old one. The public funds have proved insufficient."

"The procurator —"

"— is responsible for the in-gathering of taxes," Pilate said. "I have no power to increase them."

"Seizure of the temple funds amounts to a tax."

"Not at all. The public monies have run out. If construction is to continue, the temple must make its contribution."

"Contributions are by their nature voluntary."

"I approached you for a voluntary contribution, remember? You refused."

"The looting of the temple treasury amounts to sacrilege in the eyes of the people," Annas said. "The people won't stand for it."

"The people will stand for what they must," Pilate said.

"Remember Caesarea. People came not just from Jerusalem to protest your action. They came from every village in Judea."

"I remember Caesarea," Pilate said, his mouth stretching in a grimace. "And I assure you, there will be no repetition of the leniency I exhibited on that occasion. If you value the peace, as you say you do — if you value the privileges allowed you by Rome — you will control your people."

Annas bowed stiffly.

"Do you understand me?" Pilate said. "There is to be no disturbance."

Annas left without responding, Caiaphas coming along ponderously behind him.

† † †

Laman had gone only a few steps when he saw the stranger. He stood on the steps along the north side of the court of the women, and a crowd had gathered around him. A big crowd. John's preaching in the Judean desert, and his recent execution, had sparked the Jews' unusual interest in prophecy and fanned it into flame. Jesus himself was not unknown. Tales of miraculous healings in Galilee had been told and retold throughout Palestine. Now that Jesus was in Jerusalem, many were eager to see him and to hear him preach. Always, always, there was the undercurrent of Messianic expectation: Could this be the one? Could this be God's anointed?

"He calls himself the Son of Man," said a dark-skinned man at the edge of the crowd. "Ask yourself what he means by that. Remember Daniel. The Day of the Lord."

"Judas, think what you're saying, that this man has been seated at the right hand of God from all eternity, waiting for just this moment to appear on earth. Look at him. You can't believe that." The man was a distant kinsmen of Judas's and also a Zealot.

"It hardly matters what I believe," Judas said. "What matters is what they believe." He indicated the crowd. "They're enraged that Pilate has looted the temple treasury. Imagine the fury with which they will fight if united behind their Messiah."

Laman overheard them, but paid little attention. His gaze was focused on Jesus. "Do not think I have come to bring peace to the earth," he was saying in response to a question. "I have not come to bring peace, but a sword."

"Listen," said Judas. "Hear him. Could he be any plainer than that?"

". . . for I have come to set a man against his father, and a daughter against her mother. One's foes will be members of his own household."

"All signs of the day which is to come."

"Sir," called Laman to Jesus, pushing up through the crowd. "Good sir!"

Jesus' eyes seemed to brighten as he spotted Laman. "You look well," he said.

"Yes, for a cripple."

Several in the crowd exchanged puzzled glances.

"Please sir," said Laman. "I don't know your name."

"Jesus. Of Nazareth."

"I am Laman," the old man said, nodding his head.

"God bless you, Laman. May he bless you and keep you."

† † †

Laman went back to where he had left his mat. There were three priests surrounding it at that time, pointing to it and arguing. "There he is," said one of them, pointing at Laman. "There is the man who is littering the temple precincts."

"I only did what you instructed me to do," Laman said, protesting.

"You shouldn't have been carrying the mat in the first place."

"That's what I've come to tell you. The man who healed me, who instructed me to take up my mat and walk, he is here at the temple. Just around the corner, preaching on the steps. His name is Jesus."

It was a common enough name. "Come," said the priest. "Show him to us." Taking the old man by the arm, they started off.

"There," he said as they rounded the corner. "On the top step. The one with the black beard and the flashing eyes."

As the priests and Laman pushed through the crowd and mounted the steps, Jesus broke off in what he was saying. The crowd watched expectantly.

"They say you call yourself Jesus," said one of the priests, huffing slightly.

Jesus smiled. "It's what my parents called me," he said, and several in the crowd laughed.

The face of the priest flushed. "What do you, who pretend to be a rabbi, mean by dishonoring the Sabbath and teaching others to do so?"

"How have I dishonored the Sabbath?"

"This man says you healed him. Healing is work, forbidden on the Sabbath by the law of Moses."

"Healing is God's work, which is never forbidden."

"Who are you to disagree with Moses?"

"Where in the Torah does he forbid the healing of the sick?"

"The Torah!" the priest echoed. "You show your ignorance. The proscription is not in the Torah, but in the oral law. In the traditions of our people."

"A bad tradition, propounded in error," Jesus said.

The priest looked temporarily apoplectic. A boy pulled at Laman's cloak.

"Were you really a cripple?" he asked. "And Jesus healed you?"

"At whose feet did you study, Rabbi?" the priest said, finding his voice. "What authority can you cite for your blasphemy?"

"I have been listening to him," said a man standing in another part of the crowd. "I will say he has much learning."

The priest seemed to know him. "How such learning if he has never been taught?"

"He did not say he had never been taught," said the man. "As I recall he made no answer to your question at all."

"Well?" said the priest, addressing Jesus. "Have you been taught?"

"I have. My teaching is not mine, but that of him who sent me."

"And who is this?" the priest asked. "Who sent you, and for what purpose?"

"Anyone who has resolved in his heart to obey God will know whether my words are from God, or whether I speak on my own authority."

"You claim God sent you? You pretentious ass."

"Those who speak on their own authority seek their own glory. I seek only the glory of Him who sent me; thus shall you know my words are true."

"You have dishonored the Sabbath."

"None of you keep the law in every particular, why pick on me? Why look at me with murder in your hearts?"

"You don't even know me," said the priest. "Name a law I've broken."

"You Pharisees!" Jesus said, speaking the title like a curse. "You

Pharisees and your law!"

"My delight is in the law of the Lord," the priest said, paraphrasing the psalmist. "On His law I meditate day and night. We Pharisees seek to incorporate the law into every aspect of our lives. Surely that is to be commended."

"Surely it would be, if it were true. You use the law to hold the Lord your God at a distance. 'Thus far you may come into my life,' you say, 'and no further. I will follow your commandments, and, when I have done so, I am my own. The Lord has no further claims upon me.'"

"But that is all that is required."

"No."

The priest's lip curled in disbelief.

"It was said to men of old, You shall not kill," said Jesus. "Whoever killed was liable to judgment in the village court. I tell you, it is not enough. If you are even angry with your brother, you are liable to such judgment. If you insult your brother, you are liable to judgment by the council of elders. If you destroy his name and reputation, you are liable to the fires of hell."

"You're accusing me of violating the sixth commandment?" The priest's tone was incredulous. "By my words?"

"And your thoughts. You have violated the seventh as well."

"You're insane."

"You have never lain with a woman not your wife?"

"I have not."

"Have you ever looked at a woman and wanted to possess her? Actually fantasized about possessing her?"

The priest hesitated, and someone laughed.

"My friend," Jesus said. "You have already committed adultery with her in your heart."

CHAPTER 17

The council of the Sanhedrin met in called session. "He will capitulate," Caiaphas said of Pilate. "A display of resolve like the one we made in Caesarea, and he will capitulate."

"The last display of resolve cost my father his life," said Elionaeus, a young firebrand of the house of Boethus.

Annas inclined his head in acknowledgment of the sacrifice. "All Israel honors him for his courage."

"There are times when one man must give his life for the lives of many," Caiaphas said.

"So what do you say, Annas?" Elionaeus said. "Will he capitulate as Caiaphas says?"

Annas shrugged. "If we let this go unchallenged, it sets a precedent that may ultimately prove our ruin. If Pilate can raid the treasury for this purpose, then why not another — and another?"

"Though the aqueduct is ultimately to our advantage," said Joseph, a rich Pharisee from Arimethea, a town in the hill country of Ephraim. "And these particular funds were unsuitable for any sacred purpose because of their source."

"And we have another problem," Elionaeus said. "There is one here at the festival some say is the Messiah." He told them of the priest's report. "Each day a mob rallies around him to hear him speak."

Annas frowned. "We are familiar with this Jesus," he said. "He's been causing quite a stir up in Galilee."

"And now that he's come to Jerusalem —"

"Yes, we must follow his career closely from this point."

"What's wrong with people?" a man said. "Have they no learning? When the Messiah comes, he will appear out of nowhere."

"The Scriptures don't make that as clear as we could wish," said Annas.

"One thing is certain — he will not come from Galilee."

"No," said Nicodemus. "Not from Galilee. The Messiah will be a descendant of David, and he will come from the village of Bethlehem, which gave us David." Nicodemus stroked his dark beard.

"What are you saying?" Annas said, turning to him. "Do you know this man's origins? Is he not a Galilean?"

"His speech and his dress are those of a Galilean," Nicodemus said.

"If he looks like a Galilean and he talks like a Galilean . . ." The remark produced general laughter.

"It is not our way to condemn a man without giving him a hearing," Nicodemus. "What does he himself claim?"

"Nicodemus," said someone. "Are you too from Galilee?" There was more laughter. In the holy city of Jerusalem, Galileans were not highly regarded.

"Search the Scripture," Annas said. "You will find that no prophet is to arise in Galilee. Still, what you say makes sense. Let us have this Jesus in for questioning. Let us ask him point blank whether he is the Messiah, as we did John."

"And suppose he says he is?"

"Then we will deal with him." Annas lips stretched into a thin smile. "We'll have to. We're the only Messiah the people need."

Elionaeus shook his head. "He's a great favorite of the crowd. I don't know if it's wise to arrest him. We might provoke a riot beyond our ability to control."

"Perhaps he'll come willingly," Annas said.

"And if he does not?"

"Why shouldn't he come willingly, if he is a good Jew?"

† † †

The mob surrounding Jesus was larger than had been reported, filling the area between the sanctuary and the elegant stone partition that barred the Gentiles. The half-dozen guards sent by Annas edged through the crowd, nervous despite their swords and helmets, well aware of the black stares they attracted. Jesus fell silent as they gained the steps.

The guards stopped, conscious of the crowd's attention. Some shifted uneasily from one foot to another, their movements accompanied by the clanking of arms — an alarming sound amid the quiet.

"Yes?" Jesus asked.

The chief guard cleared his throat.

"Whom do you seek?"

A low murmur worked its way through the crowd like the rumble of distant thunder. The guard's head jerked from side to side, alert to hidden dangers.

"Are you looking for someone?" Jesus asked.

The guard mumbled something in a gruff voice that was too low to hear.

"I'm Jesus of Nazareth. Have you been sent to arrest me?"

The question seemed to produce alarm. The guard pulled his head more closely into his shoulders, and his words were lost in the renewed murmur of the crowd.

Jesus waited expectantly. Realizing that some further action was required of him, the guard decided on retreat. He jerked his head at his men and shuffled backward off the steps. The crowd seemed denser than before as the guards pushed through it.

"I may be with you for only a short time," Jesus said to the crowd. "The time will come when you look for me, but you will not find me."

Mutters of anger and displeasure swept the crowd. The guards, reaching its fringes, were pushed this way and that before breaking clear of it.

† † †

Jesus and his disciples left the city by the Fountain Gate and climbed the west slope of the Mount of Olives, across the Kidron Valley from the city walls. Today, on the last day of the festival of booths, the hillside was spotted with booths — temporary shelters constructed of leafy branches in commemoration of Israel's time in the desert before entering the promised land. Peter, stopping and looking back over them in a kind of awe at the sheer numbers, noticed the commotion before the Palace of Herod, Pilate's Jerusalem residence. "Look, Jesus," he said, pointing. "What do you think it is?"

Simon and Judas came back to join them. There was a mob in the open area before the palace gates, a mob so large as to dwarf the one that had surrounded Jesus within the temple precincts. "A riot," Simon said.

"Pilate looted the temple treasury to help pay for his new aqueduct," Judas said, amplifying. "There was a lot of anger in the crowd today."

"The people were like smoldering coals," Simon said, "wanting only a breeze to fan them into flame."

"And the Zealots have supplied it?" Jesus said.

Judas shook his head. "They're involved, certainly, but this is Annas's doing. He's hoping for another victory like that at Caesarea."

Jesus shook his head.

"It's risky, certainly, but he has little choice," Judas said. "His control over the temple treasury is at stake."

† † †

The demonstration before the palace gates continued to degenerate into chaos. Some in the crowd banged on iron pots, some hollow drums. Some hurled invectives, making wild and improbable speculations about Pilate's ancestry, about his sexual practices, about his anatomy. By dusk, negotiation had become impossible.

"They leave me little choice," Pilate said to the tribune at his side.

"Yes."

"So be it, then."

Pilate stepped up to the wall and raised his hands. The crowd saw him and, rather to Pilate's surprise, became quiet — still hostile, certainly, but apparently prepared to hear what he had to say.

He hesitated, for a moment tempted to try to reason with them, but he abandoned the thought. He had tried reason. "Disperse," he called. "In the name of the emperor, I command you to disperse."

It was not a command likely to have a soothing effect on the crowd, and it did not. A roar went up, deafeningly loud. How many tens of thousands packed the streets, Pilate wondered? How many women and children?

Many. He could see that. He stood within plain sight of the crowd, his arms still upraised. Rocks bounced off the wall below him and off the battlements around him. The clatter of a spear decided him.

Pilate lowered his arms in a swift gesture.

It was a prearranged signal. Among the sea of homespun before the gates, cloaks were thrown aside here and there, exposing steel that sparked in the torchlight. Five cohorts, half the heavy-armed infantry of the twelfth legion, were scattered among the protestors and grouped strategically. Six thousand one hundred blades slipped from their scabbards as one, each a short, well-tempered Spanish blade with a double edge, equally suited for slashing or thrusting. A few thrusts and kicks brought each cohort into its preferred formation: eight deep, a sword-length between each file of soldiers and each rank. Before the Jews realized there were enemies among them, they were boxed in against the palace walls, Roman soldiers advancing from three sides. The rocks and sticks the Jews brandished were totally ineffective against the ample bucklers, four feet in length and two and a half in breadth, against the helmets and breastplates, against the greaves protecting the soldiers' legs. The Romans attacked. Jews cursed and screamed; the Romans fought silently, striking hard and jerking their blades from the falling bodies of their victims. The spray of blood speckled the shields and garments of the soldiers, soaked through the clothing of the fallen onto the stone flagging.

In half-an-hour it was over. The few who remained alive were trying to crawl away or were groping for succor. The soldiers walked among the fallen, hacking and thrusting with their swords. At a cry from their commander, the legion reformed at one side of the square. The palace gates opened, and the soldiers went into the palace compound. The gates closed, and all was silent but for the occasional moan and the persistent dripping of blood.

† † †

Jesus and his disciples were in Bethany, in the home of Lazarus and his sisters. Mary, the younger sister, sat on the ground by Jesus' feet, gazing up at him with widened eyes.

"The priests sent the temple guards to arrest you?" she said. "What happened?"

James the elder, the son of Zebedee, answered her, giving a rather humorous account of the mumbling guards and their subsequent retreat. Mary laughed, and her eyes flashed in the firelight. James felt a warm glow at being the focus of her attention.

"They were that afraid of the crowd," she said wonderingly, unused to the idea of armed men being afraid of anything.

"They were afraid of Jesus as much as the crowd," said Simon the Zealot. "They are Jews. Even they have heard about the signs Jesus has done. They ask themselves, 'When the Messiah comes, will he do more signs than these?' They wonder about him."

A new voice cut into the conversation, a woman's, high-pitched and irritable. "Lord, there are many here to cook for, and my sister sits idle."

Jesus looked up and met the eyes of Martha, a tall, spare woman with a pale, thin mouth. "Idle, Martha?"

"She has left me to do all the work by myself, though I told her I would need her to help me."

Jesus smiled at Martha, his expression sympathetic. "Ah, Martha," he said. "You are a worrier."

"Be that as it may, Lord, I have a meal to prepare, and my sister sits at your feet doing nothing."

"Perhaps you would do well to imitate her example."

"But the dinner . . ."

"The dinner will take care of itself."

"How?" Martha asked. "And when?"

Jesus got to his feet and went over to her, grasping her arm and drawing her back to where he had been sitting. "Take my stool," he said. "Here."

"Lord —"

"Martha, you are distracted by many things, when at the moment, you need focus on only one." He sat cross-legged on the ground beside Mary.

James was on his feet. "Lord, take my place," he said, indicating his stool.

Jesus smiled and shook his head. "Sit," he said. "Sit. But the offer becomes you. All of you, if you are invited to a wedding feast, do not choose for yourself a seat of honor, because others more distinguished than yourself may have been invited. Think of the disgrace when your host comes to you, and he says, 'Give up your place to this person and move lower on the table.' If instead you sit down at the lowest place, you allow your host to say, 'Friend, move higher,' and you will be honored in the presence of all."

"That is his way," Judas said to Simon in a low voice. "He goes off into a parable on the slightest provocation."

"He seeks the teaching moment," said Simon.

"Even at the cost of an abrupt change of subject."

Judas watched Jesus' face, which seemed curiously mobile in the shifting light of the fire. He nodded to himself. "Yet," he said, "his manner adds much to his air of authority."

There were shouts on the path below the house, and Jesus broke off in his teaching. Soon a traveler came into view, flushed and disheveled. "There's been a battle," he said. "Not a battle. A massacre. Tens of thousands dead before the palace gates."

His news stunned them, sickened them.

Nobody that night had any supper.

CHAPTER 18

The road to Jericho wound its way through twenty-three miles of brown, barren mountains before reaching the lush green valley of Jericho, which lay like a sprig of parsley in the bottom of a bowl. Before descending to the valley road to begin the journey, Jesus paused on the ridge overlooking Jerusalem.

The holy city was built on two low hills divided by the Valley of the Cheesemakers, a name whose origin had been long forgotten. Facing them were the pillared porticos of the temple's east wall and beyond it the Fortress Antonio. Most of the houses visible to the left of the temple and below it were made from whitish gray limestone cut from the surrounding hills. The streets that wound among them were empty. The entire city gleamed in the first sun of the morning, its temple, consisting of marble and white limestone, seemed to sit atop it like a crown of light, too brilliant for mortal eyes.

James of Cana, standing with Jesus, was thinking not of Jerusalem but of the road to Jericho. Bandits preyed on travelers between the two cities, those traveling in small groups and without armed escort. They had never been a problem for Jesus and his disciples, but for James at least they were a recurring worry. He glanced up into Jesus' face and saw that his eyes were wet, tears running down his face until they disappeared into his beard.

"Jesus?"

Jesus shook his head. "Jerusalem, Jerusalem," he murmured.

His words attracted the attention of the other disciples as well, but Jesus seemed not to notice. "How I long to gather you to me!"

The disciples exchanged glances, associating his apparent grief with the recent slaughter. No one spoke. After several minutes, Jesus turned away in silence. He and his disciples began their descent.

† † †

Herod Antipas was in Jerusalem for the feast. He knew there had been a riot and that Pilate had suppressed it ruthlessly, but he had had no word from Pilate, no official communication, and he was still gathering intelligence, trying to piece together what had happened.

"What's the latest on the body count?" he asked.

"At least ten thousand," said an advisor. "Perhaps twice that."

"And how many of them were native Judeans?"

They had no idea on that, as yet. Jerusalem had a population of 120,000, but during festivals the population swelled to twice that, extra rooms and inns filling to capacity in Jerusalem and the surrounding villages, campers covering the hillside. Many of the pilgrims were Galileans, Herod's subjects. Many Galileans were among the slaughtered.

The sergeant-at-arms announced the arrival of Annas and Caiaphas. Herod waved for him to show them in.

They strode down the receiving hall's central aisle side by side, their gaits quick with resolve and purpose. Herod leaned back on his throne, watching.

"Your majesty," Annas said.

"Your majesty," Caiaphas boomed beside him. Annas inclined his head, and Caiaphas made a more elaborate obeisance.

"What do you want?" Herod said, sourly.

"I assume you've heard," Annas said.

"I have. What was your part in it?"

Annas shook his head. "To attempt to resolve the conflict: either to persuade Pilate to relent and return the funds to the temple treasury, or to persuade the people to leave off their protesting."

Herod made a face. "Neither, apparently, would listen to reason."

"You know how inflexible a mob can be, once it forms."

"And how inflexible a procurator can be as well," Herod said.

"We assume you and he weren't acting in concert."

Herod frowned at them fiercely. "I wasn't even informed until this morning," he said. "And then not by the procurator."

"We are petitioning the emperor for redress," Caiaphas said. "It's all we can do."

"Thousands of your tax-paying subjects have been massacred," Annas said. "Perhaps you should apply for redress as well."

Herod's gaze was fixed.

"Your majesty?" Annas said.

When Herod said nothing else, Annas turned to leave. Herod waited until they were halfway to the massive double doors. "It's a disgrace," he said thickly.

Annas and Caiaphas turned toward him.

"An absolute disgrace."

They waited.

"Be assured, gentlemen. When your complaint goes to Rome, my own will accompany it."

Annas gave a nod. When Herod said nothing else, he motioned to Caiaphas, and together they left the chamber.

† † †

Several days later, Jesus and his disciples were walking north along the east bank of the Jordan River through the Decapolis. They crossed into Galilee just south of the Sea of Galilee and spent the night with Chuza and Joanna in the city of Tiberius. The next day they continued north to Magdala, where Jesus attracted a crowd of several dozen, including Mary, who drifted up to them as they entered the city and stayed as close as possible to Jesus for the several hours they were there.

In Gennesaret, on the main street of the village, they were confronted by Jairus of the Capernaum synagogue.

"Jairus," Jesus said. "What's wrong?"

Jairus's face was pale, the cheekbones too prominent, his knuckles looking large and white in his hands. His hair stood out in all directions, and there were ashes on his face. "Jesus," he said, gasping, clutching Jesus' arm. "I heard you were coming."

"What is it, man? What's wrong?"

"Thank God you're here."

"Are you ill? Is your wife ill?"

"My daughter, Lila. She's ill to the point of death. She's dying."

"Of what?" Simon Peter asked. He shouldered back a couple of onlookers who had pressed too close.

Nathaniel asked, "Has a physician seen her?"

The crowd around them had grown, doubling from a few dozen to many dozen, and doubling again.

"The doctors tell us there is no hope," Jairus said, avoiding their eyes. "Her body burns with fever, and she shakes. For two days now we have been unable to wake her." His eyes returned to Jesus. "I have seen the wonderful things you have done."

"And you think I can help her?"

Jairus shook his head, then nodded. "Will you come? If you will come with me now, quickly, you can save my daughter."

"I will come."

"Quickly, then, for there is little time."

When they started out, the crowd started with them, buffeting Jesus and his little band of disciples this way and that, twice causing Jairus to stumble against him. The street narrowed for the length of several houses, and several of the disciples found it difficult even to breathe.

"The heat," said James the younger to John. "I feel like I'm going to pass out." John, himself flushed and sweaty, gripped James's arm and pulled him on. People pressed in on them from every side, blocking their view of anything but the cloaks that seemed to rise up around them.

Quite abruptly the whole crowd stopped, people crowding into the boys from behind and pressing them into those in front of them. They felt as if they were suffocating.

John heard Jesus say — incredibly, inexplicably — "Who touched me?"

"What do you mean, who touched you?" Peter said, expostulating. "Who hasn't touched you? Who hasn't touched you, poked you, prodded you, done all but knocked you down?" As if in illustration, the constraining force that had been building in the press of people slipped suddenly and drove them forward into a wider portion of the street. Jesus' eyes swept the faces of those nearest him.

"I'm not talking about that," he said. "I felt power go out of me." His eyes settled on the face of a woman not far away, and her distress broke from her in a great wail.

"I'm sorry," she said. "It was I. It was I who touched you."

"You, daughter?"

"I've been so ill. I bleed almost all the time, and I feel so weak."

"The doctors —"

"Can do nothing. I've been to this doctor and that one, doctors from as far away as Tiberius. I pay their fees, and I take their treatments, but none of it does me any good. I've heard of you, sir. I know your reputation. A holy man, they say. A prophet. One gifted with the powers of healing. I thought, if only I can but touch the hem of his cloak. I didn't mean to bother you, sir. I had no wish to intrude. If you only —"

"Daughter," he said again, and her flow of words stopped as abruptly as it had begun. "Peace, daughter," he said. "You have believed, and your faith has made you well."

Her face cleared. "It has? I'm well? I won't . . . I will no longer bleed?"

Jesus was smiling at her, almost grinning. "No longer," he said.

Jairus tugged at the sleeve of Jesus' cloak. "Please, sir. My daughter," he said. "There's so little time."

Jesus nodded. "Of course." He took the woman's hand and led her into the shelter of a column. With a nod and a smile of encouragement he turned, and they pressed on, leaving Gennesaret and stretching their strides as they headed along the north shore of Galilee toward Capernaum.

The crowd that followed seemed to number in the hundreds. People were laughing and joking with one another. Children skipped, and boys threw stones at the trunks of the occasional tree along the roadway and, where the road passed close to the Sea of Galilee, sent their stones skipping over the water.

"Everyone's on holiday," Andrew said in a low voice to his brother Peter.

"Yes."

"The crowd is behind him as never before."

"For now," Peter said.

"What's wrong?"

"I don't know. I don't trust the crowds, I guess. They scare me."

Judas, who had been walking nearby, said, "They'll only grow larger. It was the trip to Jerusalem. It has increased his stature among the people, just as I predicted."

A man was coming toward them, the dust of the roadway rising up around his feet and shrouding him in gloom. Though he walked swiftly, his head was down, his shoulders hunched as if in pain.

As he came closer, the crowd could see that his cloak was torn, that dirt and ashes were in his hair. Jairus, on seeing him, was shaken with a fit of palsy. "Channoch," he called out, his voice thick with grief. "No. No."

Channoch looked up and saw them, then put his head down and continued toward them. He stopped in front of Jairus, drawing himself upright with apparent effort. "Your daughter is dead," he said heavily. He looked at Jesus. "No need to trouble the teacher further."

Jesus gripped Jairus's arm. "Don't give up hope," he said.

"She's dead," Jairus said. "She's dead. If only we'd been a little sooner, I know you could have saved her."

"Take me to see her."

Jairus shook his head. "She's dead, didn't you hear him? She's dead."

"If you had faith in me once, have faith in me still."

They continued on their way, but with Jairus's head down, the trembling still in his hands.

A sober crowd entered Capernaum, Jesus leading the way, walking beside Jairus and Channoch. Behind him were his disciples, and, further back, the rest of the crowd. Long before they reached the house of Jairus, they could hear the weeping and wailing of his friends and family and of the professional mourners. When the mourners saw Jairus, and Jesus with him, the volume of their wailing increased by a factor of two as they goaded themselves toward an emotional frenzy.

Jesus pushed through them, ignoring them, his lips pressed together in a firm line. He went into the house, where he found a little girl of perhaps ten or eleven lying on a wool coverlet. He felt of her forehead, found it already cooling, bent down so that his face was against her cheek. Then he straightened.

"Let's go outside," he said. "Everyone." He herded them out so that the girl was left alone.

As he and Jairus and Jairus's wife came out through the doorway behind the others of the household, the wailing redoubled. Jesus raised a hand to silence them.

"Friends," he said. "There is no call for weeping."

They stared at him balefully with dirt-smeared faces.

"I have examined the little girl," he said. "She is not dead, but only sleeping."

His announcement was met with a silence that stretched out for two heartbeats, then three. A woman nearby emitted a high-pitched, hysterical giggle, tried to muffle it with her hand, and failed. A gust of laughter bent her nearly double, racking her frame, and the crowd stirred uneasily. The faces turned toward Jesus were now thin-lipped and angry.

"She is deep asleep," Jesus said. "She needs but a call to wake her. Come," he said, gesturing to Jairus and his wife, and to Peter and the sons of Zebedee, James and John. Others would have followed, but he held up his hand. "No," he said. "Wait and pray."

And he turned and went inside with the others.

The girl lay on the coverlet in the same position as before. No quiver of hand or cheek gave any suggestion of life. No hint of respiration moved her chest.

She looks dead, John thought to himself, looking first at his brother James and then at Peter. And dead is dead.

It was said by some that the spirit of a person lingered near its body for three days after death, hoping to be restored to it, but no tale was told of such a restoration ever occurring — except once, perhaps, in the days of Elijah. John, recalling that story, looked for Jesus to stretch himself out on the body of the little girl.

He did not. He sat beside her on the edge of the bed, took up her hand in his and with his other stroked her matted hair.

"Lila," he called softly. "Lila." Lila's body remained unmoving. He tugged at her hand. "Get up now," he said. "Get up, little one."

Her eyes were open, John noticed with a start. They had been closed, he would have sworn it, but suddenly they were open.

"Here," Jesus said, and he slipped an arm around her to help her sit up.

She looked around at her father, Jairus, then at her mother, many years her father's junior. Both stood still as stone, as if in shock.

"She's very weak," Jesus said. "She'll need some food."

The mother stirred. "Yes," she said mechanically. "Certainly." But she made no move to obey.

"But first," Jesus said. "Let's be clear on what happened here. The girl was in a fevered sleep, and I awakened her."

"Momma?" the little girl said, uncertainly.

Feeling came back to her mother in a rush. With a cry, she stepped forward and pulled the little girl up into her arms. "Lila," she murmured. "Thank God. Lila."

Jesus stood. His eyes met those of Jairus, and he smiled, a little tiredly, as they clasped hands.

Tears streamed down Jairus's cheeks, but he seemed unable to speak.

Jesus gripped his arm and, without a word, departed.

CHAPTER 19

Jesus left the premises immediately, leading his disciples quickly toward the lake. Only a fraction of those who had followed him to the house of Jairus followed now. Simon Peter's boat was there in Capernaum, drawn up on the shore. At Jesus' direction, Simon Peter, Andrew, James and John got it into the water, and all the disciples waded out to it, the mucky lake bottom tugging at their sandals.

There was a good easterly breeze, and, as Peter and Andrew hoisted the sail, the wind caught it and drove them quickly out onto the lake. Along the shore a score of people stood looking after them, their hands empty and at their sides, their faces at that distance no more than blank ovals.

Dusk came quickly, but the moon was full and myriad stars glittered high in a sky of black velvet. "Where to, Master?" Simon Peter asked him.

"The opposite shore? Just away. I'm tired."

"Away it is," Peter said. They ran before the wind all the way across the Sea of Galilee and early in the third watch pulled up on the desolate eastern shore, where cocoa-colored mountains thrust their foothills into the sea.

Half the disciples had fallen asleep during the journey, slumped against the side of the boat, and they roused themselves only enough to stagger onto the shore and to fling themselves down on the hard ground.

† † †

It was about midday when the crowd began arriving, first in groups of two or three, then in groups of as many as twenty.

"Where are they coming from?" Philip asked Andrew in some alarm. "Is there no escaping them?"

Andrew shook his head. "Jairus's daughter. They think he's raised her from the dead."

"Didn't he?"

"Ask Peter. I wasn't there."

Andrew was right about the reason the crowd had followed them. The sight of Lila had electrified them. "Just who is this man anyway?" someone asked, and the answer led to a debate over whether Jesus was in fact Elijah, or was even John the Baptizer, supernaturally restored to life.

"I've heard that Herod himself has heard of Jesus and fears him, thinking he is John returned to haunt him."

"John never performed miracles like these."

They argued and debated, but always, lurking in the recesses of everybody's mind, was the question few dared voice: Could this at last be the long-awaited Messiah?

They had set off in pursuit of Jesus, and in search of answers to their many questions.

† † †

Though the disciples tried to protect Jesus, people kept slipping past them. Among the first to find Jesus was a woman whose arm was drawn up twisted and useless at her side.

He was just finishing his morning ablutions, washing his hands and face in a bowl of water he had filled at the nearby stream. He looked at her as he flicked water from his hands and wiped his face on the edge of his cloak. "Well, daughter," he said. "You have come a long way."

She nodded, apparently too breathless to speak.

"Did you walk all night?"

Again she nodded. Andrew, stopping near Jesus, wondered if she could speak.

"How long has your arm been this way?" Jesus asked, as he reached out for it.

She jerked back, alarmed; then, with apparent effort, allowed him to touch it. He took the hand and drew the arm out straight.

"Since last year," she said, speaking in so low a whisper that Andrew barely caught it. "Last year," she repeated. "At about this time."

Jesus' face drew up in sympathy, and he stroked the arm. "Go easy on it," he said. "The arm is still very weak."

He lowered it gently to her side, and it hung there, wasted still but relaxed and straight. Andrew's eyes went to Jesus, searching out his face, but he read only compassion there, nothing else — no evidence of divinity, no conscious awareness of power.

The throng soon surrounded them. There were thousands of them, more even than had followed them to Capernaum. Most amazing of all were the lame and damaged among them: the boy hopping along on his single crutch; the blind girl led by her father; the old man bent beneath the weight of his twisted back. Jesus talked to each of them. He reached out to touch them. As he moved away, the boy followed without his crutch, though limping badly. The girl was left squinting and blinking as if dazzled by a great light. The man straightened to walk erect — to walk carefully and deliberately, but erect.

"Miracles of healing?" Simon the Zealot asked Judas.

"They think so," Judas said, nodding.

Jesus held up his hands as the people crowded close, and he prayed, "Thank you, Father, for bringing your kingdom to us. Thank you for life and health and for strength of mind. Thank you for those we love, and for those who love you." He moved into a Psalm, the transition to praise as natural to him as breathing. "Bless the Lord, oh my soul and all that is within me," he said. "Bless his holy name. Bless the Lord, oh my soul, and forget not all his benefits."

He passed through the crowd, arms outstretched. "The Lord be gracious unto you and bless you. The Lord make the light of his countenance to shine upon you and bring you peace." The blessing was one of his favorites, the blessing the Lord gave Moses to bestow on the people.

"How shall we recognize the kingdom?" called someone, and Jesus turned toward him, his eyes seeking out his face in the crowd. He found it.

"How shall you recognize it?" he asked rhetorically. "Listen. The kingdom of God is like seed someone scatters on the ground. He sleeps and he wakes, and the seed sprouts and grows, though he knows not how. First the stalk appears, then the head, then the full grain. And when the grain is ripe, he knows. He goes in at once with his sickle, because the harvest is come."

"And has the harvest come?"

"It is coming. You ask how to recognize the kingdom." He pointed at a mustard plant, one of the biggest any of them had ever seen. "The kingdom is like a mustard seed, which, when sown upon the ground, is the smallest of all the seeds on earth. When it is sown, it grows up and becomes the greatest of all shrubs, putting forth large branches." He walked to the plant and reached out to grasp one of the branches, pulling it down so that they could see the sparrow's nest attached to it. "Branches large enough that the birds of the air can make nests within its shade."

† † †

He was there one moment, and then he was gone, having stepped between Peter and Andrew to disappear from view. The disciples turned to follow him, and the crowd surged after, all but carrying them forward.

Jesus had gone up the hill, seeking out a large open space. When Peter and Andrew entered the clearing, he was there above them, seated next to Philip on a rock, using a hand to shade his eyes from the midday sun.

"Where is Judas?" Jesus asked. "Judas! Do we have enough money in the purse to feed all these people?"

"There are thousands of them," Philip answered in a low voice as Judas shook his head.

"Two hundred denarii would still be insufficient," Judas said.

"I take it, then, that we have accumulated something less than two hundred denarii?"

"Master, that would be six month's wages."

The crowd spread out across the clearing, spreading cloaks here and there on the grass to sit on. A few boys climbed up onto the twisted branches of the scrub oaks in search of a good view. A few sat on rocks and on the trunks of fallen trees. Still others remained standing.

"Pity them, Philip. They are like sheep without a shepherd." Jesus sighed, already sounding tired. "Go out among them and try to seat them in groups of fifty," he said. "Count them, if you can, to see how many there are."

As Andrew approached, Jesus said to him, "These people have traveled a long way without eating. Let's see what we have among ourselves to give them."

Andrew shook his head. "Nothing," he said. "Scarcely enough for ourselves."

Jesus looked at him

"It would be better to send them out into the surrounding villages to scour for food."

"See what we have," Jesus said.

The rest of the disciples came and sat near him. Jesus for his part sat looking around himself, making eye-contact with this one and that one and smiling. Philip and Andrew passed among the people, Philip pointing and moving his lips as he counted to himself, Andrew leaning down here and there to whisper to someone.

"What's happening?" Peter asked Jesus in a low voice. "What's going on? Andrew asked me if any of us had brought any food."

"Had you?"

Peter shook his head. "If we had, it wouldn't matter. This crowd would devour it instantly, and everyone would still be hungry."

Andrew was climbing back up the hill, and with him was a small boy. The boy stopped in front of Jesus and held up a small cloth sack.

"What's this?" Jesus asked, smiling, reaching down and lifting the boy to his knee. "What's your name?"

"Thaddeus," the boy said. He had dark, curly hair and a dimple in one cheek when he smiled.

"Thaddeus," Jesus repeated. "What an important sounding name. Do you see that fellow right there? His name is Thaddeus, too. Do you think you might grow up to be like him someday?"

Thaddeus smiled at the boy, showing a missing tooth. The boy nodded, but looked doubtful.

"Thaddeus has five small bread loaves in that sack," Andrew said. "Five loaves and two fish."

"They're barley loaves," the boy said. "My mother made them."

"Then I'm sure they're excellent loaves," Jesus said. "Where is your mother? Did she come with you?"

He shook his head, his dark eyes solemn. "My uncle brought me, my Uncle Levi." The man the boy indicated was on his feet near the edge of the crowd. His expression suggested that he was concerned that his nephew was making a nuisance of himself with the great rabbi, but was more concerned about making a nuisance of himself by coming up to inquire. When Jesus looked at him and nodded, Levi bobbed his head and took a step forward before coming to a stop again.

"His name is Levi," Jesus said to Thaddeus, pointing out Matthew.

"The fat man?"

Jesus' smile broadened. "He's much thinner now than when I met him. I worry sometimes that the wind will catch him and carry him away."

Thaddeus laughed and clapped his small hands.

"Perhaps we should tie a string to him, so we won't lose him if that should happen. Do you think we should?"

The boy nodded.

"Actually, he likes to be called Matthew, in honor of his father."

The boy whispered something in Jesus' ear.

"Is he? Is he really?" Jesus said, in a slightly louder whisper than the boy had used. "Did you know that's my name in Hebrew?"

The boy whispered something else, and a shadow crossed Jesus' face. "I'm sorry to hear it," he said. "I know you miss him."

The boy nodded.

"How about your father's father? Is he still living?"

The boy shook his head.

"So your father has gone to be with his father, just as someday you will go to be with both of them. And both of them are with God."

The boy flung his arms about Jesus' neck, and Jesus stood with him, stroking his back. "And with the great Joshua himself," Jesus said. "Joshua the son of Nun, who led Israel home again, and who is now of course with his own father." Jesus held the boy away from him to look into the small, tear-streaked face. "That would be old Nun himself," Jesus said.

Andrew was left holding the boy's sack — a small sack — and he looked from time to time down into it, not having the least idea what he should do with it. Jesus, noticing him, set little Thaddeus on the rock where he himself had been sitting. Philip came up then, panting. "Five thousand," he said. "I can't say exactly, but I think five thousand men, plus all the women and children."

Jesus took the sack from Andrew, giving him a wink of encouragement — though in truth the wink left Andrew more bewildered than encouraged. Jesus sat again on the rock beside Thaddeus. He smiled at the boy. "Five barley loaves and two fish," he said.

The boy nodded.

"All you brought with you to eat today."

Again he nodded.

"But you're willing to give it to me to help feed all these people."

Thaddeus's head turned, and his gaze swept out over the crowd. When his head turned back again to Jesus, his eyes were wide.

Jesus gave him a wink, too, and the boy smiled. "Do you think it's enough?" Jesus said, dropping his voice to a conspiratorial tone.

The boy shook his head solemnly.

"Suppose I told you it was more than enough?"

Immediately the boy began nodding, and Jesus laughed. He reached out to tousle the boy's hair. "The first rule of plenty," Jesus said. "Put all you have at the service of God. Will you remember that? Even when it doesn't seem to be nearly enough."

He stepped up onto the rock. "Fellow Jews," he said, addressing the crowd. "Sons of Abraham. We have a boy among us named Thaddeus who has graciously offered to share his lunch with us." Jesus held up the sack. "He has five barley loaves — made by his mother — and with them two small fish. Did she say what kind of fish they were, Thaddeus?"

He shook his head.

"Perch," Andrew said, and Jesus looked at him. "They're perch," Andrew repeated.

"Five barley loaves and two small perch. Is anybody hungry?"

Several looked at each other, but none responded. Jesus pointed to a man near the front, one with the barrel-shaped body of the well-to-do. "You sir, you look like a man in need of sustenance."

There was general laughter.

"Could I interest you in half a barley loaf and perhaps a bit of fish?"

There was more laughter. Several hands reached out to slap the man on his back and his shoulders. The man looked around and, in response to all the smiling faces, began smiling himself. He bobbed his head and, turning again toward Jesus, shrugged his beefy shoulders.

"First, we must thank our father in heaven, from whom comes every good thing." Reaching one hand upward, Jesus prayed, "Thank you, Father, for this gift from your bounty. Bless it to our nourishment, bless us to your service. May your kingdom grow and grow until all humanity can take shade in its branches."

He looked out again over the people. "Amen?" he said.

"Amen." In unison. Heads nodding firmly. Jesus took each of the loaves out of Thaddeus's little bag and tore it in half. He did likewise with the fish, dropping the fragments back in again and handing the bag to Andrew.

Andrew took the bag and looked at him.

"Go and distribute the food among the people," Jesus said.

Andrew hesitated. He shrugged then and went to the group nearest them. Kneeling down, he held open the bag.

"No, thank you. Martha packed us some food," the man said, nodding at his wife.

Andrew offered the bag to the next man. Who reached in and took half a loaf. Who reached in again for a bit of fish.

His wife swatted his hand. "Look how many," she said, jerking her head. But when he pulled out his hand again, he clutched a piece of the salted perch.

"Many thanks," he said. "Many thanks." His wife, despite her objections, reached in for a bit of bread. The family next to them took food as well.

As did the next.

And the next.

Andrew, moving like a sleepwalker, not daring to look in the bag, not daring even to feel of the bag to see what might be in it, moved down the line, offering it to everyone. Not everyone needed food. A surprising number had brought their own, and they were spreading their food out around them and offering it to their neighbors.

When Andrew got to the second group of fifty, someone actually put fish into the bag. Then someone gave him a basket. "Here, empty it into this," he said, but Andrew didn't dare.

Judas was standing next to Philip. "What do you think?" he asked. Andrew had moved to the third group. He still had the bag, and now the basket was full as well.

Nathaniel and Matthew and Peter were already out in the crowd, each with a basket of his own. "It's a miracle," Philip said, watching.

"Yes, but what kind of miracle?"

"Pardon?"

"Is he multiplying fishes, or is he getting a bunch of stingy Galileans to share their food?"

Philip ignored the implied criticism of his native province. "I'm needed." He broke away from Judas and went out into the crowd. Someone handed him a basket full of food. He looked into it curiously, but saw nothing but bread and fish — more specifically, nothing but salted perch and barley loaves. It was indeed a miracle. Philip took it to the group farthest from Jesus and began distributing food.

† † †

There were twelve baskets of food left over. Jesus sat on the rock before the crowd, one of the baskets between him and the boy Thaddeus, enjoying bread and salted perch as if nothing out of the ordinary was going on.

"You're the Messiah, aren't you?" the boy said, looking up into his face.

"Who is the Messiah?" Jesus asked him. "What will he do when he comes?"

"He's to be a son of David," the boy said, speaking slowly, as if by rote. "A son of David who will throw off the yoke of the Romans and restore God's people to greatness."

"Then I am not the Messiah."

Thaddeus looked hurt and sad, and Jesus placed a hand against the boy's chest. "The kingdom of God is here; it is among us," he said. "Peace with God and with each other does not depend on political arrangements. Do you understand?"

The boy looked as if he were trying very hard to. The conversation of the crowd, growing louder, suggested that others also were grappling with the Messianic question. "Is this not the one who is to come?" they were saying. "He can even make bread to feed his armies."

"It is surely the Prophet."

"He who is to come into the world."

Jesus gestured for James the younger. "Stay with Thaddeus until his uncle finds him," Jesus said.

"Where are you going?"

"Up into the mountain to pray. Wait for me until dark, then if I am not back, sail for Capernaum without me."

The crowd, louder now, more vocal, was on its feet. "King Jesus," a Judean voice shouted from somewhere in the crowd.

"King Jesus," a voice echoed.

Faces were flushed. Hands were raised. As one the crowd cried, "King Jesus, lord and savior." The crowd surged forward, and James glanced nervously toward Jesus.

But Jesus was gone.

James pulled Thaddeus close as the crowd pressed around them. In response, Thaddeus put his arms around James and pressed his chubby cheek into his cloak.

CHAPTER 20

Dusk came, and perhaps half of the five thousand had drifted away, going home to Capernaum or Bethsaida, or into one of the nearer villages in search of lodging. Those that remained eyed the disciples sullenly. Questions had been asked and gone unanswered. Where was Jesus? Didn't he want to be their king?

The disciples had no answers. Even Judas, who had kept the enthusiasm going as long as he could, had lapsed into an irritable silence.

The twelve were huddled around Peter's boat. "It's dusk, should we go?" James the elder asked. "He said we should go."

"Look," Peter said, gesturing. "Do you want to go out in that?" The wind had risen over the course of the day, and foam topped the waves.

"I think I'd rather go out in that than stay here with them," James said, indicating the crowd.

"I'm with James," Matthew said.

"You're not a boatman," Peter said.

"I'm not giving an opinion, merely stating a preference."

"Where the devil is he?" Judas said. "He had them eating out of his hand. Literally. He had the crowd with him, and now he's lost it. He'll never be able to reclaim it."

"Don't discount Jesus," Peter said.

"I'm not discounting him. He's the most charismatic leader to arise in Israel since the time of the Maccabees. They led a revolt that threw off the Greeks, and Jesus could do the same with the Romans."

"If he will," Matthew said.

"Why wouldn't he?" Judas said. "He's an Israelite, the same as the rest of us. Why wouldn't he, if he could?"

"Are you saying he couldn't?"

"No. I'm saying he had this crowd ready to make him king by acclamation and to follow him into battle. To die for him, if necessary. And he disappeared."

"This isn't getting us anywhere," Peter said. "Do we leave, or do we wait for him?"

"He told us to leave," Andrew said.

"It will mean miles of rowing."

Andrew shrugged. Rowing was nothing new to him.

"Okay, we leave," Peter said.

Judas scowled. "I'm not ready to leave. Let's put it to a vote."

Peter shook his head. "Andrew and I are taking the boat back to Capernaum. Stay if you want, or come with us."

James and John helped Peter and Andrew push the boat out into the water. Several of the others waded after them.

"Where are you going?" called someone in the crowd. "Look, they're leaving us. They're going off and leaving us in this wilderness."

Judas and Simon and all of the others entered the water and waded as quickly as they could toward Peter's boat.

Soon the land was out of sight, and clouds obscured the stars. The wind grew stronger, and it blew squarely against them. The sails were useless, and even Simon Peter and Andrew rowing together could make very little progress. The waves lifted the boat and turned it, making it hard to be sure of their way.

"What now?" Matthew shouted over the sound of the wind and waves. "Do we wait it out?"

"Can't," Peter said, gasping between pulls on a creaking oar. "If we stop moving forward, the waves will swamp us."

Matthew looked grim, his mouth tightening as he squinted into the wind.

"You wanted to do this," Peter said.

"As you said, I'm no boatman."

"Sure, blame the boatmen."

They all took turns at the oars, James and John, Nathaniel and Philip, Judas and Simon — even Matthew. By the time a gray line marked the horizon in the east, all were exhausted.

"Look," said Simon the Zealot in a low voice to the younger James. "Look — is it a ghost, do you think?"

Or the fog?" James pulled his cloak more closely about him and shivered.

"You don't see the shape of a man in the fog?"

"Maybe. Of course it can't be."

"Keep your eyes on it, boy. There's something not right about it."

"It's Jesus!" It was John, standing up in the front of the boat and rocking it precariously.

"Jesus," breathed Andrew, pausing at his oar to look.

There was no question now that it was a man coming toward them, walking on the water. "It's a ghost," Simon said hoarsely. "A ghost." And what but a spirit could walk abroad on such a night? Wading through the surf as if walking along the shoreline, the waves breaking against its body.

Andrew slipped an oar from its oarlock and pushed the oar down into the sea, testing its depth. The oar did not touch bottom.

"It's just standing there."

And it was. At this distance the face seemed sad, but it could have been angry or even expressionless. Or not a face at all.

"Master?" Peter called. He too was standing in the boat. "Master, is it you?"

The spirit lifted a hand.

"If it is you, speak to me and I'll come to you."

They couldn't quite make out the response, if in fact there was one.

Peter, straining to hear, cupped a hand behind his ear.

"Come," came the voice, all but lost in the sound of the sea.

Peter swung a leg over the side of the boat.

"No, wait." Andrew clutched for the sleeve of his robe, but he missed. Peter slipped over the side. For an eerie moment, it seemed that he, too, moved over the surface of the water, as ghostly a figure as the other.

"Look," James said. "He's —"

But he wasn't. Peter had slipped beneath the waves and was gone.

"Turn the boat," Andrew cried. "Turn it! James, John — take the oars."

Peter had surfaced, treading water. He disappeared from view again as a wave broke over his head, but fought his way back to the surface, where he spluttered and looked around blindly.

"Jesus," he called, and struck off into the fog, swimming strongly.

"Peter!" Andrew cried. James and John were beside him, peering into the mist. They could no longer see Peter, neither him nor the spirit or apparition or whatever it was. The dark waves were topped with foam, and they stretched endlessly toward the gray horizon. "Peter!"

Nothing.

Andrew pushed past James, nearly upsetting the boat. Grasping both oars, he began turning the boat.

"Wait, I'll help."

But Andrew was stroking blindly, his face wet with tears or water, his head down. He grunted with each pull of the oars. "Pull," he told himself. "Pull."

His oars left the water as the sea lifted the boat. There was a jolt, and he fell from his seat.

Peter tumbled headfirst into the boat, clothes and hair streaming water. Jesus was sitting on the starboard side, swinging his legs into the boat.

"Master?" Andrew asked.

Jesus stood in the middle of the boat, knees bent as he worked to keep his balance. "Hello," he said. "Greetings to all of you."

His cloak and tunic were soaked below the waist and dripping water from the waves that had been breaking against him. James the younger laid a hand on his shoulder.

"It's dry," he said.

Andrew fell gibbering into the bottom of the boat at Jesus' feet.

† † †

They sailed into Capernaum on a glassy sea. Jesus felt subdued. Despite the high experiences of multiplying food and walking on water, he was troubled. It was not possible to usher in God's kingdom by acclamation: The experience with the five thousand had confirmed it. His ministry was at a turning point.

"Let's stock up for a journey," Jesus said.

"Another preaching tour?" Matthew asked, in his mind already cataloging the provisions they would need.

"No, I think we need to get off to ourselves for a while. We'll go north along the Jordan, maybe as far north as Caesarea Philippi."

"We'll be leaving Galilee then," said Matthew. "I assume you have no friends in Caesarea Philippi on whom we can rely?"

Jesus grinned at him and reached out to prod his stomach. When he had turned away, Matthew said to the younger James, "I think a direct answer would have been more helpful."

"I think he'll be happy if you do the best you can."

"Yes, but will it be enough?"

James shrugged.

"Yes, I know. The salted perch and the barley loaves. We do the best we can, and we leave the results to him. I'm not comfortable living that way. Too much letting go."

"What a relief if we could let go."

"How can we? How can we dare?"

† † †

The crowd caught them before they got away, some straggling into town on foot and others arriving by boat, some passing fishermen having agreed to carry them.

They were not surprised to see Peter and the rest of the disciples; they had, after all, watched them depart by boat before them. They were astonished to see Jesus.

"How did you get here?" asked one of the more daring among them. "Did you walk all night?"

"Why are you so interested?" Jesus responded. When he got no answer, he said, "Because I was able to feed you? Don't focus so much on filling your bellies. The food you eat passes through the system and is gone. Focus instead on spiritual food, food that will nourish you forever."

"What spiritual food? Where will we get it?"

Jesus shook his head. "Did you get nothing out of the events of yesterday other than a free meal? As the Father sent manna from heaven in the days of Moses, so he now offers the true bread of heaven."

The confusion in their faces did not clear up.

"I am the bread of heaven," Jesus said. "Whoever comes to me will never be hungry, and whoever believes in me will never thirst."

† † †

Later, on the long hike north, Simon the Zealot asked him, "Why do you speak so often in riddles and parables? Why not say straight out what you mean?"

"What I am teaching can't be grasped that way," Jesus said. "I'm trying to give people the feel of a place, of a person." When Simon didn't say anything, Jesus said, "Think of the way I begin my stories. 'The kingdom of heaven is like . . .' 'God is a father who . . .' Over and over, story after story."

They walked for a while in silence. The other disciples had moved closer, wanting to hear what it was that Jesus was saying. Finally, Simon said, "Aren't you afraid people will be confused? That they won't get the point of your story?"

And Jesus sighed. "Many will not get it."

"Then why not be more direct?"

"It wouldn't help them. Those who can understand will pursue the tale to its meaning, asking whatever questions they need to. Those who cannot understand — the things of heaven are already closed to them."

"That seems harsh."

"It is the justice of heaven, and its mercy. Those who ask will receive what they ask for. Those who knock will have the door opened to them. In the end, everyone will receive what he chooses."

"So those who seek God —"

"Will find him. None of you have children, but can you imagine a child asking his father for bread and his father giving him a stone? Or a child asking his father for fish and receiving a snake?"

A reluctant smile twisted Simon's features. "Another of your parables," he said.

"And its meaning?"

"If we, who are evil, give good things to our children . . ." He hesitated.

"Yes?"

"Then God who is in heaven also will give good things to those who ask him."

Jesus' smile was radiant.

† † †

Some days later they were camping in the region of Caesarea Philippi. Nathaniel and Philip built the fire, and all sat around it talking. Twilight came and deepened into night. A companionable silence descended on the gathering.

"Does anyone know what we're doing here?" Jesus asked.

"Retreat and regroup," said Judas. Jesus answered him with a smile.

"Yes," he said.

"Why is it necessary? Only days ago, you had the crowd behind you as no one ever has."

Jesus shook his head. "The crowd was excited. I was, for a

moment, the focus of fevered imaginations."

"What do you want from them?"

"Recognition. Recognition of who I am."

"They recognize you for who you are."

"No."

"Yes."

"Who then do they say I am?"

His question brought silence.

"Anyone?"

"Some say Elijah," Matthew said, diffidently.

"Some say John, the Baptizer," said the younger James.

"I've heard Jeremiah."

The silence returned.

"And you?" Jesus said. "You who have followed me over hundreds of miles, who have heard me speak in village after village, who have seen me do sign after sign? Who do you say I am?"

"You are the Messiah."

Jesus' eyes turned toward Peter. "And when you say the Messiah," he said, "what do you mean by it?"

"I mean you."

"Yes?"

"I don't understand it all, but you're defining the term for us every day. You are the one who was to come, the one everybody's been expecting."

Jesus looked at him for a long moment. "You've been blessed, Simon Bar-Jonah," he said. "The spirit speaks through you. It is appropriate that I call you Peter, for you are the first stone, the cornerstone, of my new church."

Peter's eyes began to water as he returned Jesus' gaze.

Jesus looked around at the others. "Other stones will be added to it. Peter is the first."

Tears ran down Peter's face and into his beard. "I'm sorry," he muttered, standing and turning away, embarrassed by his tears.

Jesus stood with him and reached out a hand.

† † †

It was the next day before Judas mustered the courage to ask his question. "It is good that you state frankly that you are the Messiah," he began.

"I state it frankly to you, the twelve," Jesus said.

"But —"

"The time is not yet right to tell others. They would not understand."

"But given that you are the Messiah —"

"Yes? Given that I am the Messiah foretold of old . . ."

"What's the plan? What's our strategy from here?"

"Our goal?" Jesus asked him.

"Oh, you've stated the goal plainly enough."

"Have I?"

"To establish God's kingdom."

"And what does that mean?" When Judas didn't answer immediately, Jesus said, "You can be sure of one thing: it won't be the kingdom you've been expecting. Or even the kingdom I expected, in the beginning."

"What do you mean? What did you expect?" Peter asked, drawing abreast of Jesus and Judas on the road. John also crowded close, as did his brother James.

"I expected the people to respond to me."

"They have responded."

Jesus shook his head. "No. They're responding to someone they think can lead them against Rome."

"You can do that," Judas said.

"I could, perhaps, but I won't. I made that decision long ago."

"You did? When? Where?"

"In the desert hills north of Jericho, shortly before we met. John was preaching then, by the river Jordan: 'Repent, for the kingdom of heaven is near.' I came announcing that the kingdom had arrived, and I expected repentance — real change of heart, Judas, not a declaration of political allegiance — and joy. Instead, I found rejection."

"Only by the religious establishment, the scribes and Pharisees. The people accept you."

"No, Judas. The people are prepared to accept a leader who will return Israel to greatness."

"Because they need such a leader."

"What they need is reconciliation to God. He gave Moses the law, but who can approach even that rough approximation of righteousness? And who does not feel the guilt, the burden of their sin? I thought they would accept me joyfully, but now I think they will not."

"What will they do?" Peter asked.

"Reject me."

"What does that mean?" Judas said. "Reject you how?"

"I don't know. But I think that when I return again to Jerusalem . . ."

"Yes?" Judas prompted.

"I think the temple guards will arrest me —"

"The people will riot. They won't allow it."

Jesus looked at him. "I think the Jewish leaders will arrest me and turn me over to the Romans to torture me and kill me."

"No," Peter said.

"You'll fail?" John said on the other side of him. "You'll fail?"

Jesus turned toward him. "No, John. I won't fail."

"No, you won't," Peter said. "You must not. We'll keep you out of Jerusalem."

"How, if that's my destiny?"

"We won't allow it. God won't."

They had just crested a rise in the road, and at the top of the next rise were three crosses silhouetted against the sky. Jesus saw them and stopped. A shadow seemed to pass over him, and he shivered as if from cold.

"No," Peter said, following his gaze. "It won't happen."

Jesus looked at him.

"It can't," Peter said.

"The words of Satan," Jesus said. "Long ago."

"Satan! What are you talking about? Have you conversed with Satan?"

"And fought with him. I've called you a rock, Peter. See to it that you are a building block and not a stumbling block. Do not try to interfere with the task God has set for me."

"When will all this happen?" It was John, his voice quavering.

"I don't know," Jesus said. "I must find out." He started again along the road, toward the crosses looming above them, and his disciples followed.

CHAPTER 21

It was six days later that they made camp at the foot of Mount Hermon, by one of the springs at the headwaters of the Jordan River. The previous day they had gone into Mizpah to replenish their supplies, but, for the most part, they had been avoiding the cities and villages, keeping almost entirely to themselves. The disciples, though they discussed it much among themselves, couldn't think what to make of it. "Has he gone into hiding then?" Judas muttered.

"What else could he be doing so far north?"

They built a fire that night and sat around it in a circle until nothing was left of the fire but glowing embers. "I'm tired," Peter said, and, as he stretched, his joints popped like the knotted pine they had burned in the fire.

"Going to bed?"

"To sleep like the dead," Peter said. He wrapped himself in a blanket and lay down with his head pillowed on his arm. The others were still talking when he fell asleep.

† † †

The stars were out, glinting in a sky as dark as pitch, when Jesus shook him awake. "Peter," he whispered. "Peter."

Peter rolled onto his side and looked up, seeing Jesus only as a shadow already moving away from him. When he had gotten to his feet, he saw that Jesus was not alone, but that Zebedee's boys, James and John, were with him.

"What is it?" he whispered, sensing the secrecy of the moment. "Where are we going?"

"Up onto the mountain to pray."

"That mountain?" He pointed. The snow-capped ridge of Mount Hermon was faintly luminescent against the night sky.

"Where better? 'My soul is cast down within me,'" Jesus said, quoting from a psalm ascribed to the sons of Korah. "'Therefore I will think of you in the land of Jordan, on the heights of Hermon.'"

"'Deep calls to deep in the roar of your waterfalls,'" James said. "'As the deer pants for streams of water, so my soul pants for you, O God.'"

Jesus and Peter looked at him.

"Mother's favorite," John said.

In the darkness, Jesus chuckled. "It seems I've chosen the right companions for this adventure," he said.

† † †

They hiked long into the night, winding up the southern slope of Hermon. The mountain marked the northern-most point of Joshua's conquests. It was a natural boundary. As Peter walked, leaning into the incline, he wondered why he had been chosen for the adventure, as Jesus had called it. His arms and his legs were heavy with fatigue, and he had no poetic associations with Mount Hermon to inspire him. To him, it was a mountain, a steep one, and increasingly cold. At first leaves crackled under his feet, then the trees thinned and disappeared, removing the last protection from a biting wind. The crickets and locusts had long since fallen silent. Still they climbed on.

Strangely, as the cold increased and the climb became more difficult, Peter's lethargy increased as well. It was almost with surprise that he realized they had stopped, that James and John stood beside him on the blank face of the mountain, and that Jesus had gone on ahead of them, mounting an outcropping of barren stone. Jesus was no more than a shadow against the mountain above and beyond him.

"Father," he said, his arms outstretched at his sides with his palms facing upward. He continued, but Peter lost the sense of what he was saying, realizing only that he was speaking ancient Hebrew rather than Aramaic. As Jesus spoke he became less shadowy and more distinct, almost as if illuminated from within. He was speaking in liquid syllables, the words themselves incomprehensible, and his clothes and his face seemed to shine with a white light.

Peter blinked. He felt numbed, stupid with the need for sleep. He wondered in passing whether James and John were seeing what he was seeing, but he stood transfixed, unable to shift his gaze.

Light flashed, obscuring Jesus in what might have been a ball of lightning, and Peter fell to the ground, landing on a numb shoulder, a shoulder that might have belonged to someone else for all the feeling he had in it. The light pulsed once, and Peter held up a hand to shield his face.

There were three men on the side of the mountain rather than one. For a moment Peter thought James and John had climbed up to join Jesus, but he felt James' hand on his arm and felt John crowding close. There were three men above them, one recognizably Jesus, but with his face and garments whiter than the snow that clung in patches to the rock around him. The other two were similarly glorified, one with a full head of white hair and a long, curly beard lying full on his chest, the other with shorter, rough-cut hair and a cloak made from camel-skin.

"Elijah," John breathed beside him.

Jesus and the men with him were conversing in Hebrew, and Peter could understand no more than the isolated word or phrase. He felt himself on his feet, no more in control of his actions than if in a dream. He himself recognized the third man — or recognized rather the stone-tablets that blazed in the crook of his arm with the radiance of the sun. A golden cloud had descended on the mountain top, and the mist was filled with a flickering incandescence supernaturally reminiscent of fireflies.

"Master," he heard himself saying, his voice shaking with fright. "Master, it is good that we are here." His words seemed to him nonsensical, coming out of his mouth without conscious thought. "We can build a shelter for you, a shelter for each of you. We can make camp here tonight and start down the mountain again tomorrow. We . . ." His words cut off as Jesus looked at him, the gaze so piercing and direct that Peter found himself held by it, unable to breathe. The fog thickened, blinding Peter with the dancing lights and obscuring Jesus.

Suddenly the fog was gone. Stars shone again in the night sky. Jesus, alone, was coming toward them, once more little more than a shadow in the night. The three disciples regarded him in dumb wonder.

Jesus reached out a hand to Peter, another to John. He shifted a hand to James. "My friends," he said. "My good friends."

"What did we just see?" John said. "Was that . . ." He trailed off.

"Was that Moses and Elijah?" James said.

"You have seen a great thing," Jesus said.

Peter said, "Yes, but what have we seen, exactly?"

"Me. Me as I really am. You must not tell anyone, though, not even the rest of my disciples, until the son of man has risen from the dead."

"I thought you were the son of man," Peter said.

John said. "You summoned them, Moses and Elijah? And they came?"

Jesus moved his head toward the path and began leading them along the path that twisted down the mountain. "They came," he said.

"How?"

"Why?" Peter said.

"They brought needed counsel," Jesus said.

Peter said, "Is that what the teachers of the law were referring to, when they say Elijah must come first?"

"No. Elijah has come, and men rejected him, and they did to him as they wished."

"The Baptizer."

"John. In just the same way, men will reject me."

"No," Peter said.

"Yes. Whoever would save his life must lose it. Whoever gives up his life —"

"Isaiah said God's servant would be raised and lifted up and highly exalted."

"Yes. The day is coming when you will remember that phrase and will actually understand it."

"Why Moses and Elijah?" John asked. "Because they symbolize the law and the prophets?"

Jesus laughed out loud. "Partly," he said. "Both are great men, especially as they are now, and coming from the Father. Each is a source of valuable counsel — but, just as important, each was available."

"What do you mean, sir?" asked James, on the other side of him. "You mean both are living?"

Jesus shook his head. "All those with God are alive. Not all can be summoned back into this world."

"And Moses and Elijah?"

"Elijah, you will remember, was taken up into heaven in a chariot of fire. Like Enoch, he walked with God; then he was no more, because God took him away."

"He didn't die in the body."

"That's right. He didn't die in the body."

"And Moses?" John said. "What of Moses?"

"What does the Torah say of his fate?"

James said, "'The Lord buried him in Moab, but to this day none has been able to find his grave.'"

"Ah," Peter said.

They looked at him.

"Almost all of scripture takes on new meanings when you're around," Peter said to Jesus.

CHAPTER 22

The rest of the disciples, on waking and finding Jesus not among them, went into the nearby village of Mizpah to look for him.

"Greetings," called a tanner who was working on a goatskin in the doorway of his shop. "You're back."

"We're back. We're looking for Jesus."

"Yes," said a merchant from a nearby stall. "Where is he? I don't see him with you." He sat on a stool in the midst of his hanging meats.

"We don't know where he is," said Andrew. "We're looking for him."

Some women approached them from the well, while others disappeared into doorways or hurried off down the street calling for their husbands and children. "He's back," they were saying. "Jesus, he's come back."

"Is he back?" said the tanner. "I don't see him."

"No," Philip said. "He's not with us. We don't know where he is."

"Well, if you don't, who does?" asked the meat merchant.

"We were hoping you did, that he —"

"Hoping we did! But we haven't set foot outside this village."

"Yes, we know," Andrew said. "We thought perhaps he'd come into the vil —" He broke off. A young woman, barely more than a girl, was coming toward them. She moved with the careful gait of convalescence.

"Ah, there's Shera," said the tanner. "I can tell you, she won't be forgetting your Jesus anytime soon."

"No, I don't imagine . . . Hello, Shera," Andrew said. "Good day to you."

"Yes," she said, smiling, peering past them. "Jesus, where is he?"

"We don't know. We've come here looking for him."

"They lost him out there somewhere," said the tanner. "If you can believe it." He stood, then, laying aside his skin. He looked both ways down the street, as if half-expecting to see Jesus coming toward them. The meat merchant came out into the sun as well. In fact, a number of villagers were congregating about the disciples, mothers carrying their babies and herding their toddlers, fathers standing with their sons in front of them.

"So where is Jesus?" someone asked. "Is he coming behind you?"

"Did he come back to see Shera?"

"My baby, she seems to be hot with fever. Could Jesus —"

"We don't know where he is," Andrew said. "We've come to look for him."

"So he's here in Mizpah?"

"No, not if you haven't seen him."

"Then why are you here looking for him?" the tanner demanded, raising his chin belligerently.

Andrew felt at a loss as to how to answer him.

"And where is he?"

A man and a woman were approaching with a boy of ten or eleven, the man carrying the boy, the woman using a blanket to shield him from the sun. As they approached the disciples, the crowd shifted to clear a path for them, and everyone quieted. The man set the boy on his feet in front of Andrew and Philip. The boy stared up at them vacantly, almost as if he didn't see them.

Andrew knelt. "Hello, little fellow," he said to the boy.

There was no response.

"Jesus isn't with us," Andrew said, looking up at the parents.

"But you, you who are his disciples, surely you can do something for him. A spirit possesses him — nearly every day it seizes him and throws him to the ground."

"He struggles against it," the woman said. "Thrashing about and foaming at the mouth."

The man said, "When the spirit leaves him, it leaves him like this."

"Stupid so much of the time. Hardly aware of what's going on."

"Can you do something?"

Andrew laid a hand on the boy's shoulder. "What is your name, son?" he said, gently.

The boy looked at him.

"It's Daniel," the mother said. "Say hello, Daniel."

Andrew looked up at the villagers crowded around him, at their eyes, all of which seemed to be focused on him. He looked back at Daniel and cleared his throat.

"Demon," he said in his sternest voice. "Demon, what is your name?"

The boy continued to look at him — as did the rest of the villagers.

"You can't help him, then?" the boy's father said. He sounded resigned, too used to disappointment.

"I'm sorry," Andrew said, standing. The man turned away, guiding his son ahead of him.

"They can't help him," said a woman in the crowd.

"Well, who thought they could?" said someone else.

"Look at Shera," said the woman.

A familiar voice spoke. "Andrew, Philip?"

Andrew, jerking his head around in surprise, felt immediate relief.

"It's Jesus," said someone. "Call to Admon. Tell him Jesus is back." The crowd opened up as people pushed back against their neighbors to open a path between Jesus and Admon and his small family. They all fell silent.

Admon looked at Jesus, and Jesus looked back. Finally, Admon said, "Do you think you can help my son? Your disciples couldn't." Daniel stood squinting up at Jesus, dazzled by the sunlight beyond him.

Jesus looked at Andrew, at Philip, at all the rest of them. "Where is your faith?" he asked. "What will you do when I am no longer with you?" He turned just in time to see Daniel's eyes roll back into his head as he fell back against his father. Carefully, Admon lowered the rigid body to the ground.

"How long has he been like this?" Jesus asked, kneeling beside him.

"Since childhood." The boy's face was twitching, and his legs jerked convulsively. "The demon throws him to the ground, sometimes into the river or into the fire as if to kill him. He never leaves the house anymore unless his mother or I am with him."

Foam forced its way through the boy's clamped teeth and flowed from the corners of his mouth. Those nearby noted the smell of urine as the boy voided his bladder.

Tears were running down into Admon's beard. "For the love of God," he said, his voice cracking. "If there's anything you can do, do it now."

"Much depends on you. Do you trust God to help if we ask him?"

"I do," Admon said, thickly. "Or I want to. If it isn't enough, help me to trust more."

The boy was thrashing on the ground, his head cradled in his father's lap.

Jesus looked up. "Father," he said. "Grant the prayers of us, your children."

Everyone was watching him.

"Spirit," he said, looking down at the boy.

A spasm arched Daniel's body, lifting it entirely into the air but for his heels and his head.

"Spirit!" Jesus said. "Leave the boy and never return to him."

A moan escaped the boy. His body gave two powerful jerks, then went limp. Jesus knelt beside him. The boy's head had fallen to one side, and blood mingled with the spittle that ran from his mouth.

"He's dead," said someone in hushed tones. "The demon has killed him."

Jesus took the boy's hand, and the boy's eyes fluttered open. His expression was blank.

"He's alive, but his mind is gone," observed the same commentator.

"Daniel?" Jesus said. "Can you hear me, Daniel?"

Daniel nodded.

"He knows his name."

"Get up, Daniel." Jesus slipped an arm beneath his shoulders, and, as he raised him up, the strength returned to the boy's legs and they took his weight.

† † †

Later, when they had left the village, Andrew asked Jesus why he had not been able to drive out the demon. "I did it once before," he said, recalling an incident in the village of Jotapata, so long ago.

Jesus looked at him, and one corner of his mouth lifted in a wry smile. "No," he said. "You've never cast out a demon."

"But I —"

"God has done it when you asked him to."

Andrew was silent.

"These things can be accomplished only through prayer," Jesus said.

† † †

In Bethsaida, they went first to the home of Leah, Peter's mother-in-law, and found Salome there and also Mary of Cana, James's mother. Salome, on learning that they were bound for Jerusalem, insisted on coming.

"Me, too," Leah said. "I don't have anything to keep me here, and, from the look of you, you could use someone handy with a needle and thread."

"And I can cook," Salome said. "Better than either of my boys, if you're relying on them for that." She cast a hard look to where James stood with his brother John.

Jesus smiled. "It's hard to say just whom we're relying on for that," he said.

"No fresh meat, I'll wager," she said.

"Very little."

"Fresh fruit, vegetables? What do you men know about preparing those?"

"Not much."

"I'm coming then," she said. A statement, not a question.

"Alpheus is here in Bethsaida," Mary said. "We'll travel with you, too."

"You may find the road harder than you imagine," Jesus said.

"Likely enough. Likely enough we all will," Salome said.

† † †

The group split between Salome's house that night and Leah's. All were glad to be in out of the weather. It was the first night any of them had passed in warmth in many days. The next morning, they set off south along the lake shore, most of Bethsaida following. A couple of hours of walking brought them to Capernaum.

Jesus stopped at the well for water, greeting children by name, tousling heads, lifting toddlers high into the air while their mothers smiled proudly. People called to him, asking him to come into their homes to eat, but he and his disciples ate in the home of Jairus. The townspeople crowded into the doorway and looked in at the windows.

Jairus had a guest, a young man wearing a purple robe and a silk tunic. Over dinner, the man said to Jesus, "Good teacher —"

"Good?" Jesus said, interrupting him.

"They say so."

"Only God is good."

"I have heard you speak. You talk about the life which is eternal."

Jesus nodded, refilling his goblet from the clay jug. "Yes, always," he said. "I offer the life which is eternal."

The man cleared his throat. "I understand what you mean, of course," he said, "though I'm not entirely comfortable with that way of expressing it."

"I mean it in just the way that makes you uncomfortable."

The man sipped wine from his own goblet, eyeing Jesus over the goblet's rim. "Be that as it may," he said at last, "I'm interested in this eternal life. I want to know what I must do to procure it."

"What you must do?"

"Yes, exactly."

"You know the commandments," Jesus said. "Do not commit adultery, do not murder, do not steal —"

"Yes, yes."

"Do not give false testimony —"

"I have done none of those things, going as far back as I remember."

"Honor your father and mother."

"I do."

"Good."

"Does that mean I have eternal life?"

Jesus met his gaze. "Do you?"

"I don't know."

"You are a wealthy man as the world reckons it," Jesus said. He indicated the purple robe, the rings glittering on the young man's fingers.

The man nodded. "God is good."

"He is. But of what lasting worth are earthly treasures? Moths destroy fine clothing. Animals die. Iron rusts."

"Thieves steal," the man said.

"Thieves steal. Your wealth is temporal, and yet your whole life is wrapped up in it. It distracts you from those things which are eternal."

The man sighed, making a helpless gesture with his hands. "It can be a burden."

Jesus leaned toward him across the table. "Be free of it. You can be, you know. You can be rich in the things of heaven, can be already deep into the waters of eternity."

The man was nodding, his mouth pursed thoughtfully.

"Sell all that you have and give the proceeds to the poor," Jesus said. "Come with me now to Jerusalem."

The man's breath caught. He seemed to have stopped breathing. The gazes of the two were riveted together.

"Do it," Jesus said.

The man's mouth opened. For a moment he gaped soundlessly. "I can't," he gurgled, sounding as if he were strangling.

"You can."

"I'm not like these men." He indicated Jesus' disciples. "These others who follow you. I have a certain position."

Jesus sat back, exhaling noisily. "Ah, well," he said.

"Wealth to an extent I think you fail to comprehend."

Jesus nodded, his lips compressed in a fine line.

"Surely there is another way for those like myself to participate in the kingdom."

"For those like yourself there is no other way."

"It would mean giving up everything I have."

Jesus said nothing.

"Everything I am."

Jesus gave him a shrug of his shoulders. "We speak of eternal life, and you quibble over cost."

"It's my life."

"Those who seek to preserve their lives will find only deadness."

The man shivered. "Excuse me," he said, putting his hands on the table as if to rise.

"You don't believe me," Jesus said.

"It's not that." The man pushed back from the table. "It's just that I have to go. I have an appointment." As he stepped away from the table, he knocked over a stool that stood nearby. "Excuse me," he said to Jairus, bowing. "Many pardons." He bumped into Jairus's servant. "Clumsy of me," he said. And he passed through the door and pushed his way into the crowd.

When he was gone, all eyes turned back to Jesus. He shook his head. "It is so hard for the rich to enter God's kingdom," he said.

"But —," Jairus protested.

"But surely wealth is a sign of God's favor," said another guest.

"No. Wealth is a stumbling block. What is the largest animal found in Palestine? That's right, Jairus. A camel. What's the smallest opening you can imagine?"

Jairus shrugged. "The eye of a needle."

"I tell you," Jesus said, nodding. "It is easier for a camel to go through the eye of a needle than for a rich man to enter the kingdom of heaven."

"But . . . You're saying it's impossible."

"If the rich can't get in . . .," someone began.

Jesus finished the thought. "Then no one can? You're right. By your own efforts, it's impossible. Remember, though, that for God all things are possible, and God is acting in the present age to draw all men to himself."

Jairus's eyes had grown wide. It seemed to all present that he trembled at the very edge of some momentous understanding. Then the light in his eyes faded.

Jesus laid a hand on that of Jairus. "Good friend," he said. "Thank you for the meal and the hospitality."

† † †

When they were on the road, Peter said to Jesus, "We gave up everything we had to follow you."

"Yes."

"Though like the man said, for a lot of us it wasn't much."

Jesus laughed. "I tell you, Peter, whatever you have given up, you'll get back a hundredfold."

"In the age to come," Peter said.

"In this age," Jesus said. "And in the age to come, eternal life."

Peter remained troubled.

"What is it?"

"I don't see how we are to achieve these things."

"You're not."

"Yes, but the demands are impossible. We can't just not murder; God wants our emotions. We can't just stay away from married women. God wants our thoughts and our fantasies. Tithing isn't enough . . ."

"God wants it all," John concluded.

"God's demands are so great that they leave a man with nothing."

"Assuming we could meet his demands in the first place," John said. "When we're with you and caught up in what you're doing and what you're saying, we have trouble enough. And the strong emotions don't last, or we forget. Our old habits are back on us almost at once."

Jesus was nodding.

"Well?" Peter asked.

"Yes, something more is needed."

"What?"

"It's why we're going to Jerusalem," Jesus said. "To find it."

CHAPTER 23

They met Mary again in Magdala. The noise of the crowd alerted her. She came through a doorway, and her face lighted up when she saw Jesus. "Master," she said, and she ran toward them, her dark hair blowing around her face and her cloak flying.

"She is beautiful," the younger James murmured to John, and John grinned at him.

"She's too old for you," he whispered.

"I didn't mean," James began in an indignant whisper, but John elbowed him to silence.

"Are you staying long?" Mary asked Jesus.

Smiling at her, he reached out with the back of his hand to touch her cheek. "Not long," he said. "Passing through on our way to Jerusalem."

Her smile faltered, and he said, "Do you want to come with us?"

She threw herself into his arms and began kissing his face and beard with all the enthusiasm of an ardent puppy. Laughing, he pushed her away. Several of the women of Magdala had stopped to watch. All were smiling.

† † †

They spent the night in Tiberius with Chuza and Joanna, and the next morning crossed the Jordan to the road that ran south along the river's east bank. They camped under the stars and woke early the next day to continue their journey, Jesus walking in front with

Peter on one side of him and Judas on the other.

"What's the plan?" Judas asked him. "What can we do to help?"

"Go with me to Jerusalem," Jesus said.

"But you'll be arrested," Peter objected, not for the first time.

"I think so. Arrested. Tortured. Executed." His face was grim.

"But why?"

"I'm not sure why. And I may be wrong, even now. I hope so."

"You're not the only one," Peter muttered. He quickened his pace, wishing to avoid further conversation on the topic. As he walked, he brought each foot down hard, stinging his soles. It brought him a certain satisfaction, and he smiled grimly.

† † †

Jesus was sitting on a rock, making a lunch of dried figs and a small loaf of bread. He looked up as Salome approached, one arm hooked through that of each of her two sons. Jesus smiled. "Yes, Salome?"

She stepped forward abruptly, releasing James and John and kneeling on the ground in front of Jesus. His eyebrows climbed his forehead.

"Yes, Salome?"

"My lord," she said.

His face worked as he tried to suppress a grin. "You want something," he said. "What is it?"

"Lord, my sons James and John have followed you for some time now," she said. "Have they not served you faithfully and well?"

Jesus looked over her head to meet James's eyes, then John's. "They have," he said. "Faithfully and well."

"Could you ask for two better servants than these?"

"I could not," Jesus said.

"Then grant it that when you come into your kingdom one of my sons may sit at your right hand and the other at your left."

"Do you have a preference?"

She looked up, unsure whether or not he was taking her seriously.

"Salome," he said. "You don't know what you're asking."

"I do. I'm not asking for them lives of opulence and sloth, only challenges worthy of them."

Jesus looked past her to James and John. "Are you up to facing the challenges I'm about to face? Can you drink from the cup I drink or undergo the baptism I must undergo?"

John looked at his brother, who nodded positively. "We can," James said, and John turned his face again to Jesus.

Jesus raised an eyebrow.

"We can," John said.

Jesus smiled. "Yes, I think you can — that you will."

"Then my request?" Salome quavered, still bending low before him.

"Is, regretfully, denied." Jesus stood, brushing the crumbs from his tunic. He took Salome's arm and helped her to her feet. "What you ask isn't mine to grant," he said. "The seats to my right and left belong to those for whom my Father has prepared them."

† † †

Philip and Nathaniel, who had overheard the entire conversation, drifted away to join the other disciples. "Can you believe it?" Nathaniel said, after repeating Salome's request and Jesus' response. "Those young puppies thinking they're the greatest among us."

"It was their mother," Andrew said. "You know how mothers are."

"And Salome is more of a mother than most," Peter said, nodding.

"They were right behind her," Philip said. "You have to believe they put her up to it."

"He turned her down. That's the important thing."

"Why did he, do you think?" Philip asked. "Who is the greatest among us?"

Andrew looked at Peter.

"Peter?" Philip said.

"Jesus said his faith would be the foundation of his kingdom."

"Of his church," Nathaniel said. "Didn't he say church?"

Philip couldn't remember. "Is he planning to be king or high priest?"

"Both I think," Peter said.

"He was just using Peter's faith as an example," Nathaniel said. "Because Peter was the one who first said he was the Messiah. But any of us could have said that."

"Perhaps," said Andrew. "But not any of us did."

"So who do you think will sit at his left? You, as Peter's brother?"

James and John joined them, and everyone fell silent.

"He could make worse choices," said Peter, eventually.

"Like who?" Judas interjected. "Like me, for instance?"

"What are you talking about?" John asked.

"Like you don't know."

"For instance," Peter said to Judas.

Judas's mouth curled in a sneer.

"Where is Jesus, anyway?" Matthew said. "Has he gone off again and left us?"

After a somewhat frantic search, the younger James spotted Jesus walking along the road nearly half a mile ahead of them.

"There he is," he said, pointing.

"Where? I don't see him."

"He just went behind those trees."

Peter gathered his robe about his waist and took off running. Andrew, with a quick look at the others, pulled up his own robe and ran after him. They all followed, even Matthew, still rather portly, his heavy, white legs shining in the noonday sun.

† † †

They caught up to Jesus in a bunch, all of them sweating and blowing hard as they fought to catch their breaths. Jesus looked around at them in apparent amusement.

"You went off and left us," James said. He glanced at a small band of travelers, heading toward them along the Roman road with their families and pack animals.

"We've got ground to cover," Jesus said. "No time to spend in pointless debate."

The disciples looked at one another.

"What were you talking about back there, anyway?"

None of them answered him.

"Rest assured that it is as difficult for a great man to enter the kingdom as it is for a rich man."

The north-bound caravan had pulled abreast of them. A small, piping voice interrupted Jesus, saying, "'Scuse me.'"

"It is, in fact," Jesus continued. "Impossible."

"'Scuse me," came the voice again, more insistently. A boy mounted on a small donkey nudged his way past John into Jesus' field of vision.

"Yes, son?"

"Are you Jesus? My daddy says you're Jesus, the prophet."

Jesus smiled, his happy expression a stark contrast to the frowns of several of his disciples. A man in a worn cloak pushed toward the boy and grabbed his donkey by the bridle. "Sorry," he murmured, bobbing his head without meeting anybody's eyes. "Nuri, you're making yourself a nuisance."

"He's not a nuisance." Jesus lifted the boy off the donkey and up onto his shoulders. "Nuri," he said. "Meet Peter and Andrew and John." He inclined his head toward each of them in turn.

Each nodded.

"Great men all of them," Jesus said. "Thus all handicapped in their efforts to reach God's kingdom."

The three disciples shifted their feet uncomfortably. Behind them, Judas scowled.

"What's handicapped?" the boy asked.

"Encumbered with impediments," Jesus said.

"With what?"

Jesus laughed. "Actually, Nuri, the lesson is for them rather than you. By the way, that's a fine donkey you've got there."

The boy nodded. "I walk most of the time," he said. "But sometimes my feet get tired."

"Sometimes my feet get tired," Jesus said. "I wish I had such a fine donkey to ride." He swung the boy back astride the donkey. He smiled at the boy's father. "I'm sure you're proud of him."

A tentative smile flitted briefly across the man's face. "Yes, we are."

"I'm afraid your party's leaving you," Jesus said, pointing.

The man started, then made off after them, tugging at the donkey's reins. Soon the rise in the road hid him from view.

CHAPTER 24

They crossed the Jordan at the Hiljah Ford. It was late afternoon, and, as they walked toward Jericho, they were squinting into the westering sun.

"It's too late to make Bethany tonight," Philip said to Nathaniel, who trailed with him behind the others.

Nathaniel answered without looking up. "Yes," he said, his eyes doggedly on the road in front of him. "We can hardly count on the hospitality of Lazarus and his sisters."

They heard the clop of hooves behind them and moved to one side of the road to make way for a small brown man mounted on a camel that was striding swiftly in a high-stepping gait.

"I hope we can rely on the hospitality of someone," Philip said. "The land's all desert around Jericho. I don't think I could bear another night in the open."

Nathaniel said, "I'm used to it."

"Used to it! You look like that camel's dragged you face down in the dirt all the way from Capernaum."

"I feel like I've been dragged face down in the dirt all the way from Capernaum."

"But you said —"

"I'm used to feeling like I've been dragged through the dirt a good many miles."

A laugh would have required too much energy, and Philip was tired. He did manage a weak smile.

He and Nathaniel need not have worried. They spent the night in the home of a man named Zacchaeus, a short, round man who, like Levi (now Matthew) was a tax-collector. At first sight he made a humorous, even ludicrous, spectacle: He was perched on one of the spreading branches of a sycamore tree, craning his fat neck (if he could be said to have a neck), while his silk robes and his linen tunic flapped about his sandaled feet.

"Zacchaeus," Jesus said. "Come down out of that tree."

"Me, sir?"

"Are you Zacchaeus?"

"Yes, but . . ."

"My friends and I have need of lodging for the night. I was hoping your house was available."

"My house? Oh, yes, I'd be delighted . . . That is to say, I —" He was scooting along the branch, trying to reach the ground with a plump leg, and at that point he lost his balance and fell forward into the street.

Some members of the crowd laughed as the cloud of dust rose about him, but Jesus bent and helped him to his feet.

"I'm overcome by the honor of your visit," Zacchaeus said several times. "I mean, that you would visit me. I had always heard that you were a holy man, a good man — not that I have any reason to doubt it now, in fact quite the contrary — but I never dreamed you would be willing . . . I'm not very well liked. I mean, what will people say?"

"I imagine they'll say rather what you expect," Jesus said. "'He claims to be a man of God. What is he doing in the home of a tax collector?'"

"I was a tax collector," Matthew interjected. "Until I met Jesus."

Once they had eaten and arrangements had been made for the night, Zacchaeus returned to the subject. "Is that the requirement of righteousness? To relinquish my post?"

"No."

Judas's head swung toward him.

"Taxes must be collected," Jesus said. "And someone must do it. The reason tax collectors are held in such disrepute —"

"Is that they're flunkies of the Roman dogs who oppress us," Judas said.

"Is that so many of them cheat people," Jesus said. "They collect more taxes than the government requires and grow fat on the difference."

"You don't see honest Jews growing fat on what little you leave them," said Judas to Zacchaeus.

"Except perhaps the temple priests," said Simon, his fellow Zealot. "If we can stretch a point and call them honest Jews."

Zacchaeus's head dropped, and he regarded his rounded paunch unhappily. "I haven't always been strictly honest," he said, almost reflectively, and he raised his eyes to Jesus.

"And what are you willing to do about it?"

Zacchaeus's eyes passed over the large room, taking in the ornate furniture, the tapestries and the carvings and the accenting gems. "Not cheat in the future," he said.

"Is it enough?"

He shook his head slowly. "It is not enough. I shall make a donation to the poor."

Judas snorted.

"Half of my possessions." He was on his feet, his round body almost vibrating with sudden energy. Jesus was nodding. "And if I've cheated anyone . . ."

"If," Judas said.

Zacchaeus paced the floor. "If I've cheated anyone, I'll return their money to them. Return to them double their money. With apologies for the mistake. No, no —" He wagged his finger. "With apologies for my thievery. And double isn't enough. It must be three — no, four times the amount." The commitment, if honored, was very likely to mean financial ruin, but Zacchaeus seemed oblivious to the prospect.

Jesus stood. "Today salvation has come to this house," he said to Zacchaeus. He turned to look at the others. "That is why I am here, my whole reason for being. To seek and to save what is lost."

His eyes came to rest on Judas, who looked away.

† † †

The road from Jericho to Jerusalem rose sharply as it wound through the mountains. As they left Jericho's oasis, fed by the Fountain of Elisha just north of the city, the land became harder — not rich soil fit for agriculture, but clay and rock. The road twisted and doubled back on itself. Countless streambeds, dry except in the rainy seasons, opened off it. It was in those mountains that bandits lived, their hideouts tucked away in rocky strongholds. According to the rumors circulating in Jericho, however, the most notorious of those outlaws, a man named Jesus Barabbas, had been at long last captured and was awaiting execution in Jerusalem.

At any rate, no one bothered Jesus and his disciples on their journey. It was nearly dusk on the following day when they entered the pass that opened out within sight of the city of Jerusalem.

"It is beautiful," John said, stopping beside Jesus.

Jesus looked down at him. "It is, isn't it? Yet it will all be destroyed, in your lifetime."

John's eyes widened. "The Romans?"

Jesus' eyes were sad. "I would save it if I could."

"When?"

"Years, I think, but coming."

They stopped in Bethany, at the home of Lazarus and his sisters, Martha and Mary. "Here for the feast of Dedication?" Lazarus said to Jesus, coming out to meet them and walking with them back to the house. "I knew you'd come. Just this morning, I was telling Martha you'd come."

"I've come."

"We've been collecting candles all year to light up the house. Got a new lamp there, too."

"I see you have."

"We'll have the whole place lit up, come the twenty-fifth, and for each of the eight days following."

Some three hundred sixty years ago, Alexander the Great had conquered Palestine. In the years after his death, the Greeks' treatment of the Jews had grown more and more liberal, first under the Ptolemy dynasty, then under the Selucids. Eventually, the Jews were granted a charter to govern themselves by their own constitution, the Torah. Then Antiochus Epiphanes came to power in Syria. Insistent that everyone adopt Greek ways and worship Greek gods, he made it a capital offense even to possess a copy of the Torah. On the temple altar, an altar to Zeus had been erected, and a statue. On the twenty-fifth of the month, a pig was sacrificed on that altar. Judah revolted.

Three years later — to the day — having beaten the Syrians in several decisive battles, Judas Maccabeus reclaimed Jerusalem. He found priests who had remained faithful to the service of Yahweh, tore down the altar to Zeus, and purified and rededicated the temple in a celebration that lasted eight days. *Then Judas and his brothers and all the assembly of Israel determined that every year at that season the days of the dedication of the altar should be observed with gladness and joy for eight days, beginning with the twenty-fifth day of the month of Chislev.* So said the history of the Maccabees. The Feast of Dedication did not have the importance of the Passover, nor of Pentecost, nor of the Festival of Booths, all of which required the males of Israel to travel to the temple in Jerusalem, but it was a feast, and one Lazarus was pleased to celebrate with his friend Jesus and his followers.

On the next day, the Sabbath, Jesus and his disciples went into Jerusalem. They were entering the city by the Fountain Gate, and by the gate sat a man with a coarse blanket laid out in front of him for alms. "Please, sirs," said the man, raising his head at the sound of their approach. "I can hear that there are a great many of you. Surely some among you can spare a few coins."

Judas dropped some coins from the common purse onto the man's blanket. "How long have you been blind?" he asked.

"Thank you, sir. I was born blind. All my life I have known only darkness." He looked up with pupils so large that they seemed to bleed into the milky irises.

"Why does God allow such misery?" Andrew said, looking down at him with sympathy.

"His sins, or his parents'," Peter said, glancing at Jesus. If the beggar heard him, he made no sign.

Jesus squatted in front of the man. "Do you believe that?" he asked. "That your sin or your parents' caused you to be born blind?"

The man shrugged. There was a spastic movement of his lips, not a smile. "What else can I believe?" he said. "God is good. Would he allow such infirmity to strike the innocent?"

Jesus looked up at his disciples, at Peter and Andrew. "There are many reasons for suffering," he said. "Man is fallen, and with him all creation. Some are born blind in order that their spiritual sight not be blinded. You were born blind in order that God might reveal a mighty work." He licked his finger and touched it to one of the man's eyes. "My name is Jesus. I am the light of the world." He touched his finger to the man's other eye.

The man was blinking. Squinting. Turning his head. "I can see," he said.

The disciples looked at one another.

"Not well, not clearly, but I can see something. Shapes," he said, looking from one to another of them, following a passer-by with his eyes. His gaze was filled with wonder. "People? They must be people unless trees can walk."

Jesus spat in the dirt and stirred up some mud with his finger. With his thumb, he rubbed a little of the mud into each of the man's eyes.

"No, I'm blind again," the man said.

"I've smeared some mud into your eyes. You must go and wash it out there in the pool of Siloam." He helped him to his feet and led him into the city, sitting with him on the retaining wall of the city's reservoir, guiding his hand down into the water.

The man put his cupped hand to his eyes, and, as he scrubbed, dirt ran down his cheeks and into his beard. He blinked, then leaned over the pool to scoop up more water, water dribbling off his face and back into the pool. When the man had blinked it away, he became utterly still.

"That's me, isn't it?" he said. "My reflection in the pool."

Jesus' reflection appeared beside his own. "That's you," he said. "What do you think of yourself?"

The man shook his head, still watching himself. "I don't know. Ask me a week or a month from now."

Jesus laughed. A crowd of about a dozen had joined the disciples. The man's eyes became unfocused as his wandering gaze took in unfathomable splashes of light and color.

"Can I live like this?" he said, his voice bordering on panic. "With the world spinning around me and everything rushing in?" He blinked, almost blindly, trying to clear his eyes of the water that still ran down from his hairline, to clear his eyes of their tears. "Can I live like this?"

"Jonah?" said a man pushing his way to the front of the crowd. "Jonah, what's wrong? What are you doing there?"

"Saul?" Jonah said, standing at the sound of the familiar voice.

"What is it?" Saul said, grasping him by both arms. "What's the matter?"

Jonah moved his head, squinting, trying to make some sense of the swirl of light. He reached out blindly and touched his brother-in-law's face. "It's all right," he said. "It's all right, I can see."

Saul looked around at the crowd for an explanation of this madness. Andrew, looking around with him, realized with a start that Jesus was no longer with them.

"I can, I really can," Jonah said, almost hysterically. "Your hair," he said, touching it. "Your face." His gaze shifted. "That man is holding up an arm."

Andrew dropped it, having pulled Peter to him. "Jesus, have you seen Jesus?" he asked.

Peter's head was up, his eyes scanning the crowd. "No. Somehow he slipped away."

"Probably went on to the temple," James said at Peter's elbow.

Peter nodded. "We'd better get along ourselves." He focused for a moment on Jonah and the bewildered Saul. "A man named Jesus gave him his sight," he said, laying a calloused hand on the back of each of them. "Jesus of Nazareth. He's gone now. We're going to find him."

Peter, followed by the others, pushed away through the still-gathering crowd.

CHAPTER 25

Jonah Bartimaeus sat on a four-legged stool in the chamber of the Sanhedrin. His eyes were closed, his head tilted backward in what was undeniably an odd angle for a seeing man. Caiaphas was on his feet, pacing. Annas sat nearby, working his lower lip with his teeth as he studied Jonah. No other members of the council were present.

Caiaphas stopped in front of the man, leaning over him with his index finger rigidly extended. Jonah opened his eyes for a moment, squinting, then closed them again.

"Bah," Caiaphas said. He straightened and continued his pacing.

"You're overlooking the obvious," Annas said.

"Which is?"

"That this isn't the blind man who sits at the Fountain Gate."

"But —"

"Yes, yes. We have witnesses who say it is."

"Exactly."

"Also witnesses who say he isn't, that this is a look-alike. What better way to stir up the enthusiasm of the crowds, if you notice that one of your disciples bears an uncanny resemblance to a certain blind man?"

"Jonah's pretty well-known. For years he's been at that same gate. Since he was a boy."

Annas stood, uncoiling himself. "What did you say your name was?" he asked the witness.

The man opened his eyes. "Jonah."

"The son of Timaeus."

"Yes."

"Is your father alive?"

"Yes. He lives right here in Jerusalem."

"Your mother?"

Jonah closed his eyes again, as if the world of sight were too much for him to endure for more than a few moments at a time. "Yes," he said, his head already beginning to tilt oddly as he lost his visual point of reference. "They are old, both of them, but very much alive."

Annas looked at Caiaphas. "There you are," he said to Caiaphas, as if the man Jonah had told them anything of importance.

"Where am I?" Caiaphas said, his voice somewhat petulant.

"Have the man's parents brought here."

Caiaphas went to the door, and, while he talked with the guard, his voice rolling audibly through the council chamber, Annas stood over Jonah. Annas's chin rested in the crook of his hand between his thumb and forefinger as he studied him. "How long have you known this Jesus?" he asked abruptly.

Jonah's eyes opened, though his expression was, to Annas, unpleasantly and inappropriately vague. "I met him today," Jonah said. "I'd heard of him, of course."

"Ah, of course."

"Do you think he could be the Messiah? The one we've waited for?"

"Is that what you want us to think?"

When Jonah didn't reply, Annas said, "Let's try to avoid blasphemy, shall we? Tell me again what happened to you this morning."

"This man called Jesus —" Jonah hesitated.

"Yes, yes. This man called Jesus," Annas said, moving him along.

"He rubbed mud into my eyes and helped me to wash it out with water from the pool of Siloam."

"And you could see."

"Yes."

"And you couldn't before."

The man shook his head. "Not from birth."

"You were blind from birth. Do you realize that in recorded history there is no record of sight being restored to one born blind? Have you ever heard of such a thing?"

The door opened, and Annas whirled toward it. Nicodemus was there, and with him Joseph of Arimethea. Annas looked at Caiaphas.

"I thought a question of this magnitude should be decided by the full council," Caiaphas said.

Annas turned away, rolling his eyes in exasperation. They didn't yet know where this was leading — how best to use it or diffuse it — and his idiot son-in-law was calling in witnesses. Other members of the council began to arrive: Cephas and Talman and Baruch and Nissim. By the time the guard returned with old Timaeus and his wife, the Sanhedrin had a quorum.

† † †

"Tell us again who you are," Annas said, and Jonah told him. "And this morning you were begging as usual by the Fountain Gate?"

"I was."

"Because you were blind."

"Yes, I was blind."

"And what happened this morning?"

Jonah went over it again.

"Where is this man now?" Annas asked him. "This Jesus — did he say where he was going?"

Jonah shook his head, his eyes closing and his chin coming up in a way that was almost taunting.

Caiaphas cleared his throat, and Annas turned sourly toward him.

"He's preaching on the temple steps," Caiaphas said. "In the court of the Gentiles."

"Preaching openly, is he?" Annas said. "Well, well."

"He put mud in my eyes, and I washed," Jonah said. "And now I see."

"You've made that quite clear."

Talman, one of Annas's closest allies on the council, said, "One thing is clear. This man Jesus cannot be of God. He doesn't honor the Sabbath."

"The miraculous restoration of sight is work within the meaning of the law?" Nicodemus queried.

"Healing. A physician is prohibited from plying his trade on the Sabbath."

"This man is no physician."

"That doesn't change the nature of the action."

"You realize you're conceding the miracle," Nicodemus said. "That this Jesus gave sight to one born blind."

"Not at all, I —"

"Because if he didn't perform an act of healing, he hasn't been working within the meaning of the law." Nicodemus turned to look at the others. "If this man is not of God, how can he give sight to one born blind?"

"This isn't the first miracle of healing that's been ascribed to him," said Joseph of Arimethea.

"No, it isn't," said someone. "And that is the question we must ask ourselves: How can an obvious sinner perform such miraculous signs?"

All eyes turned to Annas.

"Get this man Jonah out of here," he said. "Send in his parents."

The guard jerked Jonah to his feet and led him to the door. As Jonah's parents entered the room, old Timaeus hobbling with difficulty, supporting himself on his wife's arm, they stopped for a long moment and looked at their son. He looked back, his gaze a little vague, but clearly seeing. Tears came spontaneously to the old man's eyes, and he shook his head.

"Go on, go on," the guard said, prodding him.

"Come have a seat here in front of the room," Annas said, indicating the stools. "Have a seat." He hesitated, glancing at his son-in-law. "Caiaphas, it's your place to question them."

Annas took a seat on one side of the council chamber, and Caiaphas strode to the center of the room. "You there, your name," he said, pointing at the witness.

Timaeus's tremor became worse, his head moving atop his thin, waddled neck. "Timaeus," he said. "This is Mary, my wife."

"You are the parents of this man Jonah, the man you passed just now in the doorway?"

"We are," Timaeus said tremulously.

"He is your son," Caiaphas said. Annas snorted audibly, and Caiaphas turned toward him.

"Go on, go on," Annas said.

Caiaphas wheeled ponderously on the couple, who sat holding hands for mutual support. "He is your son," he said again, more loudly than before.

Timaeus's head bobbed as if set atop a spring. "He is. He is our son," he croaked.

"Tell us, how long has he been able to see?"

"He has never been able to see. He has been blind from birth."

"He was born that way," Caiaphas asserted.

"Yes."

"Born blind."

Annas stood up. "For heaven's sake, sit down," he said to his son-in-law, and Caiaphas went obediently to his seat, apparently glad to be rid of the responsibility of cross-examination.

"You're aware, aren't you, that your son is no longer blind," Annas said. "He can see now."

"Yes."

"In fact, you passed him on the way into the chamber."

Timaeus nodded.

"And you looked at him."

"Yes."

"And he looked back. How do you explain that? If your son was born blind, how is it that he can now see?"

"You're asking us? It is we who should be asking you — by what means has God accomplished this thing?"

"What makes you think God has done anything?"

"Who else could have done it?"

"Perhaps a man possessed by a demon."

"Do demons open the eyes of the blind and unstop the ears of the deaf?"

Annas looked irritably toward Nicodemus and Joseph, sitting together on the front row. "Do you confirm everything your husband Timaeus has said to us?" he asked Mary.

"We know he is our son," Mary said.

"That's not what I asked you."

"We know he is our son, and we know he was born blind. But how he can see now, or who opened his eyes, we don't know. Ask him. He's a grown man and can speak for himself."

"Get out of here," Annas snarled. "Both of you."

† † †

Jonah was brought back in and pointed to the stool in the front of the room. "Sit down," Annas said. "Do you know who we are?"

The man looked at Caiaphas. "I know he's the high priest," he said, pointing.

"And I was high priest before him," Annas said. "There are Simon, Eleasor, Ismael — high priests all of them, at one time or another. We are those appointed by God to lead his people. And of one thing we can assure you, this man Jesus is not of God. He's crooked. Twisted. A sinner among sinners."

"I wouldn't know. All I know, I was blind, and now I see."

"You keep saying that, but what did this man do to you? How, exactly, did he open your eyes?"

"I've already told you."

"Tell me again."

"Why? Are you thinking of becoming one of his disciples?"

Annas turned back to the rest of the council, his arms outstretched, palms up. "There you have it," he said. "The man is a disciple of this Jesus. Even here he cannot resist the opportunity to proselytize. We can't rely on anything he tells us."

"I wasn't one of his disciples until today," Jonah said. "I was blind, incapable of following anyone."

"Why would he defend him, if he were not a disciple?" Annas asked, rhetorically.

Nicodemus spoke. "Perhaps because this man Jesus gave him his sight?"

Annas ignored him, turning again toward Jonah. "You say you are this fellow's disciple. Who is he? Where does he come from? We are disciples of Moses, and no one can doubt that God spoke to Moses. As for this fellow —"

"Are you saying you don't know where he comes from or anything about him?"Jonah interrupted, incredulous.

"No one knows anything about him. The man's a nobody, a pretentious nobody."

Jonah looked from one to the other of them, making an obvious effort to bring them into focus. "A nobody? He opened my eyes, I tell you. Could a nobody do that?"

Annas leaned over him. "He could if he was in league with the devil!" Annas shouted, spittle flying from his lips. Jonah's eyes closed, and his head went back defensively. "He could if he was possessed by Beelzebub," Annas shouted. He slapped the side of Jonah's head with his open palm. "Well?" he said. "Well?"

Jonah didn't open his eyes. "God doesn't listen to sinners," he said in a low voice that was nonetheless determined. "Only to the righteous."

"What?"

"God —"

"What does God have to do with anything? It wasn't by God's power that this Jesus did whatever it was he did to you. What do you know about the almighty God? What do you even think you know? You were steeped in sin at your birth. You —"

"We know he was steeped in sin because he was born blind," Nicodemus interjected.

"You're an ignorant . . ." Annas broke off, turning toward Nicodemus as the words penetrated. He stood for a moment without speaking, his breathing plainly audible. Then he turned back to the guards, standing one on either side of Jonah.

"Get him out of here," he said.

† † †

Jonah found Jesus where Caiaphas had said, in the court of the Gentiles. Jesus was talking to a crowd of nearly a hundred, and Jonah stopped at the edge of the crowd to listen. He was startled to hear Jesus call him by name.

"Jonah Bartimaeus," Jesus said, and many in the crowd who had heard of Jonah's healing turned and craned their necks to see him. "The prophet Daniel said that as he looked in the night there appeared before him one like a son of man coming with the clouds of heaven. If I told you I were that son of man, would you believe?"

All eyes were on Jonah, who stood by himself in the midst of a small clearing. Jonah's eyes remained fixed on Jesus. Slowly, awkwardly, he lowered himself to his knees on the tile mosaic.

To the others, Jesus said, "I have come to bring sight to the blind and blindness to those who see."

"What does that mean?" a man said.

Jesus, turning, recognized him as a rabbi, a scholar of the law.

"What category do the rest of us fall in?" the man said angrily. "The sighted blind or the blinded seeing?"

"You tell me. You think the blind have no sight because they have sinned, but I tell you, it is you who see clearly who are truly in danger of the judgment."

Passing close by the crowd came a couple of priests herding yearling lambs toward the Bazaars of Annas. As the bleating of the animals receded, Jesus walked down through the crowd to where Jonah was still kneeling. Helping him to his feet, he said, "I am the good shepherd. I know my sheep, and my sheep know me, just as my Father knows me and I know the Father. It is the good shepherd who lays down his life for the sheep." Jesus pointed back up at the Pharisee. "While the hired hand runs away," he said.

"Yes," shouted a voice in the crowd, Judas. "They sell us to the Romans for their own selfish gain." The Pharisee started, his eyes darting nervously to this man and that one.

"He's raving," he said. "Are we sheep or men? Why are we listening to him?"

"I will lay down my life for the sheep," Jesus said. "I will lay down my life of my own accord, and I will take it up again."

"He's possessed," the Pharisee said.

"For such has my Father promised."

"Get him!" Again, it was Judas, red-faced and pointing. The crowd took a step toward the Pharisee, almost as a single organism, and the Pharisee turned and ran.

"Stop!" Jesus said to the crowd, and in the answering silence only the sound of the Pharisee's retreating footsteps could be heard. "Why seek him out? I will be with you for only a short time; stay with me and learn about the one who sent me. If any of you is thirsty, let him come to me and drink. Whoever believes in me, from within him shall flow streams of living water."

He was quoting Isaiah, but to many the reference seemed cryptic, its meaning obscure. Its very obscurity, however, seemed to add to its import in the minds of his listeners.

"Surely, he is a prophet," said one.

"Or the Messiah," said another.

"He's a Galilean," protested a well-dressed man. "Doesn't Scripture tell us the Messiah will be a descendant of David, a Judean?"

Someone pointed at him. "You're one of them, too, one of the Pharisees in league with Rome."

The well-dressed man, his eyes widening in fear, took a step backward and began to sidle away through the crowd. He reached the edge of it and was gone.

CHAPTER 26

A few days later, during the Feast of Dedication, Jesus was again in the temple area preaching in Solomon's Portico. Among those who were gathered about him were a number of Jews in the employ of the Sanhedrin. One of them interrupted him to say, "Why do you speak in riddles? To build suspense, or for some other reason? If you are the Messiah, tell us, and tell us plainly."

"I have told you."

"No."

"Yes. You didn't understand because your lack of faith prevents you from grasping even the possibility."

"So you are the Messiah?"

"Not your Messiah. Some the Father has set aside for me; these are my people. I know them, and they know me."

The man who had challenged him was a lawyer. He said, "These people who cluster around you are sensation seekers. You are the curiosity of the moment. Tomorrow it will be someone else."

"Some of them are curiosity seekers, true. Others are mine. The Father has given them to me, and no one can snatch them out of my hand."

"What father?"

"My Father."

The lawyer's face didn't change.

"God," Jesus said. "The God of Abraham, Isaac, and Jacob. The Lord God Almighty. What He holds in His hand, no one can snatch away."

"You claim to be God's son?"

Jesus looked at him.

"Blasphemer." The word was a signal. Stones appeared from beneath the robes of a dozen men.

"Blasphemer," shouted another.

There was a commotion in the crowd. Jonah Bartimaeus broke through to Jesus and stood beside him. Laman, the cripple he had healed at the pool by the Sheep's Gate was beside him, too, pressing close to shield him. Those with raised stones hesitated, and in the moment of hesitation Jesus spoke.

"Cripples walk and the blind see. For which of these miracles do you stone me?"

"For neither of them," the lawyer said. "But for blasphemy. You, a mere man, have claimed to be God."

A group of temple guards were coming toward them, the tramp of their boots clearly audible.

"You are a lawyer," Jesus said. "Your law quotes God Himself as saying to men, 'I tell you that you are gods; you are all sons of the Most High.'"

It seemed to take a moment for the lawyer to recognize the quotation from the psalm of Asaph. He glanced around uneasily, realizing that most of the eyes on him were distinctly unfriendly.

"If God Himself calls men gods, what about the one whom He set apart as His very own and sent into the world? Would you stone the son of man because he calls himself God's son?"

The lawyer threw his stone, but it sailed past Jesus' head and clattered harmlessly on the tile far beyond him.

"Do not believe me if I'm am not engaged in my Father's redemptive work." He laid a palm on Jonah's back. "But even if you don't believe me, believe in the miracles. They alone should tell you that the Father is in me and I am in the Father."

The temple guards were pushing through the crowd. "Seize him," the lawyer said, pointing. "He must be taken before the high priest."

With a great deal of shoving and shouting and scuffing of feet, the crowd came together around Jesus in an impenetrable barrier.

Several of the guards fell to the ground; others staggered into each other. The crowd hemmed them in so closely that their spears were of no use to them and they were unable even to draw their swords.

"Perhaps I must be," Jesus called to the lawyer over the heads of the crowd. "But not today. And not on your order."

As Jesus moved toward the gate, pushed and jostled by the very crowd that protected him, the lawyer shouted, "You can never come back. You know that. You can't blaspheme the Lord God and show your face in here. We'll be ready for you next time. We'll be ready."

† † †

The stopover in Bethany was brief. "I'm going beyond the Jordan to the area where John preached and baptized," he told Lazarus and his sisters after recounting the events of the day. "The lawyer was right. When I appear again in Jerusalem, the Sanhedrin will move against me in force. The time isn't right for that."

"I thought it was right," Lazarus said. "I thought it was why you came back."

Jesus smiled. "The time is close."

"Close."

"Just not quite here. I'll know when it comes."

Judas said, "The time is now. You saw how the people flocked around you."

Jesus shook his head. "We came closer to stoning than you realize. The lawyer had half the crowd persuaded."

"And why? Why all that talk about being the son of God? What does it mean, anyway? 'I and the father are one. I am in the father, and he is in me.'"

"You really don't understand, do you?"

"'My sheep listen to my voice. I know them, and they know me.' Listen, Jesus. You're my shepherd. I'm part of your flock if anyone is. I'm prepared to fight to the death for you, to spill my last drop of blood."

A sad smile had appeared on Jesus' face. "And I will do the same for you," he said.

"No. I'm expendable. The movement needs you. If you die, the whole thing collapses."

"So you agree that a trip beyond the Jordan now would be advisable."

Judas scowled. "I don't know. Maybe. It wouldn't be necessary if you left off this God-talk. Nobody understands it. The Messiah is a concept people can grasp. Even the son of man. But 'I and the Father are one' doesn't mean anything to anybody."

Jesus' eyes went from Judas's face to Peter's, to Philip's, to Andrew's.

"So how long will you be gone this time?" Lazarus asked. "When can we expect you back?"

Jesus, his eyes still on his disciples, shook his head. "We've got work to do," he said. "It may be awhile."

† † †

It was, in fact, a little over three months. When the rain of the winter months had loosened the ground, Lazarus began plowing and planting, walking for long hours behind his two oxen, struggling with the single curved blade that tore farrows in the earth. First he planted his barley crop, then his wheat crop, both of which were necessary to feed his family and servants throughout the year. Early in the month of Adar, mid-February according to the Roman calendar, he was plowing his vegetable garden in preparation for planting cucumbers, garlic, onions, and leeks, when a rain-storm swept in with a cold front and soaked him to the skin. By the time he had tended to the oxen and returned to the house, his teeth were chattering and his fingers were brittle with the cold. Pneumonia set in, beginning as a fever that was soon accompanied by a painful cough. The physician who came from Jerusalem could do nothing.

"We shouldn't be surprised at his failure," Lazarus told his sisters. A fit of coughing interrupted him. "Remember King Asa. 'Though his disease was severe, even in his illness he did not seek help from the Lord, but only from physicians.' We must pray,

Mary. Martha. Pray that the Lord will forgive me my sins and heal my body."

Later that same day, his clothes and his hair wet with perspiration, he said, "I would like to see Jesus once again before I die."

Martha had been thinking much the same thing. In fact, she had been thinking that if Jesus came, Lazarus would not die. Hadn't Jesus healed Peter's mother-in-law up in Bethsaida? Hadn't she heard reports without number of paralytics who walked, of lepers made whole? If Jesus came, everything would be all right. She sent the stableboy to Bethany Beyond-the-Jordan, where John the Baptizer had lived. "Ask after him there. If Jesus is nearby, the people will have heard of him. Tell Jesus that Lazarus, his friend, is ill, ill to the point of death. He must hurry if he is to be in time to save him."

† † †

It took Martha's servant two days to reach Bethany and another day to find Jesus, who was camped some distance away with his twelve disciples. When he had heard the message, Jesus sat for a long time staring moodily into the fire.

"It's too dangerous for him to go," John said to his brother.

"Perhaps there's no need. Jesus will know how sick his friend Lazarus is."

"How will he know that?"

"The same way he knows everything. Master?" James asked, turning to Jesus. "Will the sickness end in death?"

Jesus seemed to focus on him only with difficulty. "End there? No, it will not end in death."

"So there is no need to return to Jerusalem."

"I don't know." Jesus stood. "I'm going to go away by myself a little while," he said. "Wait here till I return."

"A little while?" Peter said when he heard Jesus had gone. "A few hours? A few days?"

Martha's servant said, "Lazarus was on the point of death when I left him. If Jesus is to save him, he must hurry."

"He can't go," Peter said.

"He can," Judas said. "It's time, and I think he knows it; time to return to Jerusalem to challenge Rome."

Nobody looked happy to hear it.

"He can do it," Judas said. "It's what he's prepared for all his life."

Peter nodded, slowly. What, indeed, could Jesus not do? He could make bread to feed an army, and he could raise up the wounded from where they had fallen.

And yet —

And yet.

He couldn't help but feel it all was going to end badly.

CHAPTER 27

It was two days before Jesus returned from the hills east of the Jordan. The morning air was filled with mist, and he appeared out of it like a wraith, almost grim in his determination.

"We must go," he said.

"Will we be in time? Martha's servant said —"

"I know what he said. Each day has twelve hours of daylight to do what must be done. It is enough."

"Lazarus isn't dead then?"

Jesus laid a hand on the top of James's curly head. "Our friend Lazarus has fallen asleep. I am going to wake him."

"If he can sleep, that's good," James said. "He's getting better."

Jesus' mouth twitched. "He's dead, James. Stone, cold dead. The time has come for God to reveal his son." He bent and lifted a bag of their provisions, and he swung the strap over his shoulder. "Let's go," he said.

The disciples exchanged glances.

"He's going to his death," Peter said.

"Maybe."

Thomas said, "Let's go, too, then. So we can die with him."

Everyone looked at him.

Judas was the first to stand.

† † †

It took two days to get to Bethany. Martha's servant Jonathan, running ahead of Jesus and his disciples, found the house crowded with visitors and Martha alone in the back room, kneading dough for bread.

"Jesus is coming. He's on his way."

But Jesus was too late and Jonathan knew it. There were too many people to be visiting a sick man: neighboring farmers with their families and servants; friends from Jerusalem, only two miles away; a few of the leaders of the local synagogue; even one or two members of the priestly aristocracy, the Sadducees. Mourners. People there to comfort Martha and Mary on the passing of their brother. Martha was dressed in the traditional coarse sacking, and a line of smeared ash marked her forehead.

She took a breath, pressing her hands for a moment against her sides, leaving smudges of flour. Her arms were white with it to the elbows.

"When?" Jonathan asked, his voice cracking.

"Four days ago."

"Just as I found Jesus."

Martha's eyes closed against the tears that threatened to fall. "How far is he?" she said.

"Just outside town. No more than a mile now at most."

"Take me to him. No, the back way. Let's avoid the crowd."

† † †

Jesus saw her coming and stopped in the road to wait for her. The disciples fell silent. Martha walked straight to Jesus and put her arms around him, pressing her head against his chest. She began to shake, her face contorting with grief. Her first tears since Lazarus's death wet her cheeks. "You've come. Thank God, you've come," she said, and he stood holding her and stroking her hair.

"Martha," he said. "Dear Martha."

"Oh, Master, if you'd only been here, he wouldn't have died."

He pushed her back to look into her face, now smeared with dirt and flour and ashes. "Your brother will rise again," he said.

She nodded, sniffling. "I know," she said. "I know. Like all of us, he will rise again in the resurrection on the last day." She stepped back, making an effort to control her grief, wiping her eyes with the heels of her hands.

"I am the resurrection," Jesus said.

Martha nodded, sniffing again, loudly. "Mary will want to know you're here. I slipped out without her. Oh, Lord, there're so many people to do for."

Jesus smiled, faintly.

"Jonathan here will take you to his tomb. I'll get Mary."

† † †

"That one." Jonathan pointed to the stone blocking the entrance to one of a dozen caves in the hillside. "He's in that one."

Jesus approached the tomb and placed a hand on the heavy stone. "Oh, Lazarus," he said softly. "Lazarus."

"See how he loved him?" said the younger James to Simon the Zealot.

Simon nodded. "He could have saved him. I know that."

They heard people approaching long before anyone got there. Mary appeared at the gate, frail and wan, and the mourners who followed crowded around her.

"Mary," Jesus said. He turned and went toward her, his own eyes moist with unshed tears.

"Master." She looked up into his face and fell against him. He had to catch her to keep her from falling to the ground. Her thin body jerked with her sobbing. "Lord, if you had only been here," she said, looking up. "He wouldn't have died. He wouldn't have."

Looking past her, Jesus saw the crowd of people, pushing and craning their necks to see. His name was spoken and echoed and echoed again as those pressing from behind called for information about what was going on.

"No, not that Jesus," someone said.

"Jesus, the one who opened the eyes of the blind man," said someone else.

"— healed Jonah Bartimaeus, the man born blind."

"I heard he —"

" — there was the cripple he healed by the pool at the Sheep's Gate —"

"Surely, if he had been here, he could have kept his friend from dying."

Jesus raised his voice. "Come through the gate one at a time. Don't crowd. Give us room around the cave."

He left Mary with Martha and approached the stone over the entrance. "Can you move it?" he said to Peter. "You and Andrew together, perhaps?"

Peter set his shoulder against the stone, but it wasn't until Andrew joined him that he felt it give.

"Jesus?" Martha said, tentatively. "It's been four days since he died."

The stone lifted and fell to the side.

"There's going to be an odor," Martha said, in some distress. "A bad one."

Jesus walked back to her. "Believe," he said, softly. "Believe, and you will see God's glory." Peter and Andrew stood in the tomb's entrance, the sleeves of their cloaks drawn over their faces. Jesus looked up and said, "Father, I thank you for always hearing me."

"What's he doing?" someone asked.

"Praying. He calls God Father."

Jesus turned back to the tomb. Jesus gestured to Peter and Andrew, and they moved aside.

"Lazarus," Jesus called in a loud voice. "Lazarus! Lazarus, come out."

Silence. No movement, not even a stir of air.

"He's lost his mind," someone whispered audibly.

"His grief has unhinged him."

Silence again, and not a comfortable one. The crowd shifted uneasily. Jesus did not react to the people, if indeed he was even aware of them. A clatter of stones sounded from inside the cave, and the crowd gave a collective start.

"What is it?" said a voice, elderly and petulant. "What's he doing?"

There was another clatter of stones, this one followed by the sound of shuffling. A woman in the crowd gave a little shriek, but was quickly silenced.

For a time it seemed that nothing more would happen.

Then a man staggered into the doorway, or at least something in the shape of a man. There was a cloth over his face, and his entire body, including his arms and legs, was wrapped with strips of linen. At the sight of him, several in the crowd turned and ran blindly into those standing behind them. Others jolted forward, necks outstretched and eyes straining. Someone fell with a cry.

As the mummified corpse shuffled toward them, blindly and awkwardly, his arms raised in front of him, a hysterical screaming broke out from somewhere in the crowd.

"Lord?" the dead man said in a quavering voice, just audible over the sound of the screaming. "Lord?"

Pandemonium.

† † †

The news took little time to reach Jerusalem. By mid-afternoon, the council of the Sanhedrin was in full session.

"We have spoken against him," Annas said, after the debate had gone on for nearly an hour. "Denounced him in so far as we dared, yet he is still as popular as ever."

"Even more popular."

"The people don't like us," said a Pharisee. "They respect us, to a degree, but they have never liked us."

"Whereas they adore him."

"Exactly," Annas said. "They adore him. Their adoration only increases with time. We try to warn him off, and he keeps preaching. We try to run him off, and he returns. Now we get reports of a man raised from the dead, raised in front of a hundred witnesses. What can we say to counteract the effect of that on the people?"

"And whatever we say, even if it were enough to turn the people against him, what happens tomorrow when he performs his next miraculous sign?"

"When we denounce him, we endanger only ourselves."

Nicodemus said, "Listen to you! Listen to all of you. What are you saying? Jesus raises men from the dead, and you ask, What effect will it have on the people? Better to ask what effect it will have on us. On the whole world. If this Jesus is raising people from the dead, then the Day of the Lord is upon us. Indeed, it is already here."

"Ridiculous," Annas snarled. He bared his teeth. "You must be one of his followers."

"Ridiculous, you say," said Nicodemus. "Fine. Lazarus remains dead, and Jesus is a fraud. Let's expose him."

"Expose him how?" someone said.

"Talk to those witnesses. How many people actually claim to have seen this man raised from the dead?"

"Can we produce his corpse?" said another.

"A relevant question," Nicodemus said. "Can we? Or can we not?"

"One thing is certain, we can't allow Jesus to go on as before," Annas said. "The people believe in him. He'll raise them in revolt."

"And when Rome crushes the rebellion, it will take away all that we have."

"Take the temple away from us. Our positions."

"The very nation will cease to exist."

"Exactly," Caiaphas boomed. "Exactly. This Jesus is a threat to the nation of Israel."

They looked at him.

"Is it better for a man to die, or for a whole nation?" Caiaphas demanded.

"What are you saying?"

"I'm saying," Caiaphas said. "That Jesus must die for the nation of Israel. The next time he enters the city, our guards will seize him. He's a revolutionary. We'll turn him over to Pilate for execution."

"Seize him in public? With the crowds around him?" someone objected.

"You'll incite the very revolution you hope to forestall."

"No," Annas said. "Not in public. Not with the people around him."

"How then?"

"Where does he spend his nights? In the home of this Lazarus fellow?"

"If Lazarus is really alive."

"Let's find out where Jesus spends his nights," Annas said. "The man has friends. Surely one of them can be prevailed upon to talk."

CHAPTER 28

Jewish law required every male who could to travel to the temple in Jerusalem for the festival of the Passover, which began on the fourteenth day of Nisan. As the time neared, and Jerusalem became crowded with devout Jews, everyone looked for Jesus. Few had seen him since the raising of Lazarus.

"What do you think?" they asked each other. "Is he coming to the feast or not?"

"Not if he knows what's good for him. The chief priests and the Pharisees have offered a reward for information as to his whereabouts."

Some traveled out to Bethany to see Lazarus, whom Jesus was reported to have raised from the dead. "I won't believe it unless I see him," one would say.

"See him? What will that prove unless you had seen his corpse?"

"I would have had to have been there," said another. "I would have had to see him come to life with my own eyes."

But still they went, hoping to see Jesus, but content to see Lazarus and to talk to him, to hear him tell again the amazing story of what it had been like in the world of the dead. Many who heard believed, and, though many more did not believe, all participated in the general feeling of excitement and expectation.

† † †

The Sanhedrin, meanwhile, was again in session, Caiaphas the high priest presiding. “Everyone in Jerusalem is going to Bethany,” he said.

“Jesus isn’t there.”

“No, but Lazarus is. It seems everyone has heard of him. Everyone wants to see the man who was raised from the dead. Despite our best efforts —”

“We haven’t been able to come up with evidence to refute the claim,” said Joseph of Arimethea.

Caiaphas frowned. Annas said, “You and Nicodemus both.”

“Both what?”

“Both admirers of this Jesus. Aren’t you?”

“If he is of God, there is nothing we can do to stop him,” Nicodemus said. “And nothing we should do to try.”

“If he is of God,” Annas said in mimicry. “You believe it then.”

“And if he is not of God, he will fail all on his own, for he presumes much.”

“Too much,” boomed Caiaphas. “I hope we are still in agreement, that for the sake of all of us this Jesus must die.”

“How, if we can’t find him?”

“What about this Lazarus?” asked someone. “If we could produce his body, we could expose this Jesus for the fraud he is.”

“Lazarus is up there in Bethany tending his garden,” Annas said.

“He is now.”

“What are you suggesting? That we try to interest Rome in a farmer? Or are you suggesting something more devious?”

“Less direct perhaps —”

“We could orchestrate a stoning —”

“Or simply find someone to assassinate him.”

“We may have to,” Annas said. “If Jesus himself doesn’t surface soon, we may have to.”

† † †

Jesus had withdrawn to the village of Ephraim, not quite a day’s journey north of Jerusalem. When he returned to Bethany six days before the Passover, the curiosity-seekers were still in evidence.

Some who recognized him hurried off with news of his return. Others called out to him in hopes of getting a response; these seemed pleased when Jesus raised a hand in greeting or made in the air the sign of peace.

On seeing Jesus approach, Lazarus, who had been mending a fence to keep the goats out of his vegetables, began to wave excitedly. He started down the road toward them, then turned back as if to fetch his sisters, then turned again and strode toward them. "Jesus," he said. "I thought they'd run you off for good. You wouldn't believe all the people who've come out to see me. You'd think they'd never seen an animated corpse before." He chuckled. "Of course, I don't feel like an animated corpse. I feel amazingly good. I suppose I must die again someday — do you suppose next time I could come back fifteen years younger?" He fell in with them as they walked on toward the house.

"We killed a calf last night," Lazarus said. "We'll have us a feast — meat and vegetables until we can eat no more. Wine — I'll have to send Jonathan into Jerusalem for more wine. Your visits always leave me with a depleted cellar." Lazarus seemed half-drunk already with delight. Jesus, too, was beaming, as were most of his disciples. The sense of foreboding that had seemed to hover over them was all but forgotten.

Jonathan, before leaving for town, brought water to wash the dust from their feet. He motioned for Jesus to sit so he could wash his feet first, but Mary, Lazarus's sister, motioned him aside, and she knelt before Jesus, not with water, but with a jar of pure nard.

"Part of my dowry," she said, looking up at him shyly.

"I'm honored."

Mary poured the perfume over his feet, and the sweet scent of lavender permeated the room. Martha, coming in from the kitchen, saw what Mary was doing and opened her mouth to protest. She hesitated, then closed her mouth again without saying anything.

"Ah, that's wonderful," Jesus said, wiggling his toes. "Wonderful."

Mary smiled up at him. Then she undid her hair and shook it out. Everyone sat stunned, hardly breathing, as Mary bent over

Jesus' feet to wipe them clean with her hair.

Lazarus coughed, his face flushed with embarrassment.

Judas said, "I suppose you realize this is a terrific waste." His voice was dry.

Jesus looked up at him sharply.

"We're supposed to be in the business of bringing healing to the sick and good news to the poor," Judas said. "What better news than that we've sold a jar of ridiculously expensive perfume so we could distribute the proceeds? It's got to be worth a year's wages."

"And it's not yours," Jesus said. "Leave her alone. I won't be with you long, and the remainder of this jar will be used at my burial."

"But the poor —"

"What do you care about the poor? Don't use the faceless poor as an excuse to ignore those whom God has placed around you. Mary's act of devotion will be remembered and recounted until the trumpet blows on the last day."

"What are we even doing here?" Judas said. "We come to Jerusalem, then retreat beyond the Jordan. We return and retreat again to Ephraim in the desert. We come back and here we sit, wasting yet more time and more resources. Do you plan to lead us against Rome, or don't you?"

Mary, looking back and forth between them, began to cry, silent tears running down her cheeks, and Jesus laid a hand on her head to comfort her. "I am here to redeem Israel," he said.

"Does that mean you intend to cast off the shackles of —"

"And through her Rome," Jesus said.

"Rome," Judas repeated.

"And all the world."

"You're mad," Judas said, his voice suddenly soft.

"The work I have been sent to complete is greater than you imagine."

"A megalomaniac," Judas said.

"Will you follow where I lead?" Jesus said.

"Where are you leading? You're headed for a confrontation with Rome's Jewish puppets, and you don't even realize it. Do you expect me to pour out my life's blood for nothing?"

"If you pour it out in an attempt to destroy Rome, then it will be for nothing," Jesus said. "It is you and those like you who are driving Jerusalem to destruction."

"To freedom."

"The kind of freedom you seek is only an illusion."

"An illusion? It's my life."

Jesus shook his head, a rather sad smile lifting one corner of his mouth. "There's no life in it," he said.

Judas opened his mouth as if to reply, then turned abruptly and pushed through the door, opening it on a crowd of faces straining for a glimpse of Jesus. Then the door banged shut behind Judas, and they were alone again.

From outside came the first rumble of distant thunder.

CHAPTER 29

By the next day news had reached Jerusalem that Jesus had returned to Bethany. People got up early to go see him; those who went found still others who had camped the night there, eating the fruit and vegetables from Lazarus's garden. Martha was vexed with them, but Jesus told her to consider her garden a gift to God. "God will repay you in kind," he said. "For the rest of the season, your garden shall produce ten times the food it ever has before."

"Is that a blessing on her garden, or merely a prediction?" James asked, curious.

"Does it matter?" Jesus went to the window and held up his hand. "Blessed art thou, oh garden of Martha," he said. "From this time forth thou shalt produce much fruit." He turned back. "Satisfied?" A grin flickered at the corners of his mouth.

"I am," Martha said. "Perhaps those people out there would like to dismantle my house as well."

Everybody laughed.

"I could use a new one," she said. "Ten times the size."

More laughter.

"One with a larger cook area anyway. Perhaps with a comfortable chair for Mary to sit and keep me company while I work."

Mary blushed, and Martha touched a hand to her cheek. "I'm only teasing you," she said. "You're a big help, and you lighten my spirits besides."

Judas came in, back from Jerusalem and breathless from having worked his way through the crowd. "They're talking about you in Jerusalem," he said. "It's rumored that the Sanhedrin is looking to arrest you." His eyes scanned the room, settling finally on Lazarus. "Even Lazarus is in danger," he said. "They would prefer a dead Lazarus to a rejuvenated one."

Both Lazarus's sisters looked alarmed, but Jesus held up a hand to calm them. "He'll be all right," he said.

"What are we going to do?" Peter asked. "Advance or retreat?"

Jesus smiled. "Battle terms," he observed.

"They seem appropriate."

"Before we do anything," Jesus said, "I need you and John to run an errand for me."

"Yes?"

John stood up.

"Bethphage is only a mile from here. A man there has a donkey colt that's never been ridden. You'll see it tied to a rail as you enter the town."

They looked at him, wondering when he had seen the colt and how he could be sure it was still there.

"You want the colt?" Peter asked.

Jesus nodded. "I need you to fetch it for me."

Nathaniel stood, his expression one of awe, his eyes alight with religious fervor. "You're going to ride the donkey colt?"

"Yes."

"This is it, then."

"I don't understand," the younger James said. "What is it? Why ride a colt that has never been ridden?"

"Suitable for religious purposes," Nathaniel said. "The ark of the covenant was drawn by oxen that had never been yoked."

"Why a colt at all?"

"'Rejoice greatly, oh daughter of Zion,'" Philip said, quoting the prophet Zechariah. "'Shout out loud, oh daughter of Jerusalem.'"

Nathaniel continued the quotation: "'See, your king comes to you, triumphant and victorious, yet humble and riding on a donkey, on a colt, the foal of a donkey.'"

Jesus looked at James. "I defer to our resident scholars of sacred literature," he said. Judas stared at him fixedly, almost as if trying to read his mind.

† † †

Peter and John went out. Some boys followed them a little way, then went back, unwilling to leave the house where Jesus was staying. Fifteen minutes walk brought Peter and John to Bethphage, where they saw the colt standing in the street, just as Jesus had said they would, its halter tied to the rail of a fence that encircled a small yard.

"Hey, you there. That's my donkey. What are you doing?" someone called to them.

They turned to look. Three men were coming toward them along the street. John wet his lips and said what Jesus had told them to say: "The Lord has need of it."

"He does, does he?"

"And how would you know?" asked another of the men.

"He sent us after it."

"The Lord God sent you after it," the man said, mocking.

"The Lord Jesus," Peter said.

It served to focus their attention on him, on his thick neck and corded forearms.

"Jesus of Nazareth?" said one of them.

"Jesus of Nazareth."

The man held out his hands, palms up, in invitation.

John untied the rope.

"Let's go," Peter said, taking the rope from John and wrapping it around his fist. He tugged at the donkey, and it started off willingly enough.

The three men fell in behind them and followed them back to Bethany.

† † †

Their arrival with the colt seemed to excite the crowd. The excitement grew when Jesus came out of Lazarus's house dressed, not in his travel clothes, but in a white robe and tunic.

As Jesus came toward them, Peter said, "Wait, Lord," and he shrugged out of his cloak and threw it over the back of the donkey. John, seeing what he was doing, took off his own cloak as well.

The crowd was moving around them, not getting so close as to crowd them, but talking and calling to one another so that it was difficult for the disciples even to hear each other. Jesus lifted a leg to rest his hip on the donkey's back, and it started off, moving slowly, Jesus riding sideways with his sandaled feet dangling just above the hard-packed dirt.

The crowd's immediate reaction seemed to be puzzlement.

"Hosanna!" Nathaniel intoned, falling in behind the colt. "Lord, save us now, we beseech you."

The crowd got it, and a shout went up.

"Blessed is he who comes in the name of the Lord," Nathaniel said, shouting now to be heard over the clamor of the crowd. "Blessed is the King of Israel!"

They were words from the psalm the people had shouted and sung at the procession of Judas Maccabeus, Judas the Hammer, after he had conquered Acra and wrested it from Syrian dominion more than a hundred years before.

Judas Maccabeus, though, had been riding a war horse.

† † †

It was two miles from Bethany to Jerusalem, and the crowd walked ahead of them and all around them, growing in numbers as travelers on the road joined them and people came out from Jerusalem to see what was happening. "Hosanna! Hosanna!" the crowd shouted, their voices swelling like the roar of the sea. "Blessed is he who comes in the name of the Lord." People took off their cloaks and spread them on the road for Jesus' donkey to walk on. When he had passed, they picked up their coats again. Some ran to catch up with Jesus, to get in front of him and spread their coats on the road before him a second time, and a third. Some stripped branches from the trees and spread them on the road. Always, always, they were chanting and shouting, “Hosanna, hosanna! Blessed is he who comes in the name of the Lord.”

As they entered Jerusalem by the Fountain Gate, people were standing in the streets near their shops and their homes, craning their necks to see what was going on, to see what accounted for the noise of the crowd. When Jesus appeared, clad in white and riding the donkey, they shouted, and the shouts were heard in the temple, rumbling and crashing like thunder.

Caiaphas and Annas and others of the Sanhedrin, standing on the temple steps, saw Jesus in the street below them, the vortex of a whirling sea of humanity, surging through the streets. Nicodemus said, “At last, at last. The King of Israel.”

Annas looked at him sourly. Joseph of Arimethea, his eyes not leaving Jesus, ran down the steps and into the crowd. Jesus was coming toward them, riding the donkey up the broad steps into the court of the Gentiles, the outermost court of the temple.

“Jesus!” Caiaphas shouted. “Jesus of Nazareth.” He pushed toward him, but was soon overwhelmed by the force of the crowd.

“Caiaphas,” Annas cried. “Don’t be a silly ninny.”

But Caiaphas pushed through to Jesus and fell up against the donkey on which Jesus rode. “Jesus,” Caiaphas shouted. “Talk to them! Quiet them! Pilate’s in the city, and he won’t tolerate another riot. You’ve got to disperse the people before the streets are wet with blood.”

Jesus shook his head. “No.”

“Disperse them, I say.”

“They can’t be quieted. They can’t be dispersed. Today, Jerusalem welcomes her king.”

“Hosanna!” the crowd shouted. “Hosanna!” And like a refrain, “Blessed is he, blessed is he who comes in the name of the Lord.” Riotous shouting, the words becoming indistinguishable.

Caiaphas, a big, beefy man, grabbed the donkey’s halter and swung its head toward him. “You must, you must quiet them.”

His wrists were seized, painfully; the reins dropped from his nerveless hands. He turned to find himself looking into the broad, grizzled face of Peter.

"Control your disciples," Caiaphas called to Jesus, but whatever he said next was drowned out by the cries of hosanna. The press of the crowd was driving them forward, further into the temple.

"If everyone fell silent, the noise would continue," Jesus called to Caiaphas as the crowd forced them apart. "The rocks themselves would cry out for joy." He was grinning hugely, reaching out with his hands to touch this one and that one in the crowd. Though Peter, Andrew, and the others feared he would be torn from his donkey, he remained in his seat.

Caiaphas fell back to where Annas was standing. The old man's face was grim. "The crowd's gone mad; there's nothing we can do," Annas said. "The revolt against Rome begins today."

The people around Jesus weren't all Jews. There were dark-skinned men with smooth faces, men from Egypt and Ethiopia in their strange garb, Nabataean tradesmen, Idumaeans and Syrians and those from Asia Minor.

"It's the whole world," said Caiaphas, agreeing. "The whole world's gone over to him."

Jesus, on foot now, mounted the steps to the gate called Beautiful, and he extended his hands over the crowd. Gradually, the shouting subsided.

"The hour has come for the son of man to be glorified," Jesus said.

The crowd, which was packed shoulder to shoulder and chest to back, erupted again in noise. Still more people pressed into the temple.

Jesus held up his hands again. "A kernel of wheat, unless it falls to the ground and dies, remains only a single seed. But if it dies, it produces a multitude."

Confused buzzing. Judas, pressing close to him, said fiercely, "Don't do it, Jesus. You've got them. They're yours. Don't perplex them again and send them away."

Looking at Judas, Jesus said, loudly enough for many in the crowd to hear, "The man who loves his life will lose it. To find life, you must hold life forfeit. Give your life, and God will give you life in the spirit, which is eternal."

In the pause that followed, a voice shouted, "So fight with courage," and the clamor of the crowd broke out again full force.

Jesus raised his hands once more. When he could be heard, he said, "What shall I say? Shall I pray, Father, save me from this hour?"

"No," a man in the crowd shouted.

"No," the crowd shouted.

"No! It was for this very reason I came," Jesus cried. "Father! Lord God! Glorify your name!"

The crowd roared.

"Glory to God in the highest," Jesus shouted. "Glory be to God!"

And the thunder of the crowd echoed him. The people raised their hands in the air and cheered. "Blessed is the Lord's anointed! May he reign forever!"

Jesus turned and strode through the gate called Beautiful into the court of the women. The chief priests, Caiaphas and his fellows, closed in behind him, pulling shut the gates, and outside the guards moved into the crowd, shouting and shoving, to disperse it.

Jesus led his disciples through the court of Women and out of it again through another gate, and he slipped unnoticed through the people in the court of the Gentiles.

By nightfall, he was back in the house of Lazarus, in Bethany.

† † †

Caiaphas and Annas and a handful of others sat and paced in the high priest's chambers, where one by one the officers in charge of the temple guards reported back to them.

"He has eluded us," Annas said, finally, striking his hand on a table and getting to his feet. "Once again, he has slipped away."

"When we see him tomorrow. . .," Caiaphas began.

". . . he will again have the crowd around him."

"We can put out a reward for information as to his whereabouts," someone said, but Annas shook his head.

"We can do nothing openly. Our hold on the crowd is . . . tenuous. Perhaps nonexistent."

"Whereas he holds them in a fist of iron."

"Yes."

"So what do we do?"

"What can we do, but bide our time?" Annas said.

"And if Pilate decides we are unable to keep the peace?"

"I don't know," Annas said.

"But —," Caiaphas began.

"And you don't know either," Annas shouted, turning on him.

Caiaphas raised his eyebrows and pursed his lips, but he said no more.

CHAPTER 30

The court of the Gentiles was always crowded and busy, but at Passover, with pilgrims from all over the world, it was thronged to capacity: with Jews, certainly, because Passover was the one feast which every Jew throughout the empire longed to attend at least once in his life; but also with Gentiles, for the temple of Herod the Great was an architectural triumph, known even as far away as Rome. As always, parts of the courtyard were set aside for trading.

First, there were the money-changers. The temple tax of one-half shekel had to be paid in specific currency, stamped coins of high-grade silver. Those not possessing the appropriate currency — there were myriad currencies in use in Palestine and throughout the Roman empire — had to exchange their currency there at the temple. The money-changers charged a gerah for the transaction; if change were required, they charged another gerah for giving change. Two gerah constituted a half-day's wage for a working man: a half-day's wage for a single transaction. The money-changers, who at this time of year were making change as fast as they could count, grew rich.

The Bazaars of Annas, the private property of Annas and his family, sold animals for sacrifice. Nearly every visit to the temple involved a sacrifice. Doves were required when a woman came for ritual purification after childbirth; also when a leper came to have his cure attested and certified. Lambs were required for the Passover. All but continually, burnt offerings were made to the Lord on behalf of the people.

Any animal offered to the Lord must be perfect and without blemish. Theoretically, these could be purchased outside the temple. In practice, as they had with Lazarus, the temple inspectors rejected any animal brought from outside the temple and redirected the worshiper to the Bazaars of Annas — where unblemished animals were freely available for ten times what they would cost anywhere else.

As Jesus entered the temple precincts on the second day of the week (Moon-day by the Roman calendar), a woman and a small boy were at the inspection booth, and a priest was examining a lamb the boy held by a rope attached to its halter. "No," the priest said. "Sorry."

"But it's a yearling, and in perfect health," the woman said. Her hairline, just visible from beneath her shawl, was streaked with gray.

"Blemished. Sorry."

"Nathan raised it from birth."

The priest bent down to look her in the face. "What kind of person would wish to offer a blemished sacrifice to God?"

She blinked rapidly. Nathan, looking up, pulled at her skirt. "It's all right, mother. Please — it's all right."

Jesus held up a hand to stop his disciples, who were crowding past him.

"His father died when he was a baby," the woman told the priest.

"A lamb suitable for sacrifice can be purchased there," the priest said, pointing. "They'll probably even be willing to take your lamb as part of the trade."

"So they can resell it for a tidy profit," Jesus said, but he was too far away for the priest or his petitioners to hear him.

"What?" Andrew asked. He then noticed the woman and her son and realized at once what was going on. "Oh." He pulled a face.

"Give me your rope," Jesus said.

Peter had a bit of rope, too, shorter and heavier. Jesus stood knotting Andrew's rope to the end of it.

The woman stepped closer to the priest, talking rapidly, but in too low a voice for Jesus or his disciples to overhear.

"I can't help what you can or cannot afford," the priest said in a loud voice, stepping back.

"Momma, please," the boy said, beginning to cry.

"There are people behind you." The priest indicated another family standing with anxious faces. "Show some consideration."

The woman and her boy moved away, the woman stumbling, a hand to her face, the boy still leading his yearling lamb.

"Excuse me," Jesus said, moving in front of the priest.

"Yes? What is it?"

Jesus punched the man full in the face, knocking him backwards onto a table with enough force to break the table's legs and spill the priest onto the tile mosaic.

He looked up at Jesus with eyes wide with fright and blood welling around his teeth and running down over his lips and into his beard. "What," he said and stopped, his mouth working in a toothless, gumming motion. He spat out a tooth. "Are you possessed?" he said.

"Possessed of God," Jesus said. "You may consider this the first installment of His judgment."

People on all sides were crowding back, opening a space around them. A priest, skipping sideways, was calling for the temple guards. Jesus looked around at the nearby priests, his eyes still cold with anger. "It is written," Jesus said in a voice loud in the silence. "My temple is to be a house of prayer." He moved through the courtyard, the people crowding after him at a respectful distance. When he approached the nearest table of the money-changers, the clerks behind it stood quickly and stepped away from it. "You have made God's temple a den of thieves and robbers," he said.

He overturned the table, and the money chest fell to the floor, its lid bursting from a hinge as it hit the floor, gold and silver coins scattering over the colored tile.

"Hey, you can't —" The money-changers started toward him, but Jesus cracked his makeshift whip in the air and they spilled backward, stumbling into each other in their haste to get away. They left the entire row of tables, each burdened with a heavy chest, unmanned and unguarded.

Jesus went down the row flinging over the tables. Several of the money-changers ran at him, but he straight-armed one to the floor and opened the cheek of another with his whip. With his foot he pushed over the last table. Someone cheered. Boys dropped to all fours in a scramble to catch the rolling coins.

"You've exploited God's people long enough," Jesus shouted in the midst of the gathering crowd, his voice still angry. "How dare you rob them in God's own name? How dare you rob them in God's own house?"

The guards were coming, the people could hear them: "Move. Stand aside. Get out of the way." Some punctuated their hurled commands with shoves and expletives, and the crowd gave way, opening the path to Jesus.

"Put down the rope," said the officer in charge.

"No."

"You leave us no choice but to —" Someone pushed the guard from behind, and the guard staggered forward. It was like a stopper popping from the bottle of the crowd's fermenting resentments. Before the officer could regain his balance, he was pushed again, harder. As he fell to the floor, the people set on the rest of the guards, grappling with them to strip them of their shields and spears. Those guards who could ran off. The others lay on their faces, their arms and hands held protectively about their heads as the crowd pummeled them with ropes and sticks and whatever came readily to hand.

"Follow me," Jesus shouted, and his disciples crowded close behind him to keep from being trampled as he led the way toward the sheep and dove merchants — who saw the approach of Jesus at the head of an angry mob and fled, abandoning their tables and cages and sheep pens.

More money scattered over the tile in a cataract of gold and silver. Cages were smashed and doves took to the air. Sheep ran bleating through the temple precincts.

It took the appearance of Caiaphas himself to still the crowd. "Jesus of Nazareth," he intoned in his deep voice. "You have brought violence into the temple precincts."

"Yes," Jesus said. "To challenge the fraud and deceit which you and your family have brought into it."

"By what authority do you make this challenge?" Caiaphas asked. He made a sweeping gesture that encompassed the crowd. "Tell us by what authority you do these things."

"What authority?" Jesus said.

"By what authority," Caiaphas said. "If you have authority, someone must have given it to you; otherwise you are nothing more than a brigand and an outlaw."

The crowd, now, was still and utterly silent. Between Jesus and Caiaphas, doves strutted over the tile, pecking at the gleaming coins.

"I will answer your question," Jesus said.

"If you can."

"But first you must answer me a question. If you can," Jesus said.

Caiaphas raised his eyebrows. He held out his hands. "I can answer any question you care to ask," he said.

On the steps before the Beautiful Gate, where a cluster of loyalists from the Sanhedrin stood, Annas groaned.

"John, the Baptizer," Jesus said. "What was his authority? Did it come from heaven, or did he act on his own?"

Caiaphas opened his mouth and closed it. He turned to look at Annas.

"Go ahead," Jesus said. "Discuss it among yourselves."

Caiaphas retreated to the steps leading up to the court of women. A titter swept through the crowd.

"What do I tell him?" Caiaphas asked his father-in-law. "What shall I say was John's authority?"

"Well, you can't say it was God," Annas said. "We weren't supporters of John, and everybody knows it."

"And besides, John all but anointed this fellow," said another of the Sadducees. "He'll respond, 'Well, why then didn't you believe him?'"

"And if we say John was acting on his own —"

"Right," Annas said, grimly. "The people will stone us. They believe this John was a prophet."

"Why don't I just tell him I don't know?" Caiaphas suggested.

Annas snorted. "Right," he said. "That will satisfy them."

Caiaphas, giving a sharp nod, turned back to Jesus, not noticing that Annas grabbed for his sleeve. "We don't know," he said, his booming voice rolling out over the sea of people. "We don't know what John's authority was."

"You mean you won't say."

"I mean we don't know."

Jesus laughed, long and mockingly. "If we're not going to discuss these things honestly, there's no point in discussing them at all," he said.

Caiaphas cleared his throat. "You haven't told us your authority," he said.

"No, and I'm not going to."

"Do you think that will satisfy them?" Caiaphas asked, indicating the people.

"We'll see."

As Jesus turned to the crowd, Caiaphas turned to give his father-in-law a confident smile.

"A man planted a vineyard," Jesus said. "He rented it to some farmers and went away for a long time. All of you are familiar with absentee landlords."

There was a murmur of assent.

"Go on with your fairy tale," Caiaphas said impatiently.

Jesus turned to look at him. "At harvest time, the landlord sent a servant to the tenants to receive his share of the fruit. Instead of paying the servant, the tenants beat him and sent him away empty-handed. The landlord sent another servant, but they beat him, too, and sent him back with nothing. He sent a third, but they wounded him and threw him out."

"Your point?" Caiaphas jeered. "Are you making a point?"

"This is how Israel's religious leaders have treated God's prophets," Jesus said. "Elijah. Jeremiah. John."

The murmur of the crowd was like distant thunder. Caiaphas took a backward step, moving closer to his fellow members of the Sanhedrin and to the gate into the interior of the temple.

Jesus appealed to the crowd. "What could the landowner do?" he said. "He decided to send his own son. Surely they would respect his son, he thought."

"And?" someone called.

"What did they do to him?"

The hint of a smile touched Jesus' face, giving it a look of almost unbearable sadness. "They saw the son coming," he said, "and they recognized him. They said, 'This is the heir. If we kill him, the inheritance will be ours.' So they carried him out of the vineyard and killed him."

Caiaphas had retreated all the way to the steps. The temerity of Jesus — he seemed to be equating himself with God's own son — was not lost on him, but neither were the hostile glances of those in the crowd. Jesus had them on the verge of a full-scale riot, and the riot, if it broke out, was unlikely to leave Caiaphas unmarked and on his feet.

"What then will the owner of the vineyard do to them?" Jesus asked the crowd. "The evil tenants?"

"Kill them," said a voice from the crowd, and Jesus nodded.

"He will come with his armies and kill them," he said, pointing to the cluster of clerics on the steps of the sanctuary. "And he will give the vineyard to others who will recognize his rights in the harvest."

"Yes," a voice shouted.

"They won't get away with it."

The august members of the Sanhedrin turned and pushed their way hastily through the gate, and, as the people mounted the steps, the high, arched doors swung shut.

An overripe pomegranate hit the door's gold plating, splattering its reddish pulp in a bloodless starburst.

CHAPTER 31

That next day Jesus was back in the temple, teaching amid relative calm in the court of the Gentiles. The crowd that surrounded him was so closely packed that children had to be lifted onto their fathers' shoulders to keep them from suffocating. It was so extensive that Jesus' voice was scarcely audible at the edges of it. Questions were being asked — anxious questions, some of them — and Jesus was answering them. In mid-morning, a man said, "Teacher, it is clear you speak truth." He was middle-aged and lean, with dark eyes and an intent look. "And you speak with courage, without fear of those in authority."

Jesus met the man's gaze, his face impassive.

"Tell us," the man said. "Is it right for us to pay taxes to Caesar, or not?" His status as an agent of Annas was immediately clear.

Simon the Zealot looked at Jesus anxiously. If he answered no, then he was a revolutionary and the full power of Rome could be brought to bear. If he answered yes . . .

The people deeply resented the Roman tax. To support it could not help but diminish Jesus' popularity.

"Give me a denarius," Jesus said.

"What?"

"Give me a denarius."

The man looked to his right and his left. "Are you now charging us to answer our questions?" he said.

Jesus continued to look at him.

The man opened his coin purse and, shaking several coins out onto his palm, extracted a denarius. "Here," he said.

"Thank you. The poll tax is a denarius, is it not?" Jesus asked.

"Yes."

"The amount every Jewish adult must pay to Rome each year."

"Yes."

Jesus handed the coin back to him. "Look at it. Is there a picture on it? Someone's profile?"

"Yes."

"Whose?"

"Tiberius Caesar's."

"His profile is stamped on the face of the coin."

"Yes. It's a Roman coin."

"Then give it to the Romans."

"What —"

Jesus addressed the crowd. "Give to Caesar what is Caesar's," he said. "And give to God what is God's."

Judas, angered to the point of blind rage, pushed away through the crowd. As Judas broke through it, running and stumbling as he hurried to put distance between himself and Jesus, Simon's gaze went from face to face, evaluating the crowd's reaction.

"The demands of Caesar and the demands of God do not always conflict," Jesus said. "When they don't, you can't avoid the demands of one by appealing to the demands of the other."

There was some murmuring among the crowd, some discussion going back and forth, but no hostility. "How do we know when these demands are compatible and when they are not?" someone asked.

"Through wisdom."

"But —"

Jesus smiled. "Ask God, son. 'For the Lord gives wisdom to those who seek it, and from his mouth come knowledge and understanding.'"

"Teacher," a man said. "My brother died and left a wife but no children. The law of Moses holds that I must marry his widow now and have children for my brother."

"So what troubles you?"

"I'm the second of seven brothers. Suppose I marry her and die, and each of my brothers marries her in turn, none producing children? At the resurrection, whose wife will she be, since she was married to seven of us?" Another test.

Jesus laughed, and several in the crowd smiled with him. "A pretty puzzle," Jesus said. "Enough to make one disbelieve in the resurrection."

The man looked surprised, then gratified. He was in the employ of the Sadducees, the religious party that controlled the high priesthood and a majority of the seats in the Sanhedrin. It was one of the Sadducees' peculiarities that they denied the existence of angels and spirits and also the resurrection of the dead.

"Lazarus, come stand with me," Jesus said, and Lazarus pushed past several of Jesus' other disciples to stand next to him. His appearance produced a stir in the crowd, for there were few who hadn't heard of him and of his purported death and resurrection.

"Your question shows ignorance about that age which is to come," Jesus said. "The people of this age marry and are given in marriage. Though not everyone will have a place in the resurrection of the dead and the age to come, those that do will not marry or be given in marriage. They will not die, but will be like the angels, children of the resurrection and therefore children of God."

"But Moses," the man protested. "Moses said . . ."

"Moses himself gave evidence of the resurrection. In the account of the burning bush he calls the Lord the God of Abraham, of Isaac, and of Jacob. Is the Lord the God of the dead or of the living?"

The man's tongue appeared briefly between his lips.

"To God, all are alive," Jesus said.

"Well said, teacher," a man said, and Jesus looked at him. The phylacteries strapped to his left arm and forehead identified him as a Pharisee.

"Support comes from unexpected places," Jesus said, though it was perhaps not so unexpected: the Pharisees and the Sadducees had bitter differences in matters of religious doctrine. "Do you have a question of your own?"

The Pharisee cleared his throat, his prominent Adam's apple

rising and falling in his neck. "I do, in fact," he said. "A sincere question."

"A sincere question," Jesus said.

"Not a test. I believe it may have been asked you before, but I have never heard your answer."

Jesus smiled. "Ask the question."

"It is generally understood that the Messiah is to be a descendant of David. From Bethlehem."

"Yes?"

"Nowhere in scripture does the town of Nazareth appear."

"Ah," Jesus said. "You wonder how I can be who they say I am."

"I'm only asking," the man said.

"King David himself referred to the Messiah in the Book of Psalms. Do you remember?"

The man swallowed and again cleared his throat. "'The Lord God will say to my Lord,'" he said, quoting. "'Sit at my right hand, and I will make your enemies a footstool for your feet. I will extend your scepter from the mount of Zion, and you will rule.'"

"Yes," Jesus said. "David calls him Lord."

The Pharisee shook his head, not understanding.

"Does a man address his children or his grandchildren as Lord?" Jesus asked him. "The Messiah is greater even than David."

The Pharisee looked at him, and Jesus looked back. The Pharisee went to him and knelt in front of him, and Jesus blessed him.

† † †

Later, in Bethany, Peter asked him about his answer to the Pharisee's question. "I thought you were born in Bethlehem," he said.

"Yes."

"But you're not of the house of David?"

"I am."

Peter looked perplexed. "Then why not say so?"

"Should my claim hinge on genealogical proofs?" Jesus looked at the fire. "Besides, the lineage of David carries certain expectations.

The people are expecting a Messiah in the tradition of David."

"And you're —" Peter hesitated.

Jesus glanced up at him. "I break the mold," he said.

† † †

Judas was sitting in the antechamber of Annas, seeking an audience. A guard stood by the door, the butt of his spear planted on the ground, his eyes on Judas.

"What are you looking at?" Judas said.

The guard continued to study him. Judas shook his head. Eventually, another guard came out of Annas's chambers. "They'll see him now," he said, addressing the guard and ignoring Judas.

Judas kept his head down as he followed him though the wide double doors into Annas's chambers, where Annas stood with one withered hip perched on the corner of an ornate desk. Caiaphas was there, recognizable by his robes and his headdress. He paced back and forth, his head down and his hands clasped at the small of his back.

Judas came to a stop before them, and Caiaphas came to a halt, too, focusing on him.

"Well?" Annas said.

Judas, on seeing them at such close quarters, was consumed with an almost blinding hatred. He was there only because he hated Jesus more for abandoning his people to such parasites.

"They say you are one of his followers," Annas said. No need to say whose followers.

Judas scowled.

"A close follower," Caiaphas said.

"His treasurer. You want to be able to find him when he's away from the crowd? I can help you."

"Why would you? You say you're this man's follower. Why betray him?"

"He's betrayed me already, me and all of Israel."

Annas raised an eyebrow.

"He has the power to raise up the people against her Roman

oppressors, and he won't do it."

"You're a Zealot then."

"He has the power to seize the temple precincts and to strip you and your kind naked — to smear you with excrement and drive you through the streets."

One of the guards at the door hit him in the back of the head with the butt of his spear, throwing him forward onto his knees. Annas held up a hand.

"You're obviously not helping us out of love and abiding affection," Annas said. "What do you want?"

"Money."

"Money," Caiaphas echoed.

"For the cause. I'll add your silver to his."

"What makes you think we'd be interested in funding your activities?"

Judas smiled. "Who is more dangerous to you — Jesus? Or me with a hundred pieces of your silver?"

Annas put back his head and laughed. Judas waited.

"I didn't mean to be funny," he said at last.

"But you are. A hundred pieces of silver."

"Eighty then."

"Why are you here, Judas? Are you really here to raise funds?"

"As I've already told you —"

"Or are you here to betray your master?"

"Fifty gold pieces." Sweat seemed to pour from his hairline, making his forehead slick with it and dampening the hair at his temples.

"You're all but eaten up with the need to betray him. Aren't you? You'd do it for nothing."

Judas moistened his lips with his tongue.

"'Give to Caesar what is Caesar's.' Is that what did it for you? I knew that question would be his undoing."

"Thirty."

"What?"

"Thirty pieces of silver."

Annas's lip rose, exposing his teeth. "I'll bet it was all the God-talk. A little unnerving, wasn't it, to have a man of flesh and blood telling you he's the deity? Not just the Messiah, no, no, but God Incarnate. Gives him about as much credibility as a man claiming to be a hard-boiled egg. I'll bet —"

"Stop!" Judas exclaimed. "Just stop it, will you? He spends his nights in Bethany."

"In . . ."

"In Bethany, at the home of Lazarus."

Annas shook his head. "That information is useless to us," he said. "Do you know how big a crowd camps around him?"

Judas's eyes shifted. "Later this week, we'll be celebrating the Passover in a room provided to us by Joseph of Arimethea."

"Joseph!" Caiaphas exclaimed.

"Yes," Judas said. "One of yours."

"So it would seem."

"I'll be with them. By the time we leave the city, it will be late, the streets deserted. He can be taken on the Mount of Olives as he crosses over it to Bethany."

Annas gnawed his lip. "Others will be taking that road at night," he said. "Even if we were to lie in wait . . ."

"Tell me where you'll be," Judas said. "I'll find you and take you to him."

"Rather desperate, suddenly to be rid of him."

"You want him. Just take him, will you?"

"And for your compensation?"

"Keep it. I don't want your money."

Annas's lip curled. "You don't," he repeated. "Perhaps not. Still, services rendered should be paid for." He lifted a box from beneath his desk and, resting it on the desktop, counted out thirty coins. Judas watched, his posture still, but his hands trembling with increasing agitation and his desire to be away.

Annas swept the coins into a bag and tossed it to him, and Judas caught it against his chest. His eyes were suddenly wide.

"You know we're going to kill him," Annas said.

"Or have him killed," said Caiaphas. "If we can enlist the Romans, it will mean crucifixion."

"So what?" Judas's voice was thick, and he cleared his throat. "So you'll kill him. What is that to me?"

"You hate him so much that you're willing to sell yourself to the devil, aren't you?"

The observation sparked something in Judas. "Or to you," he said. "Little difference in either case."

Annas smiled. "Small wonder that we can do business," he said.

CHAPTER 32

Jesus didn't enter the temple at all during the next two days.

The first day of the feast of unleavened bread came on the fifth day of the week. The sky became increasingly overcast as the day wore on, and late afternoon had the half-light qualities of dusk.

Joseph of Arimethea had offered them a second-floor banquet hall in which to celebrate the Passover, and Jesus retired there with the twelve.

Everyone seemed cross and out of sorts. When they reached the upper room, they found a long table set out for them. On it were large flasks of wine, a large platter with the Paschal lamb, bowls of charoseth and of bitter vegetables for dipping in vinegar. Peter dropped onto a couch and leaned back with a sigh.

"Joseph didn't supply us with servants, did he?" Judas said. "We'll have to wash ourselves." He gestured to the large stone jar near the door.

Peter, sitting with his eyes closed, said, "Why don't you take care of that for us?" He extended a sandaled foot darkened with dust and dirt.

"For your feet I'd need a scouring brush," Judas said.

A white robe lay across one of the sofas. It was for Jesus, the head of their little family. Jesus, having removed his dusty cloak, picked it up.

"Andrew," Nathaniel said. "Be a good fellow. Stand there with the dipper and rinse our feet as we pass."

"Why should I?" He stepped back from the stone jar, lest

proximity should confer obligation.

"You have the gift of helps. I'd do it, but I'm more the intellectual type."

"And intellectuals can't dip water?"

"We could each dip our own water," said James the younger.

"We could, but we'd likely get our cloaks and tunics wet."

"You're the youngest," the other James said. "Why don't you perform the service for us?"

"Being the youngest doesn't make me your servant."

Jesus was shucking out of his tunic. His chest and shoulders, which rarely got any sun, were pale in the lamplight. "Sit down on those couches, all of you," he said. He was wrapping a towel around his waist.

"What are you doing?" Peter asked.

"I'm going to wash your feet." He ladled water into a small wooden bucket and knelt in front of Andrew.

"Not my feet," Peter said.

Jesus dipped water onto Andrew's feet. "Yes, your feet. If you have never heard a word I've said, perhaps at least you can profit by my example." He finished with Andrew's feet and extended a hand for one of Peter's.

Peter looked unhappy.

"I am about to be taken from you," Jesus said. "You're going to have to learn to wash each other's feet."

Peter grasped the dipper. "Let me," he said. "I'll do it now."

"No. This is my service of baptism. You want to be part of me? Let me wash your feet."

Peter bowed his head. "Wash me all over then," he said.

"You're not dirty all over." Jesus' eyes swept down the row of disciples. "I can't say that about all of you."

Peter looked up sharply. His eyes, too, scanned the faces of the other disciples.

† † †

Later, while they were eating, he asked Jesus what he had meant.

"What do you mean, not all of us are clean?"

Jesus, from the beginning of the meal, had seemed to him withdrawn and subdued, even sad. Indeed, thinking back, Peter thought that Jesus had been depressed all day, perhaps even for several days.

"Are you not happy with us?" Peter asked. He was sitting on Jesus' right, John on Jesus' left. Judas and Nathaniel and Philip sat directly across the table.

"My time with you is over," Jesus said. "And it seems I leave you far from prepared."

"Over! Is that what's bothering you? Nothing's over. It's just beginning."

"Prepared for what?" John said.

"Betrayal," Jesus said. "Persecution. Despair."

Judas looked at him, suddenly intent.

"Betrayal?" Peter asked.

"Yes, before the night is over."

"Some slip of the tongue, some accidental —"

"It won't be me, will it?" Philip said.

Nathaniel reached for a bottle to help himself to more wine. "I know how I can prevent any accident on my part," he said. "I just won't say anything for the rest of the night."

Philip snorted. "You not say anything? Not likely."

Jesus looked sad as he listened to them. Idly, he broke off a bit of the unleavened bread and dipped it in the vinegar sauce. Judas, reaching across the table, dipped his bread in the same bowl.

"It's you," Jesus said.

"It's who?" John asked.

"I had such hope for you."

"You mean the betrayer is here among us?" Peter said.

"The one who dipped his bread in the sauce with me."

Peter's glance slid over Judas as he scanned the table. They were all dipping their bread in the sauce, sharing perhaps half-a-dozen bowls. "One of us," Peter said to himself. "One of us dipping his bread in the sauce."

His eyes came back to rest on Jesus. "I'll stand by you, you can count on that. Even if all the others fall away, I'll be with you."

Jesus looked at him.

"You know that," Peter said.

"You will deny you even know me."

"Peter?" John asked, incredulous. "Peter will betray you?" His comment was the first to attract the attention of the entire table.

Peter looked wounded. "Never," he said to Jesus.

"This very night."

"No."

"Before the cock crows."

There was whispering among those at either end of the table. John was looking in disbelief at Peter, who was looking both hurt and indignant. Jesus looked across the table at Judas. "Are you going to do it, or aren't you?" he said.

Judas's eyes widened fractionally. "You want me to?"

"Does it matter what I want?"

Judas's face might have been a mask, so immobile was his expression.

"Go on," Jesus said. "If you're going to do it, do it and get it over with."

"It didn't have to come to this."

"Didn't it?"

"More riddles." Judas's voice was filled with disgust. He stood abruptly, pushing back from the table.

"Did we forget something?" Peter asked, wondering why Jesus would send Judas after it in the middle of the feast.

"No," Jesus said. "Everything is taken care of." He stood with sudden energy, picking up a large piece of the unleavened bread.

"He sent him to make a donation to the poor," John said to Peter, speculating, but the conversation got no further. All eyes were on Jesus, who prayed, "Father, bless that which is being offered to you." Jesus lowered his eyes and looked around at them.

"This is my body that is broken for you." With a snap, the bread parted. Jesus handed one of the pieces to Peter, another to John on his other side. "Take it and eat it," he said.

"What do you mean, this is your —" Nathaniel trailed off under the sudden focus of Jesus' gaze.

"I am the bread of life," Jesus said. "I satisfy all hungers. Today I give you my flesh to eat."

Nathaniel, who could think of no reference in either history or prophecy for such a monstrous statement, was clearly troubled, though he remained silent.

Peter, who made no pretense of scholarship, obediently broke off a piece of the flat, hard bread; then, eyeing it uncertainly, he passed on the larger piece. On the other side of Jesus, John did the same. Soon everyone had a piece; no one had yet eaten it.

"Go on," Jesus said. "Eat it in remembrance of me."

Remembrance. The word filled them with uneasiness, giving them the momentary feeling that Jesus was not only leaving them, but had already done so. Each, though, obeyed, putting the unleavened bread thoughtfully to his mouth.

Jesus poured wine into a large goblet and raised it, too, with both hands to bless it. Then he handed the cup to Peter. "This is my blood, the seal of the new covenant."

Peter stopped with the cup halfway to his mouth. He looked down into the deep red liquid and up again at Jesus.

"Go on. Anyone who eats my flesh and drinks my blood has eternal life, and I will raise him up on the last day."

"You didn't have any," Peter said.

Jesus shook his head. "No. Pass it among you. I won't drink wine again until I drink it anew in the kingdom of God."

Again everyone felt a chill, as if a cold breeze had passed through the room. Peter hesitated a moment longer, then drank, the dark wine staining his mouth. He passed the goblet to his right.

When the cup came to Nathaniel, Nathaniel hesitated some moments over it.

"Nathaniel?"

"I can't make out the symbolism here. I can't . . ."

"Nathaniel."

"What?" he said.

"Drink now. Think about it later."

Nathaniel took a breath and drank. As he passed the cup, Jesus began to chant softly, his voice deep in pitch and gaining strength. "Not to us, O Lord, not to us, but to your name be the glory." Peter joined him on the next line: "Because of your love and your faithfulness."

Thomas, wiping the wine from his mouth and passing the goblet on, sang, "Why do the nations say, 'Where is their God?'"

James's voice, thin and piping: "Our God is in heaven. He does that which it pleases him to do." Together they went through the second half of the Hallel psalms, then fell silent.

When Jesus left Jerusalem with his disciples, he crossed the Kidron Valley to the Mount of Olives, named for the olive grove that covered much of its slopes. It was a quiet grove, peaceful, with fireflies lighting up the darkness with sporadic flashes. Jesus walked through the inky tunnel formed by two rows of trees, his disciples following after him. Just on the other side of the grove was a garden, surrounded by a low stone wall. Gethsemane. Jesus had come there with his disciples several times.

Sitting with them now near a tree white with spring blossoms, he said, "Will you pray with me?"

Several of them nodded, shifting their positions to get more comfortable. Jesus looked at them a moment, his eyes passing from one to another of them. Then he turned his face up into the dark, starless sky and began to pray. "Father," he said. "My work is nearly done, and I'm ready to go home again."

Several of the disciples looked at each other, but their eyes were shadowed and their expressions unreadable. Jesus held out his hands to Peter and John, who sat on either side of him, and in response all the disciples groped for the hands of those beside them so that they sat in an unbroken circle.

"These are my friends," Jesus said. "I have kept them safe while I was with them and lost only the one doomed to destruction from the beginning. Stay with them when I am gone, and protect them from the evil one. As you sent me into the world, so I send them into the world. And the world will hate them, for they have become as unworldly as I. Sanctify them through me as I am sanctified . . ."

None of the disciples understood exactly what he was talking about: Far from giving comfort, his prayer made each of them deeply uneasy.

When Jesus was finished, he stood, and they blinked up at him. "Wait here while I go off by myself a little way," he said. "Pray for me. My hour is upon me, and I can hardly bear it."

His words seemed to have a terrible weight to them. Peter heard Andrew stifle a yawn beside him, and he felt unaccountably weary himself, as if his limbs were unusually heavy. From a distance, Jesus' voice carried to them on the still night air, but the words were indistinguishable.

"Lightning," James said heavily, as the clouds lit up above them.

Peter rested his head against the trunk of the tree behind him. "Dear God," he thought with an effort. "Father in heaven . . ."

The next moment, Jesus was shaking him awake. "Peter. John. Couldn't you stay awake with me for even an hour? James, what's wrong with you? The evil one is here; I can feel him. Keep watch and pray, lest he overwhelm you."

Jesus went away again. Peter, looking after him, was conscious of the sound of rustling foliage. He felt drugged, his mind numb, his eyes burning with fatigue. The other disciples all seemed to be sleeping.

Jesus, standing over them a little later, shook his head. He left them asleep and returned to his prayers.

"Father," he said, and again fell to his knees at the high point of the garden. "Open your mind to me; tell me why I must do this thing." He had been praying the same prayer all night, every night for the past week. It was a question that had first occurred to him on the slopes of Mount Hermon. He had expected it to be answered with the passing of time.

Now, the moment of decision was here, and still he didn't know. He was tired, disappointed in his closest disciples. Even tonight, after years with him, they were stiff-necked and stubborn, full of pride and self-will. He had offered to show them the Father, yet they remained filled with themselves, focused on their own petty ambitions.

Their failure had brought him to this moment. He must himself become their bridge to the Most High God; to do so he must undergo torture, humiliation, and death. He must clutch the pride and self-will of humanity to himself and plunge with it into the abyss. "God, Father," he said beseechingly. "I want only to do your will. Isn't there some other way — for me, for them?" He looked up into the sky, blanketed with clouds, and beyond it, trying to pierce with his gaze the very veil of heaven.

Light, the barest flicker, then a steady illumination: A man stood in the distance, his clothes, his very skin, white, almost luminescent. In his hand was a naked sword.

"Michael," Jesus said.

The man's eyes shone with reflected light, as if from unshed tears. His face was grim. As the vista opened behind and beyond him, the entire host became visible, assembled in rank after rank. A blaze of light glinted from a thousand weapons, a thousand thousand. Over and beyond the armies of heaven was a great cloud with brightness around it and fire flashing forth from the midst of it, and within the cloud were the four living creatures, each with four faces and four wings, two covering their bodies and two beating the air with the sound of thunder. Wheels within wheels were spinning around them, the rims of the wheels covered with eyes.

In the garden Jesus' breathing had become labored, rasping in his chest though he was not aware of it. Above the four living creatures was a great crystal dome, and on it was a throne, deep blue like the color of sapphire. On the throne sat a being in something like the form of a man except that his chest was gleaming amber and his legs were fire. All the colors of the rainbow blazed forth from him, blinding and intense.

"Father," Jesus said, his voice crackling as if under unbearable strain. "Father." Already the vision was receding, the hosts of heaven scrolling away from him until only Michael remained, shimmering and indistinct.

He was gone. Jesus struggled to stand, but he was weak. As he staggered, drops of moisture fell from his face, spotting the ground. He wiped at the perspiration on his face, but his wrist and the back of his hand came away streaked with blood. He sat down hard, staring at it. The air around him was heavy with the portent of storm.

Human beings, being what they were, were incapable of surrendering their wills, of submitting willingly to mortification and rebirth. The Lord of Hosts, seated above all things on his sapphire throne, was likewise incapable of such surrender. Man needed aid and direction in doing something utterly alien to the divine nature.

To save him, God had to acquire the attributes of humility, of obedience, of surrender and suffering and . . . death. It was, Jesus realized, his mission — and had been from the beginning.

"Father, not my will but thine," he said. From the garden below him came the clink of armor, the rustle of movement. He climbed awkwardly to his feet, dusting off the knees and the seat of his robe, and he went back to his disciples.

Torchlight was visible beyond them. Men approaching.

Jesus moved into the midst of his disciples, clapping his hands. "Look, the hour is here. I am betrayed into the hands of evil men."

Around him his disciples stirred.

"Come on, get up," Jesus said. "Now. Here is my betrayer."

Peter, struggling into sitting position, saw Judas standing at the head of a squadron of temple guards. They were armed with swords and torches and clubs.

"Judas?" said Simon, his fellow Zealot, rubbing his eyes.

Judas walked past him to Jesus. "Rabbi," he said, and kissed his cheek. Peter, getting to his feet, saw beneath Judas's robe the sword in its wood-and-leather sheath. He looked from it up into Judas's eyes. The guards were closing, encircling them.

"Galilean peasant," Judas said.

The next moment, Judas was on his back in the grass, and Peter stood over him with Judas's own sword. He swung the sword in the air, and the temple guards fell back. He swung it again and one of them fell to the ground with blood spouting from the side of his head.

"Stop!" Jesus ordered, gripping Peter's arm at the elbow. Lightning flashed in the sky overhead and was followed by the rumble of thunder. The temple guards froze, their eyes wide with superstitious dread.

Jesus stepped in front of Peter and knelt by the fallen guard. The blood looked black in the torchlight. Lying in the grass nearby was a human ear.

Jesus picked it up. "Peter," he said, without looking up. "Put away the sword. It's not yet your time to die."

He held the severed ear against the guard's head and, after a moment, pulled the guard to his feet.

There was still blood matting the man's hair and beard and staining his tunic, but his ear was back in place. He felt of it uncertainly, and one of the guards behind him let out a low moan of terror.

"Who are you looking for?" Jesus asked them.

"Jesus of Nazareth," someone said.

"I am Jesus."

The officer in charge looked from Jesus to Peter, standing just behind him with Judas's sword, to Judas himself, who had scooted backward along the ground until coming up against a tree. Nobody moved.

"Whom did you say you wanted?" Jesus asked. The first drops of a cold rain pelted them, and the wind stirred their hair.

The officer coughed. "Jesus," he said. "Of Nazareth."

"I am Jesus of Nazareth."

Still, they didn't move. Jesus saw out of the corner of his eye that Peter still held Judas's sword. "Peter," he said, sharply. "Don't you realize that at my command are twelve legions of angels? They are all about us, even now."

The whites of the guards' eyes were visible in the torchlight.

"Why do you come in the night with swords and clubs to capture me?" Jesus said to them. "For days I have taught in the temple courts, and you did not arrest me."

"You must come with us now," the officer said.

A smile lifted a corner of Jesus' mouth. No one moved. "Come,"

Peter said. “We can still escape.”

“No,” Jesus said. “A thousand years of prophecy are waiting to be fulfilled.”

“But —”

To the guard Jesus said, “Let’s go. End your part in this and go pray to God for the salvation of your immortal soul.”

He walked down through the guards, and the guards followed him. Their faces, visible from time to time in the flickering torch-light, looked strained and anxious.

CHAPTER 33

Peter followed the band of soldiers into the walled city of Jerusalem. He stayed in the shadows, invisible to their torch-dazzled eyes, the sound of his wet sandals on the muddy streets masked by the tramp of feet and clank of weapons and armor. His heart was beating rapidly, and he walked with the heel of his hand pressed to a pain in his side. Though the rain had stopped, his clothing was soaked, and he was cold.

He couldn't see Jesus, couldn't catch even the occasional glimpse of him in the midst of the helmeted heads of the soldiers. They turned down this street and that one, obviously taking him somewhere other than the temple. Peter quickened his pace, and, when the soldiers turned into the courtyard of Annas's house, he was all but tripping on their heels.

The soldiers passed through the gate, and a woman shut it behind them. She was old and dressed as a slave, now fit only to sit by the gate and open it as needed for those wishing to pass in and out of Annas's courtyard. She peered through the gate at Peter, but he turned his back to her, sweat springing out on his forehead despite the cold.

"Suit yourself," the woman muttered to herself. There was the clang of iron on iron as the locking pin was dropped into place.

"Peter," called a low voice. He started.

"Are you the one he calls Peter?"

Peter spotted him, a shadow in the courtyard beyond the bars.

He moved closer. The face was familiar to him; this man had been in the crowds around Jesus.

"Yes, I'm Peter."

There was a muffled clang as the man drew the pin from the lock. "He's okay," he told the old woman as Peter slipped through the gate into the courtyard. To Peter he said, "Jesus is here. I saw him as they brought him in."

"How did he look?" asked Peter.

"Grim."

"Scared?"

"No. Resigned, perhaps."

"But they haven't hurt him."

"No. Not yet, anyway."

"Hurt him!" The old woman chuckled in a cracked voice. "If he was bound and gagged, they'd still be scared to death of him."

Peter looked at the man, who nodded. "It did look that way. Maybe he'll be all right, even now."

"The both of you, you're disciples of his?" the old woman asked.

"No," Peter said. "No, we're not."

His friend closed his mouth without saying anything.

Peter rubbed his arms to warm himself and looked toward the charcoal fire in the center of the courtyard. Several of Annas's servants stood around it, warming themselves.

"Go ahead. Warm yourself," the man said. "On a night like tonight nobody's going to pay the least bit of attention to us."

† † †

Annas sat alone at his heavy oak table, watching silently as the guards filed in with Jesus, eight guards before him and eight after, packing the room.

"It takes sixteen of you to control this one prisoner?" Annas said.

None of the guards responded.

"Heavens, men, you've got him so boxed in that I can't even see him."

Pushing and pulling at Jesus, they moved him to the front, the guards in front shuffling sideways to get out of the way. Jesus looked down at Annas from a point directly in front of his table.

Annas stood. "So," he said to Jesus.

"So," Jesus said in agreement.

Annas's gaze shifted to one of the guards. "I can hardly breathe," he said, irritably. "I want you and two others to remain with me and the prisoner. Get the rest of your men out of here." His eyes went back to Jesus, and the two studied each other impassively as the guards filed out with a great rattling of swords and armor.

† † †

When the guards began coming out into the courtyard, Peter started, his shoulders tensing to the point of cramping. With a great deal of foot shuffling, everyone repositioned themselves around the fire to accommodate the soldiers. One of the servants bumped into Peter.

"Excuse me," the servant said, and Peter looked down.

"You're one of them, aren't you?" the servant said. He was small with a dark, narrow face and darting eyes. "One of his disciples." He jerked his head to the door through which the soldiers had come.

Peter shook his head, turning his back on the man.

"Aren't you?" the servant said, pulling at his cloak. "One of them?"

"No. I'm not one of them," Peter said.

At his voice, one of the guards looked sharply at him.

"You have the accent of a Galilean," the small man persisted.

The guard said, "You look familiar. You were the one with the sword."

"No," Peter said. "That wasn't me."

In the distance, a trumpet sounded as the guard changed at the Fortress Antonia.

"The cockcrow," another guard said, hearing the trumpet.

Peter started. "What?"

"The cockcrow. Every morning at the end of the third watch. A

Roman practice. What's the matter? Are you sick?"

For Peter had started to shake.

† † †

Caiaphas was in his chambers, interrogating one after another those witnesses who had been brought to his attention as potentially damaging to Jesus. The first was a middle-aged man with a weak chin and a sagging face.

"What do you have against this Jesus?" Caiaphas asked him. "I hear you witnessed a healing."

"Yes. Yes, I did." The man bobbed his head. His graying hair was layer-cut in a way that gave him an effeminate appearance, despite his beard.

"Well? What healing? When and where?"

"He healed a crippled girl."

"And?"

"She was a little thing, about twelve years old. He held her leg in his hands, rubbing it, kneading the muscles. Then he pulled her to her feet, and she could walk."

"How does this help us?"

"Pardon?"

"Are you an admirer of this Jesus or a critic?"

"Oh, a critic, certainly."

"Even though he healed this crippled girl."

"Oh, yes."

"Why?"

"I don't think it was appropriate for him to touch her leg like that."

Caiaphas pulled a face in irritation. "Thank you," he said. "We'll call you if we need you."

The guard ushered him out, then brought in another witness. After Caiaphas had questioned him, failing despite his best efforts to elicit any useful information, the guard brought in another witness, and another. This last was a middle-aged man with gray in his long beard. When the door had closed behind him, he stood just inside it, hands clasped in front of him, an expression of uncertainty on his long face.

Caiaphas nodded him toward a chair. He himself was on his feet, his hands clasped at the small of his back. "Before we start," he said, "do you have something against Jesus, or don't you?"

"I do."

"Something he did, or something he said?" He was learning to get to the heart of things more quickly. Annas would be calling him to the council chambers soon, and he needed some useful witnesses.

"Something he said," the man said. "A story, really."

"Jesus told a story?" Caiaphas's tone was doubtful.

"Yes. 'The kingdom of heaven is like a wedding banquet prepared by a king for his son,' he said."

"A wedding banquet."

"Yes, the king sent his servants to tell those who had been invited that all was ready, but the guests refused to come."

"This story doesn't sound likely to prove an indictable offense," Caiaphas said.

"Oh, I think you'll find it very offensive," the man said. "You see, the king sent more servants to tell the guests about the oxen and fattened cattle the king had butchered for the feast. One of those he invited went off to his business, another to his field. The rest seized the king's servants and mistreated and killed them."

"I don't think —"

"Don't you see? The king represents God and the wedding feast is heaven. The king's servants are God's prophets —"

"Mistreated and killed, yes."

"By those invited to the feast," the man said, nodding earnestly. "The chief priests and Pharisees."

"Did he say that?"

"Isn't it obvious?"

Caiaphas rolled his eyes heavenward. Allegories were not his strong suit.

† † †

"So," Annas said again, and this time Jesus did not respond.

"You've gathered quite an army of followers," Annas said.

Jesus shook his head. "Not an army in the military sense."

"Ah."

"I'm a teacher. Those who gather around me do so to hear my teaching."

"Ah. But surely you're aware of evoking a certain . . . nationalistic fervor? For instance, the parade into Jerusalem earlier this week."

"On a jackass," Jesus said.

"On a donkey colt, a beast associated with the house of David."

"I am of the house of David."

Annas raised an eyebrow. "Are you?" he said, real interest showing briefly in his yellowed eyes. "Are you indeed?"

"The donkey is a symbol of peace."

"And of royalty," Annas said. He sat down, leaning back in his chair to study Jesus through narrowed eyes.

"Is that all?" Jesus said. "I can go now?"

Annas showed his teeth in a mocking smile.

† † †

The Sanhedrin was gathering. The servants of Caiaphas went from courtyard to courtyard, knocking until they had awakened the steward of each house. "Annas has sent for your master. The revolutionary Jesus has been arrested."

Not all seventy-one of the Sanhedrin were summoned. No messenger appeared at the house of Nicodemus, nor at that of Joseph of Arimethea. In criminal cases, a quorum was twenty-three, and only twenty-three were summoned, those closest to Annas in sympathy or blood.

† † †

"You say you are a teacher," Annas said. "What is it you teach?"

"Why question me about my teaching in secret and at night?" Jesus said.

Annas raised a hand. "You have nothing to hide, do you? Why not speak openly?"

"I've done nothing but speak openly — in the synagogues, at the temple. I've said nothing in secret."

"You speak publicly; I understand that. What is it you say?"

"Hundreds have heard me speak. Thousands. Ask them what I've said. They can tell you."

The guard behind him hit him in the head with the butt of his spear. Jesus staggered.

"Is that how you speak to your betters? Answer the high priest's question."

Annas's lips thinned. "Well?" he said.

"And you ask why I don't speak to you openly." Though Annas continued to look up at him expectantly, he said nothing more.

"You know, Jesus? You've been nothing but an irritation to me from the beginning." Annas stood and leaned across the table, his old mouth working sourly. He spat, and the spittle hit Jesus' face and ran down into his beard.

"Violence is the fool's final argument," Jesus said.

Annas gestured to the guard. "Tie his hands and take him to the council chamber."

† † †

"A what?" Caiaphas asked, pacing before the witness chair.

"A parable. At least that's what he called it. The kingdom is like a man going on a journey —"

Caiaphas raised his hand to cut him off. "I don't want to hear it."

"But —"

"I don't care what the parable means, or what you think it means. I don't want to hear it." He looked at the guard. "Is this it? How many more do we have out there?"

"Just one, sir."

"Show him in." He looked down at the man sitting in front of him and jerked his head toward the door.

The next man who entered was young, with an open, agreeable expression that made him appear simple-minded.

"Sit down," Caiaphas said, irritably. "Don't stand there in the doorway bobbing your head. "Sit down."

"Yes, your worship." The man lowered his head and moved quickly to the chair in the front of the room; there was something crablike in the smoothness of his gait.

"You've been in the crowds around Jesus of Nazareth," Caiaphas said.

The man opened his mouth. "I —" He broke off and nodded.

"And you've seen him do things. You've heard him speak."

"Yes."

"He's a sinner," Caiaphas said. "A blasphemer and a dangerous revolutionary."

The young man nodded, his eyes wide, his mouth pursed intently.

"So what can you tell me about him?"

"I —" The man hesitated, as if laboriously working to frame his answer in his mind.

"Out with it, man. What has he done? Have you heard him blaspheme? Have you witnessed revolutionary activities?"

"Yes, I —"

"Well? Which is it?"

"I don't know, exactly. He — he said he was going to destroy the temple."

"The temple here in Jerusalem?"

The man's eyes shifted to the door of the room before returning to Caiaphas. "Is there another one?"

Caiaphas exhaled, puffing out his cheeks. "Of course there are. The Greeks have any number of temples throughout the region."

"I don't know; he just said the temple. He said he would destroy it and then rebuild it. He said it would take him three days."

"Three days?" Caiaphas said. "To single-handedly rebuild the temple that took Herod and all his minions forty-six years to complete?"

The man shrugged. "That's what he said."

"Maybe he said he would destroy it in three days."

The witness looked doubtful.

"Possible?"

"I suppose it's possible."

Caiaphas sighed. It wasn't much, but it seemed to be all he had. "Did anyone else hear him say this? Anyone with you?"

"Sure," the man said. "I was with my brother."

A knock sounded, and a soldier came into the room. "They've begun to arrive. Annas is waiting for you in the antechamber."

CHAPTER 34

The summoned members of the Sanhedrin had all arrived at the house of Caiaphas. They stood about his front hall in groups, speculating about how Jesus had come to be taken, voicing opinions as to how he should be handled. "I understand not everyone's been notified," said one. "Only enough for a quorum."

"Why do we even need a quorum? What does a quorum matter at the house of the high priest? No decision we make is valid unless we meet at the Hall of Hewn Stone in the temple precincts."

"And criminal cases cannot be tried at all except in daytime," said another.

"Criminal cases aren't permitted at all during the feast of Passover," said still another.

"Who says this is a criminal case? That's what we're here for, to decide what kind of case we have, and to do it before his disciples have time to raise the crowd."

"And then what? Even if we find him guilty of some crime, a night must elapse before a verdict can be rendered."

"To give feelings of mercy time to arise? Look around you. It's not likely."

"Perhaps we're only here to advise the high priest."

"Perhaps, but to what end?"

The conversation ceased abruptly as a guard pushed Jesus through the doorway and he staggered into the room with his arms bound behind him. Recovering his balance, Jesus walked to the front of the room and turned, almost as if he were about to address them. Caiaphas entered next. Then Annas.

Annas raised a hand. “Gentlemen,” he said. “I hardly need tell you why we are here.”

Their eyes went to Jesus. Annas went forward to stand near him.

“We’ve arrested the Galilean, but our advantage may be only temporary. The situation has the potential to escalate into something unpleasant, even dangerous.”

One of the senior members of the council cleared his throat. “I assume this meeting is unofficial.”

Annas moved his head equivocally. “I think it best if we leave our precise status indeterminate at present.”

“We can always move to the Hall of Hewn Stone at dawn to formalize any decision we make here,” someone said.

Annas smiled. “Exactly,” he said. “Exactly.” He looked at Caiaphas. “The high priest has been up all night questioning the witnesses who will testify against this Jesus. Caiaphas?”

Caiaphas moved out from the wall. “Yes,” he said. “I have a witness who can testify to the subversive nature of the defendant’s activities. I’ve sent for his brother, too, for the required corroboration.”

Annas nodded. “Let’s hear the witness.”

The man who entered, though young, was completely bald, and the top of his head was dark with freckles from the sun. “Tell us your name, please,” Caiaphas told him.

“Avram.”

“You have heard the defendant teach?”

“I’m sorry? The —”

“Defendant. This man here, Jesus of Nazareth.”

“Oh, yes. I’ve heard him speak.”

“In the company of your brother.”

“Yes. Well, on some occasions in the company of my brother, on others alone.”

“But on at least one occasion in the company of your brother.”

“Yes.”

“When was this?”

“This what?”

"This one occasion."

"Oh, we've heard him together on numerous occasions. You said at least one, and I —"

"You were just telling me about a threat Jesus made."

"I don't know that I would say threat. It came out almost as kind of a promise. Or maybe a prediction."

"What was his promise?"

"He said he would destroy the temple and rebuild it in three days."

"Let's get this straight. He was going to destroy the temple in three days —"

"No. He said he'd rebuild it in three days. I've thought about it, and that's what he said. He didn't say when he was going to destroy it."

"But he did say he was going to," Caiaphas said.

"Yes."

"When did he say this?"

"Two or three days ago. The second day of the week, I think."

"And your brother was with you."

"Yes."

Caiaphas, glancing toward Annas, saw that his father-in-law was frowning. He looked back at the witness. "Did he seem to be in his right mind?"

"My brother?" Avram looked genuinely puzzled.

"No, not your brother," Caiaphas said heavily. "This Jesus. He said he personally could rebuild the greatest of Herod's construction projects in three days. Didn't that strike you as remarkable?"

The man blinked. "It didn't at the time. I guess, now that you mention it —"

Annas interrupted. "Perhaps we should focus on the threat to the temple," he said. "This Jesus threatened to destroy it. Did he say how he was going to accomplish that?"

"No. He didn't say how."

"Was he going to set fire to it, or —"

"He really didn't say."

Annas made a face. "He threatened to destroy the temple," he said again. "We'll leave it at that. When is this man's brother supposed to get here?"

"He should be here now," Caiaphas said. "Guard!"

An officer put his head in.

"Has this man's brother been sent for?"

"Yes, your highness. He's here now."

"Bring him in."

Avram's brother looked just like him: a little smaller, perhaps, his head a little less freckled, but with the same expression of open stupidity. After identifying himself as Jotham, the brother of Avram, he conceded that he had been in the crowd with his brother three days ago when Jesus was preaching.

"That was the day he disrupted the peace and drove out the merchants from the temple precincts," Caiaphas told him. "Did you hear him make any threats? More specifically, did you hear him make any threats against the temple?"

Jotham's mouth pursed thoughtfully. "No," he said, slowly. "No threats."

"Didn't he say he would destroy the temple?"

Jotham looked perplexed.

"And rebuild it in three days' time?"

Jotham's expression cleared. "Oh, yes. He did say the temple would be destroyed. And he said he would rebuild it in three days' time."

"And who was going to destroy it? Jesus himself, was he not?"

"No."

"No?"

"I was under the impression that you were going to destroy it."

Caiaphas's eyebrows rose. "Me!" he said.

"The chief priests and Pharisees."

"We were going to destroy the temple?"

"That was my impression."

"And he was going to rebuild it in three days."

Annas stood up, scowling. "Caiaphas, sit down," he said.

Caiaphas opened his mouth to protest, but, seeing the expression on his father-in-law's face, closed his mouth again without speaking.

He sat down.

Annas went and stood in front of Jesus. "Well?" he said. "What do you have to say to these charges made against you?"

Jesus met his gaze, but he didn't speak.

"Don't you have any response?"

One of the younger Sadducees said, "I'm unimpressed with these witnesses. Do we have enough to take before the full council?"

Annas turned on him. "We have a quorum," he said. "This group here can speak for the full council."

The Sadducee looked troubled. "But without proper notice . . ." He let it trail off. There were so many irregularities in the proceeding that it seemed pointless, even finicky, to protest so small a thing as improper notice.

Annas turned again to Jesus. "Tell us," he said. "Plainly. Under oath to the living God. Are you the Messiah, or aren't you?"

Jesus didn't answer.

"You have called God Father. What do you mean by that? Are you God's own son?"

"I am all you have said," Jesus said.

Annas stared at him in wonder. Until that moment they had had no case. Jesus had just provided the critical evidence against himself.

Jesus said, "In the future you will see the son of man sitting at the right hand of the Ancient of Days. You will see him coming on the clouds of heaven."

"And who —"

"I am. I am the son of man whom Daniel saw in the night visions."

Annas gripped the collar of his tunic and ripped it open, exposing the desiccated chest beneath it. Caiaphas stood and ripped at his own tunic. The display was one which had been forbidden to the high priest since the days of Moses and Aaron, but it had an electrifying effect. One after another, the councilmen stood and tore at their clothes. Their bare chests — shriveled with age, most of them, and covered with graying hair — were heaving with emotion.

"Blasphemy," Caiaphas said.

"He openly claims equality with God," Annas said, pressing the point. “What need do we have of further witnesses?”

“Death,” someone called.

“Death?” echoed the young Sadducee who had been unimpressed with the witnesses. “But we can’t . . .”

He was shouted down. “Death.” “Death.” “Stone him.”

“Yes,” shouted Annas, his voice rising above the hubbub. “‘Anyone who blasphemes the name of the Lord must be put to death.’” He was quoting from the most unimpeachable of sources, the Torah.

The young Sadducee sat back, his eyes flickering from one to another of the angry old men around him. Mosaic procedural law had been reduced in their minds to irrelevant technicalities. There was no point in saying anything further.

In the front of the room Annas turned and did as the law prescribed, laying his hands on Jesus’ head to signal that he himself was witness to the blasphemy. “Death,” he said. He nodded to Caiaphas, who stepped up to lay his own hands on Jesus.

“Blasphemer,” he intoned.

The eldest of the Pharisees hobbled forward to lay his own hands on Jesus’ head. “I, too, am witness to the blasphemy,” he said. Others were lined up behind the old Pharisee, crowding forward in their eagerness to lay hands on Jesus.

Jesus stood impassively, apparently indifferent to them and to any verdict they might render. His indifference fueled a growing anger, at first apparent only in the faces of those who approached him. It was the third or fourth to lay hands on Jesus that spat on him as well, leaving a wad of greenish phlegm in his hair. Then the next man spat, and the next. A line of spittle ran from Jesus’ hairline. The laying on of hands became slaps, then blows. Those who had felt they had been too gentle with Jesus circled back to inflict greater punishment, striking not only at his head but at his face and neck. “Prophesy to us, Messiah. Who is it that strikes you?” said one, hitting him from the side.

A man on the other side of Jesus gave an appreciative snort as he delivered his own blow. “Prophesy to us, Messiah.”

“Prophesy,” said another, and another. Each command was

punctuated by the smack of flesh on flesh. Jesus was hit again and again, his beard running with blood and spittle as the force of the old men crowding forward pushed him back against the wall.

He made no sound and no effort to protect himself, and his calm indifference enraged them to the point of hysteria. They jerked at his clothes and his hair. They threw him onto his side, kicked him in the head and in the ribs. They beat him, punched him, pinched him, and scratched him.

When they dragged him, finally, to his feet, his clothes were torn and smeared with dirt and blood, his face discolored and swollen — all but unrecognizable.

† † †

They had the formal vote at daybreak. Not surprisingly, the verdict was the same: death to the blasphemer. The difficulty, broached first by Annas, was that while Rome permitted the Jews a good measure of self-rule through the body of the Sanhedrin, it did not permit them to inflict the death penalty. "We have to go to Pilate," Annas said. "To confirm our verdict and to carry out the execution."

One man voiced the obvious problem. "Pilate is a Roman, a pagan. What will he care about the crime of blasphemy?"

"If Jesus claims to be the Messiah, he claims to be king of the Jews. He's an insurrectionist," Annas said. "Remember the disturbances he created in the temple precincts, only days ago."

"Do you think Pilate will see it our way?"

"He may have to. Events in Rome have gone against him. The arrest and execution of Sejanus, his protector, leaves him peculiarly vulnerable. It was Sejanus, you know, who got him his present position."

"And now that Sejanus has been executed and his body dragged through the streets of Rome . . ."

"To the rejoicing of the general populace, I understand."

"Now that all his adherents are under suspicion . . ."

"Exactly," Annas said. "Another complaint to the emperor might well finish Pilate. If we press him, he'll have no choice."

"All of us should accompany the prisoner as an indication of our resolve," said Caiaphas.

"Yes. And it will help if we can collect a crowd of the common people as well. Everyone must send for his servants, for his entire household. We must hurry."

† † †

Judas was in the courtyard when they brought him out. So changed was Jesus that Judas gazed at him a moment without comprehension. Then he recognized him.

"Good God," he said.

Annas saw him. "Judas," he said. "Well done, Zealot."

Jesus turned his face toward Judas. One eye was fast swelling shut, but the eye that remained open focused on Judas's face and transfixed him. Judas opened his mouth to say something, but found he could not.

Annas had allowed the party to come to a halt. Judas felt himself sinking under the weight of Jesus' gaze. His mouth gaping soundlessly, he fumbled desperately at the cloth sack at his waist. He couldn't seem to untie it. He jerked at it in panic, finally breaking the leather string. The coin purse fell with a clink to the paved courtyard.

"God forgive me," he managed at last. "I have betrayed a righteous man."

Annas sneered. "What is that to us?" he said. "Seek your own absolution."

"Here, take your money," Judas said, lifting the coin purse. "I don't want it."

"Let's go," Annas said to the others, ignoring Judas. "We must hurry."

But Caiaphas bent to take the sack of coins. As blood money, it couldn't be returned to the temple treasury or used for any sacred purpose. There were, however, any number of profane uses to which the money might be put.

CHAPTER 35

The crowds of pilgrims had not yet filled the streets, but merchants were about, seeing to their stalls in preparation for the hustle of the day preceding the Sabbath. Jesus walked in the midst of the twenty-three members of the Sanhedrin, his hands bound now in front of him and a short rope hobbling his legs. A small contingent of soldiers accompanied them. Many on the council had sent for their servants. As these joined the party, they attracted others who didn't even know what was going on — but were anxious nonetheless not to miss out on any spectacle that might present itself.

Behind Pilate's residence rose three towers on the wall of the city. It was early, and the morning sun did not yet show above the city wall. As the crowd approached the palace, a horn sounded and a sentry cried a warning from one of the two towers flanking the palace gates.

The priests led the crowd through the gates and into the open air courtyard, which was paved with large blocks of limestone striated for the movement of horses. A Roman centurion came out of the guard room. All around were watchful legionnaires armed with javelins and short swords.

"What is the meaning of this?" the centurion said to Annas. "Disperse at once."

"We're here to see Pilate."

A sneer curled the centurion's mouth. "Who is?"

"I am Annas. This is Josephus Caiaphas, the high priest. My son-in-law. Tell Pontius Pilate — your procurator —" The words formed distastefully in his mouth. "That we are here to see him."

The centurion studied him. "Just a minute." He glanced briefly at the crowd of Jews surrounding Annas, then turned and strode away.

After a wait of roughly a quarter-hour, a tribune came out accompanied by enough soldiers to provide an escort. "The procurator will see you," he said. "Follow me."

When neither Annas nor any of his party made any move to follow, the tribune turned back. "Well?" he asked. "Do you want to see the procurator, or don't you?"

"It is the time of the Passover. We cannot enter the house of any Gentile and still participate in the festival."

The tribune came and stopped directly in front of Annas, his hands on his hips. "What?" he said.

"To enter this house would be to incur ritual defilement."

"Then what are you doing here?"

"Pilate must come out to us."

The tribune started to laugh, but his laughter died under the sober gazes of the priests. He turned abruptly and re-entered the palace.

After another quarter-hour, a contingent of soldiers mustered in front of the palace. There was a wait. Pilate himself came out of a cedar grove to the right of the palace proper. He was simply dressed, wearing a white robe with a purple sash, his hair clipped close, and his thin, bony face clean-shaven. For a time he didn't speak.

"Yes?" he said at length, his thin nostrils flaring. "I hope this is important. I was at my breakfast." His eyes focused on Jesus, standing bound and bloodied in the midst of the priests. "Who is this? A prisoner? What has he done?"

"Conspired against Rome, procurator," Annas said, heavily.

"What, raised an army? Instigated a riot? I haven't heard of any such."

"He created a disturbance in the temple precincts earlier this week. Surely you heard of it."

Pilate smiled nastily. "I did, as a matter of fact. Cost you and your family a pretty penny, I imagine."

"You could have intervened."

"Roman soldiers inside the temple at the time of the festival? No, no. Your financial interests are your own concern."

"Be that as it may, he has proved himself a threat to the peace, which you are bound under law to uphold. The man claims to be king of the Jews."

Pilate studied Jesus. "Doesn't look very kingly," he said. "Not to me."

"If he weren't a criminal, we wouldn't have brought him before you."

"If he is a criminal, what is that to me? Take him yourselves and judge him by your own law." He turned away.

Caiaphas cleared his throat. "We have already done so," he said.

"We seek the death penalty," Annas said.

Pilate turned back. "Ah."

"As you know, any execution must be approved and carried out by Rome." A pained smile twisted Annas's mouth. "By you, procurator, as Rome's representative."

"And just what has he done that merits the death penalty? Under Roman law. I'm not interested in your religious squabbles."

Annas's gaze slid sideways to Caiaphas.

"He's subverting the nation, procurator," Caiaphas said.

"That's a good one!" Pilate said. "Subverting the nation. Could you possibly be more specific?"

"He's forbidden the people to pay taxes to Rome," Annas said, recalling — and reinterpreting — a discussion Jesus had had with one of Annas's people in the temple precincts.

Pilate looked at Jesus. "Well?" he said. "Is it true?"

Jesus looked at him steadily. He didn't speak.

Pilate made a sound of exasperation.

"He says he's a king," Caiaphas said, returning to the earlier theme.

"Treason," Annas said.

Pilate made an expression of distaste. "Any madman can call himself a king," he said. "The emperor can't take an interest in all of them."

"No," Annas said. "But this one has done more than make the claim. He stirs up the people in a great religious fervor —"

"— an anti-Roman fervor," Caiaphas said.

"First in Galilee, where this man comes from, then throughout the Judean countryside —"

"— finally here in Jerusalem itself."

"A city well known for its religious fervor," Pilate observed dryly. To Jesus, he said, "You've heard the charges. What about them?"

Again Jesus said nothing.

"Are you a king? King of the Jews?"

"If you say so."

Pilate pointed a finger. "The accent," he said. "This man is a Galilean."

"Yes, procurator. We told you as much."

"Then why do you bring him to me? Herod is tetrarch of Galilee. The gods know he's complained enough about my supposed interference with his subjects. Take him to Herod if you want something done. I understand he has already arrived in Jerusalem for the festival."

"But —"

"I'm going to go finish my breakfast."

† † †

They had no choice but to go to Herod.

They weren't happy about it. Herod was known as a superstitious man, and he certainly would have followed the reports of Jesus' activities. Whether he would be willing to order his execution so soon after ordering John's was open to question. His popularity was already at low ebb.

Still, they had no choice. They marched Jesus along the road to the Hasmonaean Palace, Herod's residence, where they stated their business and requested an audience. Herod was a practicing Jew. Here at least they were spared the awkwardness of insisting on a meeting out-of-doors.

In time, they were admitted to the throne room, where Herod sat on a raised dais. His red hair served to emphasize his flushed face, and gems of every description sparkled from his clothes and fingers.

"He's been drinking," Annas said to Caiaphas in an undertone.

"Does it bode well or ill?"

Annas shook his head, uncertain.

Herod waved at them from his dais. "Come, come. You may approach me." He leaned forward on his throne, eagerly studying their prisoner as they came forward. "This is he? The one they call Jesus?"

"This is he, Majesty," Annas said. "Jesus of Nazareth, the Galilean."

"And the Messiah, some say," Herod said.

"Not those with any knowledge of the law," Annas said.

"No? What do they call him?"

"A blasphemer, my king."

"And what does he say for himself?" Herod looked at Jesus expectantly. "Are you the Messiah?" he asked.

Jesus looked up at him without speaking.

"A prophet? Do you wear the mantle of John, the Baptizer?" Herod scowled, glancing at Annas. "Doesn't he talk?"

"Oh, he talks, your majesty. He has said a great deal. For instance . . ." Annas face assumed a crafty look. "He claims kingship of your subjects."

"Does he now?" To Jesus: "Do you? Are you king of the Jews?"

Jesus' face didn't change expression, and Herod smacked his mouth in distaste.

"I hear you're something of a wonder-worker. Can you perform a sign for us?" He held out a hand. "Perform a sign, and I'll let you go. A lightning storm, perhaps? A little thunder? I've got a boil on my big toe; you could heal that. This is dull."

He looked toward his master-at-arms, standing close by. "This man's a king, perhaps the Messiah himself. Should he be clothed in Galilean homespun?"

"I think not, your majesty," the master-at-arms said stiffly.

"I think not indeed." Herod struggled to his feet, shedding his own embroidered robe. "Here, put this on him." He gave the robe to his master-at-arms. Annas and Caiaphas, standing before the dais, exchanged glances. The master-at-arms came down and held out the robe to Jesus, who didn't move.

With a shrug, the man draped the robe about Jesus' shoulders. He started back toward the throne, then, on impulse, turned and touched a knee to the floor in front of Jesus, his head bowed.

Herod cackled. "Oh, that's good," he said. "The clothes make the man, they say. I guess there's some truth in it."

"He is guilty of a capital crime, my king," Annas said.

"Yes, no doubt he is."

"And you have the power to inflict the death penalty."

"And to refuse. I've already killed one prophet, or so say some. I'm not about to kill another." He looked at Jesus. "Even a silent one." To his man-at-arms he said, "Is that a contradiction in terms, do you think? Silent prophet?"

Annas stood equivocating before the throne.

"Are you still here?" Herod demanded, noticing him at last over the rim of his jeweled goblet.

"King Herod . . ."

"Get out and take your prophet with you. I've got a lot to do. By lunchtime I plan to be as drunk as possible." He laughed, glancing red-faced at his master-at-arms. "Summon my steward; it's time I return to work."

"But —," Annas said.

"I might have a high priest put to death," Herod said, drumming his fingers on the arm of his throne. "Shouldn't be much of a popular outcry over that one."

Annas's mouth tightened, but he didn't say anything. Bowing low, he turned and strode from the throne room. Caiaphas, bobbing his head quickly in Herod's direction, followed him out. Their escort came next, and with them the prisoner.

† † †

"It's outrageous," Annas said, as they strode along the street. There was a bigger crowd around them than there had been, most of the faces unfamiliar. Pilgrims were beginning to throng the streets.

Fortunately, no one recognized the prisoner. It was hardly surprising. Jesus' hair was in disarray. His face was dirty and his beard crusted with blood. He still wore Herod's elegant robe, shimmering with color, but he looked like a prisoner — though perhaps an important one.

"We can go back to Pilate," Caiaphas said.

"What's the point? He has no stomach for death today."

Caiaphas inclined his head, indicating those around them, gaping for a better look at their prisoner. "The crowd might be a factor."

"Yes, but for or against us?"

"Perhaps a few coins, distributed strategically, could determine that."

Annas's eyes narrowed. "Perhaps they could at that," he said. Then, more decisively: "See to it."

† † †

Pilate was not happy to see them a second time. "Why are you back?" he said to Annas. "I told you, I consider the Galilean to be under Herod's jurisdiction."

"Judea and Jerusalem are under your authority," Caiaphas said.

"They are a responsibility you cannot so easily abdicate," added Annas.

"You Jews," Pilate said. "You're like terriers. You take hold of something, and you won't let go. You're worse than my wife."

"Your —"

"Yes, even my wife has an opinion in the case; I can't tell you what a joy that is. It seems she was watching earlier from an upper window, and the sight of the prisoner caused her to recall a dream she'd had."

Annas and Caiaphas exchanged glances.

"She tells me this king of yours is innocent."

"He's no king of ours."

"Be that as it may, I'm not going to execute him merely on your statement that he deserves to die."

"Then try him yourself."

"Why should I? What is he to me?"

Annas and Caiaphas stood implacably, the crowd milling behind them.

"Oh, very well." Pilate jerked his head at a guard, one of his own legionnaires. "Bring the prisoner inside," he said. "I'll question him privately." To Annas he said, "I suppose that, unlike you, he has more to worry about than ritual defilement on the eve of a festival."

† † †

Pilate reclined by an oak-shaded pool to question Jesus, who stood before him with a soldier on either side.

"You have to talk to me, you know," Pilate said. He plucked a grape from the cluster on a table that stood at his elbow. In the center of the pool behind him was the statue of a woman with a pitcher from which poured an endless stream of water. The statue was brass, glinting in the dappled sunlight that filtered through the trees.

Pilate put the grape in his mouth, biting down, then spitting out the seed. "You've admitted to being king of the Jews. What does that mean, exactly? Do you consider yourself a threat to the emperor?"

"Not in any sense he cares about," Jesus said.

"Not in a military sense, then, nor a political one."

"I've been paraded through the streets all morning. If I had military aspirations, my followers would have fought to free me."

"So how are you a king? You're going to have to speak plainly. As you can see, I'm no Jew."

"My throne is in heaven. My kingdom is God's kingdom."

"Not the emperor's?" Pilate smiled thinly, without humor. "Be honest with me now," he said. "You'd like to see your people free of their Roman shackles. You'd like to see Palestine independent with you as its king."

Jesus smiled, as if at some private joke.

"No?" Pilate said.

"I'm a teacher, not a soldier."

"So why do they hate you? What have you done to so outrage the temple leaders?"

"I preach truth."

"Truth," Pilate said. "Not a popular subject, it seems."

"No."

Pilate regarded him silently. At last he stood, shaking his head. "Truth," he said again. "People fight for it; they die for it. I don't even know what the word means."

"I don't suppose you do."

Pilate's head came up. "Save your pity, Galilean. You'll be needing all of it for yourself."

Leaving Jesus, he walked along the path until he came to an opening in the wall that looked out over the crowd of Jews teeming within his gates. He watched them for a time, lost in thought. Riots, once started, could be difficult to suppress without mass slaughter. He'd been that route before.

He came back to stand before Jesus.

Jesus met his gaze.

"You don't merit death, in my judgment," Pilate said. "I'm going to save you if I can."

Jesus said nothing.

"Flog him," Pilate said to the soldiers guarding him. He went out again into the courtyard to talk to Annas and Caiaphas.

† † †

The crowd was more unruly than it had been, and swept by dark currents of muttering. Pilate looked at the soldiers that encircled the perimeter of the courtyard and saw that they were all of them intent and alert.

"Annas," Pilate said.

"Procurator." Annas stepped forward.

"I'm going to flog the man and release him."

Those close enough to hear, all of them members of the

Sanhedrin or members of their households, exchanged angry glances. The muttering, at least in Pilate's vicinity, increased in volume and took on an ugly tone, the sound like that of a disturbed hive.

"You can't do that, Procurator. The people won't stand for it."

"They'll stand for whatever I decide," Pilate said. "I've examined the man, both privately and in your presence, and I can find nothing against him, nothing that merits death."

"He's an agitator."

"I don't believe that. He may be a trifle deluded, but his delusions seem harmless enough from the perspective of Rome. Herod must agree, or you wouldn't be back here."

"Herod's afraid of the people. He's already killed one man regarded by some as a prophet."

"I thought the people were on your side." Pilate, seeing the momentary doubt in Annas's eyes, raised his voice so as to be heard by the crowd. "It has been customary for me to release a prisoner each year during the Passover. This year, out of respect for your festival, I plan to release to you this man Jesus."

There was an interval of silence, a short one, but Annas took instant advantage of it. "Jesus Barabbas," he said loudly, naming the robber who had plagued both Jews and Gentiles on the Jericho road.

"Yes, Jesus Barabbas," echoed his steward.

"Barabbas," said a member of Caiaphas's household, and the rest of the crowd took up the shout, surging unexpectedly toward Pilate.

He retreated abruptly. On either side of the courtyard, his soldiers came forward, their shields raised and javelins lowered, prepared to crush the Jews between two walls of spikes.

Pilate raised a hand. "Close the gates," he said, and the soldiers complied, effectively cutting the Jews off from any possible reinforcement. "Control your people, if you value their lives," he said to Annas. "I'll be back shortly."

† † †

The soldiers took Jesus down to a holding area where they stripped him of his robe and tunic and chained his hands through an iron ring high on one wall. The whip consisted of long strips of leather, tightly braided and studded with lead pellets and sharpened bits of bone. Jesus gasped as the first lash of the whip opened up his back. His knees buckled with the second stroke, and his chained wrists took the weight of his sagging body. He lost control of his bladder with the third. The guard continued to beat him, applying a fourth stroke and a fifth. Blood splattered the wall and ran down Jesus' back to stain his loin cloth. Six strokes. Seven. For the first time, Jesus screamed.

Pilate, coming down the stone stairway, heard it and paused. The whip cracked against Jesus' lacerated flesh twice more. Pilate continued on to the holding area. *Crack. Crack.*

The centurion supervising the beating walked over to stand beside him. *Crack.* "Political prisoner?"

Crack. Thirteen lashes. A third of the total.

"They say he claims to be the king of the Jews," Pilate said.

Crack. Neither Pilate nor the centurion so much as flinched. This beating was no worse than dozens they had witnessed. Usually the victim lost consciousness; often he died. They stood side by side, well clear of the flying blood, as Jesus' body twisted on the chain, his head rolling loosely.

Crack.

There was a pause while a soldier threw water in Jesus' face to restore him to consciousness. The water drained from his body with mingled blood.

Crack. The flesh hung in strips from Jesus' back. "He should survive it," the centurion said.

"What's that?" Pilate said, distracted.

The centurion repeated himself.

"Yes, yes," said Pilate. "He's a strong man. How many?"

The soldier administering the beating paused for a moment, his breath coming heavily and his bare torso streaming with sweat. "Twenty-two," he said.

Pilate indicated with a gesture that he should continue.

† † †

They had to revive Jesus with water twice more. When they had finished, Pilate gave a nod to the centurion in charge. "Dress him and bring him out," he said. He himself went up to a balcony overlooking the courtyard. For a moment he stared thoughtfully down at the churning crowd. What was it about this Jesus that so inflamed them? How could they possibly prefer Barabbas to the Galilean?

† † †

Jesus, released from his chains, collapsed face down on the stone floor.

"On your feet," the centurion said. He prodded him with the toe of his boot. "Come on, get up."

With an effort Jesus got to his elbows and knees, and he straightened slowly. "Come on, come on." The centurion kicked him in the ribs, knocking him back onto his side. Jesus, closing his eyes against the pain, struggled once again to his knees.

"Get him up," the centurion said to one of his men. "Take him to Pilate."

† † †

They found Pilate on the balcony. He turned toward them as they reached the top of the stairs, dragging Jesus between them. When they stopped before Pilate, Jesus' feet found the stone flagging, and he stood upright.

"I congratulate you on your stamina," Pilate said. "It's not many men who could support themselves after such a beating."

Jesus, gasping, his eyes swollen nearly shut, didn't answer.

"You're closer to death than you realize," Pilate said. "Only I stand between you and death by crucifixion."

Jesus shook his head.

"Do you doubt me?"

"You're . . . powerless to save me."

"If I can't save you, no one can."

"And you can't. You're merely . . . the tool of those below us."

"Pain hasn't taught you tact, Galilean." He motioned to him. "Come over here."

They approached the balustrade together. For a time they stood side by side, looking down. The mob began to quiet as it became aware of them.

"Look at this man," Pilate called down to them. "Does he look like a king?"

There was a chorus of "No." Someone shouted, "Caesar," and soon the cry was echoed. "Caesar! Caesar!"

Pilate's thin lips curled in an involuntary smile. "You are Jews, and yet you acknowledge Caesar?"

"Caesar is our king," cried one.

And another: "We have no king but Caesar."

"This man then is not your king?"

"We have no king but Caesar."

"Then this man is innocent of the charges against him. I'm going to release him in honor of your Passover."

"No! No!"

"Release to us Barabbas! Jesus Barabbas!"

"What then shall I do with this Jesus you call Messiah?"

"Death!"

"Death."

"Crucify him!"

"What?" Pilate exclaimed in mock horror. "You'd crucify your king?"

"We have no king but Caesar."

In an undertone Pilate said, "You've united these people behind their emperor as I never have."

The calls of the crowd coalesced into a chant: "Cru-ci-fy him! Cru-ci-fy him!"

Pilate sighed, feeling resigned suddenly to the will of the crowd below. To the centurion he said, "Bring me a basin filled with water."

When the centurion returned with the basin, Pilate had him hold it up. In full view of the crowd, Pilate dipped his hands and forearms into the basin and held them up streaming with water. The crowd cheered and stamped its feet.

"I wash my hands of this man's death," Pilate called, shouting in a vain attempt to be heard over the hubbub. "His blood is on you. On you and on your children!"

"Shall we crucify him then?" asked the centurion beside him.

Pilate nodded. Jesus, he saw with a start, was looking at him with something like compassion, as if he, and not Jesus, had just been condemned.

"I'm sorry," Pilate said. He laid a palm on the shoulder of Jesus' robe.

When the centurion had led Jesus away, Pilate, alone on the balcony, looked down at his hand.

It was smeared with Jesus' blood.

CHAPTER 36

The chief priests and their allies withdrew from the courtyard to wait outside the bronzed gates for Jesus' appearance. Silas, the centurion to whom Pilate had given the job of crucifying Jesus, selected the men he would need to help him.

"There are two others here awaiting execution, Barabbas's men. Should they be crucified today as well?"

The centurion thought a moment, then nodded. "Why not?" he said. "There's nothing so special about this one that he should merit the honor of dying alone."

"Hah! Merit the honor, sir. That's a good one." The soldier, whose name was Rudolfus, bared his teeth, exposing a blackened one in front.

"He does claim to be a king," Silas said. He studied Jesus, who stood unsteadily in the midst of a ring of soldiers.

"A king?" said Rudolfus. "King of the Jews?"

"So they say. Where are his clothes? It's hardly appropriate that a king should go naked."

"Here's his tunic," a soldier said, holding it out. He gestured to the bundle of clothes lying nearby on the stones. "Sandals, cloak, belt, head-scarf."

"And here's that embroidered robe Herod put on him," Rudolfus said.

"Fine. He's a king; put that on him."

Rudolfus draped it over Jesus' shoulders, leaving his chest and arms bare. Jesus groped for the sleeves.

"Hail, King of the Jews," Silas said ironically.

"Your majesty!" Rudolfus said, dropping to one knee with exaggerated reverence. "All hail, your majesty." He looked up, his grin again showing the blackened tooth.

Another soldier came from behind Jesus. "I have just the thing for him." He held up a circle of dry, woven vines taken from one of the piles of kindling that lay against the stone wall. "A crown for his lordship." He jammed it down onto Jesus' head, and a trickle of blood ran down from Jesus' hairline. "I'm afraid the only crown I could find was a bit on the thorny side. Haw!" Coming around to the centurion and Rudolfus, he too touched a knee to the ground in front of Jesus. Jesus held up a hand palm out, almost as if in acknowledgment of the tribute.

"Here, what do you mean by that?" Rudolfus said. "We won't take any of your sarcasm." He stood and struck Jesus across the face hard enough to stagger him.

"Here, take this," the other soldier said, pushing a long reed at Jesus. "Every king needs his royal scepter."

"Hail, hail."

Silas watched his men pay mock tribute. He had to admit that, even half-dead and with blood trailing down his bare legs, the prisoner did look rather kingly.

He shook his head. No matter. This Jesus would be dead soon, whatever his demeanor.

† † †

Balbinus, one of Silas's men who could write more than his name, made the signs, drawing his letters with a small brush and some white paint. Dysmas was a revolutionary. On his sign Balbinus wrote his name and beneath it the offenses for which he stood condemned — treason, rebellion.

"And Cestas?" Balbinus said, looking up at Silas. "Right. Treason and rebellion. How about this Jesus, the so-called king of the Jews? Treason and rebellion as well?"

"No. Write, 'Jesus of Nazareth, the king of the Jews.'"

"King of the Jews. Won't that piss the bloody hell out of the priests who brought him here?"

Silas smiled, faintly. "Jewish bastards. Let's hope so, Balbinus. I have an idea it would please the procurator."

Balbinus, grinning, went back to his lettering.

† † †

The gates opened inward. Cestas was the first of the prisoners to be led through them. His beard was matted and stiff, gray over the chin — not from age but from foaming at the mouth during the course of his beating. There was a crazed light in his eyes as he staggered out under the weight of the crossbeam on which he would be crucified. Around him were four Roman soldiers, each forming the point of a square that moved with him, keeping him at its center. Around his neck hung the placard upon which Balbinus had inscribed his name and his offenses.

The crowd shrank back as the soldiers marched him toward them. Though the Genneth Gate was just east of the palace, the soldiers turned south.

Crucifixion was a messy, time-consuming form of execution, originating with the Persians, to whom the earth was sacred — too sacred to be stained with the blood of dying criminals. The Greeks used it little, and the Romans inflicted it only on slaves and on non-Romans guilty of the most heinous of crimes: Murder. Piracy. Treason. Rebellion. The uprights of the crosses were permanent fixtures on the provincial landscape, dark spikes thrusting up from the earth at crossroads and outside city gates. The condemned were always led to the execution site by a circuitous route so they could be seen by as many as possible. They often hung on their crosses for days before dying and days afterward — except in Palestine, where Jewish law forbade corpses to be left hanging overnight.

The soldiers led Cestas south, then west, then south again, leading him along a narrow street that curved upward through the city, back toward the palace and the Genneth Gate. Several members of the crowd followed after them, silent for the most part, grimly anticipating what was to come.

Dysmas traversed the same route a quarter-hour behind his fellow revolutionary; he too attracted a handful of spectators. Most were waiting for Jesus, his disciples among them.

When he came out, he was bent under a wooden beam heavy enough that he held it in place only with difficulty. He was in his own clothes again, without Herod's robe, and, as he staggered along, the beam rubbed and bounced against his lacerated back.

The crowd closed in behind him, following him south and west and south again, then along the narrow, twisting street that started to climb as it turned northward. The merchants watched anxiously from their stalls, pulling back their goods to keep them from being knocked to the ground and trampled. Pedestrians pressed close against the walls, making way for the soldiers.

The road climbed in a series of broad steps. Jesus' sandal caught on one of them, and he fell to his knees, crying out as the end of the beam impacted on the dusty street.

"Get up, get up," Rudolfus said, prodding him with the butt of his javelin.

Silas shook his head, aware that Jesus had carried his cross about as far as he was able. His eyes, scanning the crowd, stopped on a large man with fine black hair and skin darkened and lined from years in the sun. "You there," he said, pointing. "Come here."

The man looked instantly alarmed, but he came forward, having no choice in the matter. Rome claimed as its prerogative the right to press anyone it chose into duty at an instant's notice. Frequently, the duties imposed were menial or distasteful, and the look on the big man's face made it clear he expected the worst.

"Who are you? Where are you from?" Silas demanded of him. Jesus lay face down between them, blood soaking through the cloak that covered his back.

The man identified himself. He was Simon of Cyrene, a city in northern Africa.

"Pick up the crossbeam and carry it for that man."

Jesus, shifting the beam from his shoulders to the ground, pushed up onto his hands and knees. His eyes, when they met

Simon's, were like windows into hell.

"Who is he?" Simon asked. He noted the placard around Jesus' neck. Of the three languages employed there, he could read only Aramaic: *Jesus of Nazareth. King of the Jews.* He shot the centurion a glance as he bent over the wooden beam.

"Thank you," Jesus murmured as Simon lifted the burden to his shoulder.

Tears sprang to Simon's eyes. "What's he done?" he said, but Rudolfus only planted a foot in Simon's backside and shoved him forward.

Behind them, a woman in the crowd let out a high, keening sound that rose and fell, rose and fell on the morning air. Another voice joined in, and another: middle-aged women beating their breasts and wailing. Mary Magdalene was among them, and Salome, and Mary the mother of James of Cana. All cried and wailed and beat the breast in mourning for a man who was already dead even as he walked and stumbled before them.

The procession passed out of Jerusalem by the Genneth Gate at the third hour of the morning. The sun hung low over a hill on which the uprights of a dozen crosses stood like skeletal digits. The hill itself, Golgotha, was for the most part rocky and barren, the rock outcroppings of so light a color that they resembled bits of bleached bone protruding from ruined flesh.

The screams of dying men rent the air as they approached, the clang of iron on iron. The women and the rest of the onlookers stopped at the bottom of the hill, and only the soldiers and Jesus and Simon of Cyrene went on. Dysmas and Cestas lay on the ground, their arms outstretched, their wrists secured to the crossbeams with iron spikes. Foam poured from Cestas's mouth, and his eyes showed white.

"See, that's what we've got in store for you," Rudolfus said to Jesus. "I'll take your cloak. You're in no hurry." He laughed, pulling the cloak off Jesus' shoulders and jerking it downward.

"Here, careful," Balbinus said. "I've had my eye on that cloak."

"You can have his sandals or his belt."

Jesus was relieved of each of these and of his head scarf, and he stood upright in a seamless tunic — white, though smeared with dirt, and crimson where it stuck to his bloody back.

"Come on, come on," Rudolfus said. "Get it off."

"So," said Balbinus. "Five items of clothing and only four of us."

"We can cast lots for the tunic," Silas said. "Everything else looks to be of equal value. Let's get him up there, and then we can argue."

As Simon of Cyrene put down the crossbeam and retreated, some women of Jerusalem approached with a jar of wine mixed with incense. "Please," one of them said to Silas. "For the condemned."

Silas rolled his eyes. "Yes, yes," he said. "Get it over with."

As Jesus pulled the tunic over his head, the fabric peeled from his back as if held in place by a bloody paste. Jesus gasped. Rudolfus jerked the tunic from him, and Jesus stood naked in the morning sun.

"On the ground," Rudolfus said, grasping his shoulder and throwing him down. Jesus landed on his crossbeam.

One of the Jewish women who had approached Silas now knelt by Dysmas, holding a ladle to his lips. Though he raised his head to drink, he choked on the mixture and some of it ran down into his beard. He shook his head, gasping, and opened his mouth for more. The offer of wine and incense was an act of mercy: It served as a drug to numb the senses.

When Dysmas had drunk some, it was offered to Cestas, who slurped it greedily. The woman came to Jesus, but he shook his head.

"You'll wish you had some before this is over," Rudolfus said. He grasped Jesus' wrist and held it against the cross beam, using his knee to pin Jesus' forearm.

"Take a little of the wine," the woman said. "There's no point in suffering more than need be."

"Nail," Rudolfus called. "Hammer."

"Drink some," the woman urged, her face contorted in empathy and in her anxiety to be away.

"Go," Jesus said. "In your lifetime, you yourself will experience suffering enough. The day will come when you'll wish you had never been born."

Wide-eyed, the woman backed away from him, still holding to her ladle and her jar of drugged wine.

Rudolfus said, "I guess he wants to experience these next few hours to the full. Maybe write him a poem about them in the halls of the dead."

Balbinus laughed. He stood holding out the hammer with its heavy, iron head. Rudolfus took the hammer and, still kneeling on Jesus' forearm, positioned the point of the long, square-cut iron nail on the inside of the wrist. "One," he said, and struck the head of the nail with the hammer.

A grunt escaped Jesus as the nail drove between the two bones of his forearm and bit into wood. He fought for air, gasping for it through clenched teeth.

"Two." The nail drove deeper into the wood. "Three. There." Rudolfus stood and stepped over Jesus to grasp his other hand. Jesus' eyes rolled toward him, the whites showing in his extremity. Rudolfus planted the spike and drove it in.

When all three of the criminals had been stripped and nailed to their crosspieces, the soldiers lifted them, two soldiers to a beam, and dragged the men toward the uprights, each of which stood no more than eight or nine feet high.

"Lift on three," Silas said to Rudolfus and Balbinus. On either side of them, Cestas and Dysmas were being held against the uprights, their bodies partially supported by the bit of wood nailed to the upright at the level of their hips. The crossbeams were lashed into place.

As Jesus' crossbeam was lashed into place as well, Silas took the placard from around Jesus' neck. "We're going to nail this above him," he said to Balbinus. "Pilate admired your handiwork and wanted everyone to see it."

"These, too?" called a soldier from Cestas's team.

Silas shook his head. "No, just this one. King of the Jews."

Balbinus held one of Jesus legs against the upright of the cross, and Rudolfus put a spike through the ankle. Jesus convulsed on the cross, the nails tearing at his wrists. As they impaled the other ankle, it seemed for a moment that the cords in Jesus' neck would spring from his skin, that his eyes would rupture from the internal pressure.

Then he collapsed, hanging head down. The placard above him bore Balbinus's neat lettering. Annas and Caiaphas, seeing that all was finished, climbed the hill toward them. "I want to object to that placard," Annas said to Silas.

"What's wrong with it?"

"It should read, 'He claimed to be king of the Jews.'"

"What's the difference?"

"The difference between a boast and a fact."

"Take it up with Pilate," Silas said, and he turned away.

"Do you wish you had some of that wine now?" Rudolfus said, leaning forward to look up into Jesus' face.

Annas approached the cross as well. "A sad fate for the Messiah," he said, and, hearing his voice, Jesus raised his head to look at him.

"If you are indeed the Messiah," Caiaphas said.

"Has it all been worth it?" Annas said.

Jesus didn't respond.

"You would destroy the temple and build it again in three days. Surely such a man can save himself from death by crucifixion."

Below them, pilgrims hurried along the road into the city, some looking up at the grim spectacle, others ducking their heads to hurry faster.

"Yes," Caiaphas said, inured to the spectacle of death by the daily slaughter of lambs and doves and oxen on the temple altar. "You say you are the Messiah. Come down off the cross now so that we too might believe." He laughed.

The soldiers around them eyed the two priests with evident dislike. Oblivious to them, Caiaphas said, "Such a fate could not befall God's chosen."

Cestas, the criminal on Jesus' left, croaked, "Is he God's chosen?" He gasped in a lungful of air. "You . . . if you're who they say you are . . . then save yourself . . . and us, too."

"Come on," Annas said to Caiaphas. "The man is dying. Let's go back into the city."

"God's chosen!" Cestas's voice rose in a wild, maniacal laughter that floated out over the hillside, chilling the blood of those passing in the street below.

Dysmas turned his head, looking past Jesus at his compatriot. Cestas laughed until he began to choke and sob.

In the relative quiet Dysmas gasped, "Do you not fear God . . . even in death? Surely even you . . . have heard of Jesus of Nazareth."

Cestas's mouth worked. He spat out a mouthful of phlegm toward Jesus, but it fell short of its target.

"We knew the penalty . . . for what we were doing. This man . . . 'sdone no more than preach . . . the coming of God's kingdom."

"We're dying. What's God's kingdom . . . to us?"

Dysmas addressed Jesus. "Rabbi!"

Jesus turned his head toward him.

"Is it over? No hope . . . of the kingdom?"

"Who are you? Your name?"

"Dysmas."

"Dysmas. The kingdom . . . is here. We stand . . ." Rudolfus kicked the upright of Jesus' cross, causing him to break off in a breathless cry. ". . . within its very gates," he finished, when he could.

"Little more dying, little less talk," Rudolfus said.

There was a period of quiet. Between gasps of pain, Dysmas said, "I could more easily . . . believe us passing . . . through the gates of hell." Overborne by hopelessness, he began to sob, the sound scarcely audible over the noise of the guards or of the crowd that had crept closer to the crosses to watch the spectacle of death.

CHAPTER 37

Time passed, not quite three hours, though an eternity for those on the crosses. Dysmas hung with his face turned toward Jesus. In his pain and despair, Jesus' image seemed to change before him and to become suffused with a white light.

"Master," he croaked through a throat as dry as sand.

Jesus turned his head toward him. His own face, black with dried blood, seemed to have shriveled on his skull.

"Remember me . . . when you come . . . into your kingdom."

Jesus' expression was indiscernible.

"Master?"

"This day," Jesus gasped. "We will walk, together . . . in my Father's garden."

On the other side of him, Cestas laughed. "This day . . . you will hang . . . in agony," he said. "And tomorrow."

"Look!" The voice came from one of the spectators, down the slope of Golgotha from the three crosses. Though it was noon and the sun blazed overhead, there was a small but undeniable indentation in the sun's western rim. Rudolfus, standing with the other soldiers at the foot of the cross, glanced upward, then stared. Balbinus, following his gaze, broke off in what he was saying. The crowd of Jews and foreigners looked up from the slopes of Golgotha.

"Something's eating the blasted sun," Rudolfus said.

Behind him, Jesus pushed down on the iron spikes that held his ankles riveted to the sides of his cross, raising himself to breathe.

"Eli," he shouted, his voice cracking under the strain of torture. "Eli! Lama sabachthani."

Rudolfus felt a chill along his spine and the prickle of hair at the nape of his neck. He twisted his head to look up at Jesus, who was staring blindly upward.

"By Jupiter that gives me the creeps," he said. "You, boy. What did he say?"

James of Cana realized with alarm that the Roman soldier was addressing him. "I, I think he's calling Elijah," he said, stammering.

Rudolfus looked at Balbinus. "And who the hell is Elijah?" he said. He looked around defiantly, as if daring someone to tell him.

James's father Alpheus was there. He pulled James toward him, away from the crosses.

"He is, isn't he?" James asked his father. "Calling Elijah?" It would not be the first time Jesus had summoned him.

Alpheus shook his head. "No. It's a garbling of Aramaic and ancient Hebrew." His eyes on the cross, he murmured, "'My God, my God. Why have you forsaken me?'"

James, looking up at his father, felt a keen despair. He turned again toward Jesus.

"He echoes the psalm of David," Alpheus said.

From the cross Jesus spoke again. "Thirsty," he croaked. "So thirsty."

James, looking around, saw the woman who had offered Jesus the wine drugged with incense. He ran to her. "Please," he said. "You had a sponge; I saw it. Give it to me."

"He won't have what I have to offer, not that one," the woman said, but she gave him the sponge.

James took it and a stick from the ground, and he poured wine vinegar into the sponge from the wineskin he wore at his belt.

When James approached the cross to hold up the wine-soaked sponge to Jesus' mouth, Rudolfus said, "Here, what are you doing?"

"He's thirsty."

"Well, let him thirst awhile. Maybe this Elijah of yours will come to him." But he made no move to interfere as Jesus extended his head for the wine and sucked a little of it from the sponge. His eyes closed again, and his head fell forward.

"That Elijah'd better hurry," Balbinus said. "If he's coming."

† † †

An hour passed, the dark disk of an unseen moon moving slowly across the face of the sun until all that remained was a shining crescent. Then the light began to diminish at a noticeable rate. The sky became dark except for the horizon, which remained unnaturally bright. The color of the light changed subtly, and everyone stood mute with awe and horror.

The tiny, narrow crescent of the sun diminished and disappeared: All that remained of it was a curving line of bright specks, blinking like a necklace of brilliant yellow beads.

"It's dying," someone said. "The sun is dying."

The sun was a black disk, illuminated only by a reddish aura. The brighter stars were plainly visible. A cold wind, unexpected at midday, swirled the cloaks and robes of the onlookers about their knees. Those at the summit of the hill Golgotha looked out over the sandy plain surrounding them and saw it marked with undulating striations of light and shade.

Silas stood beside his men. "It's as if we were underwater," he said, and Rudolfus and Balbinus looked at him.

"You have killed the Messiah," Alpheus said. "God's anointed."

"God's own son," said his wife Mary.

"Do you think?" Rudolfus asked his centurion.

Silas only shook his head.

† † †

Annas and Caiaphas were in the courtyard of the palace, standing and waiting in the changing light for an audience with Pilate. "He's keeping us waiting to show us who's in charge," Annas said.

"What's happening to the daylight?" Caiaphas said. "Look at the sun."

Annas glanced upward, paying little heed to it. "He's angry after this morning. We pushed him hard."

Caiaphas was still looking up at the sky, the tip of his tongue passing over chapped, dry lips.

"Caiaphas!" called a Jewish voice. It came not from the palace, but from the gates. "Annas!"

Annas and Caiaphas turned. Nicodemus and Joseph were striding toward them, Nicodemus's face red and angry above his beard.

"Greetings, colleagues," Annas said.

"You're not a colleague worthy of the name," Nicodemus said. "Secret meetings of the Sanhedrin in the dead of night, a trial during the week of Passover. How many laws do you think you've broken in the last twenty-four hours?"

Annas's eyes went briefly to Joseph of Arimethea. "As chief priests of the nation of Israel, our first duty is to the people," he said.

"Our first duty is to the Lord God."

"And to His laws," Joseph said.

Caiaphas didn't care about any of that. "Have either of you noticed what seems to be happening to the sun?" he said.

"We can't all strain at every legal gnat that swirls around us," Annas said to Joseph and Nicodemus.

"No? Maybe not. We can all surely manage to avoid swallowing camels."

Caiaphas cleared his throat. "This was a case in which the needs of the many outweighed the needs . . ."

"Our trial procedures were laid down by Moses," Nicodemus said. "They're at the heart of who we are."

"Exigent circumstances," said Caiaphas.

"By all the gods," a new voice exclaimed. It was Pilate, coming out of the palace. "What on earth is happening to the light?"

"Procurator," Nicodemus said, ignoring his question.

"Don't take that tone with me," Pilate said. "I've given you everything you've asked for."

"I'm not with these men. I want to lodge a protest, a protest in the strongest possible terms . . ."

"The placard above his head says he's king of the Jews," Annas said interrupting.

"Well?" Pilate said. "It's my understanding that that was the basis of your complaint against him."

"Our complaint was that he claimed to be king of the Jews."

"Yes, yes."

Caiaphas said, "The point is that the claim was false."

"Procurator," Nicodemus said. "These men tried and convicted Jesus of Nazareth in violation of our law."

Pilate held up a hand to cut him off. He looked back and forth between Nicodemus and Joseph on his right, Annas and Caiaphas on his left. There was an expression of irritated bewilderment on his face. "I'm not in a position to pass judgment on your procedural niceties," he said. "Look at me. Am I a Jew? As for this Jesus' claim to kingship — whether it's valid or invalid, the interests of the emperor are the same."

"So you'll order the sign changed?" Annas demanded.

"I will not. What is written is written. Now, is that all?"

"No, not quite," Annas said.

Pilate rolled his eyes.

"If we could beg your indulgence for a moment longer."

"The point," Pilate said. "Get to the point."

"As you know, we're in the midst of a festival."

"The Passover festival," Caiaphas said.

"Yes? So?"

"Three men dying outside the city's main gate is hardly conducive to the festivities."

"A little late for second thoughts, isn't it?"

"We're not having second thoughts," Annas said.

"No?"

"But tomorrow is the Sabbath; moreover, the Passover Sabbath."

"We don't want those men hanging on the cross during the Sabbath," Caiaphas said. "It begins at sundown."

"Death by crucifixion is likely to take some days," Pilate said.

"Days of exposure, trauma, blood loss . . ."

"You could break their legs," Annas said, bluntly. "That would speed the process."

"They can be dead and removed from their crosses within hours," Caiaphas said.

"By sundown, as our law requires."

"Your law," Pilate echoed. "I'm sick to death of your law. Kill this man, it's the law. No, no — the procedures weren't followed, reference our law. Now you want him off the cross by sundown, claiming . . ."

"We apologize, Lord Procurator. We're deeply sorry to have been in any way . . ."

"Somehow I doubt that. You're a pain in the imperial arse, and I think you enjoy being a pain in the imperial arse."

"No," Annas said. "We're only concerned, as you are, with domestic tranquility. Some of those among us —" He glanced at Joseph and Nicodemus. "— the Pharisees particularly — set great store by every particular of the law. I'm afraid . . ."

"Oh, very well," Pilate said. "Very well. I'll send word that their legs are to be broken."

"And their bodies removed by nightfall," Caiaphas said.

Joseph coughed into his hand discreetly. "I'd be pleased to take possession of the body," he said to Pilate. "If you'll turn it over to me, I promise to bury him at my own expense."

Pilate looked at Annas.

"If something were to happen to the body," Annas said. "If it were to disappear somehow or something were to happen to it . . ."

"Yes?" Pilate said. "What?"

"There are some who might claim he has risen from the dead. Some who might believe it."

Pilate's laughter was harsh. "You Jews are a credulous lot," he said.

"Be that as it may —"

"I can hardly post a guard over this man's corpse in perpetuity."

"If you could post one for just three days —"

"Three days!"

Annas's gaze slid to Joseph, as if trying to read his motive, then returned to Pilate. "This Jesus boasted that after three days he would return to life," he said. "Or so some have interpreted his remarks. If you could post the guard for three days . . ."

Pilate grunted in exasperation. "Very well, three days. I'll send word to Silas. Now, none of you may have noticed, but we're standing here in the middle of the day in near total darkness discussing the possibility that an executed felon may return to life to haunt us. I have to say it's giving me a headache. If there's nothing else —" He raised a hand to forestall any possible interruption. "Even if there is something else, I'm going inside."

And, so saying, he turned on his heel, and he left them.

CHAPTER 38

Joseph and Nicodemus left the palace together; so did Annas and Caiaphas, hurrying through the dark streets, their heads down, their eyes on the shimmering street before them. There were people on the streets, though not a lot for a feast day. Myriad faces looked out from doorways and windows, and people moved about without speaking.

"I hate this," Caiaphas said. "It isn't natural."

"At least it's ending."

Caiaphas, looking up, saw that he was right. The sparkling crescent of the sun was again visible; the disc that covered it was retreating. "What does it mean, do you think?" he asked Annas.

"How should I know? Is every occurrence of the heavenly bodies imbued with meaning?"

Caiaphas frowned, cutting his eyes away. The answer to Annas's question was yes, obviously, but he didn't want to provoke his father-in-law. When they reached the temple precincts, they separated without speaking, Annas going to check on the business of the temple, the money-changing and the bazaars, Caiaphas going on into the temple proper. During the Passover festival, the Jews made more sacrifices per day than at any other time, beginning with two bulls, a ram, and seven lambs, and continuing throughout the day with individual sacrifices totaling in the thousands. Animals bellowed and bawled and bleated. Blood flowed, and smoke rose up. As high priest of the people of Israel, it was Caiaphas's responsibility to oversee it all.

† † †

It was mid-afternoon, the ninth hour of the day, and the sun again shown whole in the sky. Those around the cross were silent, strangely enervated by the celestial ordeal. Jesus himself broke the silence, raising himself again with an effort and crying, "Finished!" in a voice loud enough to be heard by those passing in the street below. Nicodemus was there, and Joseph, and perhaps half of the disciples: Andrew and Philip, Mary Magdalene, James and John and James the younger, and their mothers Salome and Mary. All looked up into Jesus' face, curious, struck by the unexpected note of exultation in his voice. His cry seemed to echo out across the mountainous desert and to bounce off the city walls below them.

Even as the cry faded, it was replaced by a rumbling and creak like that made by one of Rome's great mechanical engines. The earth itself shook, and people staggered drunkenly, some sitting abruptly, others pitching forward onto their faces.

Inside the city walls, thatched roofs fell in, and walls collapsed, raining stones. Caiaphas, inside the holy house itself, fell to the limestone floor, bruising an elbow and tearing his robe. The seven-branched candlestick fell with a clatter beside him. Rolling onto his back, he stared up fearfully at the white walls that seemed to shift and move above him with the shaking of the earth. The Babylonian veil that hid the great golden doors of the Holy of Holies tore from top to bottom; for a moment Caiaphas thought that the walls of the temple would collapse on him and he would be crushed.

But the rumbling ceased, and the floor beneath him was once again firm and unmoving. Caiaphas, trembling like a leaf shaken by the wind, got first to his knees, then, holding to the table of the shewbread, to his feet. Out on Golgotha, Jesus seemed to be gazing at something that wasn't there, at a vista beyond the horizon.

"Father," he said, his tone almost conversational. "Into your hands I commit my spirit." His head fell forward, and he was dead.

His words were spoken wholly in Aramaic. Silas, the centurion, overhearing them and understanding, stood looking up at him.

"It's been a strange day," said Rudolfus at his elbow.

"What? Yes."

"You'd think they really were witnessing the death of their king." He indicated the spectators.

Silas nodded. "Or their god."

Rudolfus looked at him.

"I think we've just executed an innocent man, Rudolfus. Perhaps a holy one."

Rudolfus, shrugging, made a face.

"I know, I know. What business is it of ours?" He sighed, suddenly weary. "We're supposed to have them off the crosses by sundown," he said.

"Time to speed up the process then."

Silas nodded. "And those two want the body of Jesus when you're through."

Rudolfus saw them at the foot of the hill, two well-dressed Jews. "And the other two? What do we do with their bodies?"

"No instructions. Throw them in the mass grave; throw on a little lime."

Rudolfus nodded and bent for the large, iron-headed hammer. "I'll get their legs."

He went to Dysmas to the left of Jesus and broke his lower legs with two blows apiece. Dysmas screamed and heaved, his face contorting into a red mask and sweat springing out spontaneously on his forehead. Rudolfus crossed the ground toward Jesus, leaving Dysmas writhing and gasping and choking behind him.

"No need," Balbinus said. "He's dead." As if in demonstration, he thrust his javelin up into Jesus chest, piercing his heart. Blood flowed out, mingled with some clear fluid.

Rudolfus grinned, exposing his rotting teeth. "If he wasn't before, he sure is now," he said. He passed Jesus by and went to Cestas. "Which shall I start with, left or right?" he asked, resting the hammer on his shoulder. "I'm feeling generous this afternoon. You choose."

† † †

The sun was low in the sky, and the day was waning as the bodies were lowered. Cestas came down first. Rudolfus pulled out the nails that held his ankles, tearing the flesh with the iron of his pry-bar. With his sword he cut the ropes that held the cross-beam in place, and Cestas fell face-first, thudding to the ground.

Rudolfus walked next to Jesus' cross and freed his ankles with the same pry-bar.

"Wait!"

Nicodemus grasped Jesus about the upper legs to support his body. "Okay."

Rudolfus cut the rope, and Joseph caught Jesus' arm and the cross-beam as his body twisted forward. "We'll remove these nails ourselves," Joseph said. The flesh on the insides of Jesus' wrists was raw and puckered.

"He's already cold," Nicodemus said.

Joseph nodded silently.

As they lowered Jesus to the ground, one of Jesus' arms came loose from the cross-beam. The hand lay curled and lifeless on the rocky ground, a hole in the wrist where the nail had pierced it.

A man stepped forward. "I can carry him for you," he said.

Joseph blinked, trying to focus on the man through his tears. "Don't I know you?"

"He called me Peter."

Joseph nodded. "Yes," he said. "Peter."

It was Peter, working carefully, who withdrew the nail from Jesus' other wrist, freeing him from the cross-beam. His face all but lifeless, drained of all emotion, Peter stood with the body, cradling it against his chest.

"Where are we taking him?"

Joseph told him. He had a tomb hewn from rock in a garden north of the city. "I'd intended it for myself and my family. I would rather Jesus . . ." His voice broke, and he couldn't finish.

Silas approached them. "I'm sending these two with you." He indicated Rudolfus and Balbinus. "We don't want you disappearing with the body."

Peter only nodded. As he descended Golgotha, a whole procession of people followed: the soldiers, a half-dozen women, Joseph, and Nicodemus, and several of their servants, each of whom carried myrrh or aloes or linen cloths with which to wrap the body. Jesus' head lolled on Peter's shoulder, and Joseph walked ahead, his brightly colored cloak flapping in the hot wind like the wings of a bird.

It was a fifteen minute walk to Joseph's garden tomb. It was a walled garden, with an arched gate. A graveled walk led among the trees and other plants. It was cool here, the path heavily shadowed and lined with bell-shaped flowers.

"Here it is. Lay him here." Joseph indicated a mossy place on the ground in the midst of fan-shaped ferns. "We'll have to move that stone."

Peter lowered Jesus to the ground, settling him gently on the soft ground. Mary of Magdala came and knelt by his head, smoothing his hair back from his forehead. "Master," she murmured. "Master."

Pilate's soldiers, who had followed them into the garden, shifted uncomfortably. "We'll open the tomb," said Rudolfus, feeling strangely affected, despite himself.

Joseph nodded.

Together Rudolfus and Balbinus braced themselves against one side of the circular stone that blocked the tomb's entrance. It was massive and heavy. Rudolfus gasped and turned so that his back was to the stone and his knees were bent. Balbinus strained, red-faced, and slowly the stone began to move along its track, rolling away from the mouth of the man-hewn cave. Dank air wafted out. Rudolfus gave a final cry and drove with his legs until the wheel-like stone sank into a slight depression and stopped.

"Thank you," Joseph said.

Nicodemus knelt beside Jesus' body. "We have to hurry," he said. "The Sabbath is almost upon us." He poured myrrh over the linen cloth. "The aloes — spread them over his body." He unwound the linen cloth.

Mary, the mother of James, said, "We need more time. We haven't time to do it properly."

"No," said Nicodemus.

"We have to do it properly."

"We'll come back."

"Tomorrow?"

"Tomorrow's the Sabbath. Day after tomorrow. The first day of the week."

They wrapped Jesus quickly, winding a cloth impregnated with the fragrant myrrh about his body, winding a smaller cloth about his head. The women cried openly as Peter lifted Jesus and carried him into the tomb, stooping to pass through the low entrance.

He laid him on a ledge cut into the rock and turned away, his face wet. When he came out, he went to the stone and set himself against it.

"Ahh!" he cried in anguish, heaving at the stone, driving it up out of the depression so that it thudded into place before the tomb's entrance. He stood blowing hard, the expression on his face completely desperate.

The soldiers looked at him.

Peter pushed through the women and walked down the path toward the garden gate, walking faster and faster until he was running.

Joseph and Nicodemus exchanged glances.

"Day after tomorrow," Nicodemus said. "I'll meet you here." He nodded to Pilate's soldiers, and he left the garden tomb, Joseph following, and, more slowly, the women.

CHAPTER 39

Throughout the Sabbath Jerusalem experienced a series of after-shocks to the earthquake of the day before. Some pottery was broken; a shop wall fell in. No one was injured. Rudolfus and Balbinus were relieved of their guard-duty at daybreak, and they came on again at dusk.

The early hours of the night passed uneventfully. Rudolfus paced, and, sometime after midnight, Balbinus fell into an uneasy sleep, sitting with his back to the trunk of a small tree. The torch sputtered and went out. The moon was nearly full; Rudolfus could see well enough in its ghostly light. Stopping near his companion, he saw that Balbinus's eyes were in shadow and that his face looked almost skull-like. Rudolfus grinned, almost savagely, then continued his pacing.

Several hours before daybreak, some time about the beginning of the fourth watch, the city experienced its largest aftershock yet. In the garden north of the city walls, Rudolfus saw the ground rise in front of him. He lost his balance and fell to one knee, cutting it as it came down on a sharp stone. Balbinus cried out and came awake, staggering to his feet.

"What is it? What's happened?" he asked.

Rudolfus was cursing, softly but eloquently. "Another after-shock."

The earth groaned beneath them, and there was a sharp crack as if of rock splitting. A thump jarred them.

"Look! Over there!"

Rudolfus turned and saw the flare of light in the direction of the tomb. “Come on,” he said.

He led the way down the pathway, drawing his sword as he ran. The stone had been shifted away from the tomb’s opening. As he entered the narrow clearing, he saw a man sitting on the stone, a man dressed in white, his clothing brilliant with reflected light.

“You! Identify yourself.”

The man turned toward him, and Rudolfus swallowed convulsively. Balbinus bumped into him. “What —” He stopped beside Rudolfus.

Dread gripped them both. Their heads swam, and darkness descended.

As the sky brightened in anticipation of the dawn, four women walked out from the city. They were burdened with fresh linen, with aloes and myrrh and other spices. The road ran along the crest of the mountain range; to its east the Jordan River valley lay green and verdant in the mist, and beyond the river rose the arid mountains of Moab.

“Do you think he’ll recover?” Joanna said to Salome. “You’ve known him longer than any of us.”

Salome shook her head. She didn’t know.

“He’s always been so strong and assertive,” Joanna said. She was the wife of Chuza. They had traveled to Jerusalem for the Passover as part of Herod’s retinue.

They were talking about Peter, who sat in the upper room where he and the others had shared their last meal with Jesus. He initiated no conversation and responded to the conversational gambits of others with no more than a word before lapsing again into silence.

“It was such a grisly death. It’s affected all of us,” said Mary of Cana, James’s mother.

“And he was closer to him than most,” Joanna said.

Mary of Magdala shook her head. “It’s more than that.”

"What?"

"I don't know. It's more than that. He feels he failed him somehow."

"How?"

Mary shook her head. "He'll tell us when he's ready."

They continued along the road in silence, each wishing they could have persuaded Peter or John or some of the others to come with them. If the guards weren't there, or if they couldn't be persuaded to roll away the great stone that blocked the entrance to the cave . . .

The garden gate hung askew, supported by only one of its leather hinges, the other broken and hanging loose. The four women exchanged glances. Mary of Magdala went first, pushing through the hanging gate and walking along the path. She stopped at the end of it.

Rudolfus lay on his back, his open eyes staring vacantly upward. Another soldier lay face down, his features hidden. The stone was rolled away, and the mouth of the tomb was dark.

"Hello?" Mary called softly.

"Shh," Joanna cautioned, coming up behind her. "Move quietly."

Huddled close for mutual protection, they crossed the narrow clearing and stopped within the opening of the tomb, craning their necks and blinking into the relative darkness.

Mary of Magdala went in. The ledge where the body had lain appeared empty, but, when she approached it, she found Jesus' grave linens. They weren't unwrapped or cast aside, but lay still in the shape of his body as if he had evaporated out of them. Tentatively, she reached out and picked up the cloth that had bound his head.

"What is it? Is he there?" Salome called from the entrance.

Mary started. "No," she said.

"They've taken him," Joanna said. "They've taken his body and hidden it from us."

"But —"

"How else to explain what's happened to the guards? Somebody's drugged them, and they've taken Jesus' body."

Mary stood in the center of the tomb, unconsciously unfolding the linen she held and refolding it.

"We've got to tell the others," said Mary of Cana, still in the clearing.

"If only Peter would rally. He'd know what to do."

Mary of Magdala stopped in the cave's entrance, looking out at the neatly tended garden, at the soldiers lying in the path, at the large, circular stone just to her right. An aura of unreality hung over the scene; in response to it she felt only a dull ache.

They had taken and hidden him. Who could have done such a thing, and why? Jesus was dead, and his disciples demoralized. All his followers were scattering. Why couldn't they let him rest? Tears came to her eyes.

There was a sound behind her, the flap of clothing or the quick beat of wings. She turned, feeling the stir of air.

There was a man in the cave, a young man, dressed in a white robe that seemed to shimmer before her eyes. The linen she held dropped forgotten from her fingers. Her lips parted, but no breath passed in or out of her open mouth.

"Don't be frightened," the man said, and her breath came back to her in a sudden gasp.

"Please, sir," she said. "Please — I'm looking for Jesus."

The man extended a hand toward the ledge where Jesus had lain. "He isn't here."

"Where —"

"Tell Peter. He isn't here."

"What have they done with him?"

A hand tugged at her cloak. "Who is it?" Salome said, pressing into the entrance of the cave. "Who are you talking to?"

"Is someone there?" Joanna said, bending to peer past them.

Mary's eyes went back toward the stranger, but the cave was empty.

"He's gone," she said.

"Who's gone?"

"Of course he's gone," Salome said. "They've taken him somewhere. We have to tell Peter."

"Yes," Mary said. "Tell Peter, that's what he said. To tell Peter he isn't here."

Joanna and Salome exchanged glances.

"Yes, we'll go to Peter," Joanna said, taking Mary's arm.

"Let's go tell Peter," Salome said.

They led Mary away from the cave. At the edge of the clearing, they had to step over Rudolfus's body to reach the path.

† † †

They told Jesus' disciples. John sat in the window. Peter sat at the table, his eyes downcast and his expression moody. Andrew was there, and Nathaniel, and Philip, and Simon the Zealot. Cleopas, a friend of Simon's who had grown up with him in the village of Emmaus, was there as well.

"He's gone," Joanna said, standing in the middle of the upper room. "The guards have been drugged and the stone rolled away . . ."

". . . and the tomb is empty," Salome said. The women were still holding onto their linens and spices.

"Not quite empty," Mary said.

Peter raised his head to look at her. Beneath his bloodshot eyes the skin was bruised, and his beard was matted. "What?" he said to her. "What was there?"

"The grave linens, of course," said Mary of Cana.

The image of those linens, still bearing the shape of Jesus' body, rose up again in the mind of Mary of Magdala. "A man," she said. "Dressed in white."

"Finding the tomb empty was a bit much for her," Joanna said. "For all of us."

"He said to tell you that Jesus wasn't there," Mary continued. "'Tell Peter he isn't here,' he said."

"Who said?" Peter straightened in his chair, his eyes on her.

"The man. The man who was there."

Peter was on his feet. "He said to tell me specifically? Did he say why?"

"What man? There was no man," Joanna said.

Mary shook her head. Peter brushed past her, heading for the door.

"Peter!"

"Go with him," Salome said to her son John, and John got up and went after him.

† † †

He caught up with Peter at the city gates. "You're going out there?"

Peter shot him a glance and quickened his pace so that John had to break into a trot just to stay abreast of him.

"Why, what's the point? He's gone, they said."

"And the Roman soldiers were drugged, and a man in white clothing mentioned me by name. I want to know what's going on." Peter broke into a trot himself, and they ran side by side along the roadway, John casting occasional sidelong glances at Peter as they ran faster and faster. John was younger and lighter, and when both men were running full out he pulled steadily into the lead, Peter huffing and gasping as he pounded along the road behind him.

Mary of Magdala, coming out of the city gates, saw the cloud of dust on the road ahead of her. She drew her headdress more tightly about her face and hurried after.

John went through the gate and down the path. He stopped at the edge of the clearing, panting as he looked for the drugged soldiers. They weren't there.

Peter shouldered him aside to get to the tomb, stooping as he went through the entrance.

Jesus' grave linens lay on the stone ledge, just where the body had lain. Peter stooped to pick up another cloth, neatly folded, from the floor of the cave. The head linen, fragrant with myrrh. Peter closed his eyes. Ah, Jesus, he thought. Where are you when we need you?

John came in behind him, and Peter turned.

"What do you think?" Peter said after a moment.

John shook his head. "Mary was right. They've stolen his body. Still —" He hesitated.

"Still?"

"I have a funny feeling."

"You, too."

"Not what you'd think."

"No?"

"Almost as if something wonderful had happened."

Peter nodded, slowly. "I wonder — why would anyone take off his grave linens to move him?" he said.

"I don't know."

They saw Mary when they came out of the cave. She was at the far end of the garden, standing beneath a cherry tree white with the blossoms of spring. Her head was down, and her shoulders shook with her sobbing. A crow, gray, with a black head and wings, perched on the branch above her head.

Peter started toward her, but John grasped his arm. "Leave her," he said. "She's suffered enough."

Peter nodded, reluctantly.

† † †

Peter and John had been gone for some time when Mary realized she was no longer alone in the garden. Thinking at first that one of them had returned, she called out, "Peter? John?"

There was no sound. She hurried along the path, stopping when she saw the man kneeling by a bed of flowers.

The gardener. "Sir!" she called. "Good sir."

The man stood as she approached.

"Sir, if you tend this garden you must know where they have taken him."

"Taken whom?"

"Jesus. His body. If you saw, if you know where he is . . . I have money. I'll give you money." She was fumbling for the purse at her belt when a word stilled her.

"Mary."

She looked up, her breath catching in her throat. "Master." She made as if to fling herself on him, but he raised a hand.

"It would be best not to touch me." One side of his mouth rose in the familiar half-smile. "I have one foot in this garden of Joseph's and the other in paradise."

"Are you . . . Will the others . . ."

He inclined his head. "Go now and tell them you've seen me; that I've been here, in the garden."

"Will they believe me?"

His smile broadened. "Does it matter?" he asked.

She shook her head, smiling happily up at him through her tears. Jesus reached out as if to touch her, but suddenly he was gone.

CHAPTER 40

The disciples were locked together in the upper room. "Caiaphas and Annas bribed the guards," James said, as they were eating. "They're saying they fell asleep and woke to see Jesus' disciples making off with his body."

"You mean us making off with his body," said his brother John.

"I mean us. They're looking for us now."

"But we didn't take the body," Salome said, her eyes going from one to another of them.

Peter met her gaze. "No, of course not."

"And Mary . . ."

They turned to look at her. She sat by the window looking out over the city. All of them had been to the window to see what she was looking at. Though it was night, Jerusalem was clearly visible in the moonlight, many of the windows glowing with oil lamps, the shop-fronts illuminated by the fitful light of passing torches. Mary seemed eager and expectant, as if in anticipation of a welcome guest.

Joanna shook her head. "I don't know what to think about Mary."

A loud knock sounded on the door, and Mary jumped up from her seat by the window to run toward it.

"No," James said. "It might be the temple guards."

But Mary was already fumbling with the latch.

Simon came through the door, his beard standing out from his chin and his eyes alight. With him was Cleopas.

"We've seen him," Simon said. "Jesus."

Nathaniel's head went back, and Philip's. Andrew frowned, but Mary clapped her hands.

"We met him on the road to Emmaus," Cleopas said.

"I don't know how," Simon said, "but at first I didn't recognize him. He didn't look the same, quite. Younger, maybe, or older."

Between the two of them, they got the story out, about how they had met a traveler along the road and walked with him, how the man seemed not to know about that week's events in Jerusalem, the raising of Lazarus and the mobbed entry into the city that followed, the clearing of the temple, the arrest of Jesus and his crucifixion. "We reached Emmaus, and he was going to go on, but we encouraged him to spend the night with us," Cleopas said.

"We sat down at the table," Simon said, "and I asked him to bless the food."

"He broke the bread and blessed it, and suddenly we recognized him."

"At almost the same time," Simon said. "There was no mistaking him."

Peter pointed out the obvious: "Yet you walked with him and talked with him for well over an hour without recognizing him."

"How could that be?" James said to Simon. "You know his face like I know my mother's."

"I don't know how it could be," Simon said. "It was, that's all."

"It's hardly an explanation," Nathaniel said.

"I didn't say it was an explanation."

"But you still claim to have seen him."

"I not only claim to have seen him; I have seen him. Cleopas, too."

"So you say."

"You doubt me?" Simon said.

"I don't doubt you're sincere in what you think you saw."

Simon's face flushed angrily. "Think I saw? And then came all the way back into Jerusalem, running half the way, to report to you my delusion?"

"Peace," said a voice from the table. "Be at peace." So familiar was the voice, so accustomed, that it took a moment for its identity to register. They turned, as one, and stared in silence.

Jesus sat at the long table in the very spot he had occupied only three nights before. He used a large spoon to lift a broiled fish from the platter in the center of the table to the plate in front of him.

"Thank you," Jesus said. "Silence is good for the digestion." He took a bite of the fish.

Simon's face was stretched in a broad grin, and there were tears in his eyes. Mary was crying happily. Everyone else seemed to be in shock.

Jesus took another bite of the fish, then put it down and wiped his fingers on a cloth.

"Are you a ghost?" Nathaniel said finally, his voice sounding as if he were strangling.

"Do ghosts have an appetite for fish?"

"I . . ." In truth, Nathaniel knew very little about ghosts.

John moved closer to Jesus. "Your wrists," he said, pointing. "The scars."

"Yes, the scars are really there." Jesus held out his arm. "Go ahead. Touch them."

John touched the injured wrist, running a finger over the indentation, now white and puckered. He took Jesus' wrist in his hands, feeling of the scars on either side. Jesus held up his other hand. "Any one else?"

Nathaniel touched it, and Philip, and James the younger. The air inside the room seemed heavy, almost too dense to breathe. Andrew looked pointedly at his feet, and Jesus laughed. "Yes, scars there, too, and on my chest, marking the soldier's spear-thrust."

Everyone realized suddenly that he or she was smiling, that all of them were, their faces stretched in big, idiot grins almost impossibly wide.

"Is everyone here?" Jesus said. "Where's Thomas?"

Heads turned in search of him, but he wasn't there.

"He went walking," volunteered James. "He got angry when Mary said she had seen you."

"'She's delusional,' he said. 'I'd know I was delusional if I thought I'd seen him — and I'd admit it.'" Nathaniel smiled. "Frankly, at the time I agreed with him: Not unless he put his finger . . ." He faltered, inclining his head to look more intently at Jesus. ". . . through the mark of the nails . . ."

". . . put his hand to the place where the spear . . ." Philip, too, faltered. Jesus was different. His face was different, both sterner and older, his deep-set eyes ablaze with something like the heat of live coals.

"Maybe he'll get that opportunity," Jesus said. His words were mild, but his voice was deep and strong — impossibly so, like the voice of the ocean itself. He sat smiling at them, and the effect on Philip was like staring into the sun shining at full strength.

"You're staying with us?" said a voice.

Philip swung his head, struck by the voice's unexpected timbre. It was John's voice, but John changed — older and heavier of body, his beard long and thick.

Philip looked back at Jesus and saw him shaking his head. "But you'll see me again," Jesus said. A light was about him, glinting from the gold circling his chest in a delicate web of metal, shining from his crown. His crown? Yes, Jesus wore a crown, unnoticed by any until that moment. It was ancient in appearance and lofty, fashioned of pearl and silver and wholly white.

All of the disciples had become aware of the changes. They stood looking at Jesus and at each other and at themselves. Peter's beard, free now of any gray, flowed down over his chest. In his hand he held a gold staff like a shepherd's, a crook at its top. Matthew was stout and strong, with no suggestion of softness or fat. The women were clad in silk robes, and precious stones glinted from their clothing. The rush of a thousand stringed instruments filled the room, which itself had opened up and out until it was a great hall, its ceiling twinkling with the very stars of heaven and supported by marble pillars as tall and as big across as the cedars of Lebanon. A host surrounded them, a veritable army, clothing and faces and weapons all emanating light.

"Or are we going with you?" James asked.

Jesus smiled at him. "Yes, but not now."

"And Thomas?" said Andrew, as tall as his brother and standing beside him.

"You must tell him."

"Will he believe us? Will anybody believe us?"

Jesus met his gaze.

"Or does it matter?"

Things were changing again. The vision was passing, the light of the gems fading, the rich colors of their clothing. Jesus was gone, and the disciples found themselves alone again in the upper room.

They looked from one to another in awe and great uncertainty, and all eyes settled finally on Andrew.

"It doesn't matter," he said. "We're going to have to tell people about this whether anyone believes us or not."

"And many won't," Nathaniel said.

"But many will."

"How do you know?"

"I don't know, I guess, but I can feel it. This is it at last, the beginning of the kingdom."

"With a transcendent king at its head," said Philip.

"A living king."

"An eternal king."

Hallelujah.